Writing Mr. Right

USA TODAY BESTSELLING AUTHOR
T.K. LEIGH

Writing Mr. Right

Published by Carpe Per Diem, Inc. / Tracy Kellam, 25852 McBean Parkway # 806, Santa Clarita, CA 91355

Edited by: Kim Young, Kim's Editing Services

Quotes from *Pride and Prejudice* by Jane Austen Copyright © 1813.

Quotes from *Ethan Frome* by Edith Wharton Copyright © 1911.

Cover Design: Cat Head Biscuit, Inc., Santa Clarita, CA

Cover Image Elements:

Copyright 2019 gstockstudio

Copyright 2019 Kanokpol

Copyright 2019 Vjom

Used under license from Adobe Stock.

To Stan and Harper Leigh…

Chapter One

Seducing My Boss

"HURRY UP. HURRY UP. Hurry up." I rocked on my heels in the packed elevator as I watched the numbers ascend at a languid pace. Carefully balancing two coffees, one on top of the other, I checked the time on my cell phone. 9:02 Monday morning. I would love to have a job where it wasn't a big deal if I ran a few minutes behind, particularly on a Monday.

Particularly after having to stop at Starbucks every day to get my boss his expected triple venti soy no foam latte, the lamest drink known to man.

Particularly after having to leave my apartment an hour earlier than normal, without pay, to stand in line at the Starbucks closest to the literary agency in Rockefeller Center where I worked to get said lame excuse for a coffee.

Particularly because I had to start ordering the same coffee for myself in case I dropped it, as happened one time. The fallout was something I'd like to avoid in the future.

I preferred a basic Americano with milk from an actual cow, not this fake bullshit. I knew all about my boss' allergies. He didn't have any sort of intolerance to dairy. He was just an asshole, and his choice in drink proved it.

Finally, the ding of the elevator snapped me out of my vengeful thoughts and I barreled through the doors into a large, modern reception area.

"9:03," the receptionist sang after me, her voice almost smug.

1

"I know. I know." I dashed past the desk with Bartlett, Derringer, and Price in big bold letters on the wall behind it, not letting anyone who exited that elevator forget where they were. I wondered if the partners were trying to overcompensate for something.

"And he's in a mood," she added in warning.

"And that's different how?" I mumbled, my voice almost inaudible.

Running past cubicle after cubicle, I prayed today wouldn't be the day I slipped on the slick marble tile and fell ass over tea kettle. Since I'd started here more than six months ago, I had that vision in my head daily.

When my desk came into view, I breathed a sigh of relief. My gaze shot past it to the floor-to-ceiling glass windows separating the big bad wolf from the rest of us sheep. I observed him on the phone, pacing his office, a fierce expression on his face. At least he was preoccupied. Perhaps he wouldn't even notice I was four minutes late.

As I set my heavy messenger bag on the ground with a thump, my shoulder screaming with reprieve from the welcome lack of weight, I realized my wish wouldn't come true.

"Avery!" his powerful voice bellowed. *"Get in here!"*

"Shit." Subtly rolling my eyes, I opened my desk drawer to retrieve a small notepad, shoving it into the pocket of my suit jacket. Running my hands over my cream-colored sheath top and gray pencil skirt to straighten the lines, I grabbed his sorry excuse for a morning beverage. I paused just outside his office door, took a deep breath, then entered the devil's lair.

"You're late," he barked at me the instant my foot crossed the threshold.

"I apologize, Mr. Price." I met his hardened gaze. All my other friends could saunter into work five, ten, maybe even twenty minutes late. When they did arrive, it wasn't expected they get straight to work. They were able to ease into the day, talk about their weekends, which bars they went to, what movies they saw.

2

But not me.

I'd considered quitting at least once a week, but reminded myself that I had a rare opportunity to get my foot in the door of an industry that typically shut people out. This was my chance to have a say in who could be the next Stephen King, Nora Roberts, or J.K. Rowling. I just needed to put in my time and learn the industry. Then I could start my own firm and, hopefully, family.

"What's the excuse this time, Miss Rollins?" He ripped the coffee out of my hand.

"No excuse, sir. I should have planned better and left my apartment earlier," I responded, all too familiar with what he liked to hear. It would have been useless to tell him the real reason — that the barista at Starbucks messed up my order twice. He would simply say I should have prepared for that to happen.

"And where is it you live exactly?" He came around from behind his desk and sat on the corner, his expression and voice softening. I glanced behind me, wondering if we weren't alone.

With his booming voice, broad shoulders, tall height, and impeccable good looks, Mr. Jackson Price had a commanding and intimidating presence. In the half-year since I began working as his assistant, a position that had been like a revolving door before I came around, he'd never exhibited anything but his egomaniacal side. Not only did he get off on being in charge, I had a sneaking suspicion he took pleasure in everyone else knowing that fact, as well.

"Miss Rollins?" He raised his eyebrows at me when I didn't immediately answer, caught slightly off guard by his change in demeanor.

"Umm… Queens, sir."

"Do you have a roommate?" He sauntered away from his desk, roaming his office. He shut the door, closing the blinds. I remained firmly planted in place, his interest in me unsettling, to say the least.

"I wouldn't be able to afford an apartment in Queens on this salary without one," I quipped, then cringed, bracing for his *response. Despite months of practice, I still had trouble controlling my innate sarcastic nature around him at times.*

His presence loomed behind me, towering over my five-foot, three-inch frame. A shiver rolled down my spine, my skin prickling with goosebumps. His coffee-laden breath heated my neck, my entire being on high alert. My reaction to him took me by surprise, confusing me. It certainly wasn't the first time we had been alone together. But today, my body buzzed with anticipation and hunger.

Perhaps it was because I'd spent my weekend reading a trashy insta-love romance where the main characters probably spent more time naked than they did clothed. Perhaps it was because I hadn't had an orgasm at the hand of another person in what seemed like an eternity. Perhaps it was because I missed the touch of a man, my boyfriend of nearly four years having recently broken up with me because I was always working. Regardless of the reason, I found myself inexplicably turned on by this complete asshole.

I continued staring at Mr. Price's immaculate desk. Fantasies of his rippling body bending me over it as he had his way with me seeped into my subconscious. I imagined he would be as demanding and assertive as he was in his professional life. He would take what he wanted and teach me things I never thought possible.

"Pity." His deep, sensual voice broke through my perverse thoughts. I tried to shove them deep down and forget they ever crossed my mind. This man was my boss.

His hand swept aside my blonde hair, exposing the back of my neck. I swallowed hard, a delicious tremor overtaking me as his breath drew closer and closer to my skin. When his heated lips landed with delicate ease on my flesh, fireworks erupted in my core. It was confusing, wrong, and desperately wanted all at the same time.

My desire for him grew with each flick of his tongue on my milky skin. A voice in my head whispered this was a bad idea. I knew it was, but damn, it felt good, as if he had an Avery Rollins

4

instruction manual and knew precisely what to do to drive me insane with lust.

His strong hand skimmed the front of my blouse. The sensation of the silky material against my bare flesh heightened my awareness. He clutched my hips, forcing me against his hard stomach. His cock pushed against my back, the reality of the situation snapping me out of my erotic daydream.

I spun around, meeting his blue eyes, my mouth agape. "Wha—"

"Don't tell me you haven't fantasized about this," he said coolly. He ran his fingers through my hair, tugging, forcing my head back. "I have been since the day I hired you. You had everything I was looking for in an assistant. Beautiful. Smart. Sarcastic. But most of all, subservient."

"I'm not—"

"You are, Avery. You may think you're a strong woman, and I'd be inclined to agree, but you have a submissive side to you. A side I'm interested in exploring deeper."

Did he have a point? Did I have a submissive side? I didn't know, but the image of this man tying me up, blindfolding me, leaving me completely at his mercy didn't turn me cold. In fact, it excited me.

He ran his tongue from my ear to my collarbone, leaving a trail of fire across my flesh. I whimpered, my eyes nearly rolling into the back of my head. The forbidden nature of what we were doing made my hunger for him grow with each nip of his teeth on my skin.

His hands found their way back to my hips. With incredible ease, he picked me up and pinned me against the wall. Hiking up my skirt, he forced my legs around his waist. I closed my eyes, an unexpected moan leaving my throat when I felt what could only be his enormous erection pushing against me. A slave to my libido, I no longer cared that this man was my boss. That this was wrong on every level. That this could jeopardize everything I had worked hard for since my freshman year at NYU. All I knew was we were both wearing far too much clothing than necessary.

Greedily, I clutched his face in my hands and forced his lips to mine, trying to prove I wasn't the submissive little girl he thought me to be. A sexy rumble fell from his chest, the kiss growing deeper. His tongue swept against mine with alarming expertise. Hands were everywhere — pinching, pulling, tugging. His teeth nipped my lips, sending a jolt straight to my core.

"Avery," he groaned, pulling away, his breath dancing on my mouth. It smelled like a combination of peppermint, coffee…and raw sewage.

Sewage?

I snapped out of the trance I was in, staring at the laptop screen in front of me, a perplexed look on my face. An abhorrent stench wafted to my nostrils.

"Oh, Pee Wee! What the hell did you eat?" I shot my gaze to the slightly overweight labrador retriever curled up beside me on my large sectional, his snores loud enough to rattle even the deepest sleeper. He ignored me, his large paws moving as if he were chasing something in his sleep. I covered my nose with my shirt long enough for the offending stench to dissipate, then returned my eyes to my laptop, trying to get back into the groove.

I stared at the words I'd just written over the course of the past few hours, trying to figure out where to take the scene, but I no longer felt it. It was all the same. Girl meets boy. Girl has no interest in boy. Boy is sexy, perhaps a bit of a player. Girl lands on boy's dick and miraculously falls in love with boy. Boy says he doesn't do romance, but something about girl, perhaps her gold-plated vagina, makes him change his player ways. Then they live happily ever after and fuck like bunnies well into their eighties.

I wasn't ungrateful. I'd made a career using this

formula, with a few variations to spice things up. My readers loved steam and angst, coupled with a hot alpha male, but this felt like every other book. I didn't know how many new words I could come up with for penis...dick, cock, shaft, love stick, man meat, beef thermometer, anaconda, bologna pony, meat popsicle, Mr. Winky. I'd been known to be very creative, but there were only so many words in the English language to describe these yogurt slingers that were the cause of the most pleasurable orgasms my heroines had ever experienced.

It was pure fantasy on every level. Based on my experience, the feat of multiple orgasms was nothing more than an urban legend, a tale men told women so they'd keep their legs spread a little longer. It was no more real than the Loch Ness Monster or Bigfoot, yet all the pocket rockets I described in my books were able to deliver not just one or two orgasms a night, but sometimes bordering on double digits. They were the Olympic gold medalists of pork swords. When did it become commonplace to orgasm that much? Who would want to have that much sex? I didn't care if you possessed the tallywacker of tallywackers. No sane woman would want her legs spread that much, unless she was getting paid.

Frustrated, I closed my laptop and glanced at the clock in my darkened living room to see it was just before six in the morning. Grabbing an oversized wool sweater draped on the back of the couch, I pulled it over my head. I smoothed my wavy blonde hair into a messy bun, then snagged a canister of M&M's off the coffee table, heading toward a pair of French doors. Opening them, I emerged onto my balcony overlooking a narrow public alley in Boston's North End, the famous Italian section of town where people from across the world came to sample some of the best cuisine there was.

I climbed on top of a small wooden table and sat facing the window just a few yards away. The moon was still out, stars twinkling in the cloudless April sky. It was cold enough to see my breath in front of me.

I loved this time of day when the city was mostly still asleep, apart from delivery trucks beginning their morning routes. The bars had closed, drunk college students had passed out somewhere, and I could just sit and enjoy the peacefulness surrounding me before our small slice of heaven was infiltrated with tourists who thought Olive Garden served authentic cuisine.

Growing up in a large Italian family, I was taught two things at a very young age. One, always say your prayers before you go to sleep. That one pretty much went by the wayside when I was kicked out of Catholic school at the age of six. Two, never date a man who considered sauce from a jar authentic. I'd been able to follow that one pretty closely. I didn't date. Period.

Grabbing a candy-covered chocolate, I chucked it at the window across the alley, a smile building on my face as I continued my relentless badgering of the glass pane. Finally, a light clicked on from what I knew to be the bedside table. Seconds later, the shades were drawn and the window opened. A mass of dark hair stuck out.

"Morning, Mols," my brother said groggily, running his hand over his face, which he probably hadn't shaved in three or four days. He was two years older and had always been ruggedly handsome. Most of my friends in high school were probably only my friends because they wanted an invite to my house so they could have unfettered access to my brother. Teenage girls should be institutionalized. "Thanks to you, I'll never have to invest in an alarm clock."

"Whatever, Drew. Like those girls of yours wouldn't wake you up soon anyway," I shot back in the peaceful early spring air.

"You're probably right about that." He rolled his eyes, feigning annoyance, but I knew nothing could be further from the truth. Alyssa and Charlotte were his life. Being a single father to two precocious girls, aged six and four, was challenging, to say the least, but the love my brother had for those kids was unlike any I'd ever seen. "Another all-nighter?"

I sighed, reminded of the reason I wanted to talk to him. My brother was one of the few people who actually knew about my alter-ego, Vivienne Foxx, author of sinfully sexy romance. Everyone knew I was a writer, but they were under the impression all I wrote were situational humor pieces for a fashion magazine. While that was true, I could pull that shit out of my ass five minutes before it went to press.

"Yeah." I tugged my sweater closer as a breeze blew through the alley, knocking long-forgotten beer bottles and coffee cups around the street two stories below us. I never understood why people littered.

"What is it this time? Bad boy billionaire? Tattooed biker? Tormented rock star?"

"Sexy boss."

"That's a new one," he mused, a smirk on his lips.

"Isn't variety supposed to be the spice of life?" I raised my brows.

"Touché. So what seems to be the problem?"

I grabbed a handful of M&M's and shoved them into my mouth, not caring that it was barely six in the morning. In my opinion, the time to eat M&M's was all the time. "What *isn't* the problem? This book feels like everything else I've ever written." I shook my head. "I have this girl jumping on her boss' dick in less than twenty pages. I'm missing something, but I don't know what."

"Romance," Drew answered quickly.

I rolled my eyes. "Romance is overrated."

"Says the romance writer."

Giving him an irritated look, I pinched my lips together, pulling my sweater tighter around my slight body.

"I love you, Molly," he continued when I didn't respond, "but your lack of love life has been apparent in your books from day one."

"I have a love life!" I argued.

"Boinking meatheads when it suits you doesn't qualify as a love life."

"Did you seriously just say boink?" I stifled a laugh.

"You're deflecting."

"I can have a love life without picking out china and drapes. And one of those meatheads happened to be one of your teammates. I *was* writing a hockey book, so a professional hockey player was the perfect muse for me."

"And I made sure to give him a black eye when I found out." He narrowed his gaze at me.

It wasn't that I slept around, although I was certain my brother thought so. I just preferred to keep my so-called relationships on the light and casual side. It was better for all involved.

"I'm in no rush to settle down. I'm only twenty-nine-plus-one——"

"Thirty," he interrupted, just like he always did. I shot daggers at him for uttering that blasphemous "t" word.

"I'm not ready to give up everything I've worked hard for and achieved for a man who thinks I should just devote all my time to taking care of a dozen kids," I explained. Throughout my twenties, I'd lost touch with too many friends to count because they wanted to settle down and have a family, forsaking all other relationships for one person and eventually a pack of screaming, puking, crying rugrats. I refused to be someone who would sacrifice everything for a guy and the promise of happily ever after.

"The right person would never ask you to give up your dreams just so he could live out his. The right person would encourage you to pursue those dreams, regardless of the cost." A forlorn expression crossed his face. I could tell he was still hurt after what he had been through with his ex-bitch, as I lovingly referred to her. Actually, bitch was probably a compliment for the woman Carla was. "And I'm pretty sure you're not going to meet him at a bar on Boylston."

"Those places are a brilliant source of material," I countered. "Do you know how many story ideas I've gotten just by eavesdropping on conversations? Hell, the book I'm working on now came to me after listening to some drunk chick tell all her coworkers she was banging their boss."

He shook his head, laughing. "Whatever you say, Molly Mae, but I've seen you work on books based on something you weren't familiar with. You do your research. You don't stop until you thoroughly understand something. Maybe you need to do the same here."

"Here?" I scrunched my eyebrows. "What do you mean?"

"You write romance. Maybe you finally need to…" He paused, shrugging, "ya know, research that."

"Like interview people about their love life? Sounds a little like *When Harry Met Sally*, if you ask me."

Confusion wrinkled his forehead.

"You've never seen it?" I asked, almost in horror.

"I'm a guy. Unless there are boobs, bullets, or bombs…or we know we're getting laid…we're not all that interested."

"Whatever." I rolled my eyes. "I'm pretty sure I saw some tears falling down those manly cheeks of yours when we watched *The Lion King* with the girls last month. You can act all tough if you want, but you're a complete softie inside."

"Having kids does that," he reminded me, as he so often did. As if I didn't hear it enough from my aunts, who warned me my ovaries were going to shrivel up if I didn't have a baby soon.

I opened my mouth to respond when the faint aroma of coffee met my senses. It must have hit Drew, as well, because his shoulders slumped slightly. "Smells like Aunt Gigi's down there."

He groaned, running a hand over his stubble. "I suppose I should make an appearance. She acts like *she* owns the place instead of the other way around."

"Do you blame her? She's worked there since she was sixteen."

Aunt Gigi, short for Giorgina, was our father's younger sister. Our great-grandfather, Alfonso Brincoli — changed to Brinks when he landed on Ellis Island — started Modern Grounds in the early twentieth century. Back then, it was just a little cart he pushed to the waterfront where he sold coffee and cookies to the fishermen. It was now one of the few non-chain coffee shops left in the city and was located in the North End of Boston, the only place in town where Mom-and-Pop restaurants and coffee shops still flourished. The café had been passed down through the generations until our father took over several decades ago. It almost went belly-up a few years ago, but Drew stepped in and bought the place, keeping the family business afloat. More importantly, keeping Starbucks out of the North End.

My great-grandfather had bought the buildings we lived in when he moved his business to its current location. Over the years, the two apartments were typically rented out to employees of the coffee shop or their friends. When Carla left Drew, he moved into the apartment above the café, and I moved into the building across the alley so I'd be around to help him with the girls. Plus, I loved being just steps away from some of the best coffee in Boston.

"Daddy!" a small voice called behind Drew. A mess of dark curls appeared beside him, peeking her head out the window, a wide smile on her face. "Good morning, Auntie Molly!"

"'Morning, Alyssa," I replied with a grin reserved only for my nieces.

"Want to come over and make waffles?"

"I have to work today, princess," I responded. "And I'm pretty sure you and your sister have school. Maybe I'll come over tonight and we can make some pizza."

"Pizza!" she exclaimed with enthusiasm. "And then watch a movie, too?"

"Of course, silly!"

I heard a shuffling inside my condo and looked over my shoulder to see a tall physique come into view. My eyes widening at his nakedness, I shot off the table,

13

nearly spilling my M&M's. "Gotta go! See you later, Drew. Love ya, Lis!"

I threw open the French doors and quickly ran inside.

"Hey, babe," Kevin said, scratching himself as I hurriedly closed the blinds so as not to scar my niece for life. Hell, I was pretty sure the size of his junk had already scarred *me* for life. "What are you doing up so early? I didn't even hear you get up."

"I've been awake for a while." I peeled my sweater off and slung it onto a chair as I walked through the cozy living area and into the kitchen. I checked the kettle, made sure there was enough water, then ignited the gas burner.

"Doing what?" He leaned his elbow on the quartz countertop. It was a little disconcerting how comfortable he looked roaming my apartment naked, his schlong blowing in the wind, so to speak.

"Not much," I lied, pouring beans into the grinder and hitting the power button. I wasn't the type of girl to spill her innermost secrets to the guy she was, as my brother put it, boinking. The details of my life were completely unrelated to Kevin's ability to perform in the sack. He was a nice distraction and open to trying new things, which was extremely beneficial in my line of work, especially when working on the steamier parts of my books. Other than that, I didn't feel much for him.

"You get up early a lot," he practically shouted over the sound of the coffee beans being pulverized.

"Just working on stuff for the magazine." Turning off the grinder, I avoided eye contact, measuring the coffee grounds into the French press.

He crossed his arms in front of his chest, his large biceps bulging. I hid my displeasure. Kevin was every

14

woman's fantasy. Toned muscles. Eight-pack abs. A few tasteful tattoos dotting his arms and shoulders. He just wasn't *my* fantasy man. I liked my men a little squishy with some imperfections. However, beer bellies and nose hair didn't sell books. People read to escape, not be reminded of their ordinary, mundane lives.

For the past several months, Kevin had been my unknowing muse for a handful of book boyfriends. It was a great arrangement, even if he remained unaware of the details. I used him as a source of inspiration to write my sizzling, ovary-combusting romances. In return, he had a girl who wouldn't pester him to meet her family and hang out with her friends. Who wouldn't stand in front of the mirror for hours asking him repeatedly if she looked fat. Who didn't need to be wined and dined so he could get laid.

"Mols?" Kevin's voice made me tear my eyes away from his chest. Meeting his gaze, a lascivious smile crossed his mouth, assuming he caught me ogling. "Did you hear me?"

"What was that?"

"I said…" He stepped toward me, resting his hands on my waist. His thumb strummed my hipbone.

A shiver rippled through my body. I mentally ran through some notes I had made about a few questionable positions. Tugging at my lower lip, I tried to remember which one I wanted to check next to make sure I got the blocking right.

"You seem to work a lot, but your columns don't appear in the magazine all that often."

His lips whispered against my neck, the touch as subtle as a light breeze. I closed my eyes, arching toward him. I was thinking maybe against the wall this time. He was tall and muscular, a stark contrast to my short and slender frame. He could easily support me with just his upper body strength, barely breaking a sweat.

"Why is that?"

"I have no control over what they publish or don't," I replied in a breathy voice, repeating the same story I told practically everyone.

"What's this new column about?" he murmured, his hands hooking into the waist of my Minnie Mouse pajama bottoms and tugging them down.

"Office romances." It wasn't a complete lie.

"What about them?" His tongue circled that sensitive spot in the crook of my neck, a tingle warming my insides.

"It wouldn't interest you." Hoping to distract him, I grabbed his cheeks, pulling his lips toward me. "Kiss me, Kevin."

I had been up half the night writing, completely uninspired. Maybe this was what I needed to power through this book. Maybe I needed to feel the illusion of love and all its false promises.

My lips a breath from his, he pushed away, his posture straightening. "Why do you do that?"

"What?" I gaped at him, surprised by his sudden serious demeanor.

He ran his hand through his light brown hair. "Whenever I try to find out more about you as a person, you push me away."

"I didn't push you away," I argued. "Hell, I was ready for you to fuck me against the wall, for crying out loud! *You're* the one who pushed *me* away."

"I'm not talking physically." His muscular stature shrank, making him appear vulnerable. "Listen…" A sigh fell from his lips. "I like you, Molly. You're a beautiful woman who knows exactly what she wants. How is this relationship going to work if I don't even know who you are as a person? Your dreams and fears?"

"Relationship?" I practically choked on my own saliva, my heart rate picking up at his use of the dreaded "r" word.

In the few months we'd been casually seeing each other, which pretty much consisted of having drinks before heading back to my place, we never got personal. I didn't know much about him, and vice versa. I liked it that way. He provided me with exactly what I needed. There had never been any discussion about what we expected from each other because I was under the impression there were no expectations.

"What are you talking about?" The tea kettle began singing, but I ignored it.

"Us." He gestured between our bodies.

"Us?" I felt like I was in some sort of parallel universe.

"What did you think I was talking about?"

"I don't know, but I certainly didn't think it was *that*. Kevin, you're a fun guy. I like hanging out, but relationship?"

He stepped back, his formerly massive erection no longer standing at attention. Regardless, it was still impressive.

"And can you please cover yourself?" I snorted out a laugh. "I can't take you seriously with your junk flopping around."

His eyes narrowed, hurt evident in his expression. "You're a piece of work," he spat in a tone that emphasized it was not a compliment. He retreated from the kitchen and stormed down the hall into my bedroom.

Shrugging, I pulled my pajama pants back up, then turned toward the stove. I shut off the gas, removing the kettle from the heat. Pouring the water into the French press, I allowed the coffee grounds to steep, shaking off the guilt that tried to force its way into my conscience. *Catholic guilt.* It wasn't my fault Kevin wanted to change the rules after several months.

"I'm out of here," he called out. I turned around to see him walking toward the front door.

"Okay." I hesitated, unsure of the protocol in situations like these. I never got close enough to someone to know how to act after a disagreement. Or argument. I wasn't quite sure which this was. "Want to come over later?"

His hand on the doorknob, he stopped. His shoulders rose and fell, then he faced me. "No, Molly. I'm not going to come over later. I'm done putting time and effort into something you won't."

"Kevin…" I approached him. "I just… I didn't think this was a serious thing."

"Well, it is…or was. For me anyway. But it's fine. I get it. I thought you were different, but you're just like the rest of the girls in this town. All you see are the muscles and nothing else." He whirled around and threw open the door, storming out of my apartment.

I stood frozen in place, unsure of what to do. Should I run after him and apologize? Why? For being me? Sure, I enjoyed his company, and he was pretty good in the sack, but that was as far as it went.

Like I heard my father say all those years ago when my mother left him because she wanted more out of life than kids, like I was reminded when Drew's ex-bitch, Carla, left him because he was no longer the hockey celebrity he once was, 'real love isn't real life'. There was no such thing as happily ever after. Humans existed only to inflict heartache on others.

Nothing would ever convince me otherwise.

Chapter Two

A PILE OF KIT Kat wrappers lay beside me on the couch, damning evidence of one of my weaknesses...delicious wafers and creamy milk chocolate mixed in one irresistible treat. Ever since Kevin left, I'd been staring at my laptop screen, trying to get back into the groove of the story. My mind kept wandering to how we'd left things and the hurt on his face. Deep down, I may have harbored some feelings for him. I was smart enough to never act on those feelings. I had all the evidence I needed that so-called committed relationships were a farce. Someone always ended up hurt. I refused to do that to myself.

But now that I didn't even have so much as a casual fling, I found myself uninspired. The words refused to flow. I tried to move on and work on a scene between my heroine and her flamboyantly gay BFF, but even that felt contrived and trivial. Then again, even when I was sleeping with Kevin, the book felt contrived and trivial. Kevin had been perfect for the past few books where my leading men were a tattooed bad boy, a tormented rock star, a leader of a motorcycle club. Kevin's muscular, blue-collar persona was exactly what I needed to inspire my writing. But now that my leading man was a billionaire businessman, the game had changed. In order to finish this book by my deadline, I needed a spark of inspiration, and fast.

Grabbing the remote, I turned on the television and curled into a ball, flipping through all the movies I had on my Apple TV. They were mostly chick flicks I used to help inspire the illusion of love in my writing. Real love wasn't real life, but I could certainly watch a Hollywood version of a cheesy romance.

Just as I settled on today's choice — *The Proposal* seemed appropriate for my storyline — my cell phone rang. I groaned when I saw a New York City area code on the screen.

Clearing my throat, I hit the answer button. "This is Molly," I said as cheerily as possible.

"Molly, it's Tara," a voice answered that evidenced a life-long cigarette addiction — low, gravelly, with an occasional cough that pierced my eardrums.

"Hi, Tara," I sang in a chipper tone. I knew precisely why she called. I had less than a month to submit the final draft of my book. I'd yet to send her anything, not even a chapter. "How are you?"

"Let's cut through the bullshit. I need a status update on this book… What is it? *Seducing My Boss*?" She made what sounded like a gagging noise. I couldn't tell whether it was natural or intentional. I assumed it was the latter. I hated the title, too.

"I'm still working on it." My voice oozed all the professionalism I could muster on just three hours' sleep.

"Then why haven't I seen anything yet? Is there something I should know?"

"Everything's going great," I lied. I couldn't exactly tell my editor I'd been experiencing one of the worst cases of writer's block I'd ever endured. Yes, I'd been writing, but for me, writer's block wasn't simply being unable to write anything. It was knowing the words I did write were complete crap, that the story had no meaning.

Truthfully, I had been feeling uninspired for a while now. I wondered if I'd ever have that drive and excitement I did when I first began writing. When I did it for me, not because I had some deadline and a contract to write a particular storyline looming over me.

"Great," she answered in a clipped voice. "Then it won't be too much trouble for you to send me what you have so far."

"Why do you need that?" I stood from the couch, heading to the French doors. "It's coming along fine. I'll make my deadline."

"I don't doubt it, but I just want to make sure we're on the same page with the direction of the book."

I rolled my eyes, biting back the sarcastic remarks begging to be set free. Every single one of the books I was under contract for had the same exact direction. In fact, each pitch was practically identical, with just a few minor details changed. I could probably submit a few chapters of my previous books, changing the names, and they'd be none the wiser.

"I'm still in the process of transferring material from my notebook to my laptop." I held my breath, wondering if she'd fall for my blatant lie. While I used my notebook to do some free writing from time to time to help get my creative juices flowing, I did most of my work on my laptop. Hell, most days, I felt like I was chained to the damn thing. If I wasn't writing, I was interacting with my readers on social media.

"So you don't have anything written."

"I do," I argued back, stepping onto my balcony. The sun was shining, warming my face. I'd grown tired of the gray skies that routinely plagued New England during the winter months. "I've got the story in my head and have pages full of notes."

"Pages full of notes does not a story make." She let out a long sigh. I imagined her leaning back in her chair and removing a pair of dark-framed glasses. "What's really going on?"

"What do you mean?" I asked in an uncertain tone, chewing on my nails.

"Molly, I've been your content editor for how long now?"

"Five years," I replied without even blinking.

"The fact we've never met doesn't matter. I like to think I know you as a person. Something's going on with you. Are you blocked?"

"What? No!" I answered, indignant. I didn't know why I lied. This was a woman who had been in the publishing industry for nearly as long as I'd been alive. I was sure she had some tricks for getting rid of writer's block. For some reason, I felt this was something personal I needed to work through without hearing everyone's tips for overcoming it.

"Let me ask you something."

I remained silent, waiting.

"Are you happy?"

"You've seen the deal my agent made with your publishing company. How could I *not* be happy with that?"

"No. Not with us. In general. Are you happy?"

I opened my mouth, shaking my head slightly as I kept my eyes trained on the street below me. A few of the neighborhood locals, Lenny and Anthony, had set up their lawn chairs on the sidewalk across the street. They waved, Anthony blowing me a kiss. The eighty-year-old man had been flirting with me since I turned eighteen.

"The reason I'm asking is I don't feel as if I really *know* you, Molly."

"You know me. You're actually one of the only people who knows Vivienne Foxx is really a woman named Molly Brinks."

"That's not what I'm talking about. I'm able to get a feel for most of my other authors by working on their books. It's subtle, but they infuse bits and pieces of themselves into their stories. Not you. Why's that?"

I swallowed, tilting my head back as if the sky would hold the answers. Many author friends of mine reiterated the idea that "you write what you know" over and over again. Not me, though. I did everything I could to write every woman's fantasy, keeping my personal life out of it.

"That could be just the ticket to overcoming whatever obstacle you're facing that's preventing you from working on this book," Tara added when I remained silent.

I sank into one of the lounge chairs on my balcony, blowing out a long breath. How could I tell Tara I was tired of writing this kind of story? So many authors would kill to have the deal I'd been able to secure with this publisher, but after five years and over a dozen books, I couldn't help but feel somewhat unfulfilled. There was part of me that wanted to use my talent to tackle serious topics, such as abuse, alcoholism, human trafficking, racism, mental illness, as I'd hoped to do when I first started out in this industry. I'd grown weary of always having to write what someone else wanted me to, not what *I* wanted to.

"So you want me to change the story?"

"No," she replied quickly. "That's not what I'm

saying. You still have an obligation to deliver the story you promised. You can make a few minor changes…"

"Minor? How so?" I asked, the wheels turning in my head.

"You know what we sell here. We sell sexy. We sell sinful. We sell seductive. Most importantly, we sell happily ever after. As long as your story has all that, along with the forbidden romance you promised, I can work with anything else."

I nodded, rubbing my temples.

"Think about your own love story."

I coughed, choking. "What?"

"I'm sure you've been in love before. Use that as a jumping-off point."

I bit my lip, remaining silent. It wasn't that I didn't love people. I loved my brother, my nieces, my large extended family, my friends. But had I ever been *in* love? I doubted my crush on Taylor Bennett in eighth grade counted. I thought it was love. He passed me notes between classes and even turned the "o" in my name into a heart, listing the reasons he loved me. Then he demonstrated his everlasting love by making out with Gretchen Wells at the Valentine's Day dance. He had claimed he'd been hit by Cupid's arrow when he saw me. I wanted to light that arrow on fire and pierce his heart with it.

"You're a damn good writer, Molly, and I know you have a wonderful imagination. I'm certain your books are probably the reason for dozens of pregnancies." She let out a cough-ridden laugh. "Get out of your house and find whatever inspires you to do what it is you do so well. I expect to see 20,000 words by Monday morning." She paused, allowing what I believed to be an impossible assignment sink in. "Have a good weekend." Then the line went dead.

How the hell was I going to find a new source of inspiration that worked for this book? And in just three days?

Chapter Three

"WHAT'S WITH THE face?" a voice said, breaking me out of the hypnotic trance the blinking cursor had put me under.

I'd been staring at a blank computer screen all morning. Not a single word flowed. Instead of resorting to my old muse hunting grounds, otherwise known as a bar on Boylston, I grabbed my laptop and headed down to the café, hoping a change of environment would help inspire me. The smell of coffee and sugar, coupled with the sounds of clattering dishes and friendly conversation, gave me a feeling of belonging, like one's childhood bedroom often did.

My dependence on a muse could have been entirely psychological, but I'd written my first book because the guy I was seeing at the time sparked a story. Ever since then, I felt like I had to have a muse in order to write. It was like a security blanket...a living, breathing, incredibly sexy security blanket.

"What face?" I shrugged out of my daydream and glanced up at Brooklyn, treating her to the worst fake smile I could muster on such short notice. She plopped into the chair across from me, waving at my brother to bring her morning dose of caffeine.

"*That* face." She grimaced at me. "You look like your dog just died or something." Her eyes widened, compassion crossing her face. "Oh, my god. Pee Wee didn't…"

"No! Do you think I'd be sitting here if he did? I'd be a complete mess!" I brought my mug, which contained probably my fourth or fifth coffee of the day, to my lips. I knew I had a serious addiction to caffeine, but I had no desire to change that at the moment. "I like that dog better than I like most humans."

"Then what's wrong?" She had smoothed her dark hair into a slick ponytail that trailed down to the middle of her back. Her vibrant green eyes stared at me with intrigue, as if they could read my innermost thoughts. They probably could.

"Nothing," I insisted. I wasn't fooling anyone, especially my best friend since our first day of kindergarten. We were kindred spirits, outsiders from the beginning. We'd watched with longing as moms doted on their kids, tears streaming down their faces. We were the only two who didn't have parents snapping photo after photo as we waited to be escorted into the school by our teacher. Brooklyn's mom had died the previous year, killed by a drunk driver when she ran out to get milk.

My story was almost the same. My mom had run out to get milk, too, as my dad had told me for years, and never came back. However, she wasn't killed by a drunk driver. She had abandoned us, said she didn't want to be saddled with a family any longer. Although, to this very day, I still received a crummy pair of slippers for my birthday every year.

She got cold feet being married to my father and raising a family. I was constantly reminded of that fact.

Every.

Fucking.

Year.

"She's a bitter cynic," Drew interjected, placing Brooklyn's mug in front of her and offering her a smile, which she was only too eager to return. Just like practically every other female friend of mine, she couldn't hide her attraction to my brother. Time and time again, I had told her if she wanted to pursue something with him, I would be okay with it. Drew's kids adored her. I had a feeling Drew adored her, too. It made sense. Regardless, she insisted our friendship was more important to her than that. Brooklyn was a rare gem in a selfish world. I didn't deserve her friendship.

"Tell me something I don't already know," she shot back, smirking at me.

"She's blocked," Drew explained, lowering his voice.

He knew the drill by now. The only people who knew what I really did for a living were within a foot of me. It wasn't that I was ashamed of my writing. I didn't have a full-time job where they would look down on me for writing books that soaked your panties. I simply preferred the anonymity.

Brooklyn leaned in. "With what? Sexy Mr. Price?" She read my stuff before everyone else, even the absolute garbage that never made the final cut and was usually complete gibberish. She had a talent for seeing things I couldn't, helping me figure out where to take the story. "If I had a boss who looked like him—"

"He doesn't exist," Drew reminded her. "You make it sound like he's a real person."

I sat back in my chair, a cocky look on my face. "That's the sign of pure brilliance, Drew," I joked. "My writing is so compelling, she believes he's real."

"If he *were* real, perhaps there wouldn't be cobwebs growing between my legs," she muttered.

29

"On *that* note…" Drew offered us a tight smile. "I'm going back to work."

I glanced at the bar, seeing Aunt Gigi and Dottie, another staple of the coffee shop, talking as my aunt wiped it down and restocked the display cases. The café was a bit different. It had the typical booths and bistro tables most other places had. When Drew took over ownership, he made one drastic change. He put in a real bar that actually served alcohol. According to Drew, who had studied business in undergrad, the profit margin on alcohol was huge.

"It's not busy," I argued. "You can sit with us for a minute. All you do is take photos and sign autographs for all the hockey fans who come in."

"That's not all I do here, Mols." He shot me a sideways glance. "Truthfully, I'd rather be called for jury duty than have to listen to you two talk about cobwebs in places I'd rather not think about."

He gave Brooklyn a small smile, then headed back to the bar, his eyes glued to one of the large televisions that was playing one of the sports networks.

"Like you don't think about vaginas all day, every day," I called after him. Instantly, dozens of customers perked up from their smartphones or laptops. "You're a guy! From my experience, guys spend, like, twenty-three hours of the day thinking about the next time they're going to get some pussy!"

"Molly!" Aunt Gigi scolded, her dark eyes shooting daggers at me. "Watch your language!"

"The other hour, they're actually *getting* said pussy." I crossed my arms in front of my chest, ignoring my sixty-five-year-old aunt. "I'm pretty sure thinking about vaginas is all part of that."

"Molly!" Drew hissed, heading back to the table.

"You're going to give Gigi a heart attack, for crying out loud," he berated me, unable to stifle the laugh struggling to escape. Drew was the typical oldest child — serious, pragmatic, methodical. I was always the wild one. The one who didn't take anything in life too seriously, including myself. Still, I loved when I could get a laugh out of him...or anyone else, for that matter.

"Like she's never heard the word vagina before. Or pussy."

He sat down in the chair next to me, leaning close. "Thanks to you, I'm pretty sure we all have at this point, along with far too many other words you have stored in your vernacular for the female genitalia. No brother should have to listen to his sister say some of the things that come out of your mouth. No brother should have to read his sister's sex-filled books, either, but I do."

I planted a kiss on his cheek. "That's because you're the best brother in the whole wide world." My voice oozed with sarcasm, although I meant every word.

Through all the ups and downs in our lives, Drew was my one constant. Men would come and go, but Drew was always there for me, even during his professional hockey career. When some of my know-it-all cousins or uncles told me a degree in journalism was a waste of time, Drew reminded me I was a damn good writer and it would be a disservice if I gave up because of a few ignorant comments from people who wouldn't know how to open a book if their lives depended on it.

"So what's the problem this time, Molly?" Brooklyn asked once Drew relented and joined our discussion.

"I got a phone call from my editor this morning."

They both perked up. "What did she have to say?" Drew asked.

"She was wondering why she hasn't seen anything from me, considering the final draft is due in a month."

"You haven't sent her anything?" Brooklyn lifted her brow. "What about all the stuff you've had me read? Granted, I've probably read about twenty different versions of the first chapter, but at least it's something."

I sank into the booth, playing with my coffee mug. "I know. I just... Like I told Drew earlier, it just doesn't feel right." I narrowed my gaze on my two confidants. "It feels like every other book I've been under contract to write. When I signed this latest deal, I thought it was perfect. All I had to do was write a forbidden romance between two people who are complete opposites...if it could even be called a romance. It's really just an egotistical prick using his position of power to seduce his assistant. It's more like sexual harassment. Throw in a conflict, which even a blind person could see from a mile away, that our heroine is somehow able to look past because she can't stand not to feel his dick inside her every day, giving her orgasm after orgasm, which isn't possible, and we have our entire story, wrapped up in a neat little package, ready to market to the masses." I rested my head in my hands. "They ate it up. They made it sound like this was a completely new concept, like it hasn't been done before. Hell, *I've* done it before...repeatedly." I let out a long breath. "Maybe I'm burnt out. And my editor expects to see 20,000 words by Monday."

Brooklyn scrunched her eyebrows. "But, Molly, it's Friday—"

I held up my hand, cutting her off. "To add fuel to the fire, Kevin walked out on me this morning. He was all wrong for this particular book anyway, but at least he was *someone*. Now I have no muse and a nearly impossible deadline hanging over me." I leaned my head back against the booth and stared at the ceiling.

"What happened with Kevin?" Brooklyn asked, intrigued.

I rolled my eyes. "That went up in a blaze of glory."

"What did you do?" Drew turned to me, his expression almost smug, as if he'd been expecting this for a while. I knew my arrangement with Kevin wouldn't last, but I hated the thought of having to search for yet another muse. I loathed having to put on a tight dress and a pair of heels just to attract some guy, but it was necessary for my art.

"He asked what I was doing up so early," I answered. "We got on the subject of my magazine articles and how there aren't exactly a lot of them. Then he started asking what I was really doing all the times I told him I was working on my column."

"And what did you say?"

"I tried to distract him." I bit my lip, feeling oddly guilty about this morning's unexpected fireworks.

"Why didn't you just tell him?" Drew pushed. "I don't understand why you don't want people to know."

"I know why." Brooklyn crossed her arms, a self-righteous look on her face.

"Oh, you do, Dr. Freud?" I loved my friend dearly, but she psychoanalyzed everything. Granted, she *did* have a degree in psychology and worked as a therapist for the Department of Children and Families. Still, I hated feeling as if she were studying everything I did and said.

"This has nothing to do with me being a therapist. It's because we've been friends since we were still pissing our pants. You don't want anyone to know what you really do for a living because you haven't written

33

anything you're proud of yet."

"I'm proud of what I've accomplished!" I shot back. "Not everyone can say they've written a book."

"That's certainly true." Brooklyn took a sip of her Americano, her eyes still trained on me. "But you said it yourself. You're more proud of the act of publishing a book than the material contained in it. If you're happy, why not use your real name?"

"I don't want to jeopardize my deal with the magazine."

"Are you kidding me?" Drew scoffed. "Their circulation would skyrocket if word got out *the* Vivienne Foxx was writing for them. Your readers would salivate over your columns... 'Overheard in the Women's Restroom', 'Molly's Misadventures on Public Transport', 'Ten Weeks to Giving Better Head', 'Confessions of a Serial Dater'. Those columns are hysterical and have such a great following. Imagine if your readers knew. It would only increase your popularity."

"That doesn't matter to me." I tapped my fingernails on the table, avoiding their eyes. "I like living in the shadows. I don't need the spotlight." I met his gaze, then glanced just past him to the walls that seemed to be like a museum exhibit.

Anyone could tell just by walking into this place how proud my father was of all Drew's accomplishments. The walls that were once covered with vintage photos of my ancestors, who built the café when they didn't even have two pennies to rub together, were replaced with a history of Drew's notoriety. There were still framed newspaper clippings chronicling his rise in the hockey world from high school to college, leading up to his professional career, which was actually much longer than most. I often caught Drew staring at them when he didn't think I was looking. I could sense he wished things were still the way they use to be, but he'd never admit it. Still, I knew he must miss the thrill of lacing up those skates, listening to the crowd go wild when he took the ice, thousands of people chanting his name.

"You know he's proud of you, too, don't you?" Drew offered, taking my hand and squeezing it. I snapped my eyes away from the framed image of the front page of the *Boston Globe* from six years ago showing Drew in his Bruins jersey, holding up the Stanley Cup, surrounded by his teammates and coaches.

"I know." Even a complete stranger could tell I just said that so we could talk about something else. My father couldn't even remember my name.

Growing up, Drew had my dad and, for a few years, I had my mom. After she left, my dad tried getting me into sports, since that was all he really knew. I gave him credit for at least making an effort, but sports just weren't my thing. Over the years, I had actually welcomed sitting in a dark corner of the skating rink, a book in my hand, while my father cheered Drew on from the front row, his face beaming with pride. The Brinks name had become well-known because of my brother, and my father didn't hesitate to tell everyone about his famous son, including anyone who stepped foot in his café. It didn't bother me. I was happy living in the shadow of his success. I'd been so accustomed to the way things were, I often responded when people shouted "Drew's sister" to get my attention.

"You owe it to yourself," Brooklyn interjected, sensing my growing unease. "You've worked too hard to just let someone else take the credit for what you've accomplished."

Noticing Aunt Gigi hovering around us like a hawk, trying to eavesdrop on our conversation, I lowered my voice. "I'm not letting someone else take the credit."

"In essence, you are, Mols," Drew replied. "By refusing to even have your face connected to your alter ego, you're letting this person you made up in your mind take all the credit. Your agent has had requests for you to go on morning talk shows, for crying out loud. Do you know how many other authors would *kill* for an opportunity like that? It could make you even more of a household name than you already are. You could become the next Danielle Steel or Nora Roberts."

"Just drop it." I was bored with this conversation. They brought it up every few months. No matter what I said, they couldn't understand why I refused to make any public appearances under my alter ego.

"I'm not going to drop it this time, Molly." Drew leaned into me. "What's the *real* reason?"

I crossed my arms, inching away from him. His eyes bored into me, making me uncomfortable in a place that had always been like a second home. Narrowing my gaze at Drew, I formed my lips into a tight line. "You are," I answered with a severe look.

Blinking repeatedly, his mouth turned into a frown. "Me?" He straightened his spine, taken aback.

"Yes, Drew." I slammed my laptop shut, my voice firm, although barely louder than a whisper. "I was there every step of the way. I shared each victory of yours. When you received the Hobey Baker award in college, I was as humbled as you. When all those coaches from the NHL scouted you, I was just as nervous sitting in the stands as you were on the ice. When you skated your way to your first Stanley Cup and were awarded the Conn Smythe trophy for being the MVP, I cried along with you. Hell, we drank beer out of Lord Stanley's cup together when it was your turn to have it! Every emotion you felt throughout your career, I felt it, too."

My shoulders fell as a knowing expression crossed his face. "All the ups and especially the downs... I felt them, Drew. I know what it's like to be on top of the world, then have that ripped away." I shook my head. "I've already been there and am not going back. *That's* why I like my anonymity. If my books stop selling, it won't be Molly Brinks who will have failed. It'll be Vivienne Foxx."

Drew and Brooklyn were silent for a moment. I didn't expect them to understand. The book industry wasn't what it once was. These days, it seemed everyone and their dog published a book. Readers had started caring less and less about the craft of writing. They wanted sexier, racier, raunchier. Just telling a great story was no longer enough. You had to push the envelope. I knew there would be a day in the near future where even my stuff would be too tame for some. I wanted to be able to walk away without too much damage to who I was as a person.

"Plus, I'm pretty sure Aunt Gigi would have a heart attack if she knew," I added, lightening the mood. Humor had always been my coping mechanism. Drew said I masked my true feelings with sarcasm. I didn't see anything wrong with that. "She already practically lives at that damn church. If she knew the things I wrote about in my books, she'd start sleeping in the confessional."

"You may be surprised," Drew answered with a smug look. "This isn't about what Aunt Gigi thinks, Mols. Sure, there may come a day when your books don't sell, but that doesn't mean you're a failure. It just means you took a risk. I took a risk on a relationship with Carla, knowing full well she was a hockey groupie. If I hadn't, I wouldn't have the two beautiful daughters I do. It's scary putting yourself out there, but the rewards you could reap far outweigh the downfalls."

"Whatever." I wasn't in the mood for his little pep talk. Nothing he or anyone said would convince me to give up my anonymity. For what? So my father would finally realize he had a daughter, too? That ship had sailed years ago.

"So what are you going to do? What's your plan?" he asked, returning to the issue at hand.

I pinched my lips and shrugged. "Go back to square one. Try to find a muse that has more of a businessman vibe to him. Not sure I'll find someone like that in my usual spots."

"Oh! I know!" Brooklyn gasped. "You should try online dating! One of the girls at the office met her husband on Tinder or something! I'll do it with you!"

Drew's eyes shot to her. "I don't know. There's a lot of freaks out there." A slight scowl crossed his unshaven face.

"We're not stupid enough to go to someone's house to meet for the first time," she assured him. "There are rules."

"Rules?" He cocked a brow.

"Yeah. You always meet in a public place, preferably for just drinks. Dinner's too much of a commitment. You can down a drink in ten minutes, maybe even less, so if he's really dull or posted a Photoshopped picture, you can get out of there quickly."

Drew and I both gaped at her, wondering how she came up with these rules on the spot.

"I've done the online thing before," she admitted casually.

"You what?!" I exclaimed. "How come you didn't say anything? If you were looking to meet someone, I would have gone bar-hopping with you!"

A faint smile crossed her face. "I'm not interested in the kind of guys you meet at a loud bar. Not that there's anything wrong with the way you typically go about things. I prefer having a connection with someone. Online dating is just as random as picking up a guy at a bar, but at least you're not under the cloud of alcohol or beer goggles. It's…safer."

"I'm safe!"

"I know you are, but I don't have your looks or personality."

"What are you talking about? You're a beautiful girl, Brooklyn."

"No. I'm unique," she emphasized, gesturing to her nearly jet-black hair, freckled face, and slender stature. "There's a difference."

"If it means anything…" Drew turned to Brooklyn. "I think you're beautiful."

She tried to hide her smile, but it was impossible. She'd had a crush on Drew since middle school. Drawing in a breath, she changed the subject as best she could. "So it's settled. We'll put up profiles on every dating site out there. You may just meet *the one*." She looked at me hopefully.

"That's not the point of this. I just need a guy with a modicum of good looks and a professional persona to help inspire me to finish this billionaire businessman romance. All I need is a little spark. Then I'll walk away."

"What if you like the guy?"

"That won't happen." I shivered in disgust at the notion.

"You act as if being in a serious relationship is a curse," Brooklyn observed. "Life isn't like *Sex and the City*, you know."

"It should be. Think of all the shoes!"

Her eyes widened. "Shoes...," she exhaled in a drawn-out voice, a look of absolute bliss on her face.

Drew chuckled, pinching the bridge of his nose. "The female gender is a complete mystery. I will never understand the fascination with shoes."

"But what if you fall in love?" Brooklyn pushed. "You're just going to walk away from that?"

"I've been doing this for years now. I've yet to find anyone with whom I wanted to pick out window treatments. And it sure as hell won't happen this time, either. Love isn't real."

"I don't know." Drew leaned back in his chair, studying me. "I think it's all a front. You act like you have no desire to be in a committed relationship with someone, but deep down, you yearn to be completely swept off your feet like happens in all those movies you constantly watch, allegedly in the name of 'research'. I think you watch them because you secretly believe your Mr. Darcy is out there somewhere."

I rolled my eyes, hating that Drew used Mr. Darcy against me. *Pride and Prejudice* was one of my weaknesses, and he knew it. "They're all just fantasies. All those movies and books are nothing more than a carefully crafted story marketed to the masses who want to feel all warm and fuzzy for a minute. There's no such thing as happily ever after. You show me the happily ever after in waking up one morning after retiring from the NHL because of an injury to find the woman you wanted to spend the rest of your life with ran off with an uninjured player, leaving you to raise a two-year-old and six-month-old."

Drew narrowed his gaze at me. "Fuck you, Molly."

I knew my words hurt him, but it needed to be said. Of all people, Drew should realize true love was just a pipe dream.

Brooklyn's eyes darted between us. "Just because some relationships don't work out doesn't mean the right person isn't out there. Yes, Drew's been hurt." She reached across the table and clutched his hand, his severe expression softening as his gaze shifted to her. "But that doesn't stop him from hoping for something better. The right woman will come along and will accept the scars, bruises, brain injuries, everything." She smiled, breaking the building tension at the table.

Brooklyn had a gift. Like all siblings, Drew and I had our fair share of arguments. Throw in our innate Italian stubbornness, and what started out as a simple disagreement could turn into World War III if it weren't for Brooklyn constantly stepping in.

"Did Carla break my heart?" Drew faced me once more, his eyes brimming with sorrow. "You better believe she did. But I don't regret a second of it because, for a short period of time, I felt something. I felt that spark people want to feel when they read your books." He lowered his voice. "And I feel bad for anyone who's never experienced that. Molly, you're thirty years old."

My eyes widened as I shot daggers at him. "Don't say that vile word!"

His lips turned into a smile. "Okay. Okay. Twenty-nine-plus-one."

"Better." I smirked.

"You're going to do whatever you want, regardless of what I say, but maybe it's time you thought about finding someone who's interested in you as a person, not just in hooking up with you. I know Mom leaving had a bigger impact on you than it did on me—"

"It didn't—" I interrupted, but Drew held up his hand. I closed my mouth.

"It did. And it scarred Dad, too. I don't think he ever dated again after that. I remember hearing him say, 'Real love isn't real life.'"

"He said that?" I scrunched my nose.

Drew simply nodded. "It must be where you got it. I love you, Molly. You're my best friend. I hate the idea of you never opening your heart, or at least your mind, to the prospect of meeting someone who could love you."

"Andrew!" Aunt Gigi yelled from behind the counter. "Break's over. It's almost noon and I need the bar stocked."

He rolled his eyes. "Who owns this place? Me or her?" He winked and got up as Aunt Gigi approached the table, holding a piece of light green paper she had ripped off the advertisement corkboard beside us.

"Here you go." She slammed the paper down on the table.

"What's this?" I picked it up, reading it.

"Speed dating," she answered. "I heard what you were talking about."

My large blue eyes grew even bigger, wondering exactly how much she had overheard.

"I wasn't born yesterday, Molly. You don't exactly have the softest of voices, my dear." She leaned down, then whispered, "And your Uncle Leo thanks you. Things have gotten...interesting since I began reading

42

your books."

When she pulled away, my face reddened with embarrassment, my mind spinning, wondering exactly which of my books my aunt had read. None were tame enough for her. *The Bible* wasn't tame enough for her.

"Start here. It could be fun." She glanced over her shoulder. "And Drew will go, too."

"Go where?" He looked away from the TV showing highlights from last night's Bruins game.

"Speed dating," I answered with a grimace. I hated making small talk, feigning interest in someone's lame story about their exciting weekend trip to Home Depot. At least with online dating, I could hide my disgust behind a computer screen.

"I'm busy," he shot back.

"You don't even know when it is." Aunt Gigi crossed her arms in front of her chest. "And it's tonight."

"I can't find a sitter on such short notice."

"I'll watch the girls."

"I don't want to put you out."

"You're not," she insisted. "You want your sister to meet someone. I want the same for you."

"I'm okay. I'm happy. I don't need—"

"Ah, ah, ah." Aunt Gigi held up her hand. "You'll go, too." There was no sense in arguing with her. It was a losing battle. "Those girls need a mother. I'll babysit. No arguments."

"Yeah, Drew," I jabbed. "No arguments. If I have to suffer through this, you can suffer along with me."

"I'm not the one who breaks out in hives at the mention of a committed relationship."

"I don't break out in hives."

"Hyperventilates then."

I bit my lip, remaining silent.

43

"Gotcha," he joked.

"Come on!" I implored. "You can size up the competition and give every guy who looks at me the evil eye."

"I'm not so sure that's a good way to find a new muse," Brooklyn added. "Drew will have every guy running for the hills."

I was about to tell Aunt Gigi it was a lame idea when the fine print on the flyer caught my eye. "It may not be a complete waste of time." I held the flyer up, pointing to the bottom. "There's an open bar."

"Fine," Drew relented.

Chapter Four

"HIYA, MOLLY," ONE OF the front desk staff members said as I entered through the automatic doors of a two-story brick building.

"Hey, Reggie," I responded to the slim, older black man, the little hair he had left graying in places. I approached the counter, taking the clipboard he handed me, all too familiar with the procedure at this point. "Catch the game last night?"

"Sure did. That team hasn't been the same since your brother retired."

A smile tugged at my lips as I signed the visitor's log. "You're just saying that so I'll get you some more signed jerseys."

"No. It's the truth," he assured me. "But I wouldn't turn down a jersey or two, either. My brother's a big fan." He placed a visitor badge on the counter and I grabbed it, clipping it to my shirt.

"How's he doing today?" I asked, my expression falling.

"He's having as good a day as he can, given the circumstances."

I closed my eyes and straightened my spine, steeling myself for what awaited me down the corridor. Drew didn't understand why I came here every day, considering I didn't see my dad that much when he still lived at the house I grew up in. I couldn't abandon my

45

father. I hated that we even had to put him in a place like this. I liked to think Vincenzo Brinks had so much more life left in him. Still, he couldn't live on his own anymore. If we didn't do this, I feared we'd check in on him one day to learn he'd wandered off, unsure of who he was and where he lived.

"Don't take it personally." Reggie clutched my hand and I opened my eyes, meeting his. "He loves you. It's the disease that makes him like this."

Forming my lips into a straight line, not showing any emotion, I simply nodded. I'd heard that same thing too many times to count.

I turned from Reggie and walked down the corridor, my knee-high boots clicking against the linoleum floor. This place had a strange smell to it. Lemon cleaner. Baby powder. School lunch turkey dinner. However, it was the best facility around for chronic neurodegenerative diseases. It just so happened the neurologist who had been treating my father the past few years was on the staff here. That made the choice in facilities a no-brainer.

I passed a few decorative trees, smiling at some familiar faces. It didn't matter how much they tried to make it look like this was just another apartment complex. It was still an inpatient facility that reminded me of the convalescent homes I visited during Christmas when I was forced to sing in my church choir as a young child.

Coming to a stop outside a white door, the number 127 on a plaque beside it, I placed my hand on the knob and turned. Upon entering, there was a small sitting area with a couch and two reading chairs directly across from a wall-mounted flat-screen television. A desk sat against the opposite wall, along with a bookcase boasting some of my father's favorites. At the far end of the room was a doorway leading to his private bedroom and en-suite bathroom. When we had to make the difficult decision to put him in here, we wanted this place to feel as close to home as possible. We'd packed up all the trinkets and photos he had displayed prominently in the house I grew up in. Glancing at them now, I realized I was only in one of them.

Walking to the bookcase, I grabbed a black-and-white photo, studying it. I couldn't have been more than two or three at the time. I sat beneath a large oak tree in one of the gated parks in the city. My mother stood behind me, staring at the camera. A huge smile lit up my face. She looked sad, lost, unfulfilled.

I ran my fingers over her face, my features nearly similar to hers. Large doe-like eyes, light blonde hair with chestnut accents, high cheekbones, fair skin. Once she left, I felt like the outcast of the family. It was apparent that Drew was my father's son. His olive-toned skin, caramel eyes, and dark hair was identical to my father's and the rest of my extended family's. I stood out like a nun in a strip club. I didn't look like I belonged. Sometimes I didn't feel like I did, either.

"Josie, is that you?"

I tightened my grip on the frame and took a deep breath, readying myself for yet another afternoon of confusion. I stared at the unhappy woman my father thought I was, then placed the photo back on the bookshelf. As I turned around and my eyes fell on my father in the doorway, my jaw tensed, my fists clenched, my pulse soared. I shouldn't have been nervous, but this man in front of me wasn't my father. He hadn't been for months now.

"Are you okay, Ms. Brinks?" The orderly pushing his

47

wheelchair looked at me with concern.

"Of course." I gave him a forced smile, swallowing hard. I was anything but okay as I looked at the shell of a man my father had become. He always seemed larger than life, his raucous laughter bellowing through the halls of the modest house in Somerville I called home throughout my childhood. He would swoop me up with little effort and hoist me onto his shoulders, racing around the halls like he didn't have a care in the world. The man staring back at me now was weak and beaten down by Alzheimer's, his once strong body frail.

I stepped toward the door, grabbing the handles of the wheelchair and pushing it farther into the sitting area. "I'll take it from here, Jeffrey."

He raised a brow. "Are you sure?" he whispered. "He's been a bit aggressive today. I can stay, if you'd like."

"He's not going to hurt me," I responded in a low voice. "He's my father."

"But he doesn't realize that."

I fought back tears I had kept at bay since we'd learned about my father's condition over three years ago. As the disease continued eating away at the man he once was, it had become more and more difficult to keep it in.

"Maybe today he finally will."

He hadn't known who I was for over a year now. Still, I held out hope something would trigger a memory the disease hadn't gotten to yet. I yearned to hear him call me Molly one more time before he was taken from me, despite the medical staff telling me the chance of that was highly unlikely. Maybe that was why I came here every afternoon and read to him. By getting lost in one of the books we'd bonded over when

I was younger, maybe he'd finally look at me and see his daughter, not his estranged wife or a stranger here to do him harm.

"Okay, Ms. Brinks. Buzz me if you need anything."

I nodded, refusing to turn back around and face Jeffrey. I didn't want to see the concern and empathy in his expression. When the door clicked, I blew out a breath, parking my dad's wheelchair in the sitting area across from one of the reading chairs.

"Would you like some water?" I headed to the small kitchenette and opened the door to the mini fridge.

"You don't have to wait on me, Josie. Come and talk to me. Ever since the baby was born, you never talk to me anymore."

I wanted to scream, *I'm not Josie! She left you years ago! I'm that baby!* But I didn't. This wasn't my father talking. Like the doctors and nurses had reminded me over and over again, it was the disease. No matter how many times I'd heard it, though, I couldn't help but feel I had done something to make myself completely forgettable in my father's eyes. How could someone simply forget a person they bathed, clothed, loved, and protected for over twenty years?

"Like I've already told you," I said evenly through the ache in my chest, "I'm not Josie." I twisted the cap off the water and grabbed a straw from the drawer, popping it in the bottle. When I glanced up, I noticed a mischievous smile tugging at his mouth. "What?"

"I get it." He winked. "Role play. I like it."

I gripped the counter, drawing in a breath, recalling Dr. McAllister's directive to switch the topic if I ever felt uncomfortable.

Ignoring his last remark, I headed toward the sitting area, bringing his water to him. "What book would you like to read today? Do you want another thriller? Or something different? You've always enjoyed military books. We could read one of those."

He grabbed my arm as I set his water on the small table beside him. "And what kind of husband would I be if I always chose what we read? No, Josie. You choose. Tell me a love story."

He began running his fingers up my arm in an affectionate manner. I ripped it away from him, wishing life weren't so unfair, wishing my father could remember me, not think I was his wife who left him over two decades ago because we weren't enough for her. The woman who refused to even return a phone call when I tried to reach out and inform her about my father's condition. The woman who broke all her promises to us.

I stepped up to the bookcase, perusing its contents. My eyes settled on the spine of a book. I pulled it off the shelf, the cover tattered and torn after being read and reread countless times during my adolescence. I remembered swooning over Mr. Darcy before I knew what swooning truly was. In my mind, no man could ever compare to him. Whenever I had a bad experience with a guy years ago, Mr. Darcy was always there for me. I was pretty sure he had ruined me for all real men. Perhaps that was why I hid behind a laptop and wrote fictional accounts of every woman's fantasy man. Because the fantasy was always better than real life.

I settled into the reading chair, subtly pushing it back just a little to keep my distance from my father, and opened the book.

"*It is a truth universally acknowledged, that a man in possession of a good fortune, must be in want of a wife.*"

It felt like I was seeing an old friend again for the first

time in years. Jane Austen's words provided me a sense of comfort, and I was able to forget about all my troubles for a minute as I returned to her world.

Chapter Five

THE SOUND OF THE door opening snapped me out of the spell Jane Austen's words had put me under. Looking up, I noticed Jeffrey in the doorway.

"Visiting hours are up, Ms. Brinks," he said. "Sundowners."

Hearing the term, which referred to Alzheimer's and dementia patients' increased irritability as the sun went down, I checked my watch, surprised to see it was already five. I closed the book and placed it on the side table, standing from the chair.

"Love you, Daddy," I whispered, leaning down, placing a kiss on his forehead. "I'll see you tomorrow."

I gazed upon my father's shrunken stature as he slept slumped over in his wheelchair. My heart ached at his appearance. He was just a few years past his seventieth birthday, yet he seemed years older than that. I wished there were a magic pill he could take that would turn him back into the man he used to be. The man who had makeup parties with me when I was a little girl. The man who spent too many nights assembling a dollhouse I just had to have for my seventh birthday. The man who attended Mommy and Me lunches during elementary school so I wouldn't feel left out. Those memories were so clear, so vivid. Why couldn't they be that way for him, too?

A buzzing snapped me out of my depressing thoughts

as I headed into the hallway, reaching into my purse. Finally finding my phone in the bottomless abyss that was my bag, I saw a text from Drew.

You'd better not be bailing on tonight. If I have to suffer through speed dating, you do, too.

I hastily typed a response as I dashed down the hallway.

Just finishing up with Dad. Be at my place at 7. I'll have Brooklyn meet us there. Make sure you wear a button-down shirt. And please shave. As much as women say they like a bit of scruff, that shit hurts when you go down on us.

I grinned to myself, imagining my brother's face turning red as he read my response. I could hear his voice in my head, exclaiming, "Jesus, Molly. Enough." Instantly, Drew's reply appeared on the screen, making me laugh.

Jesus, Molly. Enough.

I tossed my phone into my bag, about to turn down another long corridor in this maze of a building.

"Ms. Brinks!" a voice called out.

Stopping, I spun around. A man wearing a crisp blue shirt, black tie, perfectly fitted black pants, and white lab coat hurried toward me.

"Dr. McAllister," I exhaled, furrowing my brow when I noticed the concerned look on his face.

I'd always been amazed that someone who appeared so young could be one of the top neurologists in the state, if not the country. It had taken me over a year to brush off my urge to call him Doogie Howser. Granted, he had to be in his thirties, not sixteen, but I'd expected my father's doctor to be old with white hair and a beer belly, not an attractive dark-haired young man who had a perpetually windswept look about him, as if he'd just stepped off his sailboat. I imagined he looked just as good in a pair of board shorts and boat shoes as he did in a tie and jacket.

"I told you. Call me Noah," he said with a smile that highlighted his nearly perfect teeth. One of the bottom ones was a bit crooked, but I liked it. It made him seem more earthly and less god-like.

"Okay. Noah."

We had this conversation every time I saw him. Still, each time he asked me to call him Noah, all I could think of was learning about the story of Noah's Ark in first grade before one of the nun's graciously asked my father not to bring me back to the Catholic school I had only been attending for a whopping three weeks. I couldn't help but picture Dr. McAllister, wearing a dark robe and having a ridiculously long beard, surrounded by a gaggle of animals. I'd confided that in my brother, who was convinced there was something wrong with me. It was simply my coping mechanism. Dr. McAllister, or Noah, always seemed to be the bearer of bad news. Our father's condition would only worsen over time. Imagining his doctor in a humorous setting prevented me from having a complete breakdown about how unfair this situation was.

"Do you have a minute? There are a few things I'd hoped to discuss with you."

I studied him. Whatever he wanted to talk to me about couldn't be good, not after five on a Friday.

"It's regarding your father," he added.

Nodding, I followed him down several hallways, past the front desk, and through a set of doors leading to the administrative wing. We finally came to a stop outside a metal door. He pulled a set of keys out of his pants pocket, inserting one into the lock. He opened the door, holding it so I could enter ahead of him.

Lights sprang to life, illuminating the small office. To the right were a leather loveseat and sofa that sat catty-corner, separated by a simple lamp and side table. His desk stood beyond that. Medical journals and legal pads obscured most of its usable surface. A small bookshelf was positioned adjacent to the sole window. On the opposite side of the bookshelf were two framed diplomas. A Bachelor of Science from Harvard hung just below an even more impressive frame boasting a certificate from Johns Hopkins University, claiming one Noah Joseph McAllister to be a Doctor of Medicine. I'd seen the same framed diplomas in his office at his own private practice, too. Apparently, doctors had to hang their diplomas in each of their offices. I figured it was an ego thing.

"Have a seat, Ms. Brinks." He gestured to the sofa. I lowered myself onto it, trying to remain still so the leather didn't make that embarrassing sound it so often did.

"You can just call me Molly." I smiled at him, glancing around his office as he sat on the loveseat next to the sofa.

"Okay, Molly. How's everything with you?"

"Good," I answered, returning my eyes to his. "I'm on a bit of a tight deadline with work, but nothing I can't handle."

"Ah, yes. You're a writer, aren't you?"

I cocked my head.

He smirked. "I've seen your name on a few columns in *Metropolitan.*"

"Oh, of course." I laughed politely. "Your wife or

girlfriend must read it, huh?"

He narrowed his gaze, shaking his head. "No."

"So *you* read it?"

"No. What I meant to say was I don't have a girlfriend."

I raised my eyebrows, giving him a coy grin.

"Or boyfriend," he added quickly. "I mean, I wouldn't have a boyfriend. I mean…not that there's anything wrong with that. I just…" He closed his eyes, drawing in a flustered breath. "Let's start over. No girlfriend. I'm straight. Some of the nurses here read the magazine and bust a gut laughing at your column. You make them smile."

"Then my job is done." An awkward silence passed between us. I cringed at the idea he had read "Ten Tips to Giving Better Head". My columns were very tongue-in-cheek, a way for me to air my grievances with whatever was bothering me that particular day. "So, what is it you wanted to discuss with me? I doubt it was how to let a guy down nicely," I joked, recalling one of my recent columns. Of course, there was nothing nice about the advice contained in it. The article would have been more appropriately titled "Ten Reasons Dating is for Schmucks".

"Right." He paused, his expression turning serious. "I apologize for the fact I haven't had time to update you on your father's condition myself."

"I understand you're busy."

"Nevertheless, there are a few things you should be made aware of and I didn't want to wait until the next time you and your brother were scheduled to meet with me."

I remained motionless, my face heating, at complete odds with the chill running down my spine. I felt out of my element here. Drew was the one who made all the decisions regarding my father's care. He was the one who knew all the appropriate questions to ask. All I knew was my dad had a terminal illness that had progressed over the past several years, now requiring constant care.

Meeting my eyes, he licked his lips, as if bracing to deliver a fatal blow. "Your father's condition has begun to deteriorate at a much faster pace."

"I'm sorry. What?" I furrowed my brow, shaking my head.

"As you know, there are seven stages of Alzheimer's ranging from extremely mild to minutes away from death."

I nodded quickly. When my father first got his diagnosis, I picked up every book I could on Alzheimer's. It was what I did. Drew was the practical one, methodically hunting for the best neurologists and long-term care facility money could buy, hoping he'd be able to extend the death sentence my father had been given. I did the only thing I knew. I researched the disease and was forced to come to the realization that my father would soon not only forget who we were, but would no longer be able to bathe or go to the bathroom on his own.

I thought we had time. Now, looking at the forlorn expression on Dr. McAllister's face, which he probably reserved for all the families he was about to deliver bad news to, I knew that time was coming to an end. I didn't know how people in the healthcare profession got up every morning, knowing they'd likely have to face upset and grieving family members, all wanting an answer to one question... Why?

"I know all about the stages of Alzheimer's," I barked

before softening my voice. "I thought he was doing okay."

"We can't ignore the signs, as much as we want to say he was just having a bad day. He's had months of bad days, Molly. He's become increasingly violent and irritable. So much so, he's had to be restrained several times. The staff has checked for infections constantly, hoping that would explain his irritability, but he's healthy, all things considered." He shook his head, his eyes remaining glued to mine. "He's easily confused."

"He's always been easily confused," I argued, not wanting to believe my father was close to the end. "When he was diagnosed, you said he could live with the disease far into his eighties or nineties. It's only been three years."

"It's true the life expectancy can be as long as twenty years, but every case is different. There's no cookie-cutter formula here, Molly. Your father has a much better chance of living a little longer because you've made him a priority. Many patients with advanced Alzheimer's, like your father, have such a short life expectancy because there's no one around to take care of them. The staff here is the best there is, and I promise you, we will do everything we can to ensure your father's final days are as comfortable and pain-free as possible."

"Final days?" I swallowed hard, my jaw going slack.

"Since the very beginning, I've told you there's no cure. There's no magic pill out there that can stop and reverse the progression." He reached out and grabbed my hand. I shot my eyes to the contact of his skin on mine. It was oddly comforting. "We're not giving up on him. I don't want you to think we are. We will continue to do everything we can to keep his brain working." He gave me a small smile, then leaned back on the couch, releasing my hand. "Environmental stimuli seems to help him have more lucid moments."

"Like photos?" I raised my brow.

He nodded. "Yes. And reading." The corners of his lips turned up. "According to the staff, he seems to be happiest in the afternoons. Somewhere inside the confusion in his brain, he knows you'll be by to read to him."

My expression fell. "That's because he thinks I'm my mother."

"None of that matters. Don't focus on what you have no control over. Enjoy the time you spend with him. Appreciate the fact that he's able to listen to your voice, that he's still here."

I took a deep breath, allowing the truth I knew was inevitable to sink in. "Have you spoken with Drew about this?"

He nodded. "Earlier this afternoon. He was unable to come and meet with me because of childcare restraints, but he did inform me you were here. But you always are in the afternoon, aren't you?"

I shrugged sheepishly. "How long does my father—"

"Molly," he interrupted, knowing exactly what I was getting at. "Even with the best care, he could live for several more years or he could die tomorrow. There's no way of knowing. But I do know that you and your brother have done everything you possibly can to ensure your dad is as comfortable as he can be for however long he has left." He hesitated briefly, forming his lips into a tight line. "On that note, the executive director, Dr. Connors, wanted me to discuss the healthcare directive in his file."

"I'm aware of it," I replied quickly.

"I just wanted to remind you that his advance directive is, essentially, what you probably know as a DNR. We prefer to use the term AND, which stands for Allow Natural Death. Pursuant to this directive, your brother signed an AND with the facility under the healthcare power of attorney your father had granted him. In the event anything happens, we cannot perform any lifesaving or sustaining measures. His directive covers a variety of different scenarios and what measures, if any, he approves. I'm more than happy to review those with you, if you'd like."

"I know what his directive says."

"I'm sure you do." He met my eyes. "When we reach this stage, it's simply protocol to remind the family of any directives in place."

I lowered my gaze, focusing on a small coffee stain on the gray rug as I absorbed everything Dr. McAllister just shared with me. I'd known my father was sick for a while. It had simply become a part of life.

Now that the truth of the situation hung in the air, I didn't know how I was supposed to feel. Most people in my shoes would probably shed a few tears at the notion they could be saying goodbye to their loved one within the coming weeks. Not me. Displaying emotions made you vulnerable. I wasn't going to put myself in that position.

With a blank expression, I stood from the couch. "I need to get going. Thank you for the update, Dr. McAllister." I held my hand out. He eyed it, then me.

"Molly, it's okay if this news upsets you."

I tugged my jacket closer, flashing him a congenial smile. "I'm fine, Dr. McAllister."

"Noah," he corrected.

"Fine. Noah," I huffed. "Like I said, I'm fine."

Standing, he narrowed his gaze. "Are you sure?"

I stepped toward the door, holding my head high. "I'm sure you deal with upset families all day long. People asking why this disease had to affect their loved ones. How come their own father can't remember them." My voice was even, at complete odds with how a normal person should feel given the situation. I'd become an expert at masking my emotions over the years. This doctor wouldn't be the one to break me. "I've had several years to come to terms with the fact my father is dying. As far as I'm concerned, this disease has already killed him. That man I read to every day is not my father."

I turned the handle, about to open the door when I slammed into the metal, the door still firmly closed. *So much for a dramatic exit.*

"Security protocol," Noah explained, reaching past me for the doorknob. "It automatically locks from the inside and outside." He pressed a button on the knob, then turned it, pushing the door open.

My face burning, I walked into the hallway, trying to regain at least a modicum of composure.

"Molly," he called out as I was about to turn the corner that had quickly become a symbol of salvation from utter embarrassment.

"Yes?" I reluctantly spun around, plastering a smile on my face.

"Are you okay?"

I huffed, rubbing a sore spot just above my forehead. "I told you, I—"

"No. Your head." He took a step toward me, eyeing me. "I can take a look at it for you."

I quickly stopped fidgeting with my head, showing him there probably wasn't even so much as a mark.

"It's fine. It's not the first time this has happened."

His concerned eyes turned light as he crossed his arms over his chest, widening his stance. "You make a habit out of walking into doors?"

"No. Just wishing I had an invisibility cloak like Harry Potter so I wouldn't have to be bothered with such trivial things as opening doors."

A smile formed on his full lips, reaching his dark eyes. The beautiful sound of his laughter echoed against the halls. "Enjoy your evening."

Taking that as my cue to leave, I hurried down the corridor.

"Oh, and Molly?"

I spun around to face him once more.

"An invisibility cloak didn't help Harry walk through doors." He winked and retreated back into his office.

My jaw dropped. *Holy shit. He gives good wink.*

In a daze, I continued out of the building. When I got behind the wheel of my car, I could have sworn a flutter erupted in my stomach similar to that strange feeling I had written about in my books on more than one occasion. So I did what any normal twenty-nine-plus-one-year-old would. I blamed it on the Mexican food I ate for lunch.

Chapter Six

"IT'S ABOUT TIME YOU got back!" Brooklyn huffed when I opened the door to my apartment to see her and Drew sitting on the couch, waiting.

Drew had taken my advice and finally shaved. His hair was still a bit damp from a shower, and he looked nothing like the scruffy hockey player I knew him to be. He looked rather dashing in his dark jeans and yellow button-down shirt with the sleeves rolled up that made his olive-toned skin appear even darker.

"This thing starts in thirty minutes, and we still need to get to the Back Bay!" Brooklyn stood, the heels she wore making her already tall and lanky frame tower over my five-foot, three-inch height by a good six inches. She wore a pair of dark jeans and a loose-fitting emerald green sheath top she dressed up with a silver belt around her waist.

"I'll be ready." I headed toward the wet bar and rummaged through its contents to find the strongest liquor I had. If I had to pretend I was interested in finding my soul mate amongst a room full of desperate people, I was going to need a decent buzz. Plus, my father's prognosis lay heavy on my heart. I needed to dull the pain I did everything in my power to hide. "I could use a drink after today."

I felt Drew's eyes on me. I shot him a sideways glance as I set a bottle and a few rocks glasses on the counter.

"Did you talk to Dr. McAllister?"

I nodded slightly. "When I was leaving, Noah…I mean, Dr. McAllister pulled me aside." I looked at Drew. My expression said everything he needed to know.

"Noah?" Brooklyn placed her hands on her hips. "You call your father's doctor by his first name?"

"That's what he asked me to call him," I answered nonchalantly, pouring a few fingers of scotch into each glass.

Before I started writing, I never drank scotch. I felt I needed to try it for research purposes since the leading men in my books tended to drink it. I couldn't speak intelligently about it if I never touched the stuff myself. There was a lot of bad behavior I repeatedly excused away by calling it research. I did have limits, though. I wasn't about to do drugs just because I wrote about a meth addict. Thankfully, *Breaking Bad* really helped in that department.

"Really?" Drew's eyes floated to mine. "He's never told *me* that."

"That's probably because you handle shit better than I do." Leaning against the wall, I crossed one arm over my stomach, the other hand holding my scotch. "That guy is just waiting for me to crack."

"What do you mean?" Brooklyn edged toward me, scooping her tumbler of scotch off the bar.

"Nothing," I responded quickly. "It's just… Whenever he gives me news about Dad, he does so in a way that makes me feel like he's waiting for me to have a complete meltdown. 'Are you okay, Molly? Are you sure?'" I said in my best deep voice, imitating Noah's scruff tone. "It's like he wants me to lose it in front of him. Like he gets off on that shit or something."

"He doesn't get off on that shit." Brooklyn rolled her eyes. "He's probably acting that way because you've never shown him any emotion at all. He's a doctor who has to tell people on a daily basis their loved ones are dead or dying. He can probably tell when someone's pretending they're okay when, in all reality, they're not."

"Then he can probably also tell when someone *is* okay," I hissed, avoiding their eyes. I raised my glass to my lips, the scotch seeming to take forever to filter through my mouth and throat, then warm my stomach. Once all the liquor was gone, I slammed the tumbler down, holding onto the quartz counter as I drew a long breath to steady myself.

"Molly." I felt Brooklyn's presence behind me before she even placed her hand on my shoulder. I spun around and faced her. She hesitated, pulling her bottom lip between her teeth as she studied my expression. My face could be blank and emotionless, yet Brooklyn always had a way of knowing precisely how I felt. "It's bad, isn't it?"

"Some people would say it is." I straightened my posture. "This isn't a surprise to me...to either of us." I nodded at Drew, whose face seemed to show everything mine refused to — pain, heartache, longing for the way things used to be. "We knew his time was short when he was diagnosed. Since that day, he's been on borrowed time. Is it bad?" I shrugged. "How can I say it is when we knew this was the path his disease would take?"

I spun on my heels and headed down the hallway, closing the door to my room so I could have a minute to myself away from prying eyes that just itched for me to finally cry in front of them. I didn't know why everyone thought I should be upset over the predictable decline of my father's ability to function. Whether or not I exhibited any emotions had no bearing on the freight train headed straight for him. Nothing could stop it.

A blank expression on my face, I sat at the vanity against the far wall, staring into the antique mirror that had belonged to my grandmother. I grabbed a tube of eyeliner off the table and began to apply some, bringing my eyes back to life. I continued through the familiar motions of putting on blush, mascara, and lip gloss, the plain version of myself disappearing as a flirty, sexy young professional out for a good time on a Friday night took her place. I'd done this same song and dance so many times now, I was getting tired of it. I hated feigning interest in someone else's life, someone else's hobbies, someone else's passion. I hated pretending to be someone I wasn't, even around Brooklyn and Drew.

"Get a move on, Molly!" Brooklyn shouted from the kitchen.

I snapped out of my daze, jumping off the stool. Perusing the clothes in my small closet, I scrunched my nose, unsure of the proper attire for speed dating. I wondered if this was something Google could tell me. Or Siri. That bitch seemed to have all the answers. She had no problem reminding me of that fact in her smug little voice, either.

Short on time, I grabbed the staple of every woman's wardrobe...a little black dress. Zipping up the fitted dress that hit mid-thigh, I surveyed my reflection in the mirror, turning around and kicking out my leg to check the slit that exposed a little more skin, but in a tasteful manner. Pairing it with animal print heels that added three inches to my short stature, I finished the look with a long, silver beaded, layered necklace and matching earrings. I glimpsed at my reflection in the mirror and plastered a fake smile on my face, pretending to laugh at my make-believe speed date's dry sense of humor. I knew what men liked. I knew how to act, what to say, what to wear to hook whatever guy was my unknowing victim that evening.

The fake smile still plastered on my face, I sauntered back down the hallway.

"You look great, Molly," Brooklyn exclaimed when I reentered my living area.

"Not like it matters. This whole thing is a joke."

"Molly," she cautioned. "At least give it a chance. You never know who you'll meet."

I grabbed my coat out of the entryway closet and headed toward the door, my brother and Brooklyn following. "I could be wrong, but I highly doubt I'll meet anyone at speed dating who will make my stomach flutter."

I stopped dead in my tracks, instantly reminded of my afternoon discussion with Dr. Noah McAllister, M.D., and the tingling in my stomach when he winked at me, coupled with a *Harry Potter* reference. That had to be it. The sensation of little wings flitting madly in my stomach as I jumped into my car earlier had absolutely nothing to do with his sweet smile, his sinful eyes, or his husky voice. I'd always been a sucker for a man who could talk *Harry Potter* to me. I may or may not have had some rather inappropriate fantasies regarding Neville Longbottom... Year seven Neville, not year one.

"Maybe. Maybe not," Drew added, nudging me.

I snapped out of my thoughts and continued down the stairs of my building, exiting onto the street. He was probably just as skeptical about the whole thing as I was. Not to mention people actually knew who he was.

He'd already had his heart broken by a hockey groupie. I hated the thought that he'd never meet anyone who wanted to be with him for him, hated that all anyone would see when they looked at him was the hockey celebrity.

"At least this might be some good material for your column."

"You're right about that. I wonder how many guys would be desperate enough to date an escaped mental patient." I gave them a crazed look. Drew laughed. Brooklyn shot daggers at me.

"Play nice, Molly. There are still some people out there who believe in the idea of love. Maybe three minutes is all you need to know if they're the one."

I rolled my eyes as we trudged down the narrow streets of the North End, the smell of garlic, tomatoes, and spices filling the air. Tourists roamed the sidewalks, debating which restaurant to try for dinner. They couldn't go wrong. No matter which spot they chose, they'd be treated to an authentic Italian meal unlike anything they'd ever had. It was a miracle I didn't weigh three hundred pounds living in an area surrounded by all this amazing food.

"You've been reading too many of my books lately, Brooklyn." I pulled my jacket closer, a subtle wind blowing between my legs, chilling me in the cool April evening. A dress probably wasn't the best idea, but I had shaved my legs earlier this morning. I couldn't waste the opportunity. "No one looks into someone's eyes and knows, at that moment, they want to spend the rest of their life with them."

"It could be real," she offered in a quiet voice. "My dad always told me he fell in love with my mother before she even said a single word. Between classes, she worked at the library on campus. He would go there every day just to see her. It took him months to finally work up the courage to talk to her. When he finally did, well... The rest is history." She looked down. "Maybe you're right. Maybe love at first sight doesn't exist." Her eyes met mine before briefly floating over toward Drew. "But maybe people believe it does because it gives them hope they won't be alone forever."

"What's so bad about being alone?" I asked when we reached the Haymarket T station. "Why does society put so much emphasis on getting married and having a family? It's not for everyone. Some people value their independence and don't want to give that up."

"You don't have to give up your independence to be in a relationship," she argued, parroting what Drew had told me earlier in the day.

"Relationships change people, and usually *not* for the better." There was no way anyone would convince me otherwise. I'd been in my fair share of semi-relationships. There was still a little give and take involved, even in the casual arrangements I had. "I'm not willing to give up who I am just to make someone else happy." We scanned our passes at the turnstiles and headed down the stairs, the sound of metal on metal screeching in the distance. I turned to face Drew and Brooklyn as we waited for the train.

"Listen, I know you two always bring this up because you care about me and want me to be happy. I *am* happy. One day, I may find someone who's just as crazy as I am. Maybe we'll fall madly in love and have lots of crazy sex and babies. But today's not that day. The only reason I even agreed to this is because I have a deadline and am in desperate need of a muse. A professional young man who looks great in a suit."

"Can't you just find a picture of some hot guy online?" Drew asked. "You have a pretty active imagination. I'm sure you could get creative."

"I tried to write a book without a living, breathing muse once…and ended up having to do a complete rewrite."

"Why?" Brooklyn scrunched her brows.

"Because it was crap."

"No. I mean, why did you try to write without a muse? You've always seemed pretty insistent on having one."

"It was unavoidable," I lied, hiding my eyes from theirs.

I swore I'd never tell another soul what had happened with one of my arrangements. If Drew knew the shit the slimeball of a politician I was seeing tried to pull, I was fairly certain the asshole would have required facial reconstruction surgery. I knew my approach to dating was unconventional, at best, and there was a certain risk involved, but that could be said of normal relationships, as well. Regardless, the incident unsettled me to the point of temporarily ditching the whole muse thing.

"I procrastinated and had to write a book in about four days. As luck would have it, it was the four days Aunt Flo decided to come visit," I added.

Drew eyed me. "We don't have an Aunt Flo."

Brooklyn and I giggled. My brother could be somewhat naïve at times. All men wore blinders when it came to things they'd rather not think about.

"Use your brain," I encouraged him.

He shook his head, his brows still furrowed.

"My vagina was bleeding," I said loudly. Other people waiting for the subway looked in our direction.

"So there was no getting laid. I mean, I guess I could have, but my sheets would have looked like a crime scene."

"Jesus, Molly." Drew looked away, blushing, his tall stature shrinking. "A word of advice for tonight. Most men don't want to hear about...bleeding vaginas."

I placed a hand on my hip as the train came to stop. "That just proves my point." I stepped into the car and sat down. Brooklyn and Drew lowered themselves on either side of me.

"What point?" he asked.

"People are forced to change when they're in a relationship. I, for one, like talking about bloody vaginas. I refuse to change my ways just for a man who doesn't."

Brooklyn laughed. "Only you would have on your list of positive character traits: 'must enjoy talking about bloody lady bits'."

"The bloody vagina is just part of the bigger picture. I'm not willing to change who I am for anyone, regardless of the size of his one-eyed willy. The right man will want to listen to me talk about my vagina in all its states — bloody, wet, dry, hairy, shaved."

"I can't believe I'm listening to this," Drew muttered, nodding across the aisle to an older couple who were giving him that look he was all too accustomed to, like they recognized him, but weren't sure if he was someone they should know or just a random doppelgänger.

"Well, the right man for me will have no problem listening to this."

"I'm pretty sure the only man who won't have any problem discussing your intimate lady bits will be a gynecologist," Brooklyn commented, then her expression brightened. "Hey! Maybe you'll meet a doctor tonight!"

I rolled my eyes. "Don't hold your breath."

Chapter Seven

"I'M A DOCTOR," A moderately attractive man said after I asked what he did for a living.

I glanced at the table to my right, giving Brooklyn an annoyed look. The function room at a popular seafood restaurant in Boston's Back Bay had been rearranged for tonight's dating extravaganza. Small two-by-two tables were assembled into approximately four rows of five tables each, the lighting dimmed. A lone candle sat in the center of each table, offering a romantic ambiance for every three-minute session. And that was exactly what it felt like. Some of these men had serious issues. If I were a therapist, I would go to speed dating just to increase my client list. The thought of drawing up some business cards had crossed my mind more than once in the past ten minutes.

"And what is it you do?"

I turned my attention back to the light brown-haired man sitting across from me. The flickering of the candle on his skin made it appear as if he had been badly burned as a child and the flesh had never grown back. Whoever organized this event was clearly trying too hard.

"Nothing as exciting as being a doctor," I said in a sweet voice, batting my lashes. Maybe I wasn't taking this seriously, but how could I when the M.C. wore an oversized gaudy heart pinned to the lapel of his jacket?

It was all so over the top. Drew was right, though. I had gotten some great material for a column. "Tell me more about that." I leaned my head on my folded hands.

One thing I had learned over the years of being a serial dater was how easy it was to get the focus off myself by asking whomever I was with a question about their lives. Human beings were naturally egotistical and loved talking about themselves. For most people, their favorite topic of conversation was me, me, and more me. But there was nothing interesting about Molly Brinks. Having a famous brother helped. Once people figured out I was the little sister of *the* Drew Brinks, all they'd want to talk about was him.

"Oh, it's not that exciting," Mr. Doctor replied casually, brushing it off. I think he said his name was Curt. I glanced at the tag he wore over the breast of his shirt, noticing a mustard stain on the collar. I tried to ignore it, unsuccessfully. It glared against the light blue color. Did he not look in the mirror before he left the house?

"Oh, come on," I coaxed. "Stop being modest. Tell me something out of the ordinary that happened today." I raised my wine glass to my mouth, licking my lips seductively. I knew how to get what I wanted.

A nervous smile tugged at his mouth as he took a breath. "Okay. Well… This guy came in today. It was an emergency appointment. He had been trying to reattach a garage door spring. Those things are pretty heavy duty. Anyway, it backfired and smacked him right in the mouth. His six front teeth were shattered so I had to extract them, then fit him for some implants."

I straightened my spine, then furrowed my brow. "Isn't that something a dentist would do?"

He nodded. "Of course. That's why he came to me."

"Wait a minute. You're a dentist? I thought you said you were a doctor."

"Technically, dentists are doctors, too. It's an incredibly specialized field."

"I'm not discounting the fact you had to study and work just as hard as a regular physician, but what would possess you to go into a profession where you'd be despised and feared? No one likes going to the dentist."

"That's not entirely true," he argued. "There are plenty of people who don't mind it."

"I'll concede there's nothing like that fresh feeling in your mouth after having your teeth cleaned, but there's nothing fun about sitting in that chair and going through all the scraping, grinding, drilling." I shivered. "I'd rather go to my gynecologist and get a metal instrument shoved up my vagina than go to the dentist, if we're being completely honest with each other. At least that's over in about a second. Not the dentist. Oh no. That shit goes on for at least an hour."

I supposed the doctor line worked on most women. Let's face it. If you met a complete stranger at a bar or on the street and heard he was a doctor, it upped his appeal a few points. If I hadn't become such a cynic when it came to the whole dating charade, it may have worked on me, too. That ship had sailed long ago.

A bell dinged, signaling the "date" was over. Mr. Dentist-not-Doctor slowly got up from the chair.

"Hope you meet someone tonight," I said in a chipper voice.

He stared at me blankly, probably still in shock at my candor. Truth be told, for a dentist, his teeth could have used a little work. "You, too, Avery."

"Avery?" Brooklyn hissed as the men shuffled down

the row of tables and we remained seated. It was a bit old-fashioned, thinking women shouldn't be asked to get up. I would have given anything to stretch my legs and give my ass a break from sitting on this hard chair.

I turned so she could see my name tag. "I'm doing this to find a muse for my book. Why not take on the persona of my leading lady?" I beamed a wide smile at her.

"I thought you were going to take this seriously," she whispered.

"I'm taking *this* seriously, but there's absolutely no one here *I* can take seriously. It's a giant waste of time."

I noticed someone lower himself into the chair across from me. Reluctantly, I turned my attention away from Brooklyn and toward the newest man of my dreams…at least for the next three minutes. It didn't sound like a long time. In some company, feigning interest in their high-paced employment as a cold-call salesperson, three minutes was a goddamn eternity. I hated those bastards more than dentists.

Over the next ninety minutes, I saw and heard it all. There was an older investment broker who, after some digging, I found was just an embellished way of saying he'd been laid off and was playing the stock market with his 401K. There were several overweight middle-aged men who still refused to come to terms with the fact their wife left them. Then there was my favorite faction of men…the hipsters. I'd never understood the necessity of wearing a winter hat indoors or sporting a pair of dark-framed glasses with fake lenses. They weren't fooling anyone, except themselves.

"This dating thing is too much work," I said to Drew and Brooklyn after all the sessions had ended and the majority of the attendees were indulging in the open bar. It appeared as if a few connections had been made, so the night wasn't a complete waste of time. But for my little circle, it was. I didn't expect anything else and neither did Drew. Brooklyn, however, seemed a little frustrated.

"No, it's not," she insisted, sipping on her gin and tonic.

"My cheeks hurt from smiling and pretending I was interested in stamp collections and stories of college trips to Cancun." I rolled my eyes, then turned to the bar, signaling the bartender to pour me another glass of wine.

As my gaze shifted around the room to see men and women, who had been complete strangers earlier in the evening, laughing between sly glances and coy smiles, I considered perhaps Drew and Brooklyn were right, although I'd never admit it. Maybe I should keep my heart open to the possibility there was a guy out there who would be content with all my idiosyncrasies, who wouldn't be offended by my sometimes vulgar language, who would love me for me.

I just didn't see how I would meet him at speed dating or online. The man of my dreams was too good to be true, a fantasy, a work of fiction. Still, I couldn't get the image of my father all alone in the nursing home out of my mind. He probably had more visitors than most residents, but a few hours a week was nothing in comparison to the long stretches of time he was forced to keep himself and his mind busy with little outside stimuli. I couldn't help but wonder who would visit me when I was old and senile. If I continued down this path, I knew the answer. No one.

"There you two are!" a voice exclaimed, breaking me out of my thoughts.

I turned around to see the flamboyant M.C., whom I had renamed Cupid's Antichrist, running directly toward us. I flashed the bartender a smile, then raised my red wine to my lips, suppressing the urge to scribble my number on a napkin and slide it to him, along with the tip, in case I ever needed a brooding bartender as a muse.

"This is the first time this has happened," Cupid's Antichrist continued.

"What's that?" Drew asked.

With a grin, he grabbed Drew's and my hand, linking them together. "I just went through all the questionnaires you filled out at the beginning of tonight and it's too good to be true!" He brimmed with enthusiasm, bouncing in his loafers. He truly was wearing loafers. With no socks. "You two are a perfect match!"

My eyes widened in horror and disgust. Yes, I was writing a forbidden romance and the stepbrother thing seemed to be popular as of late, but there was no step between Drew and me. With haste, we both withdrew our hands, our expressions nearly identical.

"What?" he asked, looking at both Drew and me in confusion. "I thought this would be good news. See." He held up the questionnaires we had filled out. "Avery Rollins and Jackson Price are compatible in every category."

I almost spit out my wine, praying this was a good omen for my book.

"Maybe on paper," Drew responded, saving me from having to answer. "But I don't feel anything for her. In fact…" He faced me, smiling brightly. "She reminds me of my sister."

"I'm not going to force you two to do anything," the

M.C. sighed. "But you should at least exchange numbers. You never know."

"We'll be sure to do that." Laughing at the ridiculousness of the entire evening, I practically downed my glass of wine. Only alcohol could help me forget my perfect match was my brother.

"Oh, and one more thing." Cupid's Antichrist spun around, studying Drew. "I'm sure you get this a lot, but has anyone ever mentioned you look like that hockey player? What was his name?" He bit his lips. "He played for the Bruins a few years back."

"Andrew Brinks," the bartender muttered, drying a few rocks glasses.

"Yes! That's it!" he exclaimed. "Has anyone ever told you that you look like him?"

A trite smile crossed Drew's mouth. "I've gotten that a few times."

"I figured. The resemblance is uncanny." He grinned at Drew, then nodded at Brooklyn and me. "Have a good evening."

After he walked away, Brooklyn turned to us, crossing her arms in front of her chest, her lips pinched. "Why didn't you include me in your little plan?" she huffed.

"What plan?" I asked innocently.

"All of this." She gestured between us, lowering her voice. "Am I the only one who used her real name?"

Drew and I shared a mischievous look. It was true we were compatible. We grew up together. We'd been each other's rock through all of life's ups and downs. We knew what the other was thinking without either of us having to voice it.

"Honestly, Brook," I began. "We didn't plan this."

"I don't buy it. What are the chances of both of you using fake names? Then both being characters from the book you're currently working on?"

Drew nudged me. "Well, after all, we *are* a perfect match."

"Sick," I groaned.

Chapter Eight

THAT DAMN BLINKING CURSOR had been mocking me all Saturday morning as I stared at it with pure hatred. I was convinced the geniuses who developed word processing software didn't include the blinking cursor as a way to signal the user as to his or her place in the document. Oh no. Those bastards had a much more sadistic purpose…to remind those of us on a deadline of the impossibility of our task. I'd bypassed the time for fucking off on my procrastination continuum. Now was the time to do all the work while crying. Although I was pretty sure the sound escaping my mouth would be more appropriately categorized as a call of distress.

I had forty hours until I needed to hand in a rough draft of the first 20,000 words. If I didn't sleep between now and Monday morning, I would have to write 500 words an hour. It wasn't an impossible task, apart from one rather minor detail. I was still sans muse. The words that once flowed so freely and easily were hard to find. I was more than aware of the fact that it was probably all in my head, but that still didn't help me find the words. I'd lost count of the number of times I'd written several paragraphs, only to go back and delete them. It was the same crap I'd been writing for years now. I was tired of it.

In a moment of desperation, I'd broken down and signed up for several online dating sites. I'd even reached out to one of my sorority sisters, Debra. She had a marketing degree and now worked as a "dating consultant" at a high-profile dating service. Apparently, extremely wealthy men paid the equivalent of most people's yearly salary to have someone else find them potential dates. Since I had been a bridesmaid at her wedding, she owed me one and was more than happy to see if she had any clients in the area who were interested in meeting me. I *was* writing a billionaire businessman romance. What better source of inspiration than going on a date with a ridiculously wealthy businessman?

After too many hours of staring at my laptop in frustration, my projected target in the corner of the screen mocking me with a total word count of one hundred, I shoved away from my computer. In the past, some of my best story ideas came to me when I stepped back from my laptop. I needed to do that again.

The sun shining, warming the city, I decided it was the perfect weather to go roam around town and people-watch. My impetuous plan to try online dating to find a muse wasn't going to help me deliver 20,000 words by Monday morning. At this point, I needed to consider the option of just writing 20,000 words of complete crap, then rewrite it once I had a muse.

Pulling on a light jacket, I found my hobo sack of a bag and threw a notebook and pen into it. I gave Pee Wee a few kisses, trying to ignore the utter despair on his face at the thought of me abandoning him, even for a minute, then left my apartment, making sure to stop by the café to grab a coffee for the road.

"You meet someone last night?" Aunt Gigi asked before I even had a chance to say hello.

"No," I answered, heading behind the counter to

pour a coffee. "But I did end up being a perfect match with someone based on the compatibility questionnaire we all did when we signed in." I turned to my aunt, whose expression lit up.

"Really? Who?"

"Drew." I grabbed a cover and sleeve for my coffee, then headed back around the counter.

Her face fell. "How about online dating? Did you put up your profile yet?"

Taking a sip of my coffee, I tried to hide my scowl. "I'm working on it, Aunt Gigi."

"Did you make sure to include a photo?"

I scrunched my eyebrows, wondering how my sixty-five-year-old, gray-haired, bingo-playing aunt could possibly know anything about online dating...or dating in general, for that matter. She had been married to my uncle Leo for forty-five years.

"I did some research for you, Molly Mae."

I practically spit out my coffee. "Research?"

"Yes. According to a few dating... What do you call them? Bogs?"

"You mean *blogs*?" I asked in a mildly condescending tone. My aunt had trouble running the register at the coffee shop, wishing it were a purely cash business, like in the "good ol' days". I wondered how she even knew how to turn on a computer.

"Yes. That's it. Blogs. They said in order for your profile to get more attention, make sure you have a good photo, and not a selfie or a mirror photo. Your aunt Teresa just got one of those fancy Canon cameras. If you want, I can call her to come take your photo for you."

Giving her a terse smile, I grabbed a muffin, then headed toward the front door. "I'll keep that in mind."

"You'd better," she warned. "If you don't, you'll never find someone. You don't want your ovaries to shrivel up, do you?"

I groaned, rolling my eyes. "What is it with all you people and shriveling ovaries? I'm pretty sure that's not even a thing!" I opened the glass door to the café.

"Have a good day, Molly Mae," she called after me, a lightness to her voice. She knew how much I hated the shriveling ovaries comment.

I stepped onto the sidewalk, the North End burgeoning with people on a beautiful Saturday morning. Only in New England could it be in the sixties one day and snowing the next. A lot of locals complained about the weather, and I probably would have been one of them if I had a job I had to commute to. I loved watching the snow fall from the comfort of my couch as I snuggled up with Pee Wee. There was nothing like seeing the leaves change colors in the fall. I didn't even mind the humidity that made the air stagnant during the hot summer months. Despite my outward cynicism, I liked to consider myself an optimist…one grounded in realism. I didn't care if it sounded contradictory.

I navigated the few short blocks to the subway station and made my way down to the platform. I remained lost in my thoughts, trying to find a story that continued to remain hopelessly out of my grasp. Within minutes, a train arrived, filled with out-of-towners and locals alike. I stepped into one of the full cars, holding onto a rail as it sped through the darkened tunnels beneath Boston. After a short trip, the train pulled to a stop at the Park station and I squeezed out of the crowded car.

Emerging on street level, I inhaled the city air and squinted, readjusting my eyes to the sun. I headed down a paved path through Boston Common, dodging runners and cyclists. Street hawkers sold t-shirts, snacks, water, and other souvenirs with the name of my beloved city in large bold letters. This was one of the city's biggest attractions, despite it being just a bit of green space in town. With its prime location near the theaters, hotels, and shopping, it was the perfect place to people-watch and even eavesdrop on conversations.

Settling beneath a large oak tree in an area with a good view of the winding paths and pond, I pulled out my journal and pen, scribbling down whatever popped into my head. It didn't have to make sense or even be in a complete sentence. Hell, sometimes it was just a bunch of profanities strewn together. It was simply a way for me to write *something*. Many times, that something turned out to be everything.

After several minutes passed and my hand began to cramp, I flipped back through my random thoughts. It ran the gamut from why anyone would want to be a dentist, particularly if they'd sat through a crappy high school production of *Little Shop of Horrors*, to my father and the news I'd received the previous day about his deteriorating condition. I wondered if he was in any pain. I wondered what it felt like to be dying. I wondered if he wished things had been different, whether he regretted shutting people out of his life after my mother left. I wondered whether I was headed down the same path.

When a rumble ripped from my stomach, I reached into my bag, pulling out the chocolate chip muffin I'd swiped from the café. Almost instantly, at least a half-dozen ducks, which had been paying me absolutely no attention as they swam in the pond a few yards away, descended on me, eyeing my muffin as if it were the last morsel of food on earth.

"Get back," I warned them.

They only grew more aggressive, snapping at the muffin. Scenes from Alfred Hitchcock's *The Birds* flashed in my mind as I stood, clutching onto it. I refused to reward the ducks' encroaching behavior. There were very few things I held dear enough to sacrifice my own life for. Food just so happened to be on the top of that list, especially anything with chocolate. It was my weakness.

One of the larger ducks, I'd mentally named him "*El Jefe*", flapped his wings, the sound ominous. I never understood a phobia of birds until that moment. Trapped against the tree, I attempted to kick away the ducks at my feet, but the bastards were relentless. Driven by the prospect of indulging in a muffin that could only be described as pure heaven, they remained steadfast in their assault, quacking and pecking at me in the hopes I'd surrender.

Just as I considered how to work this random bird attack, which was completely unbelievable and would only happen to me, into one of my books, the ducks scattered. A tall figure clad in a pair of gym shorts and a sweat-stained gray t-shirt ran toward me, flailing his arms as he chased away my attackers that were clearly seconds away from killing me. In my book, I decided the ducks would be gang members and my damsel in distress would be saved by a mobster who was feared by everyone in the criminal underworld. It would probably play better than ducks. Anything would play better than ducks.

Smoothing the lines of my t-shirt and jacket, I met the eyes of my supposed knight in shining armor. My breath hitched, taken aback by the familiar eyes. The blue was so clear, I could almost see the reflection of flying ducks in them.

"Ms. Brinks," he said, a smile on his face. "This is quite a surprise."

"Dr. McAllister." My face flushing, I avoided his intrigued stare and gathered my notebook, shoving it into my bag.

I'd always been paranoid about anyone catching a glimpse of what that notebook contained. Even Drew and Brooklyn weren't allowed to read it. It was something I did just for me. The idea of anyone reading so much as a sentence made my stomach churn. My innermost thoughts sometimes found their way to the pages. This journal contained my true feelings...feelings I often masked with my cynicism and sarcasm.

"I promise I'm not the 'Feed the Birds' lady from *Mary Poppins*," I joked.

"Tuppence a bag," he shot back in a horrific British accent. I couldn't help but laugh at how awful it was, yet he appeared so confident and unfazed by it.

My nervous laughter fading, we stared at each other awkwardly under the shade of the giant tree. It was odd to see him dressed in something other than a suit and lab coat. He looked...athletic. Strong.

Handsome.

People ran past, others flying by on those death traps on wheels, otherwise known as rollerblades. Drew made rollerblading...and ice skating, for that matter...look so easy. I, on the other hand, had no coordination. As soon as I was up, gravity would kick in and my ass would meet the ground in a most unattractive manner. It was a wonder I'd never suffered a broken bone.

"What brings you here today?" Dr. McAllister broke through the heavy silence, widening his stance. He shoved his hands into the pockets of his gym shorts.

I surveyed his flushed appearance. His lips were parted slightly, his eyes trained on me in a way that made me feel…I didn't know…desired?

Or maybe I was so desperate to find a muse, I was drawn to anyone who even paid me a modicum of attention.

"Just trying to get a bit of work done," I answered quickly, flinging my bag onto my shoulder. I needed to find a safer, duck-free perch to people-watch and write. "Before I was unceremoniously attacked by bottom-dwelling vermin, that is."

"Did you know ducks are generally monogamous creatures?" he asked as I was about to walk away, speaking at a fast pace. "Although that typically only lasts a year." He offered me a breathtaking smile, running his hand through his dark, windswept hair. "But during that year, the male duck, known as a drake, and the female duck, which is called a hen or just a duck, are monogamous."

"Interesting," I replied in a drawn-out voice, feigning interest. I had absolutely no desire to hear about the relationship status of humans, let alone ducks.

"I have a brain full of useless information." He crossed his arms, his biceps stretching the fabric of his shirt.

My breath caught unexpectedly. A warming sensation rolled over me. I never would have imagined Dr. Noah McAllister had a decent body hidden beneath the suit and white lab coat he wore whenever I saw him. Granted, I'd always thought he was a good-looking guy, but in a "boy next door" kind of way, not in a "tie me up and spank me" kind of way. Now my imagination was on overdrive. I contemplated writing a sinful story between a patient and her doctor, who certainly knew how to steam things up in the bedroom…or exam room. I didn't care whether it was ethical or not. I usually didn't let technicalities such as that get in my way. Readers loved a forbidden romance, and I loved to write them.

"You should go on *Jeopardy!*," I told him, antsy to be on my way.

"I get that a lot." He beamed a wide smile at me before his jovial expression turned more serious, more sympathetic. I had a sneaky suspicion he was about to bring up our conversation from yesterday. Before he could pick up where we left things, I proceeded past him.

"Thanks for the help with the ducks. Have a good weekend." I headed down the slightly crested hill and toward the paved path, the sun hitting my face.

Just as I was about to round the corner skirting the pond, his deep voice called out again. "Molly! Wait up!"

Slowing my steps, I let out an exasperated sigh and turned around. A shiver ran down my spine when I was treated to the sight of Dr. Noah McAllister running toward me. His strides were long, bringing attention to his toned legs.

"Yes?" I tilted my head up at him as he slowed to a stop, his smile wide and eyes bright. I could feel the heat flowing off his body. A breeze blew, picking up an aroma that was a mixture of sweat, peppermint, and fresh-cut grass. It wasn't this overpowering scent so many other men I'd been close to gave off — an artificial stench after bathing in a horrendous body spray the advertising geniuses convinced them would help them get a date or, even better, laid. Noah's scent was natural…a welcome aphrodisiac.

Hesitating, he chewed on his bottom lip. Much to my surprise, a part of me wanted to chew on it, too. "Want to grab a coffee or something?"

I opened my mouth, caught off guard by his invitation. Was that even allowed? I had no idea, but I knew one thing for certain. I had no desire to spend any more time with Dr. Noah McAllister than necessary. I couldn't help but think he would analyze everything I said and did, simply waiting for me to snap under the weight of my father's disease. I didn't need his soothing voice telling me it was okay to show my feelings.

"I don't want to interrupt your run." I spun back around and continued toward the subway. "Nice seeing you again."

"You're not interrupting it," he called after me, catching up with ease. He came to a stop directly in front of me and widened his stance. As he crossed his arms, those toned biceps were on display once more. They weren't huge, like Kevin's, but they did tug on the fabric of his gym shirt. "I came out here to clear my head." He narrowed his gaze at me. "I'm assuming you did, too."

I shot him a sideways glance.

He shrugged. "I may have overheard you talking to your dad once or twice about coming here."

I blinked repeatedly, surprised by his admission. I'd never noticed him hanging around my father's room or the common areas of the nursing home before. In fact, I couldn't remember ever seeing him outside an exam room…until yesterday.

"That's true, but I really am on a tight deadline. Plus, I've already had three cups of coffee today. If I have any more, I won't be able to hold my pen steady." I gave him a tight-lipped smile. "Have a good weekend, Dr. McAllister." I pushed past him again, conscious of a set of vivid blue eyes following my every move.

Just when I thought I was in the clear and able to continue with my hermit-like existence, he called out yet again. He certainly was persistent. "How about some ice cream then?"

Stopping, I gradually faced him. A brilliant and somewhat cocky smirk was drawn on his face. The bastard knew my weakness. "Ice cream?"

Nodding, he approached slowly, running his tongue over his lips. He probably had no idea he was even doing it, but it made the hair on the back of my neck stand on end. "Some of the best damn ice cream you'll ever have." His tone bordered on seductive. Or maybe I simply imagined it. I did have a tendency to get lost in the world and characters I'd created, often having difficulty separating fact from fiction. If this was fiction, I didn't want to stop reading.

"I love ice cream," I breathed.

"Who doesn't?" He winked, his body just a whisper away from mine. My skin prickled with goosebumps, despite the sun warming me.

"Okay," I agreed, although one could probably argue I did so under undue influence. "But no talking about my father," I added, snapping out of my daze, my voice firm.

"I hadn't planned on it." With a smile, he headed down another path, leading the way.

"Then why did you want to have coffee with me?" I asked.

"I figured it would be a better way to spend my afternoon than looking over my students' research papers."

"Students?" I cocked a brow, studying him as we walked through Boston Common. It was one of the first spring-like days we had and it seemed half the city was out enjoying the weather.

"I teach a class on degenerative brain disorders at Tufts a few nights a week."

"Of course you do, Doogie Howser."

"Doogie Howser?" He laughed, the sound beautiful, perfect. His smile reached his eyes. I tried to remember the last time anyone looked at me the way he was, as if he were genuinely interested in what I had to say, not just watching my lips move and wondering when I'd be using them on his lower extremities.

"You don't remember that show?"

"No, I remember it. But he was sixteen or something, wasn't he? I have twenty-two years on him."

"Hmm," I mused. He was older than I had originally thought. I knew he had to be in his thirties, considering he'd have to go through undergrad, then medical school, before completing some sort of residency program.

"Hmm, what?" he asked.

"Nothing. You just look young for being twenty-nine-plus-nine."

He furrowed his brow before another laugh fell from his mouth, the sound making the butterflies in my stomach, which had been dormant for years before yesterday, flutter their wings. "Twenty-nine-plus-nine?"

"Didn't anyone ever tell you?" I looked at him, my eyes wide. "The 't' word is a bad, bad word. We don't say it around these parts."

"'T' word? You mean thirty?"

I covered my mouth with my hand, feigning horror,

lowering my voice. "Watch your language." I glanced around, gesturing with my head toward a group of guys wearing their stupid winter caps and playing Frisbee. "There are twenty-something-year-old hipsters around."

He shook his head, still laughing. "No wonder the nurses love your column. If this is just a taste of what's in there, I can't wait to read what you have planned next." He placed his hand on the small of my back, leading me away from the bandstand and up a path toward Tremont Street and the Financial District.

After a few steps, he removed his hand, a chill running down my back from the lack of contact. It was something I'd written about in my books, even though I'd always been convinced such things didn't actually happen in the real world. I told myself the chill had to be due to a slight breeze, not from the absence of a relative stranger's touch on my lower back.

I refused to believe my body could have this sort of reaction to him. It wasn't real. There was no such thing as an instant attraction to a person. It had to develop over time. No one looked at someone and immediately knew they were "the one". No one felt sparks and butterflies from the innocent placement of a hand on the back...not unless they already had a few drinks in their system. Then it would be the alcohol causing that reaction, not something else, something far more petrifying.

I hadn't touched a drop of alcohol all day, yet here I was, walking next to a man I never thought of as anything but my father's doctor before. I was conscious of everything, right down to my pattern of breathing. In the last few seconds, it had increased as I imagined how Dr. McAllister looked without a shirt on.

"Chocolate or vanilla?" I asked, breaking the silence before I began imagining other parts of him without clothes. That would have made for some rather interesting appointments with my father going forward.

"What was that?" He looked at me. I wondered what thoughts I'd snapped him out of, whether he was thinking the same things about me as I was him.

"I was wondering if you preferred chocolate or vanilla ice cream." I shrugged. "Just trying to make conversation, I suppose."

"You don't like quiet, do you?" He pinched his lips together, a playful kind of arrogance on his face.

"I spend most of my days alone."

"That's not the same thing. When you're writing your columns, do you have to have it quiet or is there background noise?"

"Background noise. Always," I answered quickly. It wasn't just when I wrote my columns, either. I had a different playlist for each of my books. Mostly really intense songs my characters could get down and dirty to. I had a phenomenal repertoire of great sex music. The silence unnerved me. I'd get sucked into my own thoughts. Nothing good ever came of that.

"You should try unplugging," he suggested. "It might help with that deadline of yours." He narrowed his gaze, giving me a knowing look.

I opened my mouth to respond that he didn't know what he was talking about, but quickly closed it. Maybe I struggled with putting words onto the proverbial digital paper because I was too distracted with everything else. Maybe I needed to unplug to get reacquainted with my characters and let them tell their story, not the other way around.

"Just a suggestion. And to answer your question, I

prefer something a little more…exotic than just plain ol' chocolate or vanilla." His mouth turned into a salacious smile, bringing forward too many doctor-patient fantasies. If nothing else, spending time with Dr. McAllister certainly got my juices flowing. All I could think of at this precise moment was a forbidden affair based solely on physical attraction.

"Variety *can* be the spice of life," I countered, "but it's sometimes nice to stick with the safe bet. With chocolate or vanilla, you know what you're getting. There's no risk involved. It's a known quantity."

We approached a crosswalk and waited for the WALK signal. He turned to me, studying me as a duck boat rolled by, giving out-of-towners a tour of the city at the heart of the American Revolution. "You don't strike me as the cautious type. If I were a betting man, I'd wager you're the type of woman who loves adventure, who couldn't possibly be satisfied with the ordinary and commonplace."

I avoided his eyes. Why did I feel like we were no longer talking about ice cream? "Taking risks never pays off. You take a risk, thinking it could be worth it, only to be left completely unsatisfied. I avoid the unknown."

"So you never try anything new?" He raised his eyebrows, glancing down at me as the light changed. We stepped off the curb, following a mass of people across the street.

"I didn't say that. I try new things. I just don't get too attached to them," I answered, now certain we were no longer talking about ice cream. I had no idea how this guy was able to turn a seemingly innocuous question, such as one's favorite kind of ice cream, into something more, something deeper.

"When's the last time you tried something new?" He opened the glass door of a quaint store, allowing me to enter in front of him. I tried to hide my surprise. I couldn't remember the last time a man held the door for me.

"Just last night," I answered. The aroma of sugar, chocolate, and a dozen other scents hit me. I licked my lips, my mouth watering.

"And what was that?"

"I went to a speed dating thing with my brother and best friend."

He raised his eyebrows. "And how did that go?"

I shrugged. "It went." I offered a wide smile.

"New material for a column?"

"That's about all I got out of it."

Keeping his eyes trained unnervingly on me, he led me to an empty table. He pulled out the chair for me, then headed toward a long counter, dozens of different flavors of ice cream on display.

"You didn't ask me what kind I wanted," I called after him.

He didn't even turn around. "I know."

Chapter Nine

"OH, MY GOD," I moaned, my eyes fluttering into the back of my head.

"You like that, don't you?" Noah's voice broke through my lust-filled thoughts. I couldn't remember the last time I'd experienced so much pleasure. Everything about this was so wrong on so many levels, but damn if it didn't satisfy me in a way nothing else in my life had recently.

"It's amazing." My voice was husky, my breathing ragged. "How did you... I need more. I can't get enough." The flavor of peppermint and chocolate made my taste buds dance, as if they'd found what they'd been craving for years. I had no idea how we even ended up here, but that didn't matter. All that did was the pure joy flowing through my veins.

"Sometimes it pays to take a risk on something new, doesn't it?"

"I don't know how you did it, but this is the best damn ice cream I've ever had." I sank my spoon into the bowl, the decadent dark chocolate syrup spilling over the sides and onto the table. I didn't care how unrefined it looked. I licked the sinful deliciousness off my fingers, not wanting to waste a drop.

I'd often passed this ice cream shop on my travels within the city, yet I'd never stepped foot inside. I'd be rectifying that from now on. It was an unassuming little place, but the sinful treat dancing in my mouth made me a believer that all ice cream was certainly *not* created equal. No disrespect to Ben and Jerry, but this put their stuff to shame.

"I'm glad you like it." He grinned, placing another spoonful into his mouth. It tasted like a chocolate-covered candy cane. I wanted more. So much more.

Barely a word was spoken as we gorged on our ice cream. When I couldn't eat another bite, I leaned back in my chair, resting my hands on my stomach. A smile on my face, I remained in an ice cream-induced coma. I couldn't remember the last time I'd felt this at ease in a stranger's company. Ever since Noah had saved me from dismemberment by a bunch of ruthless hoodlums, the stress of my impossible deadline had disappeared.

"So tell me, Molly." He dabbed his mouth with his napkin. It was nice to hear him use my first name instead of the formality of Ms. Brinks. It reminded me too much of the heroes in my books. Erotic romance readers loved something about the formality of using last names. I liked it, too, but the way my first name rolled off Noah's tongue made it sound as if we were old friends. "Did you always want to be a writer?"

I considered his question. "Honestly, I can't remember a time I didn't want to be a writer, even when most of my family told me time and time again it wasn't a real profession." I rolled my eyes. "But, apparently, wanting to be a professional hockey player was." Looking away, I tugged at my bottom lip with my teeth.

"That must have been difficult for you," he commented, sitting back in his chair.

"Nah." I shrugged it off. I didn't want him to read too much into it. It was all part of life growing up with a brother who was good at something. "I didn't mind. Actually, it was a blessing all the attention was on Drew. He couldn't get away with anything. My father always made sure he was up at the crack of dawn, getting in those miles he needed to keep up his training, even in the off-season." I toyed with the straw in my glass of water, moving the ice around. "I didn't have to put up with the constant supervision like Drew did."

I stared off into the distance, my smile faltering as I recalled how I felt when I walked across the stage at my graduation from NYU, my entire extended family, except Aunt Gigi and Brooklyn, absent from the biggest moment in my life up until that point. The Bruins had made the playoffs and had a game the same day as my graduation. I guessed being at yet another hockey game was more important than seeing me graduate at the top of my class. It wasn't the first time my father had missed one of my events in favor of Drew's hockey. I often wondered if he even knew he had a daughter, especially as I reached adulthood and the resemblance to my mother grew stronger with each passing day.

"Molly?" Noah's voice cut through my memories. I shot my eyes back to his. "Are you okay?"

I forced a smile, taking a sip of my water so he couldn't see past the façade. "Of course." I swallowed hard, straightening my spine. "How about you? Did you always want to be a doctor?"

He studied me for a prolonged moment, then lightened his expression. "Not always." I relaxed my shoulders, grateful he didn't press me to talk more about what it was like growing up in Drew's shadow. "I can't say I wanted to be a doctor when I was five. Back then, I'm pretty sure I wanted to be something ridiculous, like an astronaut or stunt double."

"What made you change your mind?" My voice oozed sarcasm. "I'm sure you would have had one hell of a career as a stunt double."

"Aside from probably never being able to get a life insurance policy, my dad kind of made me choose a different path."

"Really?"

As a writer, I liked to consider myself a casual observer of life. I'd always been fascinated how some actions could influence a person's entire life trajectory. It could have been something as simple as deciding to hit snooze on your alarm one day, or a major life event, like the death of a loved one, that put someone on a completely different path. I salivated over the prospect, wondering what events in my past put me on the course I'd been on, wondering if I'd be sitting in this exact spot today if one thing were different.

"Did he want to be able to brag about having a doctor in the family?"

He shook his head. "My parents didn't care what I did with my life, as long as I was happy. They didn't even pressure me to go to college. As long as I wasn't a complete freeloader, they supported me."

"So what made you decide to go into medicine?"

"My dad got sick." He swallowed hard, his light expression faltering. He toyed with his coffee mug. "Really sick." His voice became soft, almost inaudible.

"I'm sorry. I didn't mean to bring it up." My heart fell when I observed the pain on his face, as if whatever happened was still fresh in his mind. "If anyone understands not wanting to talk about that kind of stuff, it's me."

"Actually..." He met my eyes. "I don't mind talking about it at all."

I looked away, his intense gaze burning my skin. I hoped this wasn't another ploy to get me to finally discuss my feelings. If it were, I'd never forgive Dr. Noah McAllister. My feelings were none of his business. They were none of *anyone's* business.

"It started like it does with everyone else," he continued after a protracted silence. "Like I'm sure it did with your father."

"*My* father?" I repeated in a soft voice, returning my wide eyes to his.

"He would lose things around the house, miss appointments because he'd forgotten what day it was. We assumed it was because he was getting older. My father was in his fifties when I was born. My mother was twenty years younger."

"My father was fifteen years older than my mother," I said. "I get it."

"One day, we realized it was more than just misplacing his glasses. He couldn't remember names of people he saw nearly every day. He had difficulty doing simple math. He couldn't remember what he had for breakfast." He shook his head. "His decline was aggressive. Within a matter of months, he lost all ability to respond and communicate. I hated seeing him in that condition."

"So you decided to go to med school and find a way to prevent that from happening to anyone else?"

He stared at me, despondent. "I'm not that optimistic. With more and more advances in medicine, it may be possible one day, but probably not in our lifetime. After my dad died, I decided to specialize in degenerative neurological diseases. Alzheimer's is a bitch of a disease, if I can be so blunt." His voice grew more assured, more determined, more passionate.

"There is no cure, as you know. It's not like cancer. Even when a cancer patient is told they're stage three or four, there are still treatment options. They are given hope that the medical staff will do everything they possibly can to force the disease into remission. That's not the case with dementia or Alzheimer's. It affects the nervous system, the brain. There's no remission. The only thing we can do is try to keep our patients as comfortable as possible for as long as we can. We do everything in our power to keep their bodies in great physical health, keep their minds active. Did you know most Alzheimer's patients don't die because of the disease itself? They die because of infections, like pneumonia. Those affected by this disease lose the ability to know when something's wrong with their body, so an otherwise non-deadly illness or infection ends up killing them." He shook his head, drawing in a breath.

"That's what happened to my father. He had a UTI that caused sepsis, which ended up killing him." He reached out, about to grasp onto my hand, then stopped short. "So everything you're going through, I've been there, Molly. I used to feel so alone. Sure, I had my sisters and my mother, but I had a bond, a connection with my father. I hated witnessing how he couldn't even remember who I was."

I lowered my eyes, my hands fidgeting in my lap.

"I guess what I'm trying to say is if you ever need to talk to someone about it, I'll listen, and not as your dad's neurologist, either. As someone who's been in your shoes."

Fixing my composure, I gave him a blank stare, my lips in a firm line. "Thanks for the offer, but that's not necessary. Like I said yesterday, I knew this was a death sentence. I wasn't expecting a miracle." I remained stoic, my spine straight.

"Molly..."

"I'm fine," I shot back in a clipped voice, hoping he'd take the hint and end the conversation.

He studied me for an excruciatingly long time, then sighed. "Okay, but the offer stands." He ran his hand through his wayward hair, defeated.

Chewing on one of my fingernails, I looked everywhere but his eyes, not wanting him to see the truth I'd kept from everyone for years.

~~~~~~~~~~

WHEN WE LEFT THE ice cream shop, there was an awkwardness between us. I could have very easily headed for the closest T station, which was a block away. Instead, I stayed with Noah, strolling beside him through the Common. Despite my reaction after his offer of a proverbial shoulder to cry on, I found myself drawn to his comforting presence.

As we passed bronze statues of little ducks, a tribute to the notable children's book *Make Way for Ducklings*, which was set in this very park, I glanced at him. His eyes were trained forward, a distant look on his face, as if deep in thought. I didn't want to leave on a sour note.

I inhaled a breath of the crisp spring air, then said, "*The Diary of Anne Frank*."

He cocked a brow, remaining silent, his attentive expression encouraging me to continue.

"You asked if I always wanted to be a writer. It was *The Diary of Anne Frank* that made me want to be a writer." I was unsure why I felt inclined to tell him this story. It was something I rarely told anyone. I wasn't even sure my brother or Brooklyn knew. "I read it when I was maybe eight or nine. I was so impressed with how well-written she was at her age, I made my father go out and get me a journal so I could keep a diary of sorts, just like she did. Drew had my father and hockey to keep him company. I guess I always found writing and reading to be my companions."

"What did you write about?" A smile tugged at his lips.

I wondered if this was the sort of thing Kevin hoped to get out of me. I never had any desire to share these parts of myself with him. Noah was different somehow. I didn't feel as if he would judge me or use this information against me somewhere down the road after a heated argument.

"Nothing as notable as she did. I wasn't exactly in hiding from an intolerant government." I looked down at my flip-flop clad feet, making a mental note to get a pedicure, especially with it finally being spring. "I tried to write things that crossed my mind, make commentary about what I observed in my world. I sometimes flip through it now and laugh at the stuff I wrote about, what I considered to be important. You can only imagine the missive I wrote when the Backstreet Boys broke up."

"You still have it?"

I nodded. "I've kept all my journals."

"Do you still journal?"

"Kind of. I use it as a way to free write."

"Free write?" He shook his head slightly, a glint of interest in his eyes. "What's that?"

"It's just writing whatever pops into my head. They may not even be complete sentences or thoughts, just words. When I don't know what to write about, I free write."

"Does it help?"

I shrugged. "Sometimes. I think it's more of a comfort thing for me. My journal is like a baby's security blanket. I've been journaling for the better part of my life. When I feel stuck, I go back to what I know."

"I get it."

We continued walking through the Common, passing the scene of my unceremonious attack by a gang of lowlife city dwellers. I didn't even try to fill the void with meaningless conversation. For once, I simply enjoyed the quiet.

All too soon, we reached the edge of the park by the Arlington Street station. Noah turned to me, letting out a shaky breath as our eyes met. "I should probably get back to grading papers."

"We passed Tufts several blocks back," I commented.

He shoved his hands into his pockets. "I guess I just wanted to spend a little more time with you."

I fought back the grin wanting to form on my lips from his admission. My body buzzed with happiness and something else...something I couldn't quite describe.

"As friends," he clarified quickly, looking away.

"Of course." I was a little surprised when I felt a heaviness settle in my heart at the idea that nothing more would ever happen between us. I tried not to let on, smiling with as much confidence as I could muster. Even a complete stranger could probably sense my disappointment.

Noah returned his eyes to mine, turmoil and unease on his face. "It's just—"

"Thanks for the ice cream," I interrupted, clearing my throat. I knew what he was about to say. I didn't want to suffer through that awkward conversation. "It was…life-changing." I winked.

His lips crooked into a small smile. "So you agree that it sometimes pays to try something new?"

"I'll concede you may be onto something." I smoothed one of my wayward waves behind my ear. "But I'd need more proof to make a final determination. You are a scientist, after all. You know all about needing to test your hypothesis repeatedly to prove it. I can hardly make a determination after just one test."

His small smile brightened, reaching his eyes. I'd written about panty-dropping smiles before. They had nothing on Noah's. He had a panty-dropping "let's get married and have lots of sex and babies" smile. I actually *liked* it. He wasn't flashing those pearly whites just to get into my pants or flirt with me. It was genuine. Everything about him was genuine and real. It was a pleasant change from the other men I typically surrounded myself with.

"I'd be more than happy to help you test that hypothesis again, Molly."

He stepped toward me, our bodies nearly touching. I tilted my head back. It would have been so easy to raise myself onto my toes and press my lips against his. I couldn't stop imagining how they would taste. I contemplated it, thinking it could help break through my block. I was supposed to be writing a forbidden romance. Pursuing something with Noah was certainly forbidden.

Then a pang of guilt formed in my chest at the idea of using him for a story. Could I really put his career in jeopardy just to help me get past my writer's block? I had no problem using other men, but they were different. They were mostly twenty-somethings who were content with a casual fling. I didn't know Noah well, but I knew enough to realize he was nothing like them.

"I should probably get going," I said, breaking the tension. I stepped back before I pushed him to do something he'd instantly regret...and something I'd regret.

"Right." He relaxed his stature. "And I have papers I need to look over."

"I guess I'll be seeing you then." I hesitated, then reluctantly turned away from him.

"It was nice running into you today, Molly," he called out.

I glanced over my shoulder and offered him a congenial smile as he kept his eyes trained on me, a breeze blowing my hair in front of my face.

"I hope I'll have the pleasure of running into you again sometime very soon."

Before I could respond, he flashed me his nearly perfect teeth, then ran back through the Common. I was unable to take my eyes off him as his tall frame grew smaller and smaller, disappearing from view when he turned a corner.

~~~~~~~~~~

AS I SAT IN my apartment that evening, I read message after message from guys who had stumbled across one of my online dating profiles, but none of them seemed to catch my interest. I should have been focused on finding an attractive, professional man who would ignite the spark I'd been missing lately, but I wasn't.

With a permanent smile plastered on my face, I

brought up my manuscript on my laptop, thoughts of ice cream, *Anne Frank*, and muscular legs dancing in my head. Despite insisting I needed a muse, I did something I didn't think possible…I wrote.

Evening gave way to nighttime, yet I still wrote. The bars closed, yet I still wrote. My characters had completely taken over. It was magical, satisfying, and a bit frightening all at once. I hadn't experienced anything like this since I began writing. When I wrote for myself and no one else. When no one knew who I was.

As the sun began to rise on Sunday morning, I sipped a coffee, rereading what I had written. It was nothing like the usual garbage I churned out. It had heart. It had soul. It had an actual story.

And I had a feeling my publisher would hate it.

Chapter Ten

I BIT MY FINGERNAILS as I sat on the couch, Pee Wee snuggled against me. Actually, it was more like on top of me. He was a small dog trapped in a big dog's body and thought he could squeeze his eighty pounds onto my petite lap. Every few seconds, I glanced over at Brooklyn sitting on the reading chair opposite me, her eyes glued to the pages I had printed out for her.

Once I began putting words down, I couldn't stop. A thousand ideas raced through my head, each fighting for my attention. My fingers couldn't type fast enough to get them all down. I had no idea what direction this story was going, but it was no longer up to me. I'd given absolute control to my characters and allowed them to tell their story, which was both terrifying and fulfilling. I found myself completely obsessed with them. The few times I'd stepped away from my laptop, I thought about them, wondering how they were going to find the happily ever after I believed they deserved.

My eyes a bit droopy from having worked through the night, I waited with baited breath. Finally, Brooklyn lowered the last page, placing it on top of the pile on the coffee table. I bit my lip, praying she wouldn't think I'd just wasted the last sixteen hours churning out absolute crap. I knew I hadn't. I knew this was different from any of my other books, but I also knew it was good. In fact, I knew it was better than good. I'd taken a leap and written something different. It unnerved me and filled me with a unique sense of satisfaction at the same time.

For the first time in years, I wrote what *I* wanted. This story was tragic, real, and heartbreaking, but one I was desperate to tell. Life isn't always fireworks and fairy tales. Life can be real. Life can trip us, rip us to shreds, and knock us out. Regardless of the punches life throws, we still manage to brush ourselves off and move forward. Life is hard, but refusing to live is even harder.

"Wow," Brooklyn said, her jaw slack.

"You like it?" I looked at her, hopeful.

"Wow."

"Is that a yes?"

"That's a *hell* yes!" She bounded off the chair, tackling me with a hug. Pee Wee licked both our faces, thinking Brooklyn had intended to hug him, too. Laughing, she pulled away. "This book is incredible. Poor Jackson. Oh, I just want to hug him and put together all his broken little pieces." She clutched her hands together, deflating with a sigh. "It's really touching that you've used your own life experiences with your father."

"What are you talking about? I didn't do that. His mom—"

"It's schizophrenia, right?" she interrupted.

"Yeah," I replied. I'd added a complex layer to the story. Jackson's mother was an actress who disappeared off the face of the earth decades ago. Now she didn't know who her own son was, thinking he was some government spy out to get her. But schizophrenia was vastly different from Alzheimer's. At least in my head, regardless of the parallels with my own father. "This isn't about me."

She rolled her eyes, turning her pinched lips up at the corner. "Yeah. Okay. Whatever you say, Molly."

"It's not." My voice was firm. "Not even close. My dad isn't schizophrenic."

"I know, but there's a very strong similarity between the dynamic of Jackson and his mom and you and your father. You can't deny it."

"I'm not—"

"Why does his mom think Jackson died? I need to know more about this accident." Brooklyn settled into the couch beside me, throwing her arm over her head. "Gosh, my mind is just spinning with a thousand different scenarios." She perked up, her eyes focused on me once more. "And who did you meet?"

"Meet?" I furrowed my brow.

"Yeah. Meet," she urged. "How did you miraculously pump out over 10,000 words overnight without having met your very own Jackson Price?" She lowered her voice. "Did you call someone from speed dating? Or did someone respond to one of your online profiles?"

I shrugged. "None of the above." My cheeks flamed when I recalled my rather pleasant run-in with Dr. FineLegs, as I had renamed Noah in my mind. Despite not wanting to admit it, he was the reason for my sudden burst of inspiration. It just went to prove I didn't necessarily need a man in my life to write what I knew was going to be a heartbreakingly beautiful story. I just didn't know how I was going to convince my editor this was worth publishing when they were known for steamy, sexy, and low drama. This none of the above.

"Bullshit," Brooklyn shot back, eyes wide. "You met someone. You're glowing!"

"I'm not glowing! And I haven't met anyone!" I

argued, stretching the truth.

It wasn't as if anything untoward had happened between Noah and me. I just didn't want Brooklyn to make a big deal about it, which she most certainly would. It was simply a chance meeting between friends. We could never be anything more, not with him being my father's neurologist and me being one of the parties allowed to make healthcare decisions for him. I may have researched that when I got back to my apartment yesterday.

"How could I have when I've been holed up in here for the past day writing?"

She studied me with narrowed eyes, her lips pinched. "Fine. I'll let you keep your secrets…for now."

"I'm not keeping any secrets, Brooklyn! I haven't met anyone. In fact…" I got up from the couch and grabbed my laptop, finding an email I'd received earlier this morning.

I sat back on the couch, showing Brooklyn the profile Debra had sent me. "I have a date with him Thursday evening. One of my sorority sisters is a professional matchmaker, although she calls herself a 'dating consultant'. She set it all up. It'll actually be really good for research purposes. All the men she sets up are extremely wealthy. I think the minimum annual salary to use this service is somewhere in the seven figures. Jackson Price is a wealthy businessman, so this is a good thing."

I found it a bit off-putting that the whole thing sounded more like a business transaction than a date, but I immediately reminded myself this wasn't a typical dating service. High-powered, wealthy men used it to find the woman of their dreams…or at least a little eye candy to show off at whatever public events they had to attend.

She narrowed her gaze at me. "And since a character in your book is a wealthy businessman, you decided going on a date with this poor guy would be great 'inspiration'?" she asked in a condescending tone, even adding air quotes.

There were three things I loathed in this world. The first was snakes. No explanation necessary. You couldn't trust anything without arms and legs. The second was a man with a curly mustache. I was still traumatized after agreeing to a blind date a coworker at the magazine had set up. He sounded like a great guy...until he showed up with a huge bushy mustache that grew smaller and smaller toward the ends, curling into tiny little tips. I was pretty sure the 1860s called and needed him to go fight for the Union.

That brings us to the third, and most deadly, trespass in my book...air quotes. My roommate during my freshman year of college used them incessantly, most notably when she informed me she had "sex" with half the wrestling team for "research" purposes. I wondered if she put chlamydia in air quotes when she had to tell them she was the reason for the newly contracted infection that seemed to plague the team that season.

"It's not fair to play with people's emotions like you do." Brooklyn got up from the couch and headed into the kitchen, grabbing a couple of water bottles from my refrigerator.

"I'm not playing with anyone's emotions," I countered.

"Maybe not right now, but I know you, Molly. You will. You always do. You meet a guy and make it so they can't say no to you, then once you're no longer inspired, you kick them to the curb." Placing the bottles on the coffee table, she plopped back down on the couch. "I just…" She shook her head, then faced me, grabbing my hands in hers.

I'd been through a lot with Brooklyn. We'd been each other's rock nearly all our lives. Whenever I looked back at the defining moments that made up my life, she was by my side. When the majority of my family decided to skip out on my college graduation, she was there with Aunt Gigi, regardless of the fact she was in the middle of studying for her own finals. She had witnessed my father's slow decline and was at the table with Drew and me when we had to make the difficult decision to put him in a home. Brooklyn wasn't merely a friend. She was family.

"I'm just worried about you, Molly. I want you to be happy. I want you to be able to experience everything a real relationship has to offer. You shun the idea, but I think you're missing out on so much. If you left your mind and heart open to a real relationship, maybe you wouldn't avoid it like the plague. I want you to go places with someone, have them hold your hand in public. Things real couples do."

"I've done that kind of stuff. Kevin and I went to the movies a few times." I wracked my brain, trying to think of other things we'd done outside the bedroom. "He took me to see U2 when they were in town."

"But you never went anywhere you could just sit and talk."

"Talking is overrated," I insisted, ripping my hands away from hers. "Like you saw the other night at speed dating, all anyone ever wants to talk about is themselves. Trust me, no one there had anything interesting to say."

"Plenty of them did. You just refused to listen."

"Oh, I listened. Do you want to hear my assessment of the dentist or the accountant? Or, better yet, how about the unemployed welfare recipient who's holding out for a spot on one of those stupid reality TV shows? Now *there's* a real winner." I feigned enthusiasm in an overly dramatic way. "Do you think I should call him? Do you think he'd want to sit and *talk*?"

Brooklyn huffed, clenching her fists. This wasn't the first time we'd had this conversation, and I had a feeling it wouldn't be the last. "You're missing the point," she retorted, raising her voice as much as she ever would, which wasn't any louder than slightly above a normal talking level.

"You've done everything you can to keep people at a distance, including me. Up until now, it's been a good plan." She took a breath through a tight jaw, then smiled. "All I'm asking is that you stop toying with people's emotions in order to write a book you seem to be able to write without a muse."

I turned my eyes from hers, gulping down my water.

"Do you really want to end up alone, like your father?" she asked when I remained silent.

"He's not alone!" I argued back, my eyes boring into hers. "The only reason he's in that home is for his own safety. I go see him every day!"

Brooklyn shook her head. "I don't have kids, so I can't talk from experience, but I'm sure there's nothing like a parent's love for a child. Still, it's in our DNA to want to share our lives, our dreams, our triumphs, our failures with someone...someone we can't wait to go home to each and every night."

"That kind of love doesn't exist in the real world."

"I'm not talking about the picture-perfect kind of love you typically write about. I'm talking about the gritty kind of love. The love people have to work hard for. The love that fucking hurts and rips you in two, but you're somehow able to put yourself back together in the hopes of finding that same love again. The love it appears you're actually writing about this time…without a muse or source of inspiration, if you're to be believed, which I'm not too sure about to begin with."

I faced Brooklyn, opening my mouth, words evading me. It felt like the walls of my apartment were closing in on me, suffocating me. This woman was my best friend. I should have been able to tell her everything. How I'd spent the previous day with Dr. McAllister and had never felt so inspired before. How I didn't feel like I needed a muse, but was still going to pursue finding one in the hopes it would help me forget about the way my heart skipped a beat every time Noah smiled, the way my skin tingled when he placed his hand on my back, the way my chest ached at the knowledge we could never pursue something more.

I'd dated my fair share of men. Not a single one had a pull on me the way Noah did, especially after only spending a few hours together.

Getting up, I headed into the kitchen, tossing my now empty water bottle into the recycling bin.

"I don't know what happened between Friday night and today, but whatever it was has had a dramatic effect on your writing." Brooklyn followed me into the kitchen. "It's beautiful. It's poignant. It's so much more enthralling than anything you've ever written. I just read around forty pages and there wasn't one mention of sex or even a kiss. The characters are so well developed, and part of me thinks it's because…" She stopped short, her eyes glued to me, as if working through something in her head.

"Because why?" I pushed, my voice shaky.

"Because you're Avery," she whispered, realization washing over her.

My heart thumped in my chest at the prospect of anyone, even my best friend, figuring out what I was hiding. "I'm not—"

"You *are.*" She rushed into the living area and grabbed the manuscript off the table, flipping through it as she walked back to me. "Her character has changed from your previous drafts. She used to be kind of a weak heroine who had just gotten out of a committed relationship. She was somewhat career driven, but had hoped to have a family one day." She narrowed her eyes at me, holding up the manuscript. "That's not the same Avery I just read about. This career-driven Avery prefers a short-term casual fling with a guy who understands her professional life comes first. If you ask me, Avery sounds *a lot* like someone we both know."

I turned from her, not wanting her to see the truth in my eyes. "You write what you know. It's not that big a deal."

"Maybe. Maybe not." She pinched her lips, studying me. "I can't help but wonder who your Jackson is and whether you're using the book as a way to finally get your true feelings off your chest." She gave me a knowing look and pushed the final page toward me, pointing to the very last line.

I swallowed hard, reading my words once more.

Why was the one man who made me rethink my opinion on relationships the one man I could never have?

Chapter Eleven

I HURRIED TOWARD THE simple brick building, slugging down the remnants of yet another cup of coffee. I'd lost count how many I'd consumed in the past twenty-four hours. I was running on fumes, having no idea how I'd made the drive to the nursing home without falling asleep.

Earlier, after Brooklyn left, I tried to take a short nap, but sleep evaded me. She was right. Something *had* changed in me since yesterday. Everything in my life had been exactly as I wanted it to be. Now, it was all different. I wasn't sure about anything. All I knew was I should stay as far away as possible from Dr. Noah McAllister. He'd brought out feelings I never knew I had inside me. I needed to nip those in the bud so I could get on with a much more pressing issue...writing the story my publisher expected.

Stopping just outside the front doors, I hesitated, eyeing my faint reflection in the glass. I'd done what I could to make it look like I wasn't an extra on *Breaking Bad*, but the tired eyes forced open by the copious amount of caffeine I had consumed made me look like a meth addict, with the exception of the bad teeth. As much as I dreaded going to the dentist, I went religiously. I was a strong believer in proper dental hygiene. I even flossed daily.

Smoothing my hair and pinching my cheeks, I

opened the door and headed for the visitor's desk.

"Running a little behind today?" Reggie raised an eyebrow as I approached.

"A bit." I grabbed the clipboard and signed in. Different day. Same routine.

"Have a fun Saturday night?"

"I suppose."

I bit back a grin, thinking how my Saturday afternoon was far more enjoyable than any Saturday night in recent history...or ever, for that matter. My pulse quickened at the thought of Noah, but I suppressed it. I needed to do everything I could to relinquish the spell his vivid eyes, smooth voice, and panty-dropping smile had cast over me yesterday.

"I just stayed in and did a bit of work." I grabbed the visitor badge, placing it on my shirt

"On the column?" He sat back in his chair, crossing his arms over his slender waist. "What do you have planned this time around?"

"Another installment in 'Confessions of a Serial Dater'," I replied, although that wasn't even close to what my column this month was supposed to be about. I think it had something to do with why Brazilian waxes were a torture device most probably invented by men. I was convinced they added some sort of drug to the wax that seeped into the bloodstream through the vagina walls to encourage women to keep coming back for more. Guys didn't care whether or not a woman's pussy was shaved. It could have been the Cousin It of vaginas, but as long as they could stick their dick in it, they'd be happy.

"Can't wait to read it."

"Me, too," I mumbled, then turned down the hallway, navigating the corridors leading to my father's room. I glanced at the screen of my cell phone, quickening my steps as I fought back a yawn. A tightness formed in my chest as I thought about my dad sitting all alone, wondering if anyone would visit him today. I hated that I'd arrived here nearly an hour after I typically did. I never wanted anyone to look upon him with pity, thinking he was all alone, that he had no one left.

Opening the door to his room, I stopped dead in my tracks, completely taken aback by the sight that greeted me. I'd expected to see my father watching TV or doing a puzzle. I never anticipated Noah would be sitting with him. He peered at me, giving me a heartwarming smile, then returned his attention to the book I'd begun reading to my father on Friday.

"Elizabeth saw what he was doing, and at the first convenient pause, turned to him with an arch smile and said, 'You mean to frighten me, Mr. Darcy, by coming in all this state to hear me? But I will not be alarmed, though your sister does play so well.'"

Noah's eyes locked with mine as he continued to read.

"'There is a stubbornness about me that never can bear to be frightened at the will of others. My courage always rises with every attempt to intimidate me.'"

Unable to look away, I slowly stepped into the room, lowering myself into the empty chair beside my father. I studied Noah as he read with ease, as if he'd been reading nineteenth-century novels for years. He was dressed casually in a pair of jeans and a t-shirt, and I couldn't help but wonder why he was here. As far as I knew, he made his rounds at the nursing home on Fridays. He spent the rest of his time at his own practice by Massachusetts General in Boston, where we'd first met.

He caught my gaze once more. My stomach warmed, erasing every bit of resolve I had to avoid him. I knew I should look away, should walk out of the room and keep my distance from him, but I couldn't bring myself to do it. I didn't know much at that moment, but I knew I was inexplicably drawn to this man I couldn't have.

Bringing my legs under me, I settled into the chair my father always watched TV in at our old house. I leaned my head against the worn blue fabric and closed my eyes, the timbre of Noah's voice the perfect lullaby to sing me to sleep.

~~~~~~~~~~

A NUDGE ON MY arm startled me awake. Disoriented, I opened my eyes and took in my surroundings. A dull light shone from a lamp on a side table to my left, the rest of the room in darkness now that the sun had set. I craned my head to the source of what had stirred me. Noah loomed over me, a soft smile on his shadowed face.

"Hey," he whispered warmly.

"Hey," I replied, stretching, still a bit groggy.

"I'm sorry I woke you. I waited as long as I could, but it's almost six. Visiting hours ended at five."

"It is?" I shot up, holding onto the chair to steady myself from the headrush. "Did my dad eat?" I asked urgently, my eyes searching the room frantically.

"Relax, Molly," Noah soothed, running his hands down my arms. I immediately stopped, a heat building low in my stomach as I returned my eyes to his. "An orderly came to take him to dinner at five. That's where he is now." He gestured to the entryway of his room.

121

"He'll be back soon, and you can't be here. Sundowners."

I nodded, stepping away. I ran my hands through my blonde waves, then pulled them back into a messy bun. "When did I fall asleep?"

"Pretty much the second you sat down. One minute, you were listening to Elizabeth Bennett give Mr. Darcy what for. The next, you were sound asleep. I thought about waking you earlier, but you seemed exhausted, as if you hadn't slept in days." He stepped toward me, only a whisper separating us. My heartbeat increased when he looked down at me with sincerity. "Is everything okay?"

I opened my mouth, searching for words that just wouldn't come. His warmth and compassion cast a spell over me…a spell I reminded myself I needed to break.

"Everything's great." I turned from him and hurriedly crossed the room, grabbing my bag I had dropped by the coffee table. "I have to go. Drew's probably worried."

I scurried into the hallway. The bright lights forced me to squint momentarily as my eyes readjusted.

"It's okay. I called him."

Spinning around, I practically slammed into Noah. "Why would you call him?" I demanded, searching his eyes. I knew it would look bad. Drew would push the subject, wondering if there was something I wasn't telling him.

"I know you have family dinner every Sunday. I didn't want him to worry."

I tilted my head, furrowing my brow, studying his face. "How could you possibly know about our family dinners?" I raised my voice. "And what are you doing here on a Sunday anyway?"

Dr. Connors, the executive director of the facility, chose that precise moment to round the corner, eyeing Noah and me. Taking a step back, Noah cleared his throat. His expression turned serious, professional.

"Thanks for taking the time to come in today, Ms. Brinks." His voice was no longer soft and tender, but firm and demanding, as if we were complete strangers. Wasn't that what I wanted? "Unfortunately, visiting hours are—"

"I got it." I set my lips into a firm line, my eyes hard. I didn't know why his sudden change in demeanor turned me so cold. Maybe I wanted to believe he felt the same connection I had yesterday. Or maybe I'd been so consumed with the fantasy world I'd created between Avery and Jackson, I had difficulty separating what was real from what was fiction. Maybe I'd simply imagined everything yesterday. "Have a nice evening, Dr. McAllister."

I spun around and continued down the corridor, hurrying out the front doors and toward my silver Audi SUV — the one luxury item I'd allowed myself to buy after my first book became a bestseller. I wanted nothing more than to return to the familiarity of my apartment and my family. I needed to listen to Alyssa's stories about seeing the animals at the zoo. I needed to hear Aunt Gigi complain about the other women at her church trying to show her up by bringing the same dish as she did to the potluck. I needed to look Drew in the eye and tell him I had a date Thursday night, which I was very excited about. I prayed it would help shake away whatever I thought I felt toward Noah.

Just as I was about to get behind the wheel, a familiar scruff voice called my name. I whipped my head toward the front doors of the building to see Noah running down the steps. My hardened expression unwillingly softened as I took in his form. There was something I found extremely sexy and primal about him running toward me.

Reaching my car, he took a second to catch his breath, his chest rising and falling. I could make out the subtle definition of his pectorals through his t-shirt.

"Yes, Dr. McAllister?" I tried to ooze all the professionalism I could, mirroring his attitude toward me in the hallway just seconds ago.

He ran a hand through his hair. "Look. I'm sorry about that. I didn't mean to come off like an asshole in there. I just…" He drew in a breath, shaking his head. "You want to know the real reason I'm here today?"

I remained silent, as if I'd forgotten the thousands of words I'd amassed in my vocabulary. He stepped toward me, the heat coming off his body warming me in the cool April air. My heart sped up. I tried to think of anything other than Noah's proximity in order to halt my body's impetuous response to him. I wasn't supposed to be falling for this guy. I wasn't supposed to have any sort of reaction to this man…this beautiful, endearing man.

"This afternoon, I got into my car to run to the store and pick up a few things. Somehow, I found myself driving here instead. I went to my office first, then started wandering the halls, ending up over at your father's wing. I walked by his room and saw you weren't there." He swallowed hard as he closed the distance between us, his eyes trained on mine. "I know you're always here by two, so I decided to read to him, like you always do. I figured someone should."

As much as I wanted to melt into a puddle at his sincerity and compassion, I couldn't. I needed to stay strong and forget that yesterday ever happened.

I straightened my back, meeting his eyes with a hardened stare. "Thank you for that, Dr. McAllister. That wasn't necessary. I'll be sure to get here on time going forward so you don't feel as if you have to put yourself out." I turned back to my car, about to climb into the driver's seat.

"Molly," he said in a pleading voice.

Reluctantly, I faced him. I could have very easily gotten into my car and driven away, but something about how he caressed my name spoke to me in a way I didn't quite understand.

"I shouldn't have told you all that."

He closed his eyes briefly, an adorable air of frustration about him as he ran his hand through his dark hair, tugging at it. When he returned his gaze to mine, his eyes were intense, fiery, a completely new look. He licked his lips, stepping toward me again. It felt like a giant game of cat and mouse. I knew I was the mouse. I didn't know if I was the kind of mouse who'd be happy with the same kind of cheese for the rest of her life, though.

"Have you ever felt as if you were losing complete control of everything, but in the best way possible? Like you had these firmly held beliefs you swore you would never stray from, then almost overnight, you're ready to toss everything out the window because you want to know..." He trailed off.

"Because you want to know what?" I leaned toward him, my chest rising and falling at a faster pace. My actions were no longer of my own volition.

"Because you really want to get to know this person who is wrong for you on every level, but you can't stop thinking about them."

My breath hitched and I swallowed hard at his admission.

"Because I really want to get to know you, Molly, even though I know I shouldn't."

I pulled my lip between my teeth, then looked away. "Noah, I—"

"Ever watch a movie in a cemetery?" he interrupted, sensing my impending rejection.

"I can't say as I have," I answered in a drawn-out voice. I tilted my head to the side and wrinkled my nose, curious as to where this was going. His admission hung in the air between us. Despite what he said, I didn't see how any good could come of our friendship…or whatever it was.

"When I was at Harvard, I started going as a way to clear my mind. Back then, they only did it occasionally, but over the years, it's grown in popularity. Now they host it every Thursday from April through October."

"Like baseball season," I mused.

"Exactly." A smile spread across his lips. "Once I moved back to Boston, I continued the tradition I started at Harvard and still go every Thursday. I think they're showing *An Affair to Remember* this week, if you're interested in joining me." He lifted his brow, hope building in his gaze.

I opened my mouth, hesitating. It would have been so easy to agree to his invitation, regardless of the fact I already had plans that evening.

"As friends, of course," he added quickly. "I'm not trying to lead you on. I don't want you to get the wrong idea or…"

I closed my eyes, his words like ice water, putting out the flames that had begun to grow. That was all I needed to hear to remind me why I should keep my distance. Noah was an expert at sending mixed signals.

"Of course." I lifted my chin, making it appear as if there wasn't an ache in my chest at the thought of never knowing what Noah's lips felt like on mine. I couldn't let that affect me. I was on the brink of losing my contract with my publishing company if I didn't turn in the manuscript they'd been promised by their deadline. "I'm sorry, but I have a date this Thursday," I said proudly. I needed a new muse, a new source of inspiration, someone other than Dr. Noah McAllister. If I learned anything from Brooklyn's assessment earlier and this current conversation, it was I had to stop thinking about this man. Hopefully meeting someone else would help toward that end.

"Oh." He stepped back. "With someone from speed dating?" He shoved his hands into his pockets, rocking on his heels. I noticed a look of disappointment in his expression.

I shook my head. "It's for a story at the magazine," I lied. "I'm researching online dating, so…"

"Say no more." He held up his hands, flashing me that same smile that made a little flutter erupt in my stomach. "When your column comes out, I look forward to reading all about it."

I held his gaze as we stood in complete silence. I wondered if we were both thinking the same thing…that we wished things were different, that he wasn't my father's doctor and I wasn't the daughter of one of his patients.

"Well, have a good evening." I turned to my car and slid into the driver's seat.

He placed his hands on the top of my SUV, his t-shirt lifting up slightly to reveal a sliver of firm muscles. "If your plans change, the invitation still stands. Forest

Hills Cemetery. Seven o'clock." He flashed me a brilliant smile, then closed the door to my car. I watched him jog back toward the nursing home.

Once he disappeared through the glass doors, I leaned my forehead against the steering wheel and let out a groan, more confused than I had ever been in my life. I'd often complained about some of the characters in my books who seemed to change their mind in the blink of an eye. They were hot, then cold. They were sugar, then spice. They were black, then white. Now I knew how they felt. One minute, I told myself I needed to keep my distance from Noah and focus solely on finding a new source of inspiration. The next, I never wanted to leave his side.

I prayed this was just a temporary infatuation, the result of lack of sleep and a looming deadline. I could only hope my date Thursday night would completely sweep me off my feet so I never thought of Dr. Noah McAllister as anything other than my father's doctor again.

Chapter Twelve

"ARE YOU EXCITED ABOUT your date tonight?" Brooklyn asked Thursday evening, plopping down on my bed as I peered into my closet. Not one article of clothing I owned stood out as being appropriate for my dinner date.

Regret formed in the pit of my stomach at my hasty decision to go on this date. I blamed desperation and lack of sleep on my momentary lapse of judgment. Not just in agreeing to this, but to the whole online dating thing, in general. It seemed like a great idea when Brooklyn brought it up, particularly due to the unlikelihood of finding a nice, professional man at a bar. However, as Thursday had drawn closer, the excitement most women typically experienced at the prospect of going to dinner with one of the most desired bachelors in the Boston metropolitan area had been lacking.

Timothy Vandersmith was everything I'd been looking for...filthy rich, handsome, and a workaholic, which was why he'd paid the equivalent of what most people made in a year to have someone else find him a potential date. It reminded me too much of being an escort...and an unpaid one at that. This was just further proof of my belief that real love didn't exist.

"It's just something I have to do." I glanced back at Brooklyn. "Mr. Jackson Price is ridiculously wealthy," I reminded her, shrugging. "This date could be a good thing."

Brooklyn gave me a subtle look of disapproval, then grabbed the latest issue of *Metropolitan* magazine off my nightstand, flipping through it. I'd written a particularly riveting column about the health benefits of having an orgasm on a daily basis. I even reviewed a variety of battery-operated boyfriends for my interested readers. It was a tough job, but someone had to do it.

"Speaking of which, what did your editor have to say about the pages you sent her? Have you heard?"

I sank into a reading chair in the corner of my bedroom and met her eyes. My shrunken posture and the slack expression on my face told her everything she needed to know.

"That bad?"

I pulled my legs beneath me. "She didn't say it was horrible, but she reminded me they do sexy, sweet, sinful, and most of all...happy." I rolled my eyes, my irritation evident.

"What are you going to do?"

"I'll do exactly what I said I'd do last week. I'll go on a few dates with some handsome, professional men and hope someone out there has that certain something that makes my stomach flutter and my knees weak, inspiring me to write a sexy, sinful romance with little drama and a really upbeat happily ever after." I flashed her my best fake smile.

"You're just going to toss out everything you wrote last weekend?" She wore her disappointment on every inch of her body.

"Not everything," I assured her. "My editor wants me to get rid of the storyline with Jackson's mother. She said having a parent who couldn't remember him was too depressing." I bit my lip, my shoulders falling momentarily before I recovered. "She had a handful of other suggestions, too. Thankfully, she extended my deadline to give me time to work on it."

Brooklyn opened her mouth, her expression distant, as if she'd just been told her puppy died. "But it was really good."

"I know." I turned my gaze away from hers.

It felt like I had to cut out part of my soul to rework the pages I'd written so feverishly after running into Noah. My editor's admonition that the pages I'd submitted weren't what they published was all the encouragement I needed to keep my distance from him and focus on finding a new source of inspiration. I had a deadline I couldn't miss and a book I had to rewrite.

"Hopefully this guy I'm meeting tonight will completely sweep me off my feet and inspire me." My voice turned bright, cheerful, masking my own discouragement at tossing out what I believed to be a good story.

"I still think you met someone else and just refuse to admit it for whatever reason." Brooklyn sighed. I could feel her studying me. She had always been able to see right through me and all my lies. When the silence in the room grew to an almost deafening level, she pointed at my closet. "Try the red dress. Guys love red."

I walked to it and pulled the dress out, looking it over. It had a sweetheart neckline with off-the-shoulder sleeves. The bodice was fitted through the waist, then flared out slightly. It was the perfect combination of sexy and tasteful. It said "I have a nice rack" without looking like I wore a top several sizes too small.

Taking Brooklyn's advice, I slid into the dress and paired it with black Jimmy Choo heels. I rarely wore them, but I figured going to dinner with a man who made more money in a day than most people made in a year was good enough justification to do so.

Refocusing my thoughts on my impending date, I tried everything I could to muster some sort of enthusiasm about what awaited me. Nothing worked, not even the promise of a really fantastic bottle of wine. I busied myself with applying my makeup and pinning my hair back to keep the unruly waves out of my face. Just as I took one last look in the mirror, the buzzer sounded.

"He's here," Brooklyn sang. I continued to stare at my reflection. Instead of butterflies flitting in my stomach, I felt sick. I didn't feel like myself. I hated the idea of pretending to be someone I wasn't. I didn't know why it bothered me now. For years, I'd put on a show, usually taking on the personality of whatever type of heroine I was writing about at the time. But after getting a taste of what it was like to just be myself, attack ducks and all, I found myself hungry for more.

"What do I do?" I spun around to face her, my heart racing.

"You answer the door, Molly." She laughed at the panic in my eyes. I took a deep breath, not wanting Mr. Timothy Vandersmith to see me so rattled, then stood up.

The buzzer sounded again, echoing through my small apartment.

"You'd better get going." Brooklyn hopped off the bed and pushed me down the hallway, handing me my clutch. "I expect to hear all about it tomorrow." She opened the door and practically threw me out of my own apartment.

I faced her, struggling to come up with an excuse as

to why I shouldn't go. Like what? Because I couldn't stop thinking about my father's doctor? I wanted to keep whatever I thought occurred last weekend between Noah and me to myself. It didn't matter anyway.

"Molly, what is it?" She narrowed her gaze at me.

I tried to relax my nervous expression. "Can you take Pee Wee for a walk before you leave?"

She studied me with skepticism, then returned a small smile. "Of course. Have a good night." She closed the door, leaving me alone on the landing.

Drawing in a breath, I turned back around, steadying myself before walking down the steps. I emerged on the sidewalk, my brow wrinkling when my eyes landed on a man in his fifties with graying hair standing there. A dark SUV idled just behind him. He looked nothing like the photo Debra had sent.

"Good evening, Ms. Brinks," he said. "I'm Brody, Mr. Vandersmith's driver."

I gaped at him, as if my ears were playing tricks on me. I'd chosen the exact same name for Jackson Price's driver in my book. Maybe it was a sign this was the path I was supposed to take. Perhaps this man I was scheduled to meet tonight was exactly what I needed to get back on track.

"Mr. Vandersmith apologizes for not being able to pick you up himself. He was delayed at the office this evening. I'll escort you to dinner. He'll meet you there."

He stepped toward the car and opened the back door for me. I blindly followed, remaining silent as I slid inside.

"We'll be at the restaurant shortly," Brody said upon getting into the driver's seat, then pulled into traffic. I watched the buildings zoom by as he navigated the narrow streets of the North End, driving toward the

Back Bay area. It was a clear night, the moon beautiful against the backdrop of the large skyscrapers. My mind drifted to Noah again. It would have been the perfect evening to sit beneath the stars and watch a movie.

When the car came to a stop a few blocks away from the Common, I looked out the window at a two-story brick building, no sign out front indicating what it was. Brody opened the door for me, taking my arm to help me out of the SUV.

"This way, Ms. Brinks."

I had to admit, it felt nice to be pampered. I could certainly get used to having a driver escort me around town, although I'd miss riding the subway.

When Brody opened the simple wooden door, I stepped into a dimly lit dining room, about a dozen tables filling the small space. Candles adorned tables covered with white cloths. The all-male waitstaff was dressed in formal tuxedos and wore crisp white gloves. A beautiful baby grand piano sat in the corner, a man in a dark suit playing ambient music, setting a romantic mood. I immediately felt like Julia Roberts in *Pretty Woman*. I was completely out of my comfort zone in a place like this. I just hoped the man waiting for me would be my Edward…at least until I finished writing this book.

Almost instantly, a dark-haired man stood up, meeting my gaze, buttoning the jacket of his charcoal gray suit. He had a twinkle in his green eyes, a chiseled jawline, defined cheekbones, and a breathtaking smile. I'd seen his photo, but the real thing was much more attractive than any two-dimensional snapshot could do justice.

"Molly." He approached and placed an unexpected kiss on my cheek, lingering slightly longer than I anticipated, turning the friendly gesture into one that was much more intimate, more sensual. His lips warm on my skin, a subtle shiver traveled down my back. "You're even more beautiful in person." His voice was tender, deep, seductive. "I hope you're hungry." He pulled back, a devilish grin on his face.

"Famished," I squeaked out.

He winked, then led me to the table, pulling my chair out for me. He was the perfect gentleman, everything I'd expected him to be based on what little I knew of him. He was one of the most sought-after bachelors in Boston. He started going on about how his computer security company made him millions when he was still attending MIT. He said while he had almost everything he could ever want, something was lacking.

"And what's that?" I asked as the waiter placed raw oysters in front of me. I couldn't recall anyone taking our order. I suspected Timothy had ordered before I arrived. Still, I tried not to let that affect my opinion, especially since this guy could be the one to help me get this book back on track. On paper, he *was* Jackson Price. Rich. Handsome. Successful. I couldn't let his minor faults distract me.

"A beautiful woman." He narrowed his eyes at me, treating me to a hint of a smile.

I wanted to think his words were genuine, but I knew better than that. I'd been doing this dance for a long time. I knew a fake when I saw one, and Mr. Timothy Vandersmith was definitely a fake. Sure, he had money, charm, great looks, but I wondered if a single word he uttered was sincere. Last week, I wouldn't have cared. He could have told me he trained unicorns in Oz and I'd still let him take me to his bedroom. Something was different now...because of Noah. I doubted he had an insincere bone in his body.

Lost in my thoughts, I barely noticed when Timothy answered his phone in the middle of our lame excuse for a conversation that lacked any depth. He'd been telling me all about his plans to take his yacht to Newport the following weekend. Most women may have been impressed by his wealth — the boats, the numerous properties he owned, the private jet. Not me. A dick was still a dick, regardless of whether it pissed in a gold-plated toilet or a porta-potty.

I stared at the raw oysters sitting in front of me, feeling as if I were intruding, as if I shouldn't be here. I didn't even like oysters. Why was I eating them? To impress a guy? For what? Because he had potential to be really good muse material? What if I'd already found my muse?

As if on cue, the pianist began playing a different song. I nearly spit out the salty oyster. I listened to the haunting melody, my breathing increasing. When I heard the driver's name, I'd hoped it was a sign I was exactly where I was supposed to be. But as I listened to the pianist play the theme from *An Affair to Remember*, Noah returned to the forefront of my mind...if he'd ever left. I glanced around the restaurant, an indescribable feeling washing over me. As I studied a dozen other couples feigning interest in one another, I found myself tired of putting on the same charade I had been for years.

Realization struck me, leaving me breathless, giddy, excited. Brooklyn was right. I didn't need Timothy to be my muse. I'd already found one in Noah. He had inspired me more than anyone I'd ever met. I'd been able to write unlike I had in years, if ever. Avery and Jackson had leapt off the pages, their story alive in my mind. It had depth. It had heartache. It had pain — all things I knew my publisher would never agree to release. I no longer cared what they wanted. For the first time in years, I was going to write the story *I* wanted to tell.

Abruptly, I stood up. My sudden movement caught Timothy's attention.

"Hold on a sec," he said to whomever was on the phone. So much for him being the perfect gentleman I thought he was. "Is everything okay, Molly?"

I opened my mouth, sorting through all the conflicting thoughts circling in my head. I didn't know what came over me at that moment. Maybe it was the ridiculousness of the situation I found myself in. Wearing a dress, pretending to be someone I wasn't. And why?

"Molly?" He narrowed his gaze at me.

"I have to go," I explained, laughing slightly, a wide smile brimming on my face.

"Go?" He hung up the phone and stood. "Go where? I thought we were really hitting it off."

My smile grew even wider. I hadn't felt this alive in years, the promise of doing something for me and no one else invigorating me.

"This isn't me." I gestured to my dress, then the stuffy surroundings. "I'll be completely honest with you. I don't just write snarky columns for a magazine, like Debra probably told you when she set up this date. I write really hot, steamy romance novels, too. I had my friend pull some strings so I could meet a hot, wealthy guy, since the hero in my book is precisely that. You're definitely really hot. A week ago, I probably would have suffered through all this stupid small talk just to get you into the bedroom."

His eyes widened at my confession before his gaze hooded. "I'm more than happy to indulge you in that. We can leave right now." A carnal smile grew on his lips.

I shook my head, feeling lightheaded, but in the best way possible. "I've finally realized I can be inspired without having to take my clothes off."

I whirled around, dashing out of the restaurant and onto the street, my feet not carrying me as fast as I wanted them to. I ran to the corner and hailed a passing cab.

"Forest Hills Cemetery," I said as I slid inside, unable to hide the grin on my face. I bounced my legs, traffic seeming to crawl as the driver navigated toward the interstate. At least a dozen times during the twenty minute ride, I almost talked myself into turning around. My original plan for tonight had flown out the window in seconds. I'd hoped I could forget about Noah and find a new muse. But I couldn't. Worse, I didn't want to, regardless of the consequences. I was supposed to be writing a forbidden romance. What better source of inspiration than spending time with someone I shouldn't have? I refused to believe there was any other reason I felt compelled to spend time with Dr. Noah McAllister.

When the front gates to the cemetery finally came into view, the cab slowed to a stop. I handed the driver the cash and carefully stepped onto the pavement. As I climbed the incline toward the stone pillars marking the entrance to the historic cemetery, Cary Grant's voice found its way to my ears. I crested the small hill, seeing a large projection screen set up in the distance.

It seemed odd to host movies in a cemetery. However, judging by the number of people in attendance, it was apparently rather popular. I thought it would be disrespectful to the families of those buried here, but as I drew closer, I realized the movie was being shown in an area of the cemetery where there were no graves.

Approaching a roped off grassy area, I stood on my toes, wondering how I'd even find Noah among the sizeable crowd. As if able to sense my presence, a pair of striking blue eyes swung to me from ten yards away. He shot to his feet, completely ignoring all the shouts from others in the audience to get out of the way.

I slowly walked toward him, taking my time so as not to trip when my heels sank into the grass.

"You're here," he declared, swallowing hard. His eyes locked on mine, his broad chest heaving.

I nodded, excited, nervous...happy.

"What happened to your date?"

"I didn't want to be there and pretend to be someone I wasn't," I admitted truthfully, surprising myself.

He grinned, his smile reaching his eyes, lighting up his entire face. "Come on." He held out his hand. "You can always just be yourself around me."

I took his hand, his large fingers intertwining with mine, and allowed him to lead me to a blanket spread out on the grass. After slipping off my shoes, I lowered myself to the ground. A small tingle traveled from the tips of my fingers to my toes when Noah draped an extra blanket across my shoulders, his arms keeping me warm in the brisk spring air.

Chapter Thirteen

"SO WHAT DID YOU think of your first movie experience in a cemetery?" Noah asked as we followed the crowd out of the front gates. Some crossed the street toward a makeshift parking lot on the grass, others headed down the block to the closest subway station.

I gave him a sideways glance, grinning. "You're close to proving your hypothesis that it *does* pay to try new things."

Tonight was exactly what I needed. Sitting under the stars and watching one of my favorite movies with someone who was quickly becoming one of my favorite people was a pleasant turn of events. We'd barely spoken a word to each other, but in that silence, I felt like Noah shared pieces of himself with me. Too many times, I'd stolen a glance to see him mouthing the words to some of the lines…the same ones I mouthed the words to.

"Good," he said, then faced me, both of us slowing our steps. As if able to read my mind, he asked, "Are you tired?"

I shook my head, keeping my eyes glued to his.

His lips turned up into a smile. "Where'd you park?"

"I took a cab."

"Good. Let's go." He grabbed my hand and pulled me along. Heat radiated throughout my body as I savored the feeling of my hand enclosed in Noah's, our fingers intertwined.

"Go where?"

"You'll see." He winked. "I'm not ready for this night to be over just yet."

I struggled to keep up with his long strides. Noticing my difficulty, he slowed down, beaming at me as we walked through the rows of cars. He led me to a black Mercedes and opened the passenger door, helping me in. My body hummed with excitement, a lightness in my limbs.

When I was getting ready tonight, if you had told me I'd end up ditching my date, who happened to be worth somewhere in the eight figures, to watch a movie in a cemetery with my father's neurologist, I would have laughed. I'd sworn to do everything I could to forget about Noah. This just felt right, regardless of how wrong it was for me to have any sort of physical relationship with this man.

After a silent, yet comfortable drive, Noah pulled up to an unassuming brick building a few blocks from Massachusetts General. A valet attendant approached the car and opened my door, helping me out. Noah ran around to meet me, then grabbed the ticket from the attendant. I peered at the one-story building in front of me. It didn't look like much, but the jazz music coming from within caught my interest.

"What is this place?" I asked as Noah held my elbow and steered me toward a pair of doors manned by two very large bouncers. They nodded at him, allowing us to enter.

"My college roommate told me about this club. He studied mechanical engineering, but played in a jazz quartet during his free time. After I came with him one night, I immediately preferred it to the rest of the college bars in this city." He led me into the darkened interior. The sound of a trumpet and saxophone playing incredible jazz riffs grew louder. Regardless, Noah was still able to talk without having to shout. "It used to be a speakeasy during prohibition. Thankfully, someone felt the need to preserve its history. I was surprised it was still here when I came back. Things seem to change too fast around here. Some of my favorite restaurants in college are now all nail salons or grocery stores."

"When did you come back?" I followed him toward one of the few vacant tables in a hidden corner.

"About eight years ago." He pulled out a chair for me, then sat in his own across the small table. "I'd just finished up my residency and was offered a geriatric neurology fellowship at Tufts Medical. That prompted me to make Boston my home again. When my fellowship was over, I joined a neurology practice that was looking to expand into the degenerative disorder field. I've been there ever since."

I offered Noah a tight smile, not wanting to prod any further. I didn't want to be reminded that he was my father's doctor. For just one night, I wanted to pretend he was a handsome stranger who had no connection to my family whatsoever.

A young woman dressed in black approached our table and placed a cocktail napkin in front of each of us. "Can I get you something to drink?"

Noah looked at me, allowing me to order first.

"Manhattan. Up."

She nodded, then turned to Noah.

"Scotch. Neat."

I had to bite back my laugh. Of course he ordered a scotch.

"How about you?" Noah asked once the waitress left to grab our drinks. "Have you lived here all your life?"

I rubbed my clammy hands on my dress, fidgeting with the hem. Noah's inquisitive gaze rattled me. I'd never felt comfortable talking about myself. Typically, I'd find a way to change the subject. Everything was different with Noah. He already knew about my father. I felt like he already knew me, too.

"I grew up just outside Boston in Somerville, but I feel like I grew up in the North End." I placed my hands on the table and toyed with the cocktail napkin. "My dad owned this café that's been passed down through the generations. When he got sick, Drew bought it from him. I practically lived there when I was a little girl."

"So you've always lived in this area?"

"Yes. Apart from the four years I spent at NYU."

His interest piqued a bit, his eyebrows raised. "NYU? What was your major?"

I lowered my eyes, shrugging sheepishly. "Journalism."

"That's a great school for that."

"I guess."

He tilted his head, studying my expression. "What is it?"

"Nothing," I recovered quickly. "NYU has a great journalism program. People I graduated with have gone on to write for the *New York Times*, the *Wall Street Journal*, the *Washington Post*. It's very prestigious to have a journalism degree from there."

"But it's not what you wanted, is it?" He narrowed his gaze at me.

Chewing on my lower lip, I slowly shook my head, surprising myself with my honesty. Hell, most of the guys I'd dated never even knew where I went to college, let alone what my degree was.

"I wanted to study English literature, but my dad steered me in a different direction. He didn't see how a degree in English would be useful. Don't get me wrong," I added quickly. "He loved to read and truly valued the importance of books at a young age. He just didn't see how anyone could make a career out of studying it."

Avoiding Noah's eyes, I scanned the lounge. It was relatively dark, muted lights illuminating the few dozen tables. In the center was a small stage that could only fit five musicians. The walls were exposed brick, displaying prints of famous jazz musicians, some signed. The entire place couldn't have been bigger than my apartment, but I liked it. It was small and intimate.

The clientele spanned all age groups. There were some who appeared to be on death's door. There were others I assumed attended one of the many colleges that made up the city of Boston. Regardless, everyone seemed to be enjoying the music, the atmosphere addictive. Every other bar in this city seemed to be the same…the same people, the same drinks, the same thumping music you could barely discern because of how distorted the speakers were. Not here. The music was the reason people came, not the promise of finding someone drunk enough who'd be more than willing to make a really bad decision.

When Noah remained silent, I turned back to him. "It was certainly a bone of contention between us."

"I thought you had a good relationship with your father."

The waitress approached with our drinks, Noah smiling in thanks. She placed them on the table, then retreated. Grabbing my martini glass, I raised it to my lips. I needed the alcohol to settle the nerves in my stomach. I didn't know which set me more on edge...sharing some of my innermost secrets with Noah, or the fact that I *wanted* him to know this side of me.

"I do," I said, taking a sip of my Manhattan. "Or I did when I was younger. As I reached adolescence, it was difficult for him to find things in common with me. He tried, but there are some things a girl doesn't feel comfortable sharing with her dad." I tapped my fingernails on the table. "He usually spent all this time and effort helping Drew with his hockey. I guess I just felt left out. So when he finally took an interest in what I was going to study in college, it just felt too little, too late, ya know?"

"Yet you still visit him every day? If you ask me, that doesn't sound like someone who has a bad relationship with her father."

"I guess." I fidgeted with the stem of the martini glass. "I just hate the idea that he's all alone in a nursing home. When I was younger, I was forced to sing in my church choir. During Christmas, we'd go around to all these area convalescent homes and sing carols to the patients there. They all looked so sad and alone. When Drew and I had to make the decision to put Dad in a home, I swore he'd never become like all those people I saw when I was younger."

"What about your mom?" Noah pressed. "I've never seen her stop by."

My eyes locked with his. "She left when I was four."

Understanding mixed with sympathy washed over his expression. He reached across the table, grabbing my hand. "I'm sorry. I didn't mean to bring it up."

"It's not that big a deal. I was so young, I can't even remember what she was like. It's kind of hard to miss someone you never knew." I pulled my hand away and took another sip of my Manhattan.

"You don't even know your mother?"

"I haven't seen her since she left."

Noah shook his head, licking his lips. "Why not? If I had kids, I couldn't ever imagine abandoning them, even if I wasn't on the best of terms with their mother."

"I don't know a lot of the details. It was never really discussed much, at least not at length. All I know is my mom wasn't happy with the life my dad gave her. One day, she decided to leave it all behind. She still sends me a pair of slippers every year for my birthday. I have a box full of them."

"You've kept them?"

"I know it doesn't make any sense, but I can't throw them out. This is a woman who's never made any effort to be in my life, in any of our lives. I should hate her, but a tiny part of me feels sorry for her."

The band finished playing, the crowd applauding their incredible talent. I took the opportunity to look away from Noah and joined the audience in clapping. I could feel the heat of his gaze burning my skin for a moment. Then he joined in, as well.

When the applause died down, the sax player counted off, then started playing a slower tune. It was one I recognized from the music Aunt Gigi liked to play in the café in the morning. Jazz standards consisting mostly of Frank Sinatra and his contemporaries.

A few couples got up from their tables and headed to a bit of free space in front of the stage. They swayed to the melody as a young black woman sauntered up to the microphone and sang the first line of the song.

"I put a spell on you…"

The soulful voice definitely put a spell on me, on everyone here.

His eyes glued to me, Noah stood up and extended his hand. "Do you want to dance?" He licked his lips, hope building in his gaze. "It would be an awful waste of such a stunning dress if I didn't ask." He winked.

Nothing good could ever come from dancing to such a soulful, sensual song with a man as attractive and endearing as Noah. I simply couldn't bring myself to say no. Not saying a word, I placed my hand in his, rising from the chair. My skin prickled with heat, Noah's wanton stare making my heart speed up.

I'd always been in complete control of my faculties around men. I'd been the one in charge, the one who decided whether we danced or went back to my place. I made all the rules. With Noah, I was out of my element. This man was off limits, but dammit if I didn't want to feel his body sway and move next to mine.

Once on the small dance floor, surrounded by a handful of other couples enclosed in each other's warm embrace as they moved to the slow tune, Noah placed one hand on the small of my back, linking my hand in his free one. Draping my arm over his shoulder, I met his eyes and allowed him to lead. I could sense there were a hundred things he wanted to say, but his brain wouldn't allow it. I knew exactly how he felt. We were walking a fine line of integrity.

I liked to think I had principals, despite my pattern of using my past flings as unknowing muses for my books. I didn't see the harm in it. I'd never made any promises to take out a mortgage together and live happily ever after. There were no discussions about commitment or relationships. There were no labels. For the most part, they had been more than content with our arrangement. There was something different about Noah.

I didn't even realize when I began toying with a few tufts of his hair that hung over the collar of his shirt. It felt so normal, so perfect, so right. I could dance with him for hours and never tire of the way his body moved with such fluidity against mine. Dancing was screwing with your clothes on, an act of tantalizing seduction where the seducer gave a sneak peek of what awaited once they were alone.

My body was a respectable distance from Noah's when we started. As the song went on, his hand on my back tugged me closer and closer. His head lowered, our breath mingling.

The music grew more intense, the singer belting out the lyrics with more power, more vigor, more fury. Hypnotized, we stopped swaying to the music and simply stared at each other, our bodies fused. I swallowed hard, my chest heaving, as Noah licked his lips and slowly leaned toward me. His eyes were compelling, vivid, bold, as if in a trance...as if someone had cast a spell over him.

My lips parting, I lifted my chin. The hair on my arms stood on end, my skin tingling. I was lightheaded, breathless, warm, and a dozen other emotions I couldn't articulate at that precise moment.

Just as his lips were about to meet mine, a body bumped into me from behind, catching me by surprise. I teetered on my too-high heels, struggling to catch my balance. Noah quickly snapped into action and pulled my body flush with his before I fell to the floor.

"Oh, my god. I'm so sorry," a woman said. Judging by the black dress and small tray she carried, I assumed she was one of the servers. "Are you okay?"

I offered her a tight smile as Noah released his hold on me. "Of course. Don't worry about it. At least you didn't have a tray full of drinks."

If hearing the theme from *An Affair to Remember* at the restaurant earlier was a sign I should go to Noah, I couldn't help but think this was a sign for us to put on the brakes. As much as I wanted to know how his lips tasted, how he kissed, how his tongue would feel tangled with mine, I couldn't live with the guilt if I pushed him into that unethical situation.

I stepped away from him, studying his demeanor. His expression was difficult to read. "It's getting late," I said. "I should probably get home." I turned and headed back to the table, the band now playing a more upbeat jazz number.

"Can I give you a lift?" Noah caught up to me and threw a few bills on the table to cover our tab and a generous tip.

"That's not necessary." I grabbed my clutch, smoothing the lines of my dress. "I can just take a cab." I hurriedly skirted the tables and emerged onto the sidewalk, inhaling the fresh air. The temperature had dropped, my breath visible when I exhaled. I hugged myself, running my hands up and down my bare arms.

"Let me drive you," Noah's voice called out. I whirled around to see him approaching me, turmoil in his gaze. "It's freezing out here and you don't have a coat." He shrugged out of his jacket and placed it over my shoulders.

"I don't have one that matches this dress."

He stared at me for what seemed like an eternity before his expression lightened. "You can't visit your father if you get sick," he reminded me.

Being alone in close quarters with Noah was probably a bad idea, but the prospect of waiting for a cab or walking to the closest T station was much less appealing.

"Fine," I huffed after a brief moment of hesitation. "You can drive me home."

He offered me a tight smile. Once the valet drove up with Noah's car, he helped me in. Within seconds, I directed him toward my apartment. We didn't talk much during the short drive on the practically deserted Boston city streets at one in the morning. I considered bringing up our almost kiss so there wouldn't always be this awkwardness between us. I had a feeling that would just make it worse. It was probably best we forget it ever happened.

"You can just drop me off right here," I instructed him once he turned the corner a few blocks from my apartment.

He slowed to a stop and pulled off to the side of the road. "You live in a liquor store?" He cocked a brow, glancing at the building to my right.

"No." I laughed. "I live a few blocks up." I opened the door, about to step onto the sidewalk.

"Then I'll drive you to your place."

I sighed, my expression turning serious. "I appreciate the offer, but I live across a narrow alley from my brother. It's probably in both our best interests that I walk home myself. He shouldn't see you dropping me off."

"We're just friends, Molly. There's nothing wrong with being dropped off by your friend. Who cares if I happen to be your father's doctor?"

"See, that's the thing, Noah." I bit my lip. "You don't know me like my brother does. I'm not exactly the type of girl who hangs out with guys as just friends. Even if I were, it's not worth the potential headache. This section of town is full of Italians who are notorious snoopers. Everyone here knows everybody else's business."

He studied me for a prolonged moment, then briefly closed his eyes, his shoulders slumped. "Okay, you're probably right. For the record, I'm only doing this under protest and out of necessity. I'd much rather drive you to your building and walk you to the door."

"Duly noted." I winked, then shrugged out of his jacket, about to hand it back to him.

"Keep it," he said. "If I can't drive you back to your place, the least I can do is make sure you're warm. You can give it back to me tomorrow."

"Tomorrow?"

"I guess, technically, it's today."

"I like the sound of today better," I admitted, surprising myself. As much as I knew I should keep my distance, some outside force was at play, pulling me toward him every time I tried to back away.

"Me, too."

I wrapped his jacket around my shoulders and stepped out of the car. Just as I was about to shut the door, I leaned down. "Thanks for tonight," I murmured in a soft voice. "For letting me be me."

He offered a smile, a calmness washing over his face. "I like you as you, Molly."

Chapter Fourteen

"Why are you wearing makeup?" Drew asked from behind the counter as I burst into the café on a warm Saturday in early June.

The last several weeks had been the best I'd had in ages. I'd settled into a new routine, one that involved spending more time with Noah than I probably should. Each Thursday, I made a point to meet him at the cemetery, where we watched whatever classic movie they were showing that evening. Occasionally, we made arrangements to run into each other at the Common, where we would eventually end up at the same ice cream shop he'd taken me to after heroically saving me from a criminal biker gang named The Mallards...as the story had evolved in my head.

With each encounter, I grew more and more comfortable around him, almost to the point where I felt as if we'd known each other for years. He'd talk about what it was like growing up with four sisters. I'd share stories about my own childhood.

Every afternoon when I read to my dad, I often held out hope Noah would surprise me with a visit. He'd done just that a few times. I'd smile as he sat beside me, listening to me read to my father. Whatever was going on between us had grown into something more than a friendship based on a shared struggle, although I kept reminding myself I only spent time with him because of my book.

When I wasn't with Noah, I was glued to my laptop, Jackson and Avery's story bleeding from my fingertips. He'd become my unsuspecting inspiration for Jackson, and with each encounter, I wondered how Noah would influence the next part of their story. It was like someone had cut the chains that had shackled me to the same repetitive storyline. For the first time in years, I wrote the story I wanted to tell. I'd never felt so fulfilled and satisfied with my writing.

"What are you doing here?" I stopped in the doorway, cursing my luck. Drew typically didn't work on Saturdays. "Who's watching the girls?"

I had yet to tell Brooklyn or Drew about Noah. I hated keeping secrets from them, but they couldn't know the truth...that I was essentially using my father's doctor to write a heart-wrenching forbidden romance. For all they knew, things with Timothy had gone exceedingly well and he was my new inspiration. At some point, I knew I'd have to tell them the truth, but I wasn't ready for that just yet. I didn't need their reminder that I shouldn't be playing with someone's emotions. I knew it was wrong, but I couldn't quit seeing Noah any more than an alcoholic could stop drinking.

"Hiya, Auntie Molly!" A head with tight brown curls popped up from the other side of the counter. "We're playing here before Daddy takes us to the aquarium!" Alyssa explained as a smaller, nearly identical head appeared beside her.

"Yes, Auntie Molly! Come see the fishes with us!" Charlotte implored.

I opened my mouth, about to give them the same excuse I always did...that I already had plans. Their faces fell before I had the chance to utter a single word, as if they already knew what I would say.

"Come on, Mols," Drew said in a soft voice. "Just for a half-hour. Then you can go. I feel like I haven't seen you in a month."

I eyed my watch, seeing it was already past one in the afternoon.

"He'll be okay if you're a little late today."

I pulled my lip between my teeth, hating the disappointment etched on my nieces' faces. I couldn't remember the last time I'd gone out with them and my brother. Sure, we got together every Sunday evening for family dinner and a movie, but it had been a while since the four of us had spent any meaningful time together.

"Okay. I'll come for a little bit." I winked.

"Yay!" Alyssa and Charlotte cheered with excitement, running around the counter and flinging their tiny arms around me.

"Can we go now, Daddy?" Alyssa begged.

"Of course, munchkin." He grabbed a chocolate hazelnut pastry and handed it to me, knowing my guilty pleasure.

Ducking under the counter, he swooped both Alyssa and Charlotte into his arms with ease, carrying them out of the café. Their giggles made my heart melt. I froze in place, staring at him laughing and making up songs with his two girls. I loved seeing Drew as a father. I used to think he was put on this earth only to play hockey. He had an amazing talent unmatched by anyone else in the rink, and I wasn't just saying that because he was my brother. Still, his skills on the ice were no match to the talent he had for being a father. He loved those two girls more than he loved anything, and it showed.

Drew turned around, studying me. "Are you coming, Molly?"

"Sorry." I snapped out of my thoughts and caught up with them. "I was lost in my head for a minute."

"Thinking of the book?" Drew asked while Alyssa and Charlotte debated what we should see first at the aquarium. Alyssa wanted to visit the sea turtles; Charlotte preferred the penguins.

"What else?" A silence settled between us as we wandered through Christopher Columbus Park, the smell of the ocean growing stronger.

"You never answered why you're wearing makeup," Drew commented.

"I wear makeup all the time," I insisted.

"To visit Dad?" He lowered his voice. "Do you have plans to see Timothy tonight?"

"No," I answered truthfully, although I probably should have lied.

"Is everything still okay with him?"

"Of course. He's been swamped with work and I've been busy writing. It's actually a blessing in disguise that he's so career oriented. Then he doesn't want to see me all the time." I offered Drew a smile, hoping he wouldn't be able to see through all the lies I'd been feeding him.

"I don't know why you think you even need to date this guy. Apparently, you're doing just fine writing this book on your own. You saw Kevin at least four times a week. I can count on one hand the number of times you've seen this guy, and he's never even been over to your apartment."

I sighed, crossing my arms in front of my chest. "You wouldn't understand, Drew."

"Because you refuse to talk about it."

I stared forward, remaining silent. I could feel his eyes studying me. This whole thing was a ticking time bomb. He'd eventually figure out I'd been lying to everyone about dating Timothy. I just needed to finish this book, and soon.

"Have you ever found yourself attracted to someone you knew you couldn't have?" I blurted out as we approached the doors to the aquarium, the girls bursting with excitement.

"Why are you asking?" He looked at me suspiciously. "Is something going on that I should know about?"

"No," I answered quickly. Probably too quickly. "It's just this book." I ran my hands through my wavy hair. "I guess I'm trying to wrap my head around what would make someone sacrifice everything — their career, their integrity, their reputation — for another person."

A small smile tugged on his lips before he sighed, meeting my eyes. "You'd be surprised what people are willing to give up when they're in love."

"I'm not writing a love story," I reminded him. "I'm writing a hot, steamy romance. At least that's what I'm *supposed* to be writing." I turned my head.

"But it's not," Drew stated. "I've seen what you've written so far. It's not even close to hot and steamy."

"I just wasn't feeling it," I admitted truthfully. "So I wrote something I *was* feeling. There's more than just a superficial attraction based on looks alone. There's a connection."

"Then I think you already have your answer," Drew replied.

I looked to him, my brow furrowed. "I don't follow."

"Take the girls, for example." He gestured toward

Alyssa and Charlotte as we walked behind them past the main entrance and toward a display of penguins. Alyssa's face oozed with excitement. "What if they had some terminal illness that required a transplant? What if we found a donor, but he only agreed on the condition that you give up your writing, that you never publish another book for the rest of your life? Would you agree?"

"Of course I would," I answered without hesitation. "I'd do anything for those girls."

"Because you love them."

"Yes, but that's a different kind of love than what I'm talking about."

"That may be, but the principle remains the same. The human race is, generally, kindhearted. Most of us would gladly sacrifice everything for those we love, regardless of whether that love is based on a mutual connection, attraction, or whether it's the love of family." He tore his gaze from me, a glint in his eyes as he looked at his girls once more. "I had no idea what to expect when Carla told me she was pregnant, and I was scared shitless when she left me to raise two girls on my own, but I would do *anything* to keep them by my side."

I grabbed his hand, giving him a reassuring smile as we followed the girls through the aquarium, laughing as they scrunched their faces against the glass of some of the fish tanks.

"I guess I'm just trying to wrap my head around these characters' motivations," I said, breaking through the silence that made me feel as if my brother knew this had nothing to do with my book. "He'd have to sacrifice everything to be with her. And why? For the illusion of love? Even if there *were* such a thing as love…which, just for argument's sake, I'll concede may exist…what's her motivation? She's not sacrificing anything. She should just find someone else and forget about him."

"It seems like what her brain wants and what her heart wants are two different things, Molly."

I pulled my bottom lip between my teeth, looking around, not seeing anything. My thoughts were all over the place.

"Are you sure everything's okay?" Drew asked softly.

"Of course." I turned to him, plastering a fake smile on my face. "I'm fine. I promise."

"Okay," he sighed. "Just be careful with whatever you're doing."

"Wha—"

He held up his hand, stopping me. "I don't know what it is, but something tells me you're not giving me the whole story. I just don't want to see you get hurt, whether by Timothy or someone else." He gave me a knowing look.

Instead of feeding him the same lie I had been the past few weeks, I simply nodded. That one gesture told him all he needed to know.

"I won't," I assured him. "My heart is an iron fortress. You should know that by now."

"Even iron can melt if it gets hot enough."

Chapter Fifteen

I PUT MY CAR in park outside the nursing home, then checked my reflection in the rearview mirror. I hastily applied a bit of lip gloss before stepping out of the car and scurrying across the parking lot. Reggie looked up from his book as I walked through the front doors, heading straight for the sign-in form.

"Wait a second, Molly." He shot up, unease on his face.

I frowned, confused by this unexpected change in protocol. I'd been coming to see my father every day since we had to move him here. This was the first time anyone had tried to stop me from signing in.

"What is it?"

He blew out an uneasy sigh. "I've been instructed that your father can't have any visitors at the moment."

"By whom?"

"Dr. McAllister," he answered guardedly. "Dr. Connors, the executive director, agreed with this decision, as well."

"That's bullshit." I raised my voice, heat building in my face at the idea that Noah issued this order.

It wasn't the fact someone was trying to prevent me from seeing my father that irked me. It was the idea of him being alone with only the nursing staff to take care of him. This was precisely why I fought against putting him in a home for as long as I could. Now his own daughter was being kept from him.

"Why?" I ran my hands through my hair, seething.

"It's a safety issue," Reggie responded in a quiet voice, sympathy etched in the lines of his face. "If it were up to me, I'd let you go, but I could lose my job if I did and something happened to you."

"Nothing's going to happen to me! He's my father, for crying out loud! He never so much as spanked me when I was growing up! He's always been the most docile, congenial man I know!"

"That may be," a gruff voice said. I whirled around to see Noah approaching the front desk. "But he's not the same man anymore. You know that just as well as I do. You've said so yourself."

"Why can't I see him?"

"It's not just you, Ms. Brinks," he replied in a formal voice, a complete one-eighty from the fun and carefree version of Noah I'd been spending time with over the past several weeks. It served as yet another reminder that our friendship...I wasn't even sure we could call it that at this point...would always be second to his career. "Even the nursing staff isn't allowed to see him without security present."

"Security? What the hell is going on?" I looked from Noah to Reggie, then back to Noah again, wanting someone to tell me what had happened.

"I'd be happy to discuss this with you in private." He glowered at me, obviously upset I had raised my voice.

"I don't *want* to discuss this in private. I want you to tell me what the fuck happened in the last twenty-four hours that you're now keeping my father completely isolated!" I took a breath, stepping toward Noah. My voice barely a whisper, I added, "You know damn well how I feel about this."

Sighing, his stern demeanor cracked and he ran his fingers through his hair. "I understand." He closed the distance. His hand flinched, as if he wanted to reach out and touch me, but prevented himself from doing so. I wondered if it would always be this way between us. If he would try to hide even our friendship from everyone. I didn't know why I cared so much. I had never needed reassurance of a man's feelings toward me before. Why did I need it now?

"He's taken a turn, Molly," Noah explained quietly. "You've seen it with your own eyes these past few weeks. His speech has become impaired. He's having so much difficulty communicating, he's grown increasingly more violent, lashing out at everyone, particularly during the evening hours. I have no reason to believe he'll act any differently around you. I'm not willing to put you in that type of situation."

"Well, *I'm* willing to take that risk," I shot back. "He's my father. I'm not going to leave without seeing him. You'll have to have security throw me out." I glared at him for several long moments, then softened my expression. "Please. It's not even close to sundown yet. Maybe he just needs to know there's someone out there who still cares about him." I leaned toward Noah, my voice barely audible. "What would you have done to have just five more minutes with your father?"

I hated using his personal information against him, but I didn't know what else to do. My father needed to know he wasn't alone, even if he didn't know who I was at the moment.

Noah ran his hand over his face, his shoulders slumping in defeat. "Fine," he relented. "You can have ten minutes."

"Two hours. Like usual."

161

"One hour, and that's it."

"Fine. One hour." I stepped back to the front desk and scratched my name on the sign-in sheet while Reggie eyed both of us with intrigue. Smiling at my victory, I grabbed the visitor badge and proceeded down the hallway.

"An orderly and a security guard will be present," Noah called out.

I huffed, spinning around, watching him approach with a furtive stare. "What could have possibly happened to make you think I need protection from my own father?"

"He doesn't know he's your father." His tone was even. "He's been lashing out, refusing to eat, shouting incoherent thoughts."

"And how is that different from every other day?"

He breathed in through his nose, pinching his lips together as he stared at me, fire in his gaze. "One of the orderlies was helping him into the bathroom after lunch. She now has five stitches in her forehead."

My eyes widened as I shook my head. "That doesn't sound like him."

"It's the disease. These violent episodes never have any warning so I need to do everything I can to keep those around him safe." He lowered his voice. "I know what you're going through. I've been there. I didn't want to think my father would ever hurt me. The disease eats away at him. He doesn't know which way is up and it scares the shit out of him. So much so, he has no choice but to try to protect himself from what he perceives as a potential threat."

"I just want to read to him."

"And you can." He grabbed my hands in his. I shot my eyes to him, surprised by the sudden change.

Whenever I was at the nursing home, Noah had always made a conscious effort to avoid coming within even an inch of me. "But with people who are trained to deal with this sort of behavior close by in case he lashes out at you."

"I don't like it—"

"I know you don't," he answered quickly. A tingle spread through me when he caressed my knuckles. "But this is the only way right now. I'm hoping tomorrow will be different."

"Is this why you're here on your day off?" I asked.

"I said goodbye to the idea of days off the second I decided to go into this field. My patients are my priority. Always have been. The staff called and said your father was having an unusually bad day. It's my job to keep him safe, even on the weekends."

Footsteps sounded from down the hall and he quickly withdrew his hands from mine, taking a step back. I didn't know why I expected anything different, but it still pained me.

"Dr. McAllister," a large man in a security uniform said upon seeing us. "You requested assistance?"

"Yes. Larry, this is Molly Brinks. She'd like to spend about an hour visiting her father. I'd like you to remain in the room with her, along with Brian." He nodded at the orderly by his side.

"Certainly, sir. We'll make sure everyone remains safe."

"Thank you."

"This way, Ms. Brinks," Larry said.

I forced myself to tear my eyes from Noah's and followed Larry down the familiar hallways toward my father's room. He opened the door and allowed me to enter first, remaining within an arm's reach of me at all times. This all felt like visiting hours at a prison, but I bit back any derogatory comments. If this was the only way I could see my father, I'd suffer through.

"Hiya, Dad." I gave him a congenial smile as he sat in his favorite chair, a shape sorter on the table beside him. It reminded me of a child's toy. My heart ached thinking how low he'd fallen in such a short time. It wasn't fair.

His eyes met mine and, for a split second, I thought I saw a hint of recognition in his warmhearted gaze.

"I heard you're having a bit of a rough day." I tried to pretend nothing had changed, that this was just like any other day. "But I'm here now." I lowered myself into the chair beside him, grabbing his hand in mine.

When Larry started toward me, I glared at him. He stopped, still hovering in case he needed to quickly defuse the situation. "It'll be okay," I assured him, then returned my attention to my dad.

Eyeing a new book on the side table, as if a silent instruction to read it, I picked it up. Memories of tenth grade English class rushed forward as I flipped through the pages. Turning to the first chapter, I cleared my throat, then started reading. A heat fell on my skin, as if someone was watching me. I glanced up. Noah leaned against the doorjamb, wearing an expression I couldn't quite place. Returning his tight smile, I continued reading.

"Even then, he was the most striking figure in Starkfield, though he was but the ruin of a man."

Noah continued to hold my gaze, a pang forming in my heart as I recalled the story of Ethan Frome and Miss Mattie Silver's forbidden affections toward each other, their botched attempt to find a way to spend eternity together, and the sad result of the sled accident that caused so many girls in my high school English class to shed a few tears. Not me. I saw the book for what it was…an allegory that the illusion of love could destroy your life, although my English teacher didn't quite agree.

"Keep going," Noah's voice cut through my thoughts as I contemplated whether my English teacher was right. Maybe the lesson in *Ethan Frome* wasn't that love could destroy your life, but that life was too short not to take risks. According to her, love didn't destroy Ethan's life. It was society's limitations that forced his desire to abandon the burdens put on him. It was impossible to ignore the parallels between this book and the story I was currently writing…and living.

I shot my gaze to my father. "Did you…?" I asked with a quiver, wondering if he set this book out after hearing me tell him what I was working on. I could feel three sets of eyes on me.

It was probably nothing, but my heart filled with hope my father's condition wasn't progressing as fast as everyone believed. In my soul, I knew he'd heard me tell him the storyline of my book and remembered it enough to want to read another forbidden romance. He still had some memories. He wasn't a lost hope yet.

Returning my eyes to the page, I lost myself in Edith Wharton's tragic tale, thinking of my own book and what fate awaited Avery and Jackson. I didn't quite know how their story would end. Would they be able to overcome the limitations and expectations imposed on them by society? Or would they crash and burn like Ethan and Miss Mattie Silver?

Consumed with the story, I lost track of time. Just when things had started heating up, as much as they could in early twentieth-century literature, a loud throat clearing tore me away from the book.

"I'm sorry, Ms. Brinks." Larry loomed over me, Brian standing beside him. "Doctor's orders. Time's up."

I glanced around the room to see the doorway now empty. Nodding, I reluctantly placed a shoestring between the pages of the book. A smile tugged at my lips as I recalled my father always using an old shoestring to hold his spot…a habit I now used in my life.

I left the book on the side table, then met my father's eyes. I would have given anything to rewind the clock to those days when we would read together every night. I'd never forget the disappointment in his eyes when, as I neared adolescence, I told him I'd rather read by myself. I shouldn't have shut him out like I did. I should have granted him the one thing he had in common with me…a love of the written word.

"I have to go, Dad," I told him, standing. "But I'll be back tomorrow and we'll read some more, just like when I was little."

He gave me a lopsided smile, then mumbled something incoherent.

I was about to give him a hug when the security guard and orderly rushed toward me. I stepped back in surprise, my eyes fierce.

"What the hell? I'm just giving him a hug."

"Just a precaution, ma'am," Larry explained.

"I understand that," I hissed in a quiet voice, hoping my dad couldn't understand what was going on. "But he's my father. As you've seen with your own two eyes, he's been calm the entire time I've been here. He may be confused, but he knows I'm not here to cause him any harm. I'll be fine."

Before they could stop me, I spun back around and flung my arms around my father, wishing he could understand he wasn't alone. "I love you, Daddy."

"I love you, Josie," he mumbled, his speech slurred.

I drew in a breath. These were the first real words I'd heard him say in over a week. My teeth gritted. I hated the idea this man would die thinking I was the woman who deserted him and his family, not the daughter who idolized him.

"I'm not Josie. I'm Molly, your daughter."

"Molly?" he said, sounding almost like an infant learning to speak for the first time.

I pulled back, searching his eyes, praying for a hint of recognition. "Yes, Dad. I'm Molly."

In a flash, his serene expression turned irate. Before I could react, he wrapped his hands around my throat, his strength surprising for his frail condition. Everything else was a blur as I struggled to capture a breath of welcome oxygen. One moment, I was being choked by the man who gave me life; the next, I was pushed away violently. Unable to maintain my balance, I fell back, hitting my head on the corner of the coffee table.

Disoriented, I blinked, the bright lights in the room obscuring my vision. A dark figure leaned over me, Brian's face coming into view. Out of the corner of my eye, I noticed the security guard pinning my father's arms behind his back.

"Stop! You're going to hurt him!" I screamed, my heart pounding. "He doesn't know what he's doing!" I tried to sit up and go to him, but the room spun.

A flurry of medical staff descended on the room, ushering my dad from the sitting area and into the bedroom. Almost immediately, his irate yelling and shouting ceased.

167

"Are you okay?"

I glanced to my left, surprised to see Noah crouching down beside me. His wide eyes raked over every inch of me, his breathing ragged.

"Of course I am," I shot back, quickly standing up. Dizziness set in and I lost my balance. Noah reacted quickly and grabbed my waist, preventing me from falling.

"Get a wheelchair," he ordered Brian.

"You got it." He dashed out of the room.

"I don't need a wheelchair," I insisted, trying to push away from Noah, but he was too strong for me in my still rattled state. "It's just a little headrush. I'm fine."

"If you don't mind, Molly, I'll let a professional make that determination." His hand on my elbow, he slowly lowered me to one of the chairs.

"Who? You?" I cocked a brow at him as he kneeled in front of me, studying my face intently. My hands still shook from the unexpected attack. I didn't want to believe my father had any hatred in his heart.

"I *do* have a medical degree, after all." Noah flashed a compassionate smile, then reached for my neck, pressing against it slightly.

I flinched when he hit a tender spot.

"That hurt?"

"No," I lied. I didn't want him to feel any more guilt for what had happened than he already did. He wasn't to blame. He had tried to warn me, but I'd been too stubborn to listen. I'd pushed him. I'd used personal information I knew about his family history to persuade him to allow me to see my father when he'd insisted it wasn't safe.

"Nice try, Molly. I can't let you leave until I look you over."

I raised my eyebrows, my heart rate slowly returning to normal. Since day one, Noah had an uncanny ability to calm me. The same was true today, as well.

"Does that line work on all the ladies?" I needed to laugh about the ridiculousness of the current situation I found myself in. I didn't want to think about the possible ramifications of what had happened. I feared I'd never be able to see my father without supervision again. The disease already isolated him. Not being able to offer him any sort of love or compassion would only make matters worse.

Noah's face turned red in the most adorable way. "Not like you'd think."

Brian returned, pushing a wheelchair toward us.

"Thanks, Brian." Noah stood up, stepping away from me, his voice demanding once more. "Please wheel Ms. Brinks to an open exam room. I'll be along."

Brian took my elbow and helped me into the wheelchair. As he pushed me out of the room, I glanced over my shoulder at the open door to my father's bedroom. I could see him sitting on his bed, what looked like an old photo album splayed on his lap. There was a smile on his face.

Chapter Sixteen

I PULLED MY CARDIGAN tight around me as I waited in the chilly exam room. I wondered if this was something they taught at med school. Every exam room I'd ever been in was sub-freezing…or maybe it was simply my nerves that caused a chill to trickle down my spine.

Pacing the room, I studied the diagrams of the brain, the nervous system, and the heart hanging on the wall. Science had never been my strong suit in high school or college. As far as I was concerned, these diagrams could have been in a foreign language. A few of the terms were familiar, due to the amount of reading I'd done about the disease that now plagued my father. Still, I found myself in awe of Noah and his accomplishments at what I considered to be a young age for the medical field. He had a list of credentials a mile long. All I had going for me was my ability to write a killer sex scene. The differences in our achievements were staggering.

"What are you doing standing up?" Noah's demanding voice cut through my thoughts. I hadn't even heard the door open.

Whirling around, I blinked at his tall frame standing in the doorway. I immediately felt lightheaded, which had nothing to do with my recent fall. There was something about the sight of him, the power and compassion in his gaze, that knocked the breath out of me.

"I told you I'm fine." I cracked a small smile, recovering my composure. "Making Brian push me in a wheelchair was a bit of an overkill on your part."

"There's no such thing when it comes to you."

My breath hitched, his words taking me by surprise...in a good way.

"I need to make sure nothing got rattled," he explained. "It's protocol."

"Of course." My shoulders fell.

"Go ahead and have a seat." He gestured to the padded table, a sheet of tissue covering it.

"There?" I asked with a grimace.

"Where else?"

"*Anywhere* else."

He eyed me, intrigued. "You don't like doctors?"

"It's not necessarily that, but I'm a female."

"So I've noticed," he countered with a grin.

I bit my lower lip, completely flustered by his proximity in such close quarters. Fidgeting with my hands, I explained, "Every time I'm forced to sit on an exam table, a cold metal instrument is being shoved into my hooha. And the sound of that paper crinkling is worse than nails on a chalkboard. I'd rather not have to hop onto that sadistic device you call an exam table." I crossed my arms.

"That's okay. I'm flexible." He winked.

A sex-craved little fairy, which had taken up residence in my stomach, started flapping her wings as I wondered exactly how flexible Dr. Noah McAllister truly was. I shouldn't have had these thoughts, but I was only human...and perhaps a little horny. There was something about him — his tall stature, the roughness of his hands, the vividness and sincerity in his eyes when he looked at me — that had grown increasingly impossible to ignore over the past several weeks.

"I've heard that about you," I joked in a low voice, taking a seat on a wheeled stool opposite the exam table.

"You realize, technically, that's my chair, don't you?"

I nodded, smirking as I crossed my arms over my chest.

Letting out a sigh, he kept his eyes glued to mine, faux irritation plastered on his face. He sat in another chair, then hooked his foot on the bottom of mine, dragging me toward him.

The sudden movement caught me off guard and I gripped the sides of the chair. One second, I was in my own little world. The next, I was in Noah's atmosphere. I inhaled quickly, his peppermint breath and musky aroma invading my senses, intoxicating me. One hit of that and I was a complete goner. A dull ache settled between my legs in such an inconvenient way. I wanted to yell at my raging libido to calm herself, but I had a feeling the sex-deprived nymphomaniac had no intention of listening.

"I don't know why you're making such a big deal about this," I said, struggling to suppress the multitude of inappropriate thoughts circling my head at that moment. I had a rather vivid imagination, which was currently on overdrive. "I'm fine. It was just the shock that unbalanced me. Honestly."

He removed a penlight from the pocket of his lab coat and turned it on. "Just look straight ahead."

I huffed, following his command as he shined the light into my eyes. I didn't know what he was looking for, but I no longer cared. I'd do whatever he wanted in order for him to remain near me. We hadn't been this close to each other since that almost kiss. The warmth coming off his body was an aphrodisiac.

"From what Brian and Larry told me, you took a pretty nasty fall," he said in a soft, even voice, shining his light at a bunch of different angles while I continued to stare straight ahead. "I'm just making sure you don't have a concussion."

He turned off the light and sat back in the chair, holding up his hand. "How many fingers am I holding up?"

"I'll give you a finger."

"So original." He lowered his arm. "You're not the first one to tell me that. Remember, I deal with patients with Alzheimer's and dementia on a daily basis. Some of them are quite snarky. In fact, most of them could probably outsnark you."

"Outsnark? Is that a real word?"

"It is now."

"I'm not sure," I said in reproach. "I may have to consult Merriam-Webster, just to verify."

"You do that. Now, how many fingers?" He held his hand back up.

"Three."

"Good." He placed his hands on his legs and studied me in an unnerving manner. "How do you feel?"

Horny? I thought to myself. "Fine."

"Pick a word other than fine. You're a writer. I'm sure you have a thesaurus stored in that beau…" He stopped himself, then continued, "big brain of yours."

I flung my eyes to his, wondering if I'd simply imagined he almost called me beautiful. Imagined or not, there was something in the air between us tonight that was much more charged than it had been over the course of the past few weeks. I'd spent a great deal of time with him, but we'd kept things light and easy. He hadn't looked at me with this kind of hunger in his eyes since we shared that dance.

"It's the truth. I feel fine."

"You always say you're fine. Nothing more, nothing less. Give me something else."

"Give *me* something else to go on here. What specifically do you want to know?"

"How's your head? Any headaches or stiffness?" He cupped my face just below my jawline and tilted my head from side to side, looking for any indication the movement caused me pain.

"My head is just dandy." I smirked, avoiding the use of "fine".

"Better." He removed his hands from my face. "How about any nausea?"

I shook my head. "None."

"Okay. Can you stand up for me?"

Eyeing him, I slowly stood from his chair.

"Walk a straight line."

"Is this a DUI checkpoint? Do you want me to recite the alphabet backwards while I'm at it?"

"No." He smiled. "Most people can't even do that sober."

"And most people can't really walk a straight line all that well sober, either, especially when they're wearing chunky shoes." I gestured to the wedge sandals with a rather impressive heel I wore to give my meager height an added boost.

"Okay. I'll let you slide." He stood up, peering down at me. "Any dizziness?"

I shook my head, my chest beginning to rise and fall in a faster pattern.

Leaning closer, he continued his questioning.

174

"Numbness?"

"No," I whispered, a dull fire igniting in my bloodstream.

"Any tingling in your limbs?" His voice grew quiet, serene. He ran his tongue across his lips, his eyes locked with mine.

Dazed, I shook my head again.

"Are you feeling tired or drowsy?"

"No," I breathed. An outside force made me shorten the distance between us. I should have done something, anything, to break the building tension. This was wrong. It was selfish of me to push the boundaries Noah had obviously been struggling with, but I'd never felt so inspired before. "I feel…"

He leaned down, his sweet breath mixing with mine, our lips a whisper away. A voice in my head screamed at me to walk away, but I physically couldn't. I was frozen in place, unable to put on the brakes. Noah was like a drug I'd grown addicted to. I'd become desperate to spend time with him so I could go home and write until my fingers bled. I hoped that was the only reason I couldn't stop thinking about him anyway. I didn't want to consider the possibility there was a deeper, scarier reason for my infatuation.

"Yes?" He inched closer, his mouth nearly brushing mine.

My lips tingled, anticipation and yearning bubbling deep within. I'd imagined what Noah's kisses were like. I even tried to use that to write Jackson and Avery's first kiss. No matter how many times I'd imagined it, though, the words I wrote seemed lacking. It wasn't right. There was no spark, no electricity, no euphoric sensation I felt all over from them finally acting on their impulses after weeks of torturous buildup. If I could just have one taste, I could get it right. Then I'd be satisfied and could move on.

"Fine," I finished my thought.

A smile broke out on his lips. Before he had a chance to retreat, I clutched his cheeks in my hands, forcing his mouth to mine. A shiver ran through me as my tongue traced his lips, begging for permission to enter, urging him to drop all his apprehensions. There was no turning back after this. I understood why Adam and Eve ate the forbidden fruit. Now that I had finally gotten a taste of something I wasn't supposed to have, I wanted more.

A low groan escaped his throat as he deepened the kiss. He pulled me closer, wrapping my hair around his hand, blissfully trapping me to him. His tongue explored my mouth, as if imprinting each crevice and dip to memory, thoroughly examining everything I had to offer. Part of me wished I had a way to take notes of everything I thought and felt so I could reference them later. The other part was lost in the moment. My body arched into him, a raging fire inside me. Weeks of pent-up yearning — the sideways glances, the occasional innuendo, the random brush of our hands — had culminated in this kiss. It was more passionate, more sensual, more heated than I could have imagined.

He moved his hands to my hips and lifted me with extraordinary ease, forcing my legs around his waist, propping me on the exam table. Tiny synapses erupted in my core as he gently pulsed against me. The feel of his arousal between my legs made me want more of him. More of his kisses. More of the feel of his body against mine. More of his calloused hands brushing against my skin in the most reverent, yet prurient manner. His movements were measured, forceful, greedy. It didn't matter I had initiated the kiss between us. He made it clear he was in charge. It made me burn for him in a way I didn't think possible. My mind was blank, my brain silent for the first time in years. All I could hear was a voice inside me begging for more. God, I wanted more of him, more of this, more of everything that made me feel alive.

I reached for his belt, tugging at it. Our kiss became frantic as we carelessly attempted to remove every barrier between our bodies. As I was about to rip my shirt over my head, a loud beeping pierced the sound of our heavy breathing.

Noah jumped back, snapping out of whatever trance he was in. His wide eyes met mine, horror plastered in the lines of his face. Frozen in place, he simply stared at me.

I had no idea what to do. I should have said something, but what? *Don't worry about it. I just kissed you because I'm using you for my book.* I had a feeling that wouldn't go over well at all.

When his phone beeped again, he pulled it from the clip around his belt. Looking at the screen, his brows furrowed.

"I have to go," he said quickly, avoiding my eyes. He readjusted himself, then headed for the door.

"Noah, wait." I jumped off the exam table I used to loathe. However, it now held some rather pleasurable memories. I'd never look at an exam table the same way again.

He paused just as he was about to turn the knob. He glanced over his shoulder, looking at me as if I had an infectious disease. A pang of guilt seeped into my chest when I saw the turmoil radiating from every inch of his body.

177

"This shouldn't have happened." His voice was firm. Straightening his spine, he smoothed the lines of his shirt and pants, then left the room, closing the door behind him.

Chapter Seventeen

"THERE SHE IS!" DREW exclaimed as I hurried into the café the following afternoon. I wanted to smack the smile off his face. I felt worse than I did getting ready for an eight a.m. class on a Friday after having been out drinking until the early morning hours. This time, though, I hadn't touched a drop of alcohol.

I'd tossed and turned all night. No matter what I did, I was unable to stop thinking about my kiss with Noah. The feel of his lips were burned on mine. Every time I closed my eyes, I could almost imagine him beside me, kissing me with an unquenchable thirst.

I'd used my insomnia to my advantage and worked on my manuscript. The uncertainty Noah's reaction left me with had consumed me. Reading through it earlier this morning, I didn't know what to make of everything. It was as if a stranger wrote it, the thoughts foreign to everything I believed. I kept seeing the final line I'd written flash before me, making me sick to my stomach.

It was the knowledge that, despite years of thinking real love wasn't real life, I'd fallen for the one man I could never have.

I refused to believe any of it was my subconscious rearing its ugly head. It was a work of fiction, nothing more. So what if I had Jackson freak out after his first kiss with Avery? So what if he said it shouldn't have happened just like Noah had? Avery and Jackson weren't real. They were simply products of my imagination.

"I wondered when you would show your face. It's past one."

"Sorry," I offered. "I've just been a little distracted lately, I suppose." I avoided Drew's eyes, grabbing the paper coffee cup he held out to me. I stared out the front windows of the café. Unmoving, I took a long sip of my coffee, trying to hide the bitter look on my face from the sick taste in my mouth. It had nothing to do with the coffee and everything to do with me.

I hated deceiving my brother. I'd never kept anything from him before. When I had sex for the first time, he was the first person I told…before he threatened to head over to the poor kid's house and make him wish he'd never heard the name Molly Brinks. When I stumbled into the house after a high school party during my freshman year, he held my hair back as I prayed to the porcelain god all night, then never said a word about it again to me or my father. When I thought about choosing a different career, he was the one who convinced me to keep going, who told me to ignore everyone, who insisted I had a talent that shouldn't be wasted. Maybe that was why this current deception tore me apart.

"What is it?"

I swung my eyes to his. "What is what?" I swallowed hard.

"You're acting…weird."

"No, I'm not," I argued, laughing nervously. "*You're* acting weird. I'm just tired. This book is kicking my ass."

"Oh yeah?" He crossed his arms in front of his chest. "Do you have more pages for me to see?"

I pulled my lip between my teeth. My limbs grew

jittery at the thought of anyone reading what I'd written last night, especially Drew or Brooklyn.

"Not exactly."

"Then what were you doing up all night?"

"How did you—"

"I just know these things, Molly, so fess up."

I turned from him, plopping down in an empty booth. Drew followed, sliding in across from me. I tapped on the lid to my coffee, unsure of how much to tell him.

"Before I say anything, you cannot tell a soul."

He opened his mouth, but I cut him off.

"I'm not even sure I'm going to tell Brooklyn."

He narrowed his gaze, knowing it must be serious. "What's going on, Mols?" He reached across the table and grabbed my hand in his, stopping me from fidgeting. "Whatever it is, you can talk to me about it. I won't judge you."

I shook my head, trying to collect my thoughts. I prayed I'd feel less guilty if I just told someone what had been going on. My eyes trained on Drew, I finally broke the stiff silence. "The day after speed dating, when I went to the Common to clear my head, I ran into someone."

"Who?"

I chewed on the inside of my cheek, unsure how much I should disclose. One thing was certain. I didn't want to see Noah hurt in all this. "A guy I work with," I lied.

"At the magazine?"

I nodded slightly.

"I didn't know any guys worked there. At least not straight ones," he joked.

"There are a few."

181

"What does he have to do with anything?"

I let out a heavy sigh. "That's who I've been spending time with these past few weeks, not Timothy. That date was over before it even began."

Drew stared, his mouth slack. Then he leaned back in the booth, shaking his head. "I had a feeling something was up, something you didn't want to tell me. I'm assuming this relationship is frowned upon."

"Of course. I'm not comfortable saying who it is just yet, so I don't want to disclose his exact title. He's someone who decides what gets published and what doesn't." I hoped he wouldn't see through this lie, too.

"Then it's similar to the forbidden relationship you're writing about in your book." He formed his lips into a tight line, giving me a hardened stare.

"That's not the only reason I started spending time with him," I insisted, although I wasn't sure whether that were true. "His father had Alzheimer's, too, so I guess it's kind of refreshing to spend time with someone, besides you and Brooklyn, who understands." At least that had some truth to it.

"That explains the strange questions yesterday."

"You said you weren't going to judge."

Drawing in a deep breath, he kept his eyes focused on me, unnerving me. This was his older brother stare, the look that said *I'm not going to tell you what to do, but you probably shouldn't be doing what you are.* He smiled at an older couple as they passed us, then returned his attention to me, lowering his voice. "Have you slept with him?"

"No," I replied hurriedly. "I mean, I wanted to, but he got a call on his phone before things could get too carried away."

"How far did things go?" he asked in a guarded tone.

"We kissed."

"That's it?"

"Yes." I held up my hand when I saw the disbelief on his face. "Hand to God, Drew. We made out for, like, two minutes." I brought my coffee to my lips, trying to hide my smile. "A damn good two minutes," I murmured.

"Then what happened?"

I relayed a modified play-by-play of the previous afternoon...from the kiss to an even deeper kiss, then to the phone interruption and the sudden chill that seemed to come over me.

"When he left he told me the kiss shouldn't have happened."

"And he's right, Molly."

I chewed on my bottom lip. I couldn't remember ever feeling so out of sorts.

"I didn't realize you actually went into the office," Drew commented after a prolonged silence. "I thought you submitted all your work remotely."

I tore my eyes from his, a crack of thunder sounding as a rainstorm rolled over the city. People on the sidewalk began flooding into the café to stay dry. "Oh, we've run into each other outside the office."

"Except for yesterday." He narrowed his gaze at me, making me worry he had caught me in my lie.

"Obviously." I wondered if I'd already said too much. I didn't mind Drew thinking I was having an affair with one of my coworkers, but he couldn't find out about Noah. He could make a lot of trouble for him.

"My advice, Molly?" Drew said as he stood from the booth to give Aunt Gigi a hand with the sudden rush. "Let it go. This isn't your full-time job like it is this

183

guy's. Not to mention there's a double standard in these types of things. They'll automatically assume he used his position of power to entice you to become intimate, regardless of the fact that it was just one kiss. Find another muse. Maybe call Kevin and apologize."

"Kevin's wrong for this book. I need young, professional."

"Then give online dating another try. If you think I can't read between the lines here—"

"What are you talking about?"

"You're Avery," he accused, as if it were common knowledge.

"No, I'm not. Jackson's the one with a mom who has memory issues, not Avery."

"That's a mere technicality. You've always refused to express your true feelings, except through your writing. It's a bit suspicious that this story took on a completely different tone around the same time it seems you began getting close to this guy at work. It's a damn good book, don't get me wrong, but it's not your typical style. Hell, I've read how many pages now? There hasn't been so much as a kiss between these two. And why? Because I keep reading about Avery's concern that she'll ruin this man's career. You're Avery."

"No, I'm not," I argued, standing up and straightening my spine, although my meager five-foot, three-inch frame was no match for his intimidating six-foot, two-inch stature.

"You like to conceal all your feelings, put them in a little box, and do everything within your power to make sure they stay locked up tight. *That's* why you write. So you'll never have to admit you're anything but fine, which couldn't be further from the truth."

"So just because I'm not breaking down every day at

the thought that my father can't even remember my name and tried to strangle me yesterday afternoon, you think I'm not okay?" I seethed.

"Wait... What?" He frowned.

My breath caught, realizing what I had just said.

"I thought you were at the magazine yesterday."

"Yeah." I tore my eyes from his. "I stopped by the office after leaving the nursing home."

He eyed me, skeptical, then asked, "What happened?"

"Drew!" Aunt Gigi bellowed out. We both snapped our heads in her direction.

"Just a second!" we shouted in unison. A little boy stood by the counter with a hockey puck and marker in his hand, obviously wanting an autograph.

She opened her mouth to respond, but shut it when she saw the heated expressions on our faces.

Drew turned to me, placing his hand on my bicep, his eyes awash with compassion. "Are you okay?" He surveyed my body, as if looking for a bruise or scratch.

"I'm fine. It's the disease that makes him act out sometimes. Dr. McAllister checked me out and made sure there was no damage. It's my fault. I had been warned. They tried to turn me away. They said it wasn't a good idea for him to have any visitors, but you know how stubborn I can be. I pushed and wouldn't let it go. When I went to give Dad a hug before leaving, something snapped, making him feel vulnerable, and he squeezed his hands around my throat."

"Who let you see him?" A vein in Drew's neck pulsed, a telltale sign of his anger.

"Honestly, Drew, it's not a big deal. The man is our father and I wasn't going to let anyone tell me I couldn't see him. Dr. McAllister made sure security was in the room, just as a precaution."

He shook his head, stewing. "It never should have happened in the first place. Everything makes sense now."

"What does?" I frowned.

"I got a phone call from Dr. McAllister this morning informing me he'd no longer be Dad's neurologist."

"He *what*?" I couldn't mask the surprise in my voice.

"It seemed a little unorthodox to me, but he said, based on the fact that Dad's Alzheimer's has advanced so rapidly, it was in his best interests that Dr. Farell take over his care. Now I get the feeling it has something to do with you."

My heart skipped, all the blood rushing to my face at the idea that Drew was on to me and my lies. "Something to do with me?" I repeated, swallowing hard.

"After Dad attacked you, what other explanation is there?"

I opened my mouth, speechless, then spun on my heels. "I have to go." There *was* a completely different explanation, one that made much more sense than my dad's advanced Alzheimer's that prompted a physical attack.

"Where are you going?" Drew called after me.

"Where do you think?" I shot back. "It's almost two."

"Molly." He ran to catch up to me, grabbing my arm and spinning me to face him. "Do you think that's a good idea?"

"Of course I do, Drew. He's our *father*," I spat. "I'm not going to ignore him simply because he's not the same person he was when we were kids. Maybe he's having a good day today."

He dropped his hold on me and narrowed his eyes.

"When was the last time he had a good day? I can't even take the girls to see him anymore because they're scared of him."

"But *I'm* not. It may have been a while since he's had a good day, but I'm not going to abandon him. I'm not going to let him die thinking there's no one left who gives a shit about him. I understand you need to put your girls first, but I'll be damned if Dad thinks he has no one left."

~~~~~~~~~~

I SLAMMED MY CAR door and hurried through the parking lot. The rain stinging my face, I pulled my coat tighter. However, it was still no match against the heavy downpour. Noah wasn't usually at the nursing home on Sundays, but something told me he'd be here. Tearing up the steps, I stormed up to the security desk, not caring that I was dripping water everywhere.

"I need to speak with Dr. McAllister immediately," I barked at Reggie, who seemed a bit alarmed to see me in such a state.

"I'm sorry, Molly. Dr. McAllister isn't seeing anyone today. You can go visit your father, though, if you'd like. He's having a much better day than yesterday."

I tried to calm my temper, not wanting Reggie to grow suspicious of my reaction. "This is really important." I should have walked away, but I needed to see Noah.

"It's okay, Reggie," a voice called out. I shot my eyes to the door leading to the administrative wing. Noah stood there, dressed casually. "We'll just be a minute."

"Yes sir, Dr. McAllister." He eyed me as I headed toward Noah and followed him down the brightly lit corridors.

Silence stretched between us while we walked past several darkened rooms and into his office. Instead of closing the door to give us privacy this time, he kept it open, almost as if he didn't trust himself…or, worse, *me*. He stepped behind his messy desk and sat down, gesturing to one of the chairs on the other side.

I lowered myself on unsteady legs, unsure of what to say. I had been impulsive when I demanded to speak to him. Now I found myself without a plan.

Noah's voice broke through the silence. "I assume you're here because your brother informed you that Dr. Farell will now attend to your father."

I crossed my arms over my chest. "You assumed right."

"Like I told your brother…," he continued, exuding all the professionalism he could muster.

I clenched my fists at his tone. I hated everything about this. I wanted the caring, charismatic man who made me laugh. I wanted Noah, not Dr. McAllister. I had a feeling there would be no more Noah. I felt like I was mourning the death of a friend, knowing there'd be no more ice cream, no more classic movies in the cemetery, no more daring rescues from murderous ducks. For once, I'd formed a relationship with a man based on something other than sex. The idea of that ending made me feel empty.

"Your father's progression has been so aggressive, I felt it necessary to transfer his care to Dr. Farell. He's one of the top neurologists in the country. It usually takes six months to even get an appointment with him. He's on the staff here, as well."

Glowering, I asked, "Is that the *only* reason?"

His hardened gaze met mine. After what seemed like

an eternity, his expression cracked, a softness returning to his eyes. "You know that's not the only reason." He shook his head, his voice barely above a whisper. "Something horrible could have happened to you yesterday. My judgment was clouded because of our friendship." He squeezed his eyes shut, his posture becoming slack. "I should have walked away when I saw you at the Common," he murmured. I wondered if he meant for me to hear it.

"But you didn't." I reached across the desk and grabbed his hand.

His eyes flung open and he quickly withdrew from me, leaving me feeling cold, unwanted, dejected. "No, but I can make things right going forward." His voice turned determined once more.

"What do you mean?"

He shuffled some of the papers on his desk, then stood up. "I'm sure you'll find Dr. Farell to be a wonderful addition to your father's care team."

Staring at him with cold eyes, I shot up from the chair, the vein on my forehead throbbing. I spun from him and stormed down the hallway, not wanting him to see how much his words and actions hurt.

Approaching the security desk, I did my best to hide my anger with a forced smile as I signed in. I was grateful my father was able to have visitors today. I didn't know how I would react if that weren't the case. I didn't know if I could handle any more bad news in one day.

~~~~~~~~~~

WHEN I ARRIVED HOME after seeing my father, I sat in front of my laptop and stared at the scene I'd written

189

the previous night. A lump formed in my throat at the memory of Noah's vivid blue eyes, his warm embrace, his knee-weakening kiss. Continuing with the manuscript in its current state would force me to remember all those things and more every time I looked at it. I couldn't do that to myself. I had no other option but to erase Noah from my life, just as he had erased me from his.

My heartbeat echoed in my ears as my finger hovered over the mouse. I hesitated, debating whether this was the correct course of action. Reaching for my wine glass, I downed a hearty sip, then closed my eyes, clicking my mouse.

When I looked at my laptop again, I tried to settle my panicked breathing. I'd just erased every last trace of Avery and her Mr. Jackson Price. I hoped I wouldn't come to regret this decision.

Chapter Eighteen

I SHOT UP IN bed as the door to my apartment burst open, heavy footsteps stomping down the hallway. My ferocious dog lay snoring beside me, obviously ready to attack my intruders at a moment's notice. But I knew there weren't any intruders, at least not in the criminal sense. Just by the sound of their footsteps alone, I could always tell when Drew and Brooklyn let themselves into my apartment.

They appeared in the doorway, their eyes raking over the mess that had become my bedroom during the past two weeks. My garbage bin overflowed with takeout containers, candy wrappers, and empty water bottles. I promised to buy a few carbon offsets to make up for the amount of plastic I would be tossing into a landfill.

"What's going on with you?" Brooklyn asked, her tone harsh.

"Nothing," I replied, as if it were completely normal for me to be lounging in bed at five on a Friday evening.

"No. There's something going on," she pushed, storming into my room and plopping down on my bed. "Since you were facing a deadline, I've let it slide the past few weeks, but that deadline has come and gone."

"And it played such a beautiful melody as it floated right by me," I retorted with a dreamy look on my face.

Brooklyn scrunched her brows. "What do you

mean?"

Drew sighed, stepping toward the bed and lowering himself on the other side of me. "You missed your deadline, didn't you?"

I pinched my lips together, nodding slightly.

"How?" Brooklyn asked. "I thought the book was going great."

"It was." I shrugged. "But it wasn't the story my publisher wanted. I tossed the whole thing."

"You *what*?" She shot off the bed, her eyes on fire. "Are you crazy? That story was phenomenal. I've been dying to know what happens between Avery and Jackson. I need to know if they get their happily ever after!"

I grabbed my remote, turning up the volume on my television. I'd hoped something would inspire me to write again, keeping my television tuned to the classic movie channel nearly around the clock the past few weeks. Now, as luck — or maybe fate — would have it, I was staring at Deborah Kerr and Cary Grant as they said their final farewells before disembarking from the ship, promising to meet each other on the top of the Empire State Building. *An Affair to Remember* used to be one of my favorite movies. Now it only reminded me of stupid Noah. And stupid cemeteries. And stupid dancing. And stupid kissing. I didn't care if I sounded like a petulant child.

"They don't get their happily ever after," I replied, my voice monotone. "There's no such thing, not with the direction their story was heading. My publisher needs happily ever after, so I'm starting from scratch."

She eyed me guardedly, lowering herself back to the bed. "Can I read what you have so far?"

A hopeful smile crossed my face. "Of course. I'd love

to know what you think. I could use some feedback." I grabbed my laptop and opened it. "Let me just find it... Here it is." I handed Brooklyn my computer.

She scowled. "What is this?"

"My manuscript. What do you think? I've been working on that for two weeks now. It's really compelling, isn't it?"

"Molly...," Brooklyn said in a cautious tone. "It's blank."

I threw my head back on my pillow, laughing uncontrollably. "I know."

"Is this because of that guy at the magazine?" she asked.

I shot my eyes to her, then Drew. He gave me a smug look. "I told her."

"I don't know why I tell you anything when you obviously can't keep your mouth shut. You're worse than a teenage girl."

I didn't know why I hadn't told Brooklyn about my supposed coworker. Maybe I was worried she'd be able to read between the lines and figure out it was a lie. Drew was a smart man, but he was often too distracted by his own crazy life as a single dad to give mine too much attention. Brooklyn didn't have that problem. I feared if I told her too much, she'd eventually figure out the truth.

"And I don't know why you don't talk to me about this stuff, too." Brooklyn placed her hand on my arm, getting my attention. "I get that you and Drew have a weird bond. I don't know what that's like." She looked away before recovering her composure. "And, to be fair, Drew put up a wicked fight, but I eventually beat the truth out of him." She winked at him, grinning, then faced me. "Have you spoken to this coworker of yours since you kissed him?"

I shook my head. "When I went in the following day, I learned he was taking some vacation time and had decided to transfer to a different department," I told them, stretching the truth in a huge way. I didn't know how much longer I'd be able to keep my story straight.

Brooklyn studied me for a protracted moment, her bright green eyes unnerving me. "You liked him, didn't you?" she finally said.

"What? No!" I grabbed a Snickers bar off my nightstand and peeled off the wrapper. Chocolate was the only thing that would help me handle this conversation. In truth, alcohol would have been better, but chocolate was more accessible at the moment. I'd have to walk a whole thirty feet into the kitchen for alcohol. "I like him as a person, but not like you think."

"Then why are you still hung up on him?" Drew's eyes were heavy with skepticism.

"That's ridiculous. I'm not—"

"That's why you tossed the manuscript," Brooklyn stated rather matter-of-factly. This was the precise reason I didn't want to tell her everything. She had an uncanny ability to uncover the truth...the truth I'd spent two weeks convincing myself was anything but.

"No, it's not. I'm starting over because it isn't the type of story my publisher wants!" I argued.

"No. It's because you actually have real, honest-to-goodness, boyfriend/girlfriend feelings for this man."

I jumped off the bed. "That's ridiculous."

"Then why have you been cooped up in your apartment, living off bad takeout and candy?"

"It has nothing to do with your preposterous idea that I had feelings for this guy." I went to the en-suite bathroom and splashed water on my face. "The only reason I decided to spend any time at all with him was because I thought it was necessary for the book I'm supposed to be writing." I reappeared in the doorway. "I was able to channel my characters' thoughts so easily. *That's* the only reason I kissed him. I should have listened to my editor weeks ago. But I'm listening to her now and am starting over."

Drew rolled his eyes. "The old Molly would have been at the bar the same day he transferred in search of a new muse."

"*You're* the one who told me I needed to stop looking in bars for sources of inspiration, that I was getting too old for that."

"And you are," Brooklyn agreed.

I stared at them for several long moments, my jaw tightening, my fists clenched

"So what's your plan for finishing the book?" Drew lifted a brow.

Softening my expression, I returned to the bed, plopping down between Brooklyn and him. "My publisher extended my deadline, but only because I used Dad's deteriorating condition as an excuse. I hated doing it, but I just need a little bit more time to get back on track. This whole experience has taught me I should just stick to the way I've always done things." I looked away, my voice less than enthusiastic. "Find a muse. Write my book. Walk away."

"So back to the bars then?"

I released a long breath. "I'm not going to find the type of guy I need for this book at a bar. I've been messaging a few from the online profiles I set up all those weeks ago. You're right. I'm getting too old for the bar scene. No one wants to be that wrinkly, gray-haired old woman who still dresses in mini-skirts and lets the lips of her vag hang loose for all to see."

"Oh, Jesus," Drew groaned, playfully shoving me. "You're disgusting."

"If the lips of your hooha are visible beneath your skirt, you have bigger problems," Brooklyn added.

"You can't even say it, can you?"

"Say what?"

"Vagina."

"I can." Her cheeks turned red as she avoided my eyes.

"Prove it."

"I don't need to prove it. I read your books. That should be proof enough."

"Whenever you give me feedback, you never say vagina. You always say something like hooha or lady bits or whatever dainty phrase you come up with. I've never heard you say vagina."

"What difference does it make? So what? I prefer calling it a hooha. That has no bearing on our conversation right now."

"Say it," I pushed.

"Why?" Brooklyn groaned.

"I just want to hear it. That's all. It may just be the cause of my writer's block," I said sarcastically.

"No. Your problems run much deeper," she joked.

"You're probably right." Inching closer, I stared at her, waiting.

"Fine!" she exclaimed finally, her face turning red. "Vagina! Happy now?"

The room erupted in laughter, startling Pee Wee from his slumber. I hadn't laughed so hard in weeks. It was amazing how something as simple as a laugh could make you feel as if you could overcome all your problems. It gave me a renewed drive to find a new muse and write the book I should have been writing before one Dr. Noah Joseph McAllister ruined my plans.

"Did you ever consider that maybe your writer's block is all in your head?" Drew asked once our laughter died down. "Maybe you should stop this useless search for someone who inspires you to write a particular story. Maybe you just need to find someone who inspires *you*." He paused as I simply stared back at him. "Unless you already have..."

Chapter Nineteen

"WHERE ARE YOU GOING all dressed up?" Drew asked as I let myself into his apartment a week later. It had been a surprisingly productive week, at least in terms of my writing. While the words that ended up in my manuscript were, in my opinion, complete crap, my editor would love it. It was exactly what they wanted...a weak, inexperienced heroine who had a connection to her boss the second they met each other, but a coworker with a grudge threatened to destroy both of them if they ever acted on their attraction. It wasn't what I wanted to write, but I had a contract to think about.

"On a date," I replied in a very matter-of-fact voice, as if it were an everyday occurrence. In truth, I didn't know what had possessed me to agree, especially after having turned away dozens of other potential suitors over the past few weeks.

I have a work thing. I'm going out of town. I've taken a vow of celibacy.

"With whom?" Drew lowered his voice as he searched his refrigerator, taking out some sliced cheese.

"A guy." I headed toward his wet bar and poured myself a glass of cabernet, the full-bodied red exactly what I needed tonight.

"No shit. Who?"

"Someone I met online."

"So you're still blocked?" He grabbed some bread, put a cheese slice between two pieces, then turned to the stove, igniting one of the burners and placing a fry pan on top.

"Actually, no. I mean, this book isn't going to win me a Pulitzer, but at least I'm writing." I sat down on one of the barstools at the peninsula and took a long sip of my wine, the smell of grilled cheese making its way to my senses. Part of me considered canceling and spending the evening with the girls and Drew.

"Then why the date?"

I avoided his eyes, toying with my wine glass. "I'd been talking to this guy for a while." I shrugged. "I figured it was finally time to meet up."

He narrowed his gaze. "And it has nothing to do with the falling out with your coworker?"

"Of course not. He hasn't crossed my mind all week." I straightened my spine. I refused to acknowledge the likelihood I'd agreed to this date because I still found myself thinking about Noah.

"Molly," Drew said, his voice soft. "It's okay to admit you were hurt by this guy's rejection."

"He didn't reject me. All we did was kiss, and the only reason I even did that was for my book. I felt nothing," I insisted, glaring. I didn't know if I said that for Drew's benefit or my own. Maybe I hoped the more I said it, the more I'd believe it.

After a heated moment, he sighed. "I'm not going to push it."

I raised my wine glass back to my lips, practically downing the entire thing in one gulp.

"So meeting up for drinks?" he inquired.

"Dinner, actually," I answered, wiping my mouth. "If he's a complete bore, at least I'll only waste an hour or so of my life." I returned to the wet bar and poured myself another glass.

"Good thing you're not just meeting for drinks. At the rate you're going, you'll be two sheets to the wind by the time you get there."

"Just settling my nerves. Online profiles can be deceiving. This guy could be a serial killer. It's the nice ones you have to watch out for. They could be complete psychopaths. Take Ted Bundy. He was quite the charismatic charmer, ya know."

"Way to make me feel good about this," he joked, flipping the sandwiches before stirring a pot of tomato soup that had begun to bubble.

"Anytime." I gritted a fake smile at him, then took several more sips of wine, the alcohol beginning to work.

"Auntie Molly!" two small voices exclaimed. I whirled around as Alyssa and Charlotte came barreling down the hallway and wrapped their arms around my legs.

"You look so pretty!" Alyssa said, eyeing my flowing knee-length light blue dress with flutter sleeves. I figured I couldn't go wrong with a casual dress I made appear more formal by adding pieces of well-appointed jewelry — diamond bracelet, pearl necklace, and teardrop pearl earrings.

"Thanks, Alyssa."

"Why are you all dressed up?" Charlotte asked.

"I'm meeting a friend for dinner."

"Who? Auntie Brook?"

I shook my head. "No. Someone you haven't met yet. A boy."

"What's his name?" Alyssa pushed.

"Yeah." Drew walked around the peninsula, carrying

two plates with grilled cheese toward the dining room table. "What's his name?"

"Paul," I answered.

"Is he nice?" Charlotte asked, allowing Drew to help her into her booster seat. Alyssa plopped into the chair beside her, biting into her sandwich.

"Yes, he is. He takes care of kids all day."

"He's a teacher?" Alyssa mumbled around a mouthful of food.

"No. He's a pediatrician." It wasn't a coincidence I'd decided to break my dating hiatus by agreeing to dinner with a doctor.

"What's that?"

"You know how your daddy takes you to see someone when you're not feeling well?" She nodded. "That's a pediatrician. He's a special kind of doctor for little kids."

"Oh," they said simultaneously.

"I don't like the pedilician," Charlotte said, unable to pronounce it correctly. "She sticks me with needles."

"It's just to keep you healthy, Char," Drew reminded her. "Now, eat up."

"On that note, I should probably go. Don't want to be late for my date." I made an exaggerated nervous face, biting my nails. Drew chuckled and I placed a kiss on his cheek. "See ya later."

"I want a full report tomorrow!" he called after me as I started toward the front door.

"Are you sure you'll want a *full* report?" I wiggled my eyebrows at him.

"On second thought, absolutely not. I'll just take the bullet points."

"That's what I thought." I blew Drew and the girls one last kiss, then closed the door behind me.

Butterflies fluttered in my stomach as I walked down the stairs and onto the street. The thought of blowing off this date crossed my mind when I eyed the door to my building across the alley. A Saturday night spent in a pair of oversized pajama pants on my couch while watching home improvement television and gorging on ice cream sounded so appealing. But something pulled me away from the familiarity and comfort of my apartment and into a cab.

"The things I do for my art," I murmured.

~~~~~~~~~~

"MOLLY?" A VOICE ASKED as I entered the foyer of a sushi and tapas restaurant a few blocks from Boston Common. It sounded like a strange combination, but the food was fantastic. If I was going to do the "real date" thing, I figured I could ease into it with tapas. I didn't know if I could sit through a five-course dinner, considering the last time I had a similar plan, I'd unceremoniously left the poor sap. Tapas was a good compromise.

"Paul?"

A man with dark hair and chocolate eyes headed toward me. He was dressed in a pair of gray pants and a light blue button-down shirt. A rather large bouquet of flowers in his hand practically obscured his face. I had to fight my natural instinct to roll my eyes. I hated flowers. I never understood why women lost their shit when their significant other sent them. All you could do was watch them slowly die. I'd much rather get something useful, something that truly does say how much a man cared for me...like a vibrator. There's no greater gift than that of a battery-powered orgasm.

"These are for you." He handed me the flowers and I hesitantly took them, feeling like an out of place bridesmaid carrying her bouquet. I could almost hear "Canon in D" in the background. I had to fight my urge to step, pause, step, pause as I had learned to do when my sorority sister, Debra, had decided to sell her soul to the devil and get married. I'd agreed to be a bridesmaid, thinking all it entailed was a bunch of parties, including a wild bachelorette trip to Vegas. I couldn't have been more wrong. The movies lied. I had hoped for a female version of *The Hangover*. All I got was a toned-down version of *Steel Magnolias*.

"You look beautiful," he commented.

"Thank you." I offered a forced smile. "The flowers are beautiful." It was true. I just wasn't a flowers kind of girl.

"Are you hungry?"

"Famished."

"Good." There was a gleam in his eye when he winked.

Placing his hand on the small of my back, he led me past the hostess stand and into the dining area. It had a modern feel to it, the décor angular and bright. Booths lined the walls with tables in the center, most of them occupied with other patrons seeming to enjoy their food and drinks.

He pulled out a chair for me at one of the tables in the center. I offered him a smile before sitting down, then placed the flowers on the vacant chair beside me. He sat across from me, meeting my eyes before he turned his attention to the menu.

An awkward silence passed, accompanied by the stereotypical sounds of a restaurant — dull background conversation, forks hitting plates, low music. Tapping my fingers on the white table, I glanced around, trying to come up with some sort of conversation that was appropriate for a first date. I didn't think vibrators qualified…at least not yet.

"I have to say," I began when he continued to stare at his menu, as if he'd be quizzed on it later. "I'm actually a little relieved."

He cocked his head. "Why's that?"

"It's a bit of a crapshoot, isn't it? The online thing? You could very well be a serial killer."

"Or worse," he added with a smile. "A Democrat."

I scrunched my nose. I could have been wrong, but I was fairly certain two topics should never be discussed during first dates, or ever…religion and politics.

"It's nice to know the person matches the photo," I continued, ignoring his comment. Now was probably not the right time to tell him I typically voted Democrat, although I was a registered Independent.

"Likewise," he stated with a smile, just as a waitress approached.

"Can I start you off with something to drink?" She looked at me.

"I'm happy with just water," Paul said. "How about you? Would you like an iced tea or anything like that?"

"We do have quite an extensive drink menu," the waitress said to me, although I'd been here enough times to know their wine list by heart. "We even offer a tasting menu of several different wines."

"That's not necessary," Paul interrupted. "We don't drink."

I raised my brows, taken aback by his bold assumption. He seemed rather confident in his statement and I wondered why he would think that to be true. More intrigued than anything, I decided to play along for the moment. I turned to the waitress. "Sparkling water, please."

Once she left, I looked at Paul, trying to remember precisely which website I'd met him on. I'd signed up for far too many to recall with any accuracy. "Will you excuse me? I just need to go use the little girl's room." I flashed him a smile.

"Of course."

I pushed back my chair and headed through the dining area, past the bar, and down a set of stairs toward the restrooms. Withdrawing my phone from my purse, I scanned my email. After several minutes, I finally found the messages between Paul and myself, which had originated from some website called Soul Mate.

It sounded innocuous enough. Nothing about it gave me any clue as to why he would assume I didn't imbibe in the nectar of the gods...or alcohol, as it was more commonly referred to. Then I clicked on the link to the website. It wasn't one of the more popular sites, but it did pop up when I'd conducted my initial search for online dating. It boasted a significant number of subscribers, but beyond that, I hadn't really looked into it. As I navigated to the site's "About" section, I instantly knew why Paul didn't think I drank.

Soul Mate is a Mormon dating service. Find the eternal match for your soul today.

I shook my head, uncontrollable laughter consuming me. How could I have made a profile on a site like this without realizing it? I'd never even touched a *Bible*, let alone read one. Hell, after getting kicked out of Catholic school at the ripe age of six, my only exposure to any of those stories came in the form of seeing *Jesus Christ, Superstar* years ago. It came as a total surprise to me that, right before Jesus' crucifixion, Judas didn't come back to life accompanied by a group of backup singers with whom he belted out the title song with incredible soul. Don't even get me started on Joseph and his coat. And a Mormon? I was going to have trouble not cracking lines from *The Book of Mormon*, and I wasn't talking about the actual book, but the tongue-in-cheek musical I went to see every time it came to Boston.

Trying to settle myself, I drew in a breath and placed my phone back in my purse. If nothing else, this could make for an amusing anecdote if I were to ever write a romantic comedy.

I headed back up the stairs, hesitating as I stared between the exit of the restaurant and the dining room. It would have been so easy to walk out those doors right now. I could imagine Paul's face if I divulged what I did for a living. As it was, he obviously hadn't Googled me. If he had, he would have come across the columns I'd written for *Metropolitan*, each one containing no less than a dozen expletives.

Deciding to cut my losses and mark this date as a flop, I stepped toward the exit when the rumble of a familiar laugh made its way to my ears. My heart rate immediately picked up, a heat prickling my skin. The butterflies that had been absent for the past several weeks reappeared as I slowly turned around. My eyes fell on a tall man with dark hair and full, kissable lips sitting at a table across from a rather attractive blonde. I blinked in shock at Dr. Noah McAllister.

Flustered at my unbelievable luck, I opted for door number three…the bar. I signaled the bartender, ordered a whiskey, then proceeded to gulp it down the second it appeared in front of me, all the while doing my best to stay out of eyesight of both Paul and Noah.

I hadn't even so much as seen Noah in the nursing home these past few weeks. Now, as I watched him interact easily with such a beautiful woman, an ache formed in my chest. What would have happened if I didn't kiss him? Would we still be friends? Would we have kissed eventually anyway? What if I'd waited for him to initiate it? Would he still have reacted the same way?

I hated to admit it, but I actually missed spending time with him. I missed seeing his smile as he surprised me at the Common. I missed hearing him laugh at some story I told about an odd run-in on the subway. I missed sitting in complete silence and watching classic movies in a graveyard.

This was all just another reminder of why I needed to be on this date. I needed to pretend I didn't have these feelings, pretend I never kissed Noah, pretend he didn't mean anything to me.

Armed with a dose of liquid courage, I popped a mint into my mouth, then headed toward the dining room.

"Sorry about that," I offered to Paul as I approached the table and sat down.

"Is everything okay?"

"Yes. I'm fine. Just saw someone I knew," I answered honestly as I raised the sparkling water to my lips. I hoped Paul hadn't noticed my flushed skin or trembling hands. "So..." I inhaled a breath, trying to settle my nerves. "Have you always wanted to be a pediatrician?"

"Gosh, yes. I've always loved kids. When I decided to go to med school, I knew I wanted to focus on pediatrics. How about you? You're a writer, correct?"

"Yes."

"And it's a full-time thing?"

"It can be."

"Have you written anything I might have heard of?"

"Nah. Just a bunch of smut and sex with not much story." I gave him a wide smile.

He furrowed his brow, studying me, then broke into a hearty laugh. "You're funny, Molly. After reading your profile, I had a feeling you'd have a sense of humor."

I brought my glass back to my mouth and muttered, "You have no idea."

We continued to make small talk, discussing how long we'd been in the city, our families, what we did for fun, although I let Paul do most of the talking. All the while, I was cognizant of Noah's presence. I tried to shake it off, but it was impossible. I felt like I was barely paying attention to anything Paul said, like I was in an alternate universe. I didn't know how much longer I'd be able to fake an interest. Just when I debated leaving, our server appeared carrying a few small plates.

"I hope you don't mind that I took it upon myself to order a few things," Paul explained. "You mentioned you were hungry. I'll let you pick the next round."

"It's fine," I assured him. I reached for one of the arancini balls, then spooned a bit of the marinara onto my plate to avoid the first date faux-pas of double-dipping.

"Silly me," Paul interrupted as I was about to bite into fried risotto and cheese nirvana. "I forgot the blessing."

"The what?" I looked up at him, the aroma of the arancini mocking me. My stomach growled, sounding like the roar of a lion. Being so close to tasting pure bliss had me on edge.

He narrowed his gaze at me, as if it were completely foreign to him that I'd want to put these delicious balls into my mouth without blessing them first. I was pretty certain they'd taste the same, blessing or not.

"Oh, of course."

Playing along, I lowered my fork back to my plate. Rubbing my hands on my skirt, I wasn't sure what I was supposed to do. My aunt Gigi went to church on a weekly, sometimes daily, basis. But she left her beliefs at the door, not trying to indoctrinate me or anyone else. She always said she wasn't one to judge, but that I'd have to deal with God, or something to that end, as she pointed her finger at the sky.

If there *was* a God, I'd love for someone to explain His purpose for my father's illness.

Surveying Paul, I followed his lead, folding my hands on the table in front of me. I couldn't help but feel as if people were staring at us. I'd eaten out on countless occasions and had never, in all my twenty-nine-plus-one years, seen people pray in a restaurant, except for one time in a small town in Georgia. Then again, I couldn't even get a margarita there on a Sunday, so I figured the patrons were praying for something a little stronger than just sweet tea.

He opened his mouth, then abruptly closed it, his eyes meeting mine. "I'm sorry. How rude of me. Would you like to say the blessing?"

Visions of the senile Aunt Bethany from *National Lampoon's Christmas Vacation* appeared in my head. Maybe I'd lead us in a stirring rendition of the "Pledge of Allegiance", too.

"Oh," I began, playing it off. "I wouldn't want to take the honor away from you." I didn't give a fuck whether we prayed or burned in hell. I'd gladly take that chance so I could finally have a mouth full of balls…deliciously cheesy risotto balls.

"I'd feel better if I allowed you the chance."

Willing to do anything so I could eat, I lowered my eyes. "The devil sucks. Amen," I said with strong determination in my voice, mimicking the preacher in *Footloose*. It was the only recent exposure I'd had to anyone praying.

Before Paul could respond, I stuffed a risotto ball into my mouth, my shoulders relaxing. I'd just experienced what blue balls felt like.

He cocked his head, eyeing me as he carefully cut his own arancini into four precise quadrants. "That was…interesting."

"Thanks." I looked away, catching a glimpse of Noah at the exact moment he reached across the table and clutched his dinner companion's hand. I almost choked on my food.

"Are you okay?" Paul asked.

Quickly turning my attention back to him, I nodded, taking a sip of my water. I blamed the heaviness in my chest on a bit of gas building up in my esophagus from inhaling arancini balls. Noah didn't matter anymore.

"You're much different from most women I've had the pleasure of meeting through Soul Mate," Paul remarked after we'd been through another round of tapas.

"Why's that?"

"You eat." He laughed. "It's refreshing to be out with someone who will eat more than a salad."

"I've been blessed with a fast metabolism," I explained. "And, I mean, it's no secret that everyone eats. Without food, you die, right?"

"That's correct. There's only so long a person can

survive without adequate nutrition."

"My point exactly." I dipped a tortilla chip into the buffalo chicken fondue. And yes, it was just as delicious as it sounded.

"Paul?" a voice interrupted as I was in the middle of a fondue-induced moan.

I glanced up, cheese lining my lips. My face flushed when I saw Noah and his date standing by our table. The woman wore a congenial smile, her attention devoted to Paul. She didn't notice her date staring at me.

"What a small world!" she said.

Paul stood up and kissed the blonde's cheek. Noah and I gaped at each other with unease. Before the kiss heard around the world, or at least felt around my mouth, I could usually tell what he was thinking just by the expression on his face. Now, I was at a loss.

"Not that small of a world, Piper. You *did* turn me on to this place."

"It's the best kept secret in this area, although Noah would argue it's the ice cream shop a few blocks from here." She nudged Noah in the stomach. He tore his eyes from mine, looking fondly at the woman.

"Oh, so *you're* Noah." Paul held his out hand. "I've heard a lot about you."

I watched the whole interaction with intrigue and confusion. Noah had never mentioned a Piper to me. Maybe I'd been wrong about everything. Maybe the reason he wanted to keep his distance from me was because he had a girlfriend, although he'd said he didn't. Maybe I'd been living in the fantasy world of my books so long, I imagined his interest in me.

"Hi. I'm Piper." The soft voice cut through my thoughts and I snapped my head toward her, not giving her the courtesy of standing up.

"Molly." I loosely shook her hand before returning my attention to the food in front of us, which was growing cold. There was a special place in hell for people who interrupted one's dinner.

"Piper and I work in the same medical complex." Paul smiled, obviously sensing the awkward tension at the table. "She's an OB-GYN. Actually, she's delivered a number of my patients."

"Do you like staring at vaginas all day?" I asked, unable to help myself. It was something I'd always wondered, but never had anyone to ask. I couldn't pass up this opportunity.

"Being an OB is a lot more than just staring at the female reproductive organ," she answered in an irritatingly pleasant voice.

Paul furrowed his brow at me, then looked back at Piper and Noah. Their couple name would be "Noper". Or "Pipah". What crappy couple names. "Noah, it's my understanding that you're a neurologist. You work mostly with Alzheimer's and dementia patients?"

"That's correct," he replied. His eyes locked unnervingly on mine, a hint of amusement in the lines of his face.

"Well, I feel like an underachiever being surrounded by doctors," I mumbled. I would have paid a small fortune to have a glass of wine to guzzle.

"And what is it you do?" Piper asked with a tight smile.

"Molly's a writer," Paul answered quickly, a nervous expression on his face as he ran his hands over his pants, smoothing the lines. I had a feeling he was worried I might say something that would paint him in a bad light. He was right.

"And that's successful for you?"

"I just whore myself out on the street to make up for any shortfalls each month," I answered cheerfully.

Noah shook his head, biting back a smile. It warmed my heart that I could still make him laugh.

Paul looked between Piper and me, teetering on his feet, then forced a fake chuckle. "Molly has quite the sense of humor."

"We'll let you get on with your evening," Noah said, his eyes narrowed at me. "It was a pleasure to see you."

His gaze lingering on me for a prolonged moment, he then placed his hand on Piper's back and led her out of the restaurant. Just before he turned the corner and disappeared from view, he glanced over his shoulder, our eyes locking once more. A pit formed in my stomach at the uncertainty I saw. It was as if he were trying to tell me something. I just didn't know what.

Chapter Twenty

"SO..." PAUL TURNED TO me after leaving the restaurant.

"Thanks for tonight," I said in a chipper voice. A few light raindrops began to fall, so I pulled my umbrella out of my bag, thankful I'd actually paid attention to the local meteorologist who mentioned the possibility of a passing thunderstorm this evening.

"I really enjoyed spending time with you. You're different than most girls I've met." He shuffled his feet, shoving his hands into the pockets of his pants. He looked adorably nervous. "Would you like to go to church with me tomorrow?"

Once the initial shock of his invitation waned, my expression fell, my shoulders slumping. After all the shit I did and said throughout the evening, I thought he'd never want to see me again.

"Paul, listen..."

"Those aren't good words," he remarked, avoiding my eyes.

I shook my head, sighing deeply. "I'm going to be completely honest with you, which is something I normally don't do with guys I meet." I looked away momentarily, gathering my thoughts, then returned my gaze to his. "I don't know why I feel bad saying this, but... I'm not Mormon. In fact, I'm not even religious. At all. I'm pretty sure I'd spew pea soup if anyone tried to throw holy water on me or some shit. I didn't realize that dating site was for Mormons."

"That's okay," Paul said, making me feel even worse. It was true what they said about Mormons. They were all really fucking nice. "It's never too late to open your arms to God's love."

"See, that's the thing. When people go all God and religious on me, it makes me uneasy."

"Are you..." He swallowed hard, then lowered his voice, as if speaking a horrible truth, "an atheist?"

I formed my lips into a tight line, a contemplative expression on my face. "I don't know what I am, but I *do* know I'm not going to change who I am for someone else."

Briefly closing his eyes, he nodded, hailing a cab. When one stopped, he grabbed my hand and led me over, opening the rear passenger door for me. I kept my eyes glued to him the entire time. If he was upset I led him on throughout the course of our date, he didn't let it show.

He helped me into the back seat, then leaned down, placing a soft kiss on my cheek. "You'd be surprised what you're capable of sacrificing when you meet the right person." He stood back, a small smile tugging at the corners of his lips, then closed the door. I stared at him through the window, considering his words.

"Where to?" the driver asked.

Snapping my eyes away from Paul's, I told him my address. The driver pulled into traffic as I leaned against the window, staring at the falling rain. Paul's words seemed to play on repeat throughout the drive. I didn't want to believe there was any truth to them. I could never sacrifice who I was as a person for a temporary moment of supposed happiness.

A bolt of lightning flashed in the distance, making me recall how much I loved stormy nights like these as a child. From the comfort of our screened in back porch, Drew, Dad, and I would watch lightning streak across the sky, the air thick with moisture. We would eat marshmallows and listen to the sound of the rain. Having to raise two kids on his own wasn't easy, but my father never let on.

As much as I told myself time and time again that his condition didn't affect me, it did. I wished he could recollect some of these moments we shared. I sometimes wanted to shake him and force him to remember. How could someone just forget these memories I held so very dear to me? Moments I always went back to when having a particularly hard day and just wanted to feel as though someone cared.

After a longer than normal ride due to a short deluge of rain, the cab slowed to a stop in front of my building. I reached into my purse, then handed the driver enough cash to cover my fare and tip. Leaving the flowers on the seat, I stepped onto the wet sidewalk and looked up. The rain had subsided for now. I wished I could rewind the clocks to those stormy nights I spent as a child with my father. It was true what they said. We never truly appreciate what we have until it's gone.

With a heavy sigh, I turned toward my building, fumbling for my keys. I considered heading over to Drew's, but talking was the last thing I wanted to do right now. Noah seemed to still have a strange hold over me. I needed to shake it. The only way to do that was to go back to what I knew...writing. I'd burn the midnight oil writing a sham of a love story because that was all I was good at.

Inserting my key into the lock, I nearly jumped out of

216

my skin when a voice startled me.

"How was the date?"

I whirled around, my heart racing, adrenaline spiking. I placed my hand on my chest, struggling to calm my breathing as I laid eyes on Noah's tall frame leaning against the side of the café.

"What are you doing here?" I hissed. "How did you know where I lived?"

"It's in our files." He pushed himself off the wall and started toward me.

"I told you my brother lives across the alley." I nodded at the windows above the café, my voice barely above a whisper. "He could see us."

Noah continued toward me, each step he took making my heart rate increase. He remained quiet, like a lion stalking his prey.

"Unless the only reason you were concerned about anyone finding out what happened between us is because of your girlfriend, not your relationship with my father." He took another step toward me, his sly gaze unnerving me. "Not that it's any of my business. It was only a kiss."

"It didn't mean anything to you?" He had an air of confidence about him, a slight smirk drawn on those lips I'd had the distinct pleasure of tasting for a blissful two minutes. Seven Minutes in Heaven had nothing on Two Minutes with Noah.

"I really don't think it's that big a deal." With each step he took, my heart rate increased until he was standing just inches away on my front stoop. Trapped, my breathing became ragged, a subtle fluttering starting in my chest. "It was entirely forgettable, if we're being completely honest with each other."

He loomed over me, resting his hand on the door

behind me. "Forgettable?"

My lips parted as I gave a small nod, my knees weakening under his intense stare.

Disappointment fell over his entire body, the heat in his eyes vanishing. "I'm sorry you feel that way." He hung his head.

When he started to turn away, I opened my mouth to stop him. Before I could, his lips met mine, taking me by surprise. He pressed his body into me, pinning me against the door. I stiffened, a thousand different thoughts circling my head. Noah was kissing me. On my front stoop. Where anyone could see.

After my initial shock waned, I stood on my toes and melted into him. His soft lips moving against mine felt so right, so warm, so perfect. I ran my fingers through his hair, tugging him toward me, deepening the kiss. No matter how close we were, it wasn't enough.

All too soon, Noah pulled away and stared at me, his expression unreadable. I worried he'd have the same response he did all those weeks ago.

"What did you say?" he said finally, nuzzling my neck. "The kiss was pretty forgettable?"

I nodded, swallowing hard. "Yes."

"Maybe for you, but it wasn't for me. That's all I've been able to think about."

I lowered myself down to my heels, remembering the cold shoulder he'd given me. "You have a funny way of showing it."

"And I apologize for that. I was stupid."

"You can say that again," I muttered.

"I've never allowed my feelings to interfere with any of my patients' care before."

"It was just a kiss." I spun around, turning the knob of my door to reveal a darkened staircase. I didn't want

Noah to see the truth in my eyes. That his kiss was a culmination of something that had been growing inside me since he saved me from the genetically modified killer ducks at the Common.

"It wasn't just a kiss to me. And I could be wrong, but I'm pretty sure it wasn't just a kiss to you, either."

I faced him, about to protest, but he cut me off.

"I know this is wrong..." He ran his hand down my cheek, the contact making the hair on my nape rise. A current flowed through my veins, igniting a fire that had been smoldering for weeks. "But being with you, spending time with you, laughing with you... It feels so right."

"What about your girlfriend?"

A brilliant smile crossed his face. "You mean Piper?" I nodded. "She's not my girlfriend."

"You mean to tell me you were out to dinner on a Saturday night with a woman who's *not* your girlfriend?"

"You were at dinner, too," he reminded me.

"It didn't work out," I responded. "What's your excuse?"

"No excuse. But I could never date Piper."

"Why not? She's very pretty. And she's a doctor. I'm sure you would get along famously."

"It would be illegal."

"Illegal?" I scrunched my eyebrows.

"Piper's my sister. So, you see..." He closed the distance between us again, brushing a few strands of hair out of my face. "She's not my girlfriend."

"Oh." I swallowed hard, biting my lip. "And Paul is, like, *really* Mormon, so..."

Noah raised his eyebrows. "That explains the prayer during dinner."

A shy smile tugged at my lips. "The devil sucks. Amen."

"That's what you said?"

I shrugged.

He studied me momentarily, then burst out laughing. I remained still for a moment, then followed suit, the ridiculousness of the evening catching up to me. I should have walked out of that restaurant the moment I realized the website I met Paul on was geared toward Mormons. But then I wouldn't have noticed Noah, and he wouldn't have seen me. We probably wouldn't be here, enjoying the easy conversation that had been lacking over the past several weeks.

When our laughter finally died down, he leaned toward me, his expression turning serious. "I missed this."

"Me, too."

Taking his time, he lowered his mouth to mine, a breath away. "God, Molly, you have no idea how much I've missed this."

Bliss rolled over me as our lips met again. Clutching his face between my hands, I pulled him closer, deepening the kiss. What started out as a sweet exchange turned into a heated moment of unmatched intensity and rapture as we feverishly tried to make up for the lack of contact over the past few weeks.

Desperate to feel more of him, I raked my nails through his hair, tugging at him. He groaned, the kiss becoming more primal and animalistic. His lips never leaving mine, he pushed me into the darkened stairwell of my building. Our tongues continued their well-choreographed dance, as if they'd been made to do precisely this. My core ached to feel his hands on my flesh, for him to be delicate and dominant, sweet and sinful, to feel pleasure and pain. I wanted everything he could give me. Even when he was done, it wouldn't be enough. Every flick of his tongue, every stroke of his finger, every tug of my hair made my hunger for him build until nothing would satisfy it.

Dizzy, I tore out of the kiss and struggled to catch my breath. Eyeing him with lust, I began up the steps, then paused to glance over my shoulder.

A heated expression grew on his face as he studied my every movement, a hunter out for the kill. I continued up the stairs, hoping he would get the hint and come rambling up behind me. A fire burned inside me I didn't think anyone could put out, but I hoped Noah would be up to the challenge.

I unlocked the door to my apartment, scrambling to pick up the mugs and candy wrappers strewn on my coffee table. Just as I tossed the evidence of my less-than-stellar housekeeping skills into the garbage, I heard the boards of the second floor landing creak.

Feverishly surveying my living room to make sure there wasn't anything I didn't want Noah to see, I stopped in my tracks when he appeared in the doorway. His presence was formidable. Without saying a word, he closed and locked the door, his eyes trained on me. A chill rolled down my spine.

Rattled, I headed toward the wet bar, trying to keep calm.

"Drink?" I poured scotch into two tumblers, bringing one to my lips. I stopped when I looked up to see Noah standing just inches from me. He reached for my glass and set it down on the bar. My tongue darted out, licking my lips, the taste of scotch and Noah still lingering.

His eyes unwavering, he shrugged out of his suit

jacket, then hung it over the back of one of the barstools by the peninsula. Silence stretched between us. It was neither awkward nor comfortable. It was something else entirely…charged, intense, electrifying.

I'd always held the upper hand in all of my previous arrangements. I'd always been the one to decide when we saw each other, how we fucked, and when we were done. With Noah, though, I felt completely out of my comfort zone. I wasn't the one calling the shots. I was simply following his lead, allowing my brain to stop thinking for once, able to act on mere impulse.

Placing his hand on the small of my back, he forced my body against his, our eyes locking. He wrapped my hair around his free hand, tilting my head back. I was blissfully trapped in his arms, unable to escape. He lowered his lips back to mine, this kiss just as exciting and unique as all the ones that had come before it. He was reserved, the way his tongue dipped into my mouth guarded, controlled, restrained. It wasn't enough for me. I needed the intensity, the passion, the fire. I tried to deepen the kiss, but he fought back with measured movements, his tongue barely brushing mine, teasing me. Every inch of my body was on edge, the simple act of his mouth moving so delicately and softly against mine making me lightheaded. An unquenchable thirst flamed in my core, in my heart, in my soul.

"Bedroom?" he murmured, his lips not breaking from mine.

"At the end of the hall," I answered in a husky voice. My heart thumped in my chest, my breathing increasing. I'd never been this jittery when I'd brought other men into my bedroom. But those other men weren't Noah. In that moment, I knew the connection I'd felt to him from day one wasn't simply because he helped me get over my writer's block. This was something bigger.

In one swift motion, he swept me into his arms, carrying me down the hallway. When he placed his hand on the knob and began to turn, a ferocious barking startled both of us. I'd nearly forgotten about Pee Wee in my Noah-induced desire.

"Shit." I fought against Noah to put me down. He lowered my feet to the floor. "Let me move him. Hope you don't mind dogs." When I opened the door, Pee Wee's barking stopped as he rolled over, expecting to get a belly rub.

"Not at all. If I didn't have such a busy schedule, I'd have one myself."

I offered him a smile, then opened the closed door to the right of my bedroom. I turned on the light and called Pee Wee over to his bed. When Noah stepped in behind my dog, my heart fell to my stomach as he studied the bookshelves containing dozens of copies of each of my books waiting to be signed and sent out.

With a furrowed brow, he continued past the bookshelves toward the far wall, a framed copy of the *New York Times* bestseller list from the first time one of my books appeared on it. Accompanying that were various announcements of publishing deals — foreign language translations, film and television options, and the like.

He turned around, looking at me in a completely different light. "What is all of this?"

"It's me," I replied with a shrug. I could have mustered up a lie, but for some reason, I didn't mind him knowing about this part of me. "Vivienne Foxx is a pen name I write under."

His eyes widening, he turned back around, studying

each frame. When he reached the last one, he stopped, then read it out loud. "So it goes."

"From Vonnegut's *Slaughterhouse Five*," I explained. "I've always found those three words strung together in that order so haunting. They occur each time there's a death in the book, the end of something. There's just so much emotion and lack of emotion at the same time. I guess it's just a reminder that nothing lasts forever, that everything will eventually come to an end... Including all this." I gestured at my surroundings.

Considering my words, his eyes roamed back to the bookshelves. "So you wrote all these?"

"It's really not that big a deal." I tried to usher him out of the room. "They're labeled romance, but it's more erotica than anything else. That's what my publisher likes. Short, sexy, sinful, seductive."

"But what does *Molly* like to write?" He raised his brows.

I couldn't help but think back to the manuscript I'd tossed. How it was anything but short, sexy, sinful, and seductive. Sure, there were some sensual moments between my hero and heroine, but it was a rather big departure from what I typically wrote. And it was my best work to date.

"I'm still trying to figure that out."

"Why didn't you ever tell me about any of this?"

"Like I said, it's not that big a deal. Plus, I don't like a lot of people knowing." I grabbed his hand and pulled him out of the room, shutting the door behind me. "So can we just forget about it for now?"

He shook his head. I feared he'd want to spend the evening discussing why I didn't like people knowing about my alter ego. Then his eyes turned conniving. "Tell me more about this so-called erotica."

I stood on my tiptoes. "Kiss me and I'll give you a lesson." Grabbing the back of his head, I forced his lips to mine, a low groan rumbling from his chest. It was a sense of pride to know I caused this kind of primal and guttural reaction from him.

He pushed me into my bedroom, kicking the door shut behind him. Excitement bubbled in my veins. When the back of my legs hit the bed, he leisurely pulled out of the kiss. The feel of his lips still lingered on mine. Keeping my eyes locked with his, I reached for the zipper on the back of my dress.

"Wait a minute," Noah said in a smooth voice.

Grinning a lascivious grin at me, he spun me around so I faced away from him. His fingers expertly swept my hair over one shoulder, exposing my nape, his breath dancing on my skin. Tremors rolled over me, moisture pooling between my legs. Closing my eyes, I clenched every muscle in my body. I was desperate for release from the pressure building inside me. I couldn't remember ever needing an orgasm as badly as I needed one at that moment.

His lips feathered kisses across my shoulder blades as he murmured, "That's my job."

My eyes fluttered into the back of my head, each drawn-out second that passed as he lowered the zipper of my dress with torturous apathy one second closer to me combusting from all the sexual tension. Noah didn't need a lesson from me. He was a master in the art of delayed gratification, able to build me up when all I wanted was to feel him inside me. I imagined he fucked the way he seemed to do everything else in life…with intensity, with passion, with incredible sophistication.

Shrugging my dress off my shoulders, I allowed it to pool at my feet, then laboriously turned to face Noah once more. His eyes raked over my body as I stood before him in a white lace bra, matching panties, and a pair of ridiculously expensive black stilettos. I'd never felt so exposed, yet so secure with a man.

Returning his heated eyes to mine, he ran a finger across my collarbone. "You're even more breathtaking than I imagined."

I raised myself onto my toes. Pressing my lips to his, I murmured, "You imagined?"

I felt a smile crawl across his mouth. "Since the first day I set eyes on you. I fought it for so long, but I'm done with that. Something draws me to you. I need to taste you, feel you, devour you." His voice was a growl, so primal and wanton. It reminded me that, when you removed all the sophistication the human race had developed over centuries and centuries, we were still animals driven by one thing only…satisfaction.

I grasped the back of his neck. He moved his lips against mine with a passion unmatched by any of his previous kisses. I didn't know how much longer I could survive without feeling him inside me, on top of me, below me. I didn't care about the logistics, as long as I felt him. I never wanted to stop feeling him. I was intoxicated by his lustful kisses and sensual body pressed against mine. I needed more.

With incredible ease, he lowered me onto the bed. Kicking my shoes off, I slid away from the edge, our lips remaining attached as if we'd done this a hundred times before. We were able to read each other's bodies without saying a word, without passing a look. It felt so right, so perfect, so natural. I wrapped my legs around his waist in an attempt to flip him and pin him beneath me, but he wouldn't budge from his position looming over me.

"I want to taste you," he whispered in a breathy voice. His mouth roamed from my lips to my collarbone. When he tugged on my earlobe, I threw my head back, unable to focus past the thousands of sensations flowing through me. I couldn't even tell precisely where his hands were, every inch of my skin on fire.

His tongue continued its slow, agonizing journey down my neck, stopping to savor my flesh in all the right places. He knew exactly where to kiss me to drive me even more crazy with desire and need. I'd written about contact-less orgasms in my books, thinking they were simply a myth, but Noah was proving me wrong. He wasn't even touching me below the waist, yet I felt as if I were about to shatter into a million pieces. I didn't want to think about how quickly I'd fall apart when I finally felt him between my legs.

With incredible agility, he reached behind me and unclasped my bra, sliding it down my arms and tossing it to the floor.

"Practice much?"

A self-confident smirk formed on his lips. "Actually, yes. Like everything, I tend to think practice makes perfect." He lowered his mouth to my chest, his tongue continuing its tantalizing exploration of my body. "When I was twelve, I stole one of my older sister's bras and practiced unhooking it for hours. I can now do it blindfolded in some rather awkward positions."

I smiled at him before throwing my head back as his tongue traced my nipple, lightly tugging it with his teeth. He knew exactly what to do to set me off. "I'm looking forward to testing your abilities," I remarked, curious as to how I was able to form words in the state of hyper-arousal I found myself in at the moment.

My breathing grew more rapid and uneven as he journeyed down my body, taking his time to savor each dip and valley, seducing me at a languid pace. A delicious shiver ran up my spine with each lick, each nip, each nibble. He knew I was on the edge of losing all control, but that didn't faze him. He'd made it clear from the beginning that he was in charge. I had no problem submitting myself to his talented tongue and hands.

Finally, his fingers hooked into my panties. I lifted my hips off the bed.

"Anxious?" He grinned from between my legs.

"Not anxious, but if you don't get on with it, I'm going to lose my fucking mind," I breathed.

A laugh rumbled in his chest as he slowly lowered my panties down my legs.

"Nice wax job." He threw my legs over his shoulders, his mouth just a breath away from the spot I needed it. Synapses fired all over as I struggled not to squirm under his touch.

"It was for my column," I explained in a small voice.

"I know. I read it."

"You did?" I raised a brow, craning my neck to meet his eyes.

He nodded. "I thought I'd read everything you've written. I guess I was wrong. I plan on rectifying that soon." His tongue pressed against my clit, the warmth of that very talented muscle causing my entire body to stiffen. "You're incredible, Molly," he murmured, the vibration of his seductive voice against me almost unbearable.

I had no idea who Molly was. My brain was complete mush, unable to force my mouth to form words. I was motivated solely by the effect the stroke of his tongue, the caress of his hands, the warmth of his body had on me.

Too soon, my stomach clenched. I knew my undoing was inevitable. I tried every trick I knew to prolong the immense pleasure flowing through me. "Dead puppies," I breathed. "The Yankees winning the World Series. Closing down Disney World."

"What are you doing?" Noah asked with a chuckle.

I glanced at him, my heart skipping a beat at the adorable comical look on his face. "Trying to not come," I answered. "I want this to last." I reached down, running my fingers through his silky hair.

He grinned a mischievous smile at me. "Oh, don't worry. It will absolutely last." He returned his tongue to me. I let out a sigh at the gentleness with which he worshiped me. Then his pace and ferocity increased, catching me completely off guard. My body convulsed, waves of incredible pleasure rolling over me. I struggled to breathe as I arched my back off the bed, wrapping my legs around his neck.

My heart racing, I slowly returned from planet Orgasm and opened my eyes. I unhooked my legs and allowed them to fall slack on the bed. I had no idea what just happened, other than having a mind-erasing experience, but I wanted more, the ache still building in my core.

Tugging at his blue tie, I pulled him back up the length of my body, forcing his mouth to mine. "You're wearing far too much clothing," I commented, nibbling on his lower lip.

"I'm in complete agreement with you, Ms. Brinks," he replied in a sly voice.

With clumsy fingers, I tugged at the buttons of his shirt, just wanting to cut the damn thing off him. When he loosened the tie, I ripped it off, about to toss it to the corner of the room. He grabbed my hand, preventing me.

"This may come in handy." He winked.

"Oh, Dr. McAllister…" I gave him a coy look. "Do you have a bit of a kinky side?"

"I prefer to think of it as knowing what I like and being secure in my sexuality." He narrowed his gaze at me. "Something tells me the same goes for you. Am I right?"

"Perhaps." I grabbed the back of his neck, bringing his lips back to mine. "If you're interested in some real fun, I've got a toy chest." I shot my eyes to the corner of my room where a simple black chest sat. He followed my gaze, then met my eyes once more. "Research," I explained with a shrug.

He groaned, kissing me with greed and lust as he slid his pants down his legs without breaking contact. "I think I'm really going to like research," he murmured against my lips.

"I think you are, too."

"Let's save that for later, though. I just want to feel you right now. Unless…"

"That's what I want, too," I said quickly. For some reason, I didn't think I needed any of those bells and whistles I found necessary with all the other men. If the way Dr. Noah McAllister used his tongue on me was any indication, I had a feeling I was in for quite the ride, no pun intended.

"Good," he breathed, pulling away. The loss of contact sent a chill through me, but my moment of sadness was soon replaced with unmitigated desire as I took in Noah's naked form kneeling on the bed. He didn't have eight-pack abs, but there was still some tone and definition to his chest and abdomen. He was human, his slight imperfections perfect in my mind.

Reaching into the pocket of his discarded pants, he pulled out a foil packet. Ripping it open, he slid it on without breaking eye contact. There was something about that moment, neither one of our bodies touching, that was so intimate, so pure, so carnal. He was prolonging the inevitable and I enjoyed every drawn-out second of the anticipation.

He situated himself between my thighs, hovering. He rubbed himself against me, teasing, a coy expression on his handsome face. I couldn't help but giggle. I was certain most men with whom I had arrangements in the past would grow uneasy, perhaps even upset if I laughed when they were about to fuck my brains out — at least I hoped that was what Noah intended to do. This was different. Our relationship had been built on something other than physical attraction. There was a shared understanding between us, a friendship. Despite only knowing him as Noah, as opposed to Dr. McAllister, for a few months, I felt as if I had an awareness of who he was as a person. And I had a feeling he felt the same about me.

"Tease," I muttered.

He nibbled my earlobe. "Oh, baby, you haven't seen anything yet. I can do this for hours. Build you up to the point of completely unraveling, then draw back."

My eyes rolled into the back of my head. I didn't know what I expected from him, but I didn't anticipate him having such a way with words in the bedroom. Most men I'd been with needed some encouragement and a little direction in that department. Not Noah. He was one of my leading men brought to life. He was everything that made me swoon, that made my knees weak. The truth struck me hard... Perhaps I'd found my fantasy man. My body immediately tensed up.

Noah leaned back, noticing my reaction.

"Are you okay?" he asked in a soft voice.

I searched his eyes, overwhelmed, then pulled him back to me. "Yes."

I raised my hips to him, needing to get back to the familiarity of the physical aspect of sex. It was what I was used to. I'd been able to stay detached for so long, knowing real love wasn't real life. I couldn't let a few erotic words weaken my resolve in that matter. Love was a temporary insanity, and I wasn't going to let its illusion trap me.

Feeling the burn of his eyes on me, he slid into me, filling me. Tension rolled off my body. I needed this, the simple act of using each other to find that moment of bliss that drove all humans to behave as they did. Meeting his body thrust for thrust, nip for nip, grunt for grunt, I could forget everything else. That, in the back of my mind, I knew Noah was so different from all the other men. That I actually *cared* for him.

That this wasn't going to end well.

Digging my nails into his back, I wrapped my legs around his waist, the feel of him driving inside me with gentle, yet determined thrusts pushing me higher and higher. A low tingling built inside me and my breath caught.

"Don't fight it," he grunted upon noticing my body tighten. He increased his pace. "Let yourself go."

I shook my head. "It's not possible," I breathed.

"Don't think." He dragged his tongue across my collarbone. "Just feel." His teeth grazed my skin, then latched onto me, setting me off. An orgasm unlike any I'd ever experienced ravaged through me, my body writhing below Noah as he continued pushing into me, his teeth clamped on my neck.

"God, Molly...," he moaned, then his own body rocked and shook on top of me as he found his own release, pleasure rolling over him.

Finally, his rigid body grew slack. He kissed me sweetly, yet still filled with so much passion. Pulling away, he removed the condom and disposed of it in the garbage. He returned to the bed, taking me in his arms and throwing the duvet over both our bodies.

"I thought it was a myth," I breathed, my mind still spinning.

A low chuckle escaped him. "What?" He peppered kisses across my shoulder blades.

"Having more than one orgasm. I write about it. Hell, in one of my books, my heroine has, like, four or five orgasms in a row, but I didn't think it was something that happened in real life."

He forced me to my back, hovering over me as he peered into my eyes. "Then you've been with the wrong boys, Molly. And that's precisely what they were. I'm not saying I'm God's gift to women. I'm sure there's quite a lot I still don't know, but I believe having a healthy relationship starts with being open to what we like and what we don't. And I love watching you come." A devilish smile tugged at his lips. "So I'm going to do everything I can to see that as much as possible."

"Oh really?" I wiggled my eyebrows at him.

"Really." He fell beside me and drew me into his arms, my back to his front. "But Sir Braveheart needs a break."

I quickly rolled over to face him. "You named your love stick Sir Braveheart?"

He pulled me against his chest, trailing his finger up

and down my side. "He's quite the warrior, you know."

Giggling, I snuggled against him, the steady rhythm of his beating heart lulling me to sleep.

Chapter Twenty-One

THE BRILLIANT SUN BEAMING through the curtains in my bedroom forced my eyes open. Flashes of the previous night came in pieces as I scanned the current state of my bedroom. My stomach knotted. The evidence of my sexual conquest lay on the floor, topped with the piece d'resistance...the ripped condom packet. I didn't know if I should be relieved or horrified with the knowledge I was sober last night. Well, at least sober enough to know my judgment had not been impaired by liquor. Instead, the cause of the impairment of said judgment lay solely in a pair of crystal blue eyes, a talented tongue, and an erotic voice that had me dropping my panties and spreading my legs faster than the school slut on prom night.

I remained completely still for several seconds, perhaps even minutes, listening for any breathing coming from my king-sized bed. I didn't know if I was ready to roll over and stare into Noah's eyes. It wasn't that I regretted what happened last night. It was far too enjoyable. He had completely hypnotized me, made me want to bear my soul to him. No man had ever been able to crack through the fortress I'd erected. This was precisely why I needed to keep my distance. I liked intimacy without commitment. I liked sex without the trappings of love. I liked fucking with no expectations. I'd never strayed from my well-established rules in all my twenty-nine-plus-one years. I couldn't do so now.

I clenched my legs, my bladder pleading with me to empty it. I gingerly propped myself up with what I believed to be stealth-like movements, but were probably erratic convulsions that made it appear as if I were suffering from a seizure.

My eyes landed on the opposite side of my bed. I blew out an enormous sigh of relief when I saw it was vacant. I didn't know if it were possible to do a walk of shame from my own house, but I was sure as hell ready to do so to save myself from having to face Noah in the light of day.

Rushing to the bathroom, I went about my business, then splashed some water on my face, slowly returning to the land of the living. I stumbled back into my bedroom, threw on a t-shirt and pair of shorts, then padded down the hallway on light feet to see if Noah was still here. Thankfully, my living room and kitchen were just as empty as my bedroom.

As I prepared my morning coffee, a folded piece of paper on the kitchen peninsula caught my attention, particularly once I saw my name scrawled on the outside.

Don't open it. Don't open it. Don't open it, a voice in my head teased.

I was never good at listening. I picked it up.

> *Molly,*
>
> *As much as I would have loved to stay with you all day, I got called into the hospital. I'll swing by at seven to take you to dinner. Until then, I'll be thinking of you and that amazing mouth.*

I sank onto one of the barstools, burying my head in

my hands. I couldn't do this. Noah was everything I'd ever imagined my dream man would be — handsome, smart, funny, sexy, caring, genuine. But commitment was a losing game. My mother left my father. Carla left Drew. I had no desire to put my heart on the line with anyone, particularly Noah, a man who could decide at any minute to put his career ahead of me, which he should have done anyway.

As I waited for the kettle to boil, I concocted a new plan. Avoid Noah. Forget about Noah. Hide away so I could focus on finishing my new manuscript. Then, next time I see him, tell him it's best we go our separate ways and pretend last night never happened.

But I knew damn well that plans were meant to be broken. I just wondered how long it would take before I again wanted to experience that unparalleled high I felt last night as I fell asleep cocooned in Noah's warm embrace.

~~~~~~~~~

HAVING FINALLY WASHED MY indiscretions off my body, I grabbed my bag and threw my journal into it. I couldn't be in my apartment right now. Everywhere I turned, I was faced with another memory of Noah. He'd even infiltrated the one room of my home no one else, other than my brother and Brooklyn, had been allowed into. My office was no longer the safe haven it had once been. Noah's scent was ingrained in my nostrils. His rough hands were burned on my skin. His kisses were recorded in my memory.

Needing to talk to someone, I barreled through the glass doors of the café, searching for any sign of Drew. I'd tried to get in touch with Brooklyn earlier, but she was in the field all day, accompanying a few social workers on home visits. It was just my luck. Whenever I actually needed to talk about guy problems, my usual confidantes were nowhere to be found.

"Good morning, Molly Mae," Aunt Gigi called out from behind the counter. "How was the date?"

"It was…" I trailed off, hesitating briefly, "good," I finished in an unsure voice. "Where's Drew?"

"He took the girls to the Museum of Science." She came out from behind the counter and pulled me toward a booth. She slid in, then stared at me, waiting for me to do the same. "I want to hear about this date of yours."

Reluctantly, I lowered myself into the booth, glancing around the busy café, many patrons stopping by to get their Sunday morning pastries after leaving church.

"What's his name?"

"No… Paul."

"Nepal?" She narrowed her inquisitive gaze. "Like the country?"

Besides my brother and Brooklyn, Aunt Gigi knew me better than anyone else. Hell, she'd stepped in and helped my father with us after my mother left. When it was time for "the talk", it was Aunt Gigi who had the pleasure of having it with me. When I told my father I'd gotten my period, he was on the phone in a flash, calling Gigi to come over.

"Just Paul," I corrected.

"Mmm-hmm." She angled her body away from me, squinting. "And what does this *Paul* do for a living?"

"He's a doctor." I rubbed my clammy hands on my jeans. Growing up, Drew and I often joked Aunt Gigi had eyes in the back of her head. Now I was beginning to believe the validity of our childhood belief.

"What kind of medicine does he practice?"

I reminded myself to answer her questions as if speaking about Paul, not Noah. It couldn't be too hard, could it? Hell, I made up stories for a living.

"He's a pediatrician," I answered with confidence.

"Mmm-hmm." She crossed her arms, pinching her lips. "Now, tell me why you were so frantic to see Drew. You appear a bit flushed this morning, Molly."

I pulled my bottom lip between my teeth, avoiding her gaze.

"I see." A slight grin formed. "So you invited Dr. Nepal up for a nightcap?"

"You could say that. And his name is Paul," I added quickly.

"Of course it is, dear. And when do you plan on seeing *Paul* again?"

"Hopefully never," I muttered.

"The hanky-panky was that bad? What about it didn't satisfy you?"

"Aunt Gigi!" I exclaimed, my face burning. "I'm *not* going to discuss this with you! And no one says hanky-panky anymore! We call it what it is. Sex. Fucking. Banging. Bumping uglies!"

I expected to get a reaction from her. Instead, her expression remained unnervingly composed. "I've read your books, dear." She placed her hand over mine. "Nothing you say can shock me. So tell me what happened that makes you not want to see him again, even after making love."

My eyes widened, my heart racing. "Oh no. We did *not* make love. No, no, no, no, no."

A sigh escaped Aunt Gigi's mouth as she gazed upon me fondly. "You know I love you like I do my own children, don't you?"

"Of course. And I love you as if you were my mother," I answered.

"Your father loved your mother very much."

"Too bad she returned that love by completely shattering him."

"No, Molly." She shook her head. "She shattered *you*. You were so young when she left, it affected you more than it did Drew or even your father. They still missed her, but they didn't act out like you did." She let out a small laugh. "At first, your father simply thought it was your personality coming through, but there were only so many times he could make excuses when he received a phone call from the principal of your school claiming you'd been teasing other kids who had been dropped off by their mothers, sometimes to the extent of physical altercations."

I bit my lip, remembering that like it were yesterday. It wasn't my proudest moment, but I hated hearing how all the other kids in my class got to do fun things with their moms when I didn't even know where mine was.

"We finally made the decision to put you in therapy."

My eyes widened. "Wait. What? I never went to therapy! I'd remember being on some shrink's couch, spilling my guts, him constantly asking me how everything made me feel."

She smirked. "Child psychologists are a bit different, Molly. Remember when you used to go see Miss Margaret?"

I nodded. "She was my babysitter. Dad took there so he could go to hockey practice with Drew. We played with toys and she asked me about…" I trailed off as realization washed over me. "You guys *tricked* me?"

"You made incredible progress in such a short

amount of time as Miss Margaret helped you work through all your abandonment issues. She was able to direct all your anger into something that made you happy."

"Which was?" I felt like Aunt Gigi was talking about a complete stranger, not me.

"Reading and writing. When you were eight or nine, she sent you home with *The Diary of Anne Frank*."

I stared off into the distance, then returned my eyes to her, my brow furrowed. "What does any of this have to do with Dad and my mom?"

"Molly, your father loves you and Drew more than anything, although he probably can't remember what love is anymore. When you and Drew were younger, he didn't really date because he didn't want to put you through any more heartache. Your well-being was always his priority. He dated casually, but never got serious, although there were quite a few women with whom he wanted to take things to the next level."

"So you're telling me *I'm* the reason my dad became cynical about love?"

Aunt Gigi shook her head. "Your father was never cynical about love."

"Then why would he say 'real love isn't real life' all the time?"

"It was something your mother used to say."

I furrowed my brow, this new information turning everything I thought to be true on its head. All my beliefs, all my actions were now put under a different lens.

"Do you know how they met?" Gigi asked, a nostalgic smile on her face.

I slowly shook my head. I didn't know much about my mother or her short-lived romance with my father.

241

"They met right here."

"Really?"

Gigi nodded. "He'd just taken over running the café. She worked as a waitress in one of the restaurants around here and would come in every day to get a coffee before her shift. One thing led to another and, well… She ended up pregnant about six months later. Before that, she was a bit of a wild child, a free spirit." Her lips turned up into a small smile. "I see a lot of her in you."

I scowled, not wanting to be compared to the woman who broke my father's heart…who broke my heart.

"Now, you can imagine it was quite the scandal, especially considering she was twenty-five and your father had fifteen years on her. Sure, it was the eighties, so having a baby out of wedlock wasn't that big a deal, but she was from a rather devout Roman Catholic family, just like the one your father and I grew up in. Her father was a Marine, a Vietnam veteran, who was incredibly strict. There wasn't much of a choice but for your mother and father to get married. They went to City Hall and were married by the Justice of the Peace. Five months later, Drew was born." She let out a sigh. "I think your father hoped once the baby arrived, things would improve, but they never did. She never glowed when she held Drew in her arms. It was almost like she couldn't bear to look at him, let alone touch him. You can imagine our surprise when, eighteen months later, she announced she was pregnant again."

"Wait." I took a sharp inhale of air, blinking rapidly. "If she wasn't happy with my dad, then…"

"Don't worry," Aunt Gigi answered quickly, obviously aware of what I thought. "He made sure he was the father. Even if he wasn't, he wouldn't care. He would still love you as if you were his. You and Drew are the reasons he never regretted the time he'd spent with your mother. After she left, he didn't think he'd ever hear from her again. One day, she called and asked to see you and Drew."

My mouth opened. "She did?"

"And your father, being the compassionate and understanding man he was, agreed. She never showed. She called a week later with some excuse. This happened over and over again. Each time, he tried to convince her to come back, try to work things out. Your mother would simply tell him his feelings for her weren't real, that 'real love isn't real life'. Regardless, he did love her. When they were together, he doted on her, gave her everything she ever wanted. He looked at her pregnancy as a blessing. She looked at it as a prison sentence."

I leaned back in my seat, processing all this information. Most of the decisions I'd made throughout my adult life, as it related to my arrangements, were based on the idea that I didn't want to end up hurt like my father and Drew. Not getting romantically involved seemed like the only solution. Never in a million years would I have thought I'd turned into my mother instead…a woman who ran from love.

Abruptly standing up, I grabbed my bag. "I have to go."

Gigi slid out of the booth and stepped in front of me, placing her hands on my shoulders. "I understand this is a lot of information to process, but I thought you should know before you make a decision you'll regret."

"I'm scared," I admitted through the heaviness in my throat. It was the first real thing I'd said in years, if ever.

"I know you are, Molly Mae." She squeezed my

243

arms. "If you're not, it's not love."

Nausea formed in my stomach at that blasphemous word. I spun from her, dashing out of the café. Feeling big, fat raindrops start to fall, I pulled my umbrella out of my bag. I glanced at the door to my building. Memories of Noah kissing me there less than twenty-four hours ago rushed forward. I tried to suppress them, needing to clear my head and sort through all this new information. I had a plan before talking to Aunt Gigi. Now I didn't know much of anything.

Chapter Twenty-Two

A SLIVER OF SUN peeked out from behind heavy clouds, shining a small beam of light onto the tall buildings behind me that made up the city of Boston. I'd lost track of how much time I'd spent locked in my own thoughts throughout the day as I walked from one spot to the next. No matter where I went, something made me think of Noah. How could I figure out what to do about him if I was constantly reminded of him?

A little voice in my head told me that, in itself, should have been my answer, but I ignored it, like any sane person would. It was now after six in the evening and I'd finally found somewhere that hadn't been marked, somewhere I could think clearly...or as clearly as possible with my libido reminding me of the ecstasy I'd experienced the previous night.

Looking over the harbor from my bench in Christopher Columbus Park just a few blocks from where I started this morning, I saw a plane landing at Logan Airport. I entertained the idea of going home, packing, and hopping on the next flight to some exotic locale.

My thoughts were all over the place. One minute, I never wanted to see Noah again, despite the improbability of that happening. The next, I recalled the previous night and how perfect it felt to have his arms wrapped around me.

Aunt Gigi's story had thrown everything into a tailspin. The motto I'd lived by, that love was simply an illusion, had been crushed into tiny little pieces all over the floor of the café. I was more confused than ever. Even putting all my thoughts down in my journal didn't help.

"There you are," a deep, breathy voice called, interrupting my plans of escape and living on a remote island, complete with a native manservant to bring me drinks at my bidding.

I snapped my head to the right. When I observed Noah jogging up the harbor walk toward me, my heart fell to the pit of my stomach. Although he was a few yards away, his vibrant eyes stood out.

I quickly shot up, my limbs jittery. "What are you doing here?" I looked around, feeling exposed. "How did you know I'd be here?"

He came to a stop in front of me. "When you didn't stop by the nursing home this afternoon, I was worried."

I chewed on the inside of my cheek, avoiding the look of concern and worry on his face. "I've been a bit preoccupied today," I admitted truthfully.

When he stepped toward me, I backed up. I wanted to run away. At the same time, I craved the feel of his arms around me. If this was what it felt like to be in a relationship, I was glad I'd stayed away from it. I felt bipolar, maybe even manic. The swing from my highs to lows were wide and without warning.

"Is this about last night?" He raised his brow, his voice soft, gentle, beautiful.

"No," I answered quickly. "I just have a lot on my plate right now. I already had to ask my publisher for an extension to finish this book. I'm still behind."

"So you came here?" He cocked his head, eyeing me.

I pulled my bottom lip between my teeth. "Well, I went to the Common first. Then a coffee shop. Then a bar. That one turned out to be a really bad idea, so I ended up here." My heart rate picked up as my vision raked over his full lips, his vivid, yet uneasy eyes, his slight smile. "But I really do have a lot to do, so I need to get going." I snapped out of the spell Noah's presence cast over me and spun on my heels, darting down the path.

"Why do I get the feeling you're running away from me?" he called out.

Heat washing over me, I stopped. I knew my behavior made no sense to someone like Noah, who probably never had difficulty forming strong and lasting relationships with people. I, on the other hand, had only dated casually, and I used the word "date" very loosely. A date had always just been a means to an end for me, not a device to bear my soul. There had never been a connection...until Noah. I wasn't too proud to admit all of this scared me shitless. Before this began, I had a plan, and falling for Noah wasn't part of it.

"I'm not running from you," I replied in a low voice, facing him.

He took several deliberate steps toward me. As much as I wanted to retreat, a force outside my control kept me glued to that spot.

"You are, Molly. After last night, I thought..." He ran his hand through his dark hair, tugging at it slightly as he tried to compose his thoughts. He drew even closer, the heat of his body sending a ripple through me. He tilted my chin, forcing my eyes to his. "I thought we were on the same page," he said in a quiet voice.

"Noah, I…" I blinked repeatedly, unable to look away. "I'm not the woman you think I am."

A soft smile cracked his lips. "And what woman do you think that is?"

"I don't know." I swallowed hard. "But I can assure you, I'm not her." I backed away from him. "I'm not the type of girl a guy like you dates. Hell, I asked your sister if she ever got tired of looking at vaginas all day. I'm not exactly someone you'd want to introduce to friends and family."

"Why not?" He closed the distance between us again. "Because you ask the questions everyone else is too shy to? That's a positive character trait, if you ask me."

"That's what you say now, but at some point, you won't like it anymore," I explained, an urgency in my tone. "And the lack of a filter is just one of my many quirks that should send you running for the hills. There are plenty of other women out there. Women who wouldn't put your job in jeopardy." My expression turned serious. "Maybe it's best we forget last night ever happened. You can go find someone who's at least in the same intellectual sphere as you…maybe another doctor. Then you can have lots of doctor sex and little doctor babies."

A low chuckle rumbled from his chest. He slid his hands down my body, landing on my waist, pulling me against him.

"But I don't want to have doctor sex." He slowly shook his head, his voice sensual. My resolve to walk away melted in a puddle in the middle of Columbus Park. I was complete putty in his hands. His touch was all I needed to agree to whatever he wanted. "I want to have Molly sex. Lots and lots of Molly sex."

"But how would you even introduce me to your

friends? 'Hi, this is Molly. She writes smut'?" I rolled my eyes. "I'm sure that'll go over well in all your doctor circles and doctor parties."

"Stop labeling everything. Stop putting the two of us in categories. You're a writer, a brilliant one, and I decided to make a really bad financial decision and became a doctor. How we make a living doesn't define us. You're just trying to come up with every excuse out there about why we shouldn't be together."

"And there are a lot, Noah. I'm sure I could fill pages with all the reasons we shouldn't be together, the most pressing of which being the fact you were my father's doctor."

"What if your pages full of reasons we shouldn't be together are no match for my one reason we should? What if all your reasons, taken as a whole, pale in comparison?"

My heart drummed at the sincerity in his eyes, his face, his body. "And what's that?" I swallowed hard.

He ran his finger over my lips, sending a tremor through me. "That something about you has drawn me in since the day I first saw you reading to your father. That, despite trying, I haven't been able to stop thinking about you for months. That I firmly believe fate intervened and forced us together that day all those weeks ago when I saved you from a gang of ruthless miscreants."

"Otherwise known as ducks," I muttered, a lightness in my chest.

"Just a tiny, insignificant detail." He brought his lips toward mine. "I knew I'd regret it every day of my life if I didn't say fuck it and just be with you, despite all the complications surrounding a potential relationship with you. I've never been as happy in my life as I am with you…even when we're fully clothed."

I allowed a laugh to escape my throat. "But I like it when there's no clothes, too."

"As do I." He paused for a beat, his lips a whisper away from mine. "So…"

"So…," I breathed.

"So…"

"So." I tangled my fingers in his hair, pulling him toward me. Gently, he pressed his mouth against mine, his kiss unhurried. Even with the most innocent of kisses, he seemed to invade every inch of me. I felt him on my skin, in my core, in my heart.

He leaned his forehead against mine, licking his lips. "I get it, Molly." With a firm grip, he cupped my cheeks. The intensity in his eyes was unwavering. "I'm scared, too. It's hard for me to describe. I've dated many different women in all my thirty-eight years—"

"Twenty-nine-plus-nine," I corrected.

"Yes. Twenty-nine-plus-nine," he said with a smile before his expression turned serious once more. "And not one of them has left the same imprint on me that you have. I'm not just saying that to get into your pants again." He paused, his eyes becoming hooded. "Although I'd really, *really* like to get into your pants again."

I laughed, my heart brimming at his ability to make jokes during a serious conversation, as if he knew I needed it. It was as if he always knew exactly what I needed.

"I'd really, *really* like that, too."

A smile tugged at his mouth. "Molly, what I'm trying to say is…" He took a deep breath, wetting his lips again. "I want to be able to call you my girlfriend and have a smug look on my face when all my friends find

250

out you can write one hell of a sex scene and use me as a very willing guinea pig."

I pouted playfully. "Are you just using me for my mommy porn?"

"No. Never." He grinned. "Maybe just a little."

Arching my body into his, I forced his head toward me. "You can use me any time you'd like," I murmured flirtatiously.

Groaning, his mouth moved against mine once more. All my worries momentarily left me. I'd often rolled my eyes in romance novels, including my own, when the heroine claimed all her fears were miraculously erased after the hero touched or kissed her, but I understood it now. It wasn't that I had no more concerns or trepidations. It was the knowledge I wasn't alone in my fear, that we were in this together.

"So... Dinner?" He raised a brow, looking down at me.

I gestured to my jeans and ratty t-shirt, not to mention the hair I'd haphazardly knotted in a bun on top of my head. "I'm not exactly dressed for it."

"Don't worry about that." Winking, he grabbed my hand and tugged me with him. "I know the perfect place."

My stomach fluttered when he glanced at me with more adoration than anyone ever had. I couldn't remember anyone ever looking upon me with such devotion.

"So... You never answered my question," I said, breaking through the silence as he led me toward Hanover Street and the North End. "How did you know where I was?"

He grinned. "Your brother."

I stopped dead in my tracks, pulling my hand from

his. "Drew? But won't he think something's going on between us?"

Noah held my arms, a satisfied expression on his face. "I *want* him to think something's going on between us. I said I wanted to be with you, Molly, and not just behind closed doors. I want to go out in public with you. I want to hold your hand everywhere we go. I want everyone to know how incredible you are. I'm not going to hide you away like some secret I don't want anyone to find out about."

I tugged my lip between my teeth. "But what if you get in trouble? Isn't it frowned upon for a doctor to form an intimate relationship with someone involved in the decision-making process for one of his patients?"

He cocked his head.

"Google." I shrugged.

A peaceful look crossed his face. "It is, which is why I am no longer your father's neurologist. Since it's a bit of a gray area, I sought an opinion from the medical board. As long as I shield myself from anything to do with your father's care, it wouldn't be unethical for me to be involved with you, considering he's now a *former* patient."

"But when we kissed the first time, you *were* my father's doctor. What if someone finds out?"

"I'll deal with it if and when the time comes. Right now, I just want to be with you. There's no telling what the future holds. I'm not going to worry myself with a bunch of what ifs. Not right now. I just want to hold your hand as we walk through the city streets, then have dinner with you. I don't care who sees us. In fact, I want *everyone* to see us," he declared with such joy, such fervor, such zeal. No one had ever fought so hard for me before and it chipped at another piece of the wall

252

I'd erected around my heart. "Okay?"

"Okay," I said in a small voice, blindly allowing him to lead me down a few side streets I knew like the back of my hand.

In a daze, I didn't notice when he turned down my street until the familiar scent of my family's café found its way to my nostrils. I gave Noah a smile, grateful he knew my perfect idea of dinner was an appetizer of takeout with him as my main course.

I dug through my bag, searching for my keys.

"We're not going to your place." He grabbed my keys, tossing them back into my bag. Clutching my hand in his, he continued past my front stoop, dragging me up the steps of Drew's apartment building.

My eyes widened. "What are we doing here?"

"Don't you do family dinner every Sunday?"

"Yes, but——"

"I know how important family is to you. I won't come between that."

"You think this is a good idea? I mean…" I avoided his eyes, not knowing how Drew would react to this rather drastic change of events. I knew I'd have some serious explaining to do, but I wasn't sure I was ready for that just yet.

"I do. Your brother did, too. He's the one who invited me, although he *did* warn me if I ever do anything to hurt you, he'll make sure I pay for it dearly."

"That sounds like Drew," I mumbled, nausea filling my stomach, my mouth suddenly dry.

"It's okay," Noah encouraged. "It'll all be okay." I had no idea why he was reassuring me when this was my family. You'd think it would have been the other way around. Wasn't he supposed to be the nervous one? "This is all part of being in a relationship. But if you're not ready, we can do something else."

I sighed. "Then I'll never hear the end of it from Drew and Brooklyn. Drew would just hunt me down and haul my ass over here anyway." I faced the door and placed my hand on the knob. "I just need to warn you. My family can be a bit…loud."

"I wouldn't expect anything else."

"At least I know Drew has plenty of wine."

Noah chuckled as I opened the door, the sound of boisterous voices filling the stairwell. As we headed up the stairs, I could hear my uncle Leo telling another one of his fishing stories. I wanted to turn around and run, the prospect of introducing Noah to my family as my boyfriend making my stomach roll. I didn't see how this could possibly go well. Worse, I knew Drew and Brooklyn would put two and two together and figure out there was no coworker. They'd realize it was Noah all along. I feared one of them would slip and Noah would find out I only wanted to spend time with him in the beginning to use him as inspiration.

For the first time I could remember, I actually *wanted* to be with him. I'd never felt a pang in my chest at the prospect of any of the men I dated walking out on me. With Noah, it wasn't just a pang. It was a full-on gripping ache.

Drawing in a breath, I pushed open the door to Drew's apartment. Silence fell over the living room as we stood in the doorway. I felt like I'd just shown up to a party naked. I glanced down to reassure myself that wasn't the case.

"Molly Mae!" my uncle Leo bellowed, breaking the stiff silence. "Get in here, peanut! You're letting in a draft."

Gritting a smile, I pulled Noah into the modest living area of my brother's apartment, shutting the door behind us. Only my uncle Leo would complain about letting in a draft in June. Careful to avoid any of the girls' toys strewn about, I led Noah toward the peninsula where everyone was congregated, laughing over appetizers of calamari and mushroom canapés.

"Don't be rude, Molly," Gigi said. A smug, yet satisfied expression broke out on her face. "Aren't you going to introduce us to your friend?"

"Like he even needs an introduction. I'm pretty sure you all know him already." I looked at all the familiar faces. For years, it had been a tradition to get together at Drew's every Sunday with a sliver of my huge family, which consisted of me, Drew, the girls, Aunt Gigi, Uncle Leo, and Brooklyn. She wasn't related by blood, but she was part of our tribe.

"Good to see you, Dr. McAllister," Drew said, breaking the tension, holding out his hand to Noah, who took it, giving my brother a smile.

"It's Noah. Please, just call me Noah."

"I'm sure you remember Aunt Gigi and Uncle Leo." I gestured to a short, balding man with glasses, then the petite sixty-five-year-old graying brunette at his side.

"Of course. Pleasure to see you both again," Noah replied with a smile.

"Oh, the pleasure is all ours." Aunt Gigi winked.

"And this is Brooklyn." I nodded at my best friend, who looked like she had a thousand questions she was bursting to ask. I wanted to dig a hole and bury myself in it.

"Nice to meet you," Noah said cordially.

Brooklyn simply studied him, her lips pinched. I'd expected Drew to be the one concerned with this

255

arrangement. I didn't anticipate Brooklyn to have reservations.

"If you'll excuse us for a minute." She offered a tight smile, then gripped my arm, tugging me away.

I glanced over my shoulder as she led me from the kitchen and toward the hallway. "I'll be right back."

Noah gave me an understanding look. Relief washed over me when Drew slung his arm over his shoulder and led him toward the wet bar, asking what he'd like to drink.

Brooklyn pushed me into Drew's bedroom, then practically slammed the door. She whirled around. "What the hell is going on, Molly?"

"It's kind of a long story, Brook. One I'd rather not get into tonight."

She crossed her arms, standing in front of the door to prevent me from leaving. "I'll take the bullet points. How did you go from pursuing a coworker at the magazine, to going on a date last night with some guy you met online, to now dating your father's doctor?" She narrowed her eyes. "Is this because the guy at work rejected you? So what? You find someone else who's off limits to use as a muse?"

"Shh!" I pulled her away from the door and toward Drew's bed. "It's not like that."

"Then tell me exactly what it's like. From where I'm standing, it looks like you're willing to let that poor guy jeopardize his career just for a stupid book. I've stayed quiet for years, but I'm done, so you'd better have a damn good explanation for what the hell is going on."

Dropping onto the bed, I hugged one of Drew's pillows to me, trying to collect my thoughts. "There never was a coworker." I peeked over the pillow.

Silence rang in the room.

"That day at the Common, when I was trying to overcome my writer's block, it was Noah who saved me from being mauled by a bunch of savage miscreants."

"Or ducks." She sat on the edge of the mattress.

"Details." I shot her a smile, a dreamy look crossing my face. "We hung out for hours just talking about whatever popped into our heads. After I left, I couldn't wait to get home to write. I'd never felt so inspired before, and that's when my book took on a completely different feel." I sighed. "Maybe my reasons for spending time with him were selfish at first. So many times when I'm writing, I get distracted by everything else. After spending time with Noah, I didn't give in to those distractions. I couldn't stop the story that bled from me."

"It was a damn good book, one you never should have tossed out," Brooklyn admitted. "So when you said you kissed your coworker and he pushed you away..." She raised her brow.

"It was Noah." I shook my head. "After my dad grew violent with me that time, Noah wanted to make sure I hadn't suffered a concussion or anything from falling and hitting my head. He took me to one of the exam rooms." A tingle spread through my limbs as I recalled our first kiss, the adrenaline of it being wrong, the fullness in my heart making me feel more satisfied than I ever had.

"So he took advantage of your injured state?" she hissed, her expression cold, her lips pinched. "Real stand-up guy."

"He didn't take advantage of anything, Brook. *I* was the one who kissed *him*. *I* initiated it. Sure, he kissed me back, and it was fucking amazing, but he came to his senses and stormed out of the room. I confronted him the following day after I found out he had my father's care transferred to a different neurologist. I didn't see him again...until I went out with Paul last night. By the way, did you know that Soul Mate is a Mormon dating website?"

Her eyes widened in surprise as she studied me, then burst out laughing. "You went out with someone from there?"

"I had no idea. He didn't come off as all holier-than-thou when we messaged each other. But when the waitress came to take our orders, he said we didn't drink. I knew something was up, so I hid away in the bathroom to find out where I'd met him. Brook, he asked me to say the blessing before we ate."

Brooklyn giggled. "I would have paid to see this. I'm pretty sure a church would erupt in flames if you ever stepped through the doors."

"Well, the date definitely went up in flames."

"How does Noah figure in to all this?" She leaned closer, engaged in the story. Her fury from earlier had begun to wane, and it was comforting to see the version of my friend I was used to.

"He was at the same restaurant with this gorgeous blonde, who also happened to be a doctor and knew my date. As they were leaving, they stopped by our table."

"What did you do?" she asked, her attention rapt.

"I was surrounded by all these wicked smart doctors, so I did what I always do when I feel uncomfortable." I shrugged.

"Oh, my god. You made a tasteless joke," Brooklyn said, horror on her face. She knew me better than I knew myself sometimes.

"The blonde was a gynecologist, so I asked if she ever got tired of looking at vaginas. Honestly, I was curious.

I don't know if I could deal with looking at beavers all day."

She burst out laughing, shaking her head. "Only you."

"I didn't know what else to say. Noah stood less than a foot from me with this tall, strikingly beautiful doctor. I couldn't compete with that."

Brooklyn's jovial expression fell as she placed her hand over mine. "You're a beautiful, smart woman, too, Molly. Who cares if you didn't go to med school?"

I smiled, offering her a silent thanks.

"So what happened next?" she inquired after a long pause.

"Like I said, the date was a flop, although he wanted me to go to church with him this morning." I cringed. "I debated on giving him Aunt Gigi's number to see if she'd be interested in converting to Mormonism."

Playfully hitting me, she chuckled. "Stop it."

"When I got back home and started up my steps, I heard a voice call my name."

"Aww," Brooklyn cooed, resting a hand over her heart as she fell onto Drew's bed. She rolled onto her side, propping herself up on her elbow. It reminded me of all the nights we spent sleeping over at one another's houses in middle school, gossiping about boys. "How romantic."

"He told me how he couldn't stop thinking about me. That he was sorry for ignoring me the past few weeks, but he was just scared. Then I invited him upstairs."

She narrowed her eyes. "Answer me this. After he apologized and probably poured his heart out to you, although you're conveniently leaving those details out of this retelling, what was your intention?"

"What do you mean? What intention?"

"You know exactly what I'm talking about. Did you only invite him upstairs because he inspired you to write? Do you plan to just toss him out when that's no longer the case?"

"No!" I exclaimed, then drew in a long breath. "I mean, when I invited him upstairs, it might have been."

"You understand this man is potentially risking his career just to be with you, correct?" Her tone was direct, harsh, abrasive, at odds with the light and carefree Brooklyn I was used to.

"I understand that! But something changed. I actually felt something when I was with him."

"An orgasm?"

"No, Brook. *Something*. It was beautiful and wonderful and everything I imagined it would be. So naturally, in the light of day, I realized last night was a monumental mistake."

"Oh, jeez," Brooklyn muttered, rolling her eyes. "So what did you do? The walk of shame from your own house?"

"Thankfully, I didn't have to, although I had planned my escape. When I finally summoned the courage to roll over in my bed, it was empty. He got called into work. I spent all day figuring out how to avoid seeing him again."

"Well, from the looks of things, you did a great job."

I laughed. "He went to my place looking for me when I didn't go visit Dad today."

"You didn't go see your dad?" Her eyes nearly popped out of their sockets.

Biting my lip, I slowly shook my head. "I've never allowed a man to come between me and my friends or family before. I had no desire to see Noah, so I ditched my father to avoid running into him. I don't know what

I was thinking, but I knew last night was a bad idea. At least I thought it was...until I talked to Aunt Gigi this morning."

"Wait a minute." Brooklyn shot off the bed. "You talked to your aunt about hot doctor sex and not me?!"

"You were working!" I argued in my defense, pulling her back onto the bed. "And she didn't know it was hot doctor sex. I mean, I don't *think* I mentioned sex. Maybe I did. I don't know. Anyway, she told me about my mom and dad. She said a lot of things that made sense..." I looked away. "Too much sense. Now I wonder whether I wasted the best years of my life hung up on some crazy motto I thought my idol, my father, lived by. It wasn't a motto at all, but a reminder of why the love of his life, the mother of his children, didn't want him. *That* was why he had said 'real love isn't real life'. It wasn't because he believed the words to be true. It was because my mother had told him those very same words each and every time he tried to convince her to come back. She broke his heart, but you know what? He never gave up on her." I fidgeted with my hands in my lap.

"So when Noah found me in Columbus Park toying with the idea of jumping on a plane... I don't know. I'm scared, but like Gigi said, maybe that's how I know it's real."

Brooklyn sighed, then clutched my hand in hers. "I honestly never thought I'd see the day when Molly Brinks, *Metropolitan Magazine's* own serial dater, would settle down."

"Hey! I'm not settling down! I'm still the same Molly. Being with Noah isn't going to change me."

"I think he already has." She winked just as a soft knock sounded on the door.

261

Drew poked his head in. "Everything okay in here?"

"Of course." I smoothed my jeans and stood from the bed. "Sorry. We kind of got carried away."

"Don't be." He offered me a smile. "Dinner's almost ready."

I looked at Brooklyn. "Are we good?"

She got up from the bed and wrapped her arms around me. "Of course we are." She squeezed me tight, then headed out of the bedroom. Drew and I followed down the hallway. As we were about to rejoin the crowd, he pulled me aside.

"I'm happy for you, Molly," he offered, surprising me.

"You shouldn't have found out like this. I should have told you the truth from the very beginning."

He lifted a brow, smirking. "Do you honestly think I fell for your little story about a coworker you never spoke of before?"

"You knew?" My eyes widened. "For how long?"

"Long enough."

"Why didn't you say anything?"

He shoved his hands into his pockets. "I don't know. I thought if I didn't pry, if I didn't push, maybe this one would be different than all the others." A wide smile crossed his face. "I guess I was right."

He grabbed my elbow and tugged me into the living room. My heart warmed when my eyes fell on Noah sitting on the floor with Alyssa and Charlotte, having a pretend tea party.

"Don't let it go to your head," I muttered.

"Too late." He handed me a glass of wine as I leaned against the peninsula, not wanting to take my eyes off how comfortable Noah looked surrounded by relative strangers. It was as if he belonged here.

Chapter Twenty-Three

"SHE WAS PROBABLY FOUR or five at the time," Drew said in a boisterous voice, trying to hold in his laughter. "God, she was so mad! She was dancing around in the basement to Air Supply, building something with her blocks. I have no idea what."

"It was a wall to keep stinky brothers away," I shot back with a smirk, catching Noah's enamored gaze out of the corner of my eye.

"She never even saw it coming. As she was in mid-spin, I knocked her hard work down. She chased me all over the basement, screaming, 'Give you to me!'"

Even though they all knew the story, everyone laughed...except Noah. His hand brushed my leg beneath the table.

"Give you to me?" he mused in a sexy voice, raising his brow.

I shrugged. "It was before I became so eloquent with words." I took a sip of my wine. "All these years later, whenever I get mad at him, I still say that." I winked at Drew, who wore a satisfied expression on his face as he looked between Noah and me.

"Although these two barely ever fight," Brooklyn interjected. "They have an oddly close relationship." She paused briefly. "How about you, Noah? Any brothers or sisters?"

"Four sisters," he answered. "Molly met one of them.

Piper."

"She's a doctor, too. A gynecologist," I added.

Brooklyn's eyes shot to mine as she put two and two together. "Who you asked…?"

I nodded. Sensing Noah's eyes on me, I turned to him. "I gave her the bullet points about last night."

"I figured as much." He winked.

"Did you grow up in Boston?" Uncle Leo asked.

"No, sir," Noah answered respectfully. I marveled at how well mannered he was. He had held my chair out for me as I sat at the table, even in the relaxed atmosphere of my family. It was such a small thing, but it spoke volumes as to the kind of man he was, how different he was from all the others who'd come before him. They'd never opened or held the door for me. They'd never shared their umbrella with me when we got caught in the rain and I forgot mine. They'd never thought about anyone but themselves. I supposed I hadn't, either…until now.

As I surveyed Noah's silhouette, unbeknownst to him, I considered the possibility there was a reason I never wanted anything more than an occasional fling before. Maybe I knew those guys weren't enough for me. Maybe I had been subconsciously waiting to find a man who would treat me the way a woman deserved to be treated…like a queen in public and a goddess in private. I craved the moment Noah would worship at my altar again.

"I grew up in New York."

Gigi gasped, as if he'd confessed to murdering children. Clutching Uncle Leo's hand, they looked at Noah. "New York? You're not…" She trailed off, unable to finish the words.

"No, ma'am. I am not a Yankees fan."

She breathed a huge sigh of relief, doing the sign of the cross. Baseball was as hallowed as religion in our family. "Thank God."

"Yeah!" Alyssa said, finally taking a break from stuffing her face with homemade spaghetti. "No Yankees fans are allowed in here. Daddy already told me I'm never allowed to date anyone who's a Yankees fan...or Canadian."

"You're never allowed to date, period," Drew corrected with a smile. "But if you do, it's not all Canadians. It's Montreal Canadien fans." He returned his attention to Noah, shrugging. "Old hockey rivalries never really die."

"Speaking of which..." Noah raised his wine glass to his lips, taking a sip to wash down the hearty Italian meal. I couldn't help but think there was something incredibly erotic about the way he swirled his wine, savoring the robust cabernet sauvignon he chose to pair with his Braciole, my aunt Gigi's specialty. "Ever think of getting back in the game?"

Drew lowered his head, staring at his plate as he toyed with the noodles, twirling them around his fork. "I've had some offers to coach, but I need to put my girls first. Coaching would mean being away from home for weeks—"

"Not if you coach college," Gigi interrupted.

Drew shot daggers at her. I got the feeling they had this conversation many times before. Drew was just as stubborn as I was. It was nearly impossible to convince him to change his mind once it had been made up. His love for his girls was unmatched, but it was clear how much he missed the thrill of being around the ice, although he'd never admit it. He'd bought the café from my dad when he could no longer manage it on his own due to his illness. Drew didn't really run it any more than my father did. That was all Aunt Gigi.

"I'd still have to be away from the girls. Maybe not for weeks at a time, but still longer than I'd like. Coaching is out of the question." He glared at Gigi, silently telling her to drop it. Then he turned back to Noah, anxious to change the subject. "Do your parents still live in New York?"

"My mother does." He stabbed his fork into his salad. "My father passed away when I was in college."

"I'm sorry," Drew offered.

"Alzheimer's," Noah added. Every pair of eyes in the room shot in his direction. "He's the reason I chose the path I did."

"Grandpapa has old-timer's, too!" Alyssa's voice cut through the solemn air at the table, a smile on her face. I wished she could always stay young and innocent, that the cruelty of how easily people could leave and forget you never really affect her as it had me. "He forgets a lot and it makes him angry." She tilted her head at Drew. "Isn't that right, Daddy?"

Drew nodded with tight lips. "He doesn't mean anything by it. It's just the way his brain is wired."

"Is my brain wired the same way?" Her eyes grew wide, her soft chin trembling. "I'm not going to forget and be mean, too, am I?"

"Of course not, pumpkin."

"Promise?" Her eyebrows furrowed, concern etched on her face. "Because I really don't want to forget you or Auntie Molly. Or Auntie Brook or Charlotte."

Noah squeezed my hand under the table, able to sense my unease as I bore witness to Drew's exchange with Alyssa. I'd constantly been on Drew's case that he didn't visit our father nearly enough. This conversation

266

put it all into perspective for me. I didn't have anyone I had to explain my father's deteriorating health to. Everyone I was close to understood what was going on. Alyssa and Charlotte were too young to truly grasp the concept. For them, their grandpapa was no longer the same man one day. He was no longer there to take them to the park and push them on the swing. He was no longer around to play make-believe with. He was no longer around to fill their bellies with gelato and other sugary treats. My heart went out to Drew at what awaited him somewhere down the road…having to explain what death was to two beautiful, innocent souls.

"I promise." Drew leaned over to kiss Alyssa on the forehead, then got up from his chair, doing the same to Charlotte. He walked to the wet bar and grabbed a few more bottles of wine. I had a feeling every single adult at the table wouldn't turn down more alcohol as we all silently considered the probability that my father's time was nearing the end.

"Hey, Alyssa." Noah's voice cut through the heavy atmosphere as we all stared at our plates, avoiding each other's eyes.

"Yes?" She perked up.

"Do you like jokes?"

"Yes, sir," she answered politely.

"Why is Peter Pan always flying?"

Alyssa contemplated it for a minute, then shook her head. "I don't know."

"Because he Neverlands."

She giggled, her expression brightening. "Tell me another one."

"Okay."

I glanced at Noah, who seemed as comfortable as if he were interacting with two little girls he'd known his entire life. I never pegged him as the type of man who was a sucker for kids, not with the intellectual persona he tended to exude, but he was a natural. In my opinion, he would have made one hell of a pediatrician.

"What runs but doesn't get anywhere?"

Alyssa rolled her eyes. "*Everyone* knows this one, Dr. Noah. A refrigerator!" She and Charlotte burst out laughing.

"You're too smart for me," Noah replied. "Maybe you can teach *me* a few jokes."

Alyssa scrunched her nose and looked at the ceiling, as if a joke would be scrawled on it. Finally, after much thought, she looked back at Noah, grinning. "Why can't you write with a broken pencil?"

Noah draped his arm over the back of my chair, his fingers brushing against my shoulder lightly. The subtle contact warmed me, my face flushing. He winked at me, then turned his attention back to Alyssa.

"I don't know. Why can't you write with a broken pencil?"

I felt a kick from across the table. I shot my eyes to Brooklyn, who simply mouthed, *Oh. My. God*, then feigned swooning. I bit back my smile. I absolutely adored Alyssa and Charlotte, thought of them as my own. My heart was full as I watched Noah interact with them. His interest in my family plowed through the armor around my heart.

"Because it's pointless!" Alyssa exclaimed, her giggles echoing in the room.

"You got all those jokes from Molly, didn't you?" Drew asked Noah.

He furrowed his brow, glancing at me, then back at my brother. "No. Why?"

"Really?" Drew was taken aback. "You two are made

for each other." He shook his head, laughing. "Molly has a thing for stupid humor. She got it from my dad. Besides their love of reading, the other thing they have in common is jokes. They'd sometimes have entire conversations with stupid one-liners."

Noah looked at me. "Really?"

I bit my bottom lip, then shrugged. "Yup."

"Daddy!" Charlotte said. "It's your turn! You tell a joke!"

As Drew tried to come up with an age-appropriate joke on the spot, Noah leaned toward me, his breath hot on my neck. "Perhaps I've met my match."

When he ran a light finger down my arm, my body practically fused into the chair.

Perhaps you have, I thought.

~~~~~~~~~~

EMERGING ONTO THE SIDEWALK, I drew in a long breath of the humid Boston night air. An uncontrollable smile formed on my lips as warmth radiated through every inch of my body. Tonight was better than I could have imagined. Watching Noah converse so effortlessly with the most important people in my life meant more to me than I think he realized.

My fingers intertwined with Noah's as we shuffled the few steps from the front door of Drew's apartment building, past the entrance to the café, and toward my apartment. I unlocked the door, pulling Noah alongside me. To my surprise, he withdrew his hand, hesitating on my front stoop.

"What is it?" I turned to face him, my brows furrowed.

"Molly..." He brought himself up to the same step I

was on, brushing an errant curl behind my ear. I loved the feel of his fingers on my skin. It made me feel alive. I met his eyes, a look of complete satisfaction staring back at me. "I'd love nothing more than to come up, but I don't think I should."

"You don't want to sleep with me?" I swallowed hard, wondering whether Brooklyn or Drew had said something to change his mind since our conversation in the park.

"That's not it at all." He dragged my body to his. Leaning down, he softly tugged on my earlobe with his teeth. His tongue traced circles, igniting the fire in my core. "I want nothing more than to sleep with you, to make your body do things you never thought possible." He abruptly pulled back. His sensual tone turned endearing. "But I want to prove to you that I want you for you, not for any other reason."

"I know that," I replied. "You don't have to prove anything to me." I wrapped my arms around him, pulling him closer. His lips were a whisper away and I was desperate to taste them again, to taste every inch of him.

"Let me do this." He gazed upon me with earnest. This was obviously important to him. "I don't want you to think I'm only spending time with you in the hopes of ending up in bed together. I want to show you we can have just as much fun outside the bedroom as we can inside." He pulled back, clutching my hands in his. "I don't want to just have a fling with you. I want to date you. So please, let me date you."

A satisfied smile crossed my mouth as I stood on my toes. Meeting his crystal blue eyes, I did something I'd never done before. I gave a very handsome man a kiss goodnight after he walked me to my front door. I went to bed more fulfilled with just that one kiss than I ever thought possible.

Chapter Twenty-Four

"YOU LOOK FRUSTRATED," A voice interrupted my thoughts as I sat beneath the same tree that had been the scene of my unceremonious duck attack all those weeks ago. I tore my eyes away from the lackluster story I attempted to write on my laptop. When I was treated to the image of Noah walking toward me, I couldn't contain my excitement.

"What are you doing here?" I wrinkled my nose, then checked the time. We had plans to get together for dinner. While it wasn't impossible for me to be so consumed with writing that I'd lost track of time, I knew that wasn't the case here. This story just didn't feel right. I found myself constantly thinking back to the original draft of Jackson and Avery's story.

"I was able to move some of my appointments to earlier in the day so I could surprise you." When he lowered himself next to me, I closed my laptop, wanting to devote my full attention to him. He leaned closer, his lips a whisper from mine. His voice turned husky. "I couldn't bear to be away from you a second longer than necessary."

I closed my eyes, allowing the sincerity of his words to bathe me with warmth. Running my hands through his hair, I pulled him to me, our mouths meeting. It had been less than twenty-four hours since he kissed me goodnight at my door, but it felt like an eternity without his touch. Not caring we were in public, I deepened the kiss, our tongues tangling.

"I like where this is going," he groaned, his hand clutching my hip.

I didn't know if he was talking about the kiss or our relationship. I figured it was both. I kissed him again, more forceful, wanting him to know how much I needed him, how much I craved him after spending the night without him. Our bodies fell onto the grass. He loomed over me, delicately running his hand up and down the exposed flesh of my legs. With each journey, he hiked my skirt up a little more, his fingers coming closer and closer to the spot I wanted him to touch. I momentarily forgot where we were, the feel of Noah's mouth on my mouth, his skin on my skin intoxicating my senses. I was completely disoriented, but in the most satisfying and delicious way.

When a few passersby whistled, I felt Noah smile. He reluctantly pulled away. "To be continued," he murmured, then lay on the grass beside me, gazing up at the clouds.

"When?" I asked, my chest still heaving.

"Soon."

"You do know you're driving me crazy with this whole dating and not fucking thing, right?"

"It's driving me crazy, too," Noah admitted, linking his fingers through mine.

"Then why don't we just have sex?" I glanced at him. "We've already done it. It's not that big a deal."

"But it should be, Molly." He paused, his voice turning sincere. "You're a treasure, and I plan on treating you as such."

"You could treat me like a treasure and still fuck my brains out." I smirked. His expression was unreadable, then he burst out laughing, the sound tugging on my heartstrings.

"I love your mouth." He leaned closer to me, his breath hot on my neck. "And I plan on fucking your brains out, Molly, but not yet."

"Then when?" I whined.

"All in good time." He smiled coyly, winking.

I huffed in playful annoyance. "Give me some sort of time frame. I need to know if I should stock up on batteries. Just having this conversation is making me wet."

"Really?" He cocked a brow, licking his lips. The heat in his eyes was carnal. I had a feeling most women Noah dated in the past probably weren't as open about their sexuality as I was. What did he expect? He knew my secret. He couldn't have expected anything less from me.

"Really." I nodded slowly. "So I think we should just get out of here, go back to my place…or yours…and do a little research." I wiggled my brows. "It may just help with this book. I'm in a bit of a rut."

He drew closer to me, his fingers brushing up and down my side. "I'd love nothing more than to help you, Molly." His tongue traced circles against my neck. "But not yet. Like I said…" He tugged on my earlobe, his teeth nipping my skin, sending sparks through me. "All in good time." He pulled back, leaving me incredibly frustrated.

"You're the worst," I groaned, throwing my hand over my head. "I've got a raging case of blue bean, but you're doing nothing to help."

It was silent for a moment. "Blue bean?"

"Yeah. The female equivalent of blue balls."

Noah stared at me, then laughed, his smile reaching

those devilish eyes of his. "I have a feeling I'll be adding a lot of new terms to my vernacular as I spend time with you." He turned his eyes back to the sky, a serene look crossing his expression. As much as I would have loved nothing more than to haul Noah back to my apartment and feel his body writhing on top of or below me, this moment was perfect. We simply gazed at the clouds floating above us, basking in the feel of the grass below us, the sounds of the city the perfect ambient music.

"This reminds me of growing up," I commented after a long pause.

"How so?" Noah glanced at me briefly.

"I remember Drew and me lying on the grass in our back yard or at one of the neighborhood parks in the North End and looking at the clouds. Sometimes, we'd pick out the different shapes we saw. Other times, we'd just sit in silence, especially if one of us was having a bad day. There were times I'd get home from school and he could tell I had a rough day. All he had to do was grab my hand and bring me outside. Instantly, things would be better."

"You two are pretty close, aren't you?"

"I guess." I shrugged. "Dad worked a lot when we were growing up so it sometimes felt like it was just us." I swallowed hard. "Then when Drew started getting good at hockey, it was just me." My voice trailed off, but I quickly readjusted my composure. "How about you? Are you close to your sisters?" I looked at Noah.

"As close as any guy can be in a house full of women."

"Where do you fall in the spectrum? Oldest? Youngest?"

"Right in the middle. My oldest sister is forty-six, and

the youngest is thirty. There's a big age span between all of us."

"Is Piper older? Younger?"

"Younger," he answered. "By two years."

"Your mom must be proud with two doctors in the family."

"She's proud of all of us."

I nodded and looked back at the sky, one of the clouds looking too much like a penis. Even the clouds mocked my starving libido.

"So why are you in a rut with your book?" Noah asked out of nowhere.

I glanced at him, exhaling. "It's nothing. Just something I have to work through."

"Anything I can do to help?"

I gave him a lascivious smile.

"Except that," he replied, laughing slightly. "Naughty girl."

"If only you were interested in finding out how naughty I can be."

"I am, but only when the time's right."

I sighed. "I don't think there's anything anyone can do to help me with this book. It just feels like every other book I've written for this imprint." I shook my head, my frustration returning. "When I first started out, I had all these grand notions of how I could use my talent to bring attention to different issues going on in the world today. After all, I have a degree in journalism."

"What kinds of issues?"

"I don't know." I lay on my side and propped myself up on my elbow. "Human trafficking. Abuse. Addiction." I pulled at a few blades of grass. "What it's like to have a parent who's unable to remember you."

"Molly…" He ran his hand up and down my arm, comforting me.

"I was working on something like that," I added quickly. "It was still a romance, but the focus wasn't on how kinky I could make the sex. Instead, it was a love story between two people who society said shouldn't be together."

"Like us?" Noah remarked.

"Yeah. Like us." My lips turned up slightly in the corner, a tingle running down my spine as a relished in the feel of his fingers tracing circles on my flesh. "The mother of one of the characters was schizophrenic and was convinced her son wasn't who he said he was. It's not the same as having a father with Alzheimer's, but it was close."

"It sounds like you're passionate about that story."

"I can't stop thinking about it."

Noah sat up and I followed. "Why did you stop working on it?"

I hesitated. I considered telling him the truth, that I'd used him as my unknowing muse for weeks, but I doubted that would go over well.

"When I sent the first few chapters to my editor, she reminded me it wasn't the kind of story they published." I shrugged, focusing my attention on the grass in front of me. "Hopefully, one day, I'll finally be able to write something I can be proud of, but right now, I'm under contract to deliver five books with pre-approved storylines. Until I've done that, I have an obligation to write what I've agreed to."

I could feel Noah's gaze studying me, scrutinizing me, unnerving me. When the silence grew to a deafening level, I looked at him. He stood up, holding his hand out to me.

"Come on."

I scrunched my brows. "Where are we going?"

"You'll see."

I warily put my hand in his, allowing him to help me to my feet. I didn't question him as he led me to the closest T station and we boarded a train that seemed to be overflowing with people wearing Red Sox paraphernalia. After a few stops, we disembarked, following the gaggle of baseball fans obviously heading to Fenway for tonight's game. I kept thinking we'd turn away from the crowd at some point, but we continued down Commonwealth Avenue, turned onto Brookline, and headed up the hill toward Fenway Park. Approaching Yawkey Way, Noah pulled out his wallet and handed the gate attendant two tickets. A thousand questions were on the tip of my tongue, but I remained silent.

I followed Noah under the grandstand of one of the oldest baseball parks still standing. Several years ago, the city proposed tearing down Fenway. The fans revolted, the idea of demolishing this park akin to ripping out the heart of the city. As I passed food stands, the smell of hot dogs and pretzels making their way to my senses, I couldn't imagine seeing a Red Sox game without Fenway Park.

Curious, I stole a glance at Noah. He appeared to know precisely where he was going, as if he'd already walked this path hundreds of times. I never pegged him for a baseball fan, but I guess learning all these quirks and idiosyncrasies was part of being in a real relationship.

Skirting through the crowds of people, he led me up a ramp, placing his hand on my lower back. Still not saying a word, he directed me to two seats on the aisle about five rows up the third base line. He gestured to one of the seats. I lowered myself into it, staring at him with intrigue as he sat in the one next to it.

After several intense moments of even more silence, I finally opened my mouth. "Noah—"

"It's in our DNA to try to fill every waking moment with things to do," he interrupted, staring straight ahead. It looked like he was watching the game, but I had a sneaking suspicion that couldn't be further from the truth. "Humans have a tendency to be so busy with work and families, we never take the time to do what we want, do we?" He looked at me, raising a brow.

I wrinkled my nose, unsure where this conversation was headed. All I knew was Noah had taken me to Fenway Park to watch a Red Sox game. From the way he seamlessly found these seats without so much as glancing at any of the overhead directional signs or row numbers, I came to the conclusion he probably had season tickets.

"We're all guilty of it, including me." He lowered his voice. "Especially me." He turned his attention back to the game. "My father was so proud when I got into Harvard. My family didn't have much money. My parents had to work extremely hard to make ends meet. I applied to Harvard just to see if I could get in. I was my class valedictorian, had a list of extra-curricular activities a mile long. Even if I did get in, I knew my parents couldn't afford to send me there. I was the third to go to college. I didn't even know how they were able to afford to send the first two."

I stared at him with rapt attention. For all I knew, we were in my apartment with the game on in the background. I was curious as to why he dragged me here, but I knew there had to be a reason.

"When I showed my father that acceptance letter, there was no arguing. I *was* going to Harvard. He didn't care if he had to take out a second mortgage on the house I grew up in, he was going to make sure I had this opportunity most people would kill for. I'll never forget the look of pride on his face when we said goodbye after he helped me move into my apartment freshman year." He glanced down.

I heard the crack of the bat somewhere in the distance, but couldn't tear my eyes away from Noah. The fans surrounding us stood up, their cheering growing louder and louder, but I kept my gaze glued to the turmoil and regret covering Noah's face. It nearly broke my heart.

"We came here that weekend. He'd always wanted to see a game at Fenway, but never had the chance. When I was growing up, he was always so busy with work that we rarely spent much time together. That weekend, that game, was one of the few times we were able to enjoy as father and son. I wished I had known then what I know now, that it would be the last time I would see my father smile. That it would be the last time he knew who I was." Inhaling a long breath, he shook his head.

"I was so preoccupied with studying and assimilating to college life, I ignored everything else going on, including the people who were making huge sacrifices just so I could be there. My father kept reaching out to me, saying he hoped to take some time off from the second job he got, in order to afford my tuition, and visit me so we could catch another game together. Instead of agreeing, I made excuses. I had to study. I had plans. I had a date. I had to work. I'd see him during the next school break." He ran his hand over his face. "Then I stopped answering his calls altogether.

"I'd made a new life for myself up here. I had new friends, a job in a research lab, a girlfriend I thought I'd spend the rest of my life with. Those were my priorities when it should have been my family. It took my dad's diagnosis to make me realize I had everything backwards." He looked at me, a fierceness in his expression.

"When I went home the following summer, the disease had begun to take its toll. He was confused. He didn't know who I was. All the things I said we'd eventually do were thrown out the window." He returned his attention to the game.

"That October, I got the phone call I'd been dreading. I remember sitting in my bedroom, not knowing how I was supposed to feel. I knew I needed to go home to be with my mother and sisters, but I somehow found myself wandering to this area of town. It was almost like an outside force pulled me here. I bought two tickets from a scalper and watched the Red Sox play the Yankees in the playoffs. It may sound strange, but I felt my father with me during that game. I come here as much as my schedule allows because it's the one place I can still feel him."

I reached out and grabbed his hand. He offered me a small smile, then his eyes became intense, almost pleading. "There will always be an excuse for why you can't do something, why you have to wait. You can tell yourself you'll do it eventually, that you'll get to it someday. What if there's no tomorrow?" he said passionately.

I furrowed my brows, confused.

"I would give anything to be able to sit here with my father and watch the Sox play," he added with a subtle quiver. Taking a deep breath, his intense eyes locked with mine. "What I'm trying to say is I think you owe it to yourself to do what makes *you* happy, not someone else. If going back to the initial draft of your book is what makes you happy, that's what you should do. There are too many people who have been beaten down by their jobs and other responsibilities." He leaned toward me, the depth and fire in his gaze making my hair stand on end. "Don't make the same mistakes I did, Molly."

~~~~~~~~~~

"I'M GOING TO DO it," I said to Noah as he walked me up the front steps of my building.

We'd stayed for the remainder of the game, the heaviness between us being replaced by the fun atmosphere of the ballpark. Regardless, his plea consumed my thoughts all evening. I'd often felt writing no longer held the passion and zeal it did when I first started. Back then, I couldn't wait to get in front of my laptop to write. I'd often woken up in the middle of the night just to get in a few hundred more words. Now, everything felt forced...except for the previous draft of Avery and Jackson's story. That was the first real thing I'd written in years. The spark and excitement I felt when I first began writing had returned.

"Do what?" Noah cocked his head at me.

"I shouldn't wait to write what's in my heart. I'm going to write what *I* want to write, not what my publisher wants. You never know." I shrugged. "Maybe once they see the final draft, they'll actually like it." I just hoped I'd be able to find the draft on one of my hard drive backups. Even if I had to start again from scratch, it would be worth it to finally write something real.

A brilliant smile crossed his face as he drew me into his arms. "I can't wait to read it."

"Me, either," I replied, less than enthusiastically. I didn't see how I'd ever be able to share this story with Noah. It would be clear as day I used him as my inspiration.

He pulled back, studying me. "Is everything okay?" he asked guardedly.

I put on a fake smile. "Of course."

"Are you sure?"

I reached up and toyed with the little tufts of hair that fell over his collar. "It's just a little scary pushing the boundaries."

"If no one pushed the envelope, we'd still be living in the dark ages. Just remember that."

"I'm not sure I could survive without internet," I responded, lightening the mood. "Could you imagine a world with no cell phones?"

"Or phones in general."

"It's certainly not a world I'd want to live in." I grinned, staring at Noah for several protracted moments. Then my expression turned serious. "Thank you for tonight, for sharing all that with me, for opening my eyes."

"You've opened my eyes more than I think you know," he murmured. His words chipped at another piece of the wall around my heart.

I stood on my toes and our lips met, the kiss soft, unhurried, perfect. I'd never been kissed the way Noah kissed me...with tenderness, with passion, with heart. He wasn't just kissing me as a means to an end. He kissed me in a way that made me think he couldn't go another second without providing me the warmth and affection only his kisses could give.

"Do you want to come up?" I asked in a breathy voice.

He closed his eyes, leaning his forehead on mine. "You know damn well I do, Molly." He released a heavy sigh. "But not tonight."

Arching my body toward his, I tugged on his belt. "You can't stand there and tell me you don't want me," I murmured, nibbling on his bottom lip. "I can feel how much you do." My hand brushed the erection forming in his pants.

He grabbed my wrist and forced me against the door, pressing his body into mine. "You're not playing fair." His eyes grew hooded.

"I've been a bad girl. I think I need a spanking." I raised my brows.

"Fuck," he exhaled through gritted teeth. "You're making this extremely hard for me."

"No pun intended?" I traced circles against his neck with my tongue, savoring the slight stubble on his chin.

"Pun *definitely* intended."

"I can help take care of that little problem," I reminded him in a sweet voice. "Or, if memory serves me correctly, not so little problem."

"And I want you to." He gently thrust against me, his breathing growing ragged. "But not tonight." He stepped back, releasing his hold on me. I was surprised at the strength of his resolve.

"Why?"

He studied me, and I could sense his reluctance. "What I said last night *is* true, but it's not the only reason," he admitted finally. "I *do* want to date you without you thinking I expect something in return.

284

Your presence and company is all I ever want."

"What's the other reason?"

He paused, then licked his lips. "I don't want you to run again," he answered softly.

"I didn't—"

"You did, Molly," he interrupted. "Something spooked you in the light of day yesterday morning. So much so, you didn't go visit your father. You've never missed a day in all the months he's been at the home. Call me crazy, but I have a feeling it had to do with what happened between us." He clasped my hands in his, looking at me with earnest. "I don't want you to get scared again. I need you to know this is the real deal, Molly. I've got both feet in."

The remnants of that wall around my heart came tumbling down. I flung my arms around him, happy to remain in his embrace. I marveled at how different everything was with him. It was oddly refreshing to be able to stand by my front door, a beautiful man's arms wrapped around me, with no expectations of anything more than a breathtaking kiss.

Before Noah, I felt like a tourist in my own life, each guy I slept with just another site to see in my travels. Now, as I relished in the warmth of Noah's caring embrace, I felt like I'd finally found my way back home.

Chapter Twenty-Five

A SUBTLE KNOCK SOUNDED on my apartment door and I rushed down the hallway, carrying a pair of strappy heels. I checked my reflection in the mirror, my smile wide. Tonight marked Noah's and my one month "dating, not fucking" anniversary. I had a good feeling tonight would finally be the night he caved. It didn't matter that Noah and I had already had sex and had been doing plenty of other things over the past few weeks to satiate our thirst. Excitement had bubbled in my veins all day as I wrote Avery and Jackson's first sex scene. Thankfully, I'd been able to find a recent version of my original draft on one of my backups.

Turning from the mirror and smoothing the lines of my silky red gown, a long slit showing off my leg, I opened the door. It felt like the breath was knocked out of me when I was treated to the sight of Noah in a tuxedo. I'd seen him in suits almost daily, but there was something about the crisp lines and contrast between the deep black and stark white that made me completely weak in the knees. He took tall, dark, and handsome to the next level.

"Wow," I exhaled.

A smile tugged at his full lips as his eyes raked over my body. "I could say the same about you." He leaned toward me, his breath warming my neck. "You look good enough to eat."

"Molly's House of Pussy is open twenty-four hours a day," I murmured, lost in the feeling of his lips on my skin. I was ready to combust with the amount of sexual tension that had built between us for the past month. I felt like a virgin who was about to offer her body and heart to the man she thought she'd spend the rest of her life with. In fact, I couldn't remember being this eager when I had sex the first time. Then again, there was nothing romantic about losing my virginity in a fraternity house my senior year of high school. He thought we were soul mates. I just used him for his fake ID.

"I'll keep that in mind." He pulled back, winking, then handed me a long, narrow box.

"What's this?"

"Just a little something I thought you should have."

I tugged the ribbon loose and opened the box, my eyes falling on the silky royal blue material. I pulled it out, giving Noah a coy look.

"You thought I should have your tie?"

"That's not just any tie," he reminded me.

"Oh, I know that. I have an impeccable memory." I'd never forget tugging on this exact tie the night we'd first slept together.

He licked his lips. "Then you should recall I wanted to save that for later."

I nodded, my heart rate picking up at the hunger and yearning in his clear blue eyes.

"I believe later has arrived, Ms. Brinks."

A chorus in my head began singing "Hallelujah!" as electricity ran through me. I wanted to do a happy dance and tell the world I was finally getting laid tonight.

I grabbed his hand and started toward the bedroom.

I didn't care about the dinner for some foundation he was on the board of. I didn't want to waste a second.

"Whoa!" Noah pulled his hand from mine, then locked me in an embrace. "First things first." He planted a benevolent kiss on my lips. "We have to get through this evening."

"Why?" I whined. "Do you have any idea how frustrated I've been?"

"All part of my master plan."

"Your master plan sucks."

"Perhaps, but just imagine how amazing it's going to feel later on tonight." He grasped my hand again, pulling me toward the front door. Spotting my overnight bag, he grabbed the handle. "Ready?" He raised a brow.

"More frustrated than anything," I huffed.

"You and me both." Winking, he stepped out of my apartment. I slipped on my shoes and found my clutch, then locked the door behind us. I followed him onto the street where a limo waited, much to my surprise.

Thinking of all the fun we could have in the back seat, I didn't even notice when I almost ran into someone.

"Shit. Sorry," I offered, then did a double take. "Drew?" I cocked a brow, studying his appearance. His normally scruffy hair was short and well-groomed, his beard gone. He wore a charcoal, tailored suit that looked impeccable on him. I hadn't seen him this dressed up since his hockey days. "What are you doing wearing a suit?"

"Molly." He drew in a shaky breath. "I...," he stammered. "I just had some business to attend to." He tore his worried expression from mine. "Good to see you, Noah."

"You, too, Drew."

"Are you sure everything's okay?" I asked. It felt like I hadn't seen much of him lately. Between my deadline, spending time with Noah, and the girls being out of school for the summer, both of our lives had been hectic.

"Yeah. Everything's great. Better than great." He smiled, reassuring me. "Listen, there are a few things I need to talk to you about."

My breath caught, unease visible on my face.

"It's nothing serious," Drew interjected quickly. "But let's try to get together for a drink sometime next week, okay?"

My shoulders relaxing, I stood on my toes, planting a kiss on his smooth cheek. "You got it. Love ya, Drew."

"Love ya, too, Molly Mae. You look great tonight," he whispered. "Noah looks good on you."

"I think so, too." I gave him a smile, then walked to the waiting limo.

"Ready?" Noah asked.

"Yes," I answered, although I really just wanted to get this dinner over with so I could spend the evening in a luxurious hotel room where Noah and I would do anything but sleep.

He helped me into the limo, then slid in beside me. Once settled, the driver pulled into traffic.

When Noah had asked me to accompany him to this gala, my gut instinct was to tell him no. I'd be surrounded by people on a completely different intellectual level than I was. I couldn't help but think bringing me to something like this would make Noah realize I wasn't good enough for him. Thankfully, Brooklyn had come to the rescue and convinced me nothing could be further from the truth. Now, as I looked down at my dress, I found myself reconsidering.

"Everything okay?" Noah asked, cutting through my thoughts.

"Of course," I answered quickly.

"Molly…," he countered, a hint of caution in his tone. Regardless that we'd only been dating for a month, he somehow always knew when I was lying. Apparently, I had a really shitty poker face. "What is it?" He linked his fingers with mine. The contact comforted me, but it was short-lived.

"Are you sure you really want to take me to this thing? You can drop me back off at my apartment. I'd completely understand."

His brow furrowed. "Why do you say that? You're my girlfriend, Molly. Like I've told you before, I want everyone to know you."

"But this is different than just going to dinner with your college friends. You're on the board of this amazing foundation that's done so much to advance research to try to prevent Alzheimer's. You've done so much with your life." I lowered my eyes, avoiding his gaze. "I can't compete with that. All I've done is write a bunch of books that are filled with a lot of kinky sex."

"Oh, is that all?" I could hear the sarcasm in his voice. "Most people couldn't even fathom being able to do what you do. To make people fall in love with your words, to feel what your characters feel, to cry, laugh, and cheer with them." He leaned toward me, his lips a breath from mine. "To be so turned on, they go jump on their spouses. That's a fucking gift." He ran his fingers down the line of my neck, the contact light as a feather. "*You're* a fucking gift."

Noah's lips met mine, his kiss tender, soft, reverent. I didn't know how he did it, but he always seemed to know exactly what I needed to hear. For years, I'd masked my fears and insecurities in my sarcasm and writing. It was freeing to be able to finally give a voice to all these things I'd kept locked inside.

"Are you sure I can't persuade you to skip tonight and just go straight to the hotel room?" I nibbled on his lower lip.

"And waste such a stunning dress?" His hand skimmed my stomach, making me desperate for more of him. "I've been looking forward to dancing with you all week."

"I know a few horizontal dance moves we can do instead." I wiggled my brows.

He laughed, his smile reaching his eyes. "I don't doubt that. Believe me, we'll get to those. All in due time, Ms. Brinks."

Chapter Twenty-Six

"THIS WAY," NOAH INSTRUCTED as he led me into the lobby of a luxurious hotel across the street from the Common. My heels clicked on the marble tile of the cavernous entrance, people dressed in designer clothes surrounding me. He steered me down a long corridor and toward a palatial ballroom. Crystal chandeliers hung overhead, servers roamed the room carrying champagne on trays, and guests wearing beautiful gowns and perfectly tailored tuxedos milled about.

Spotting the bank of restrooms just past the entrance, I turned to Noah. "Can you excuse me for a minute?"

"Are you okay?"

"Of course. I just need to reapply all the lipstick you kissed off in the limo, you fiend."

"I don't think you'll be complaining about that later tonight."

"Or sooner, if I have *my* way." I winked.

"Is that a challenge?"

I gave him a demure look, then walked away. Able to feel a pair of lust-filled blue eyes watching my every move, I swayed my hips a little more than necessary and slipped into the restroom. Once inside, I locked myself in a stall, shimmying out of the pair of red silk panties. I grinned as I considered how Noah would react when he found out I wasn't wearing anything under my dress.

I scrunched my panties in my hand and left the restroom, spotting Noah chatting with a group of people. When he saw me walking toward him, his smile brightened and he excused himself from whomever he was speaking to.

"What is it?" he asked, noticing the conniving expression on my face.

"Let the games begin, Dr. McAllister," I whispered, shoving my panties into his hand.

He looked down, toying with the soft fabric, then shot his eyes toward mine. Stuffing them into the pocket of his pants, he bit his lip, his nostrils flaring. He brought my body against his, gripping my hip hard. "Are you telling me you have nothing on underneath this gorgeous dress of yours?"

"How observant of you."

His hold on my hip tightened as he blew out a heavy breath. "You're killing me, Molly."

"That's the point." I smirked.

"You'll pay for this later." His tone was deep, guttural, hungry.

"I do hope so."

"Dr. McAllister!" a voice called out.

Noah shot his head in the direction of the voice, secretly adjusting himself. He cleared his throat. "Daniel!" He placed his hand on the small of my back and leaned toward me. "I'll deal with your panty issue later," he muttered. "For now, there's someone I'd like you to meet."

"Great." I plastered a smile on my face. Once I gave Noah my panties, I'd hoped we'd rush straight upstairs. No such luck. I was going to have to up my game.

Skirting the tables and the hundreds of guests, Noah led me across the floor toward a man of average height with broad shoulders, sandy hair, and narrow eyes. When his features became clearer, I inhaled quickly, my heart dropping into the pit of my stomach. Bile rose in my throat.

"Good to see you again, Dr. McAllister," he said, shaking Noah's outstretched hand.

"You, too, Daniel. I appreciate the mayor taking the time to make some remarks here tonight."

"Not at all. As you know, his mother suffered from this horrible disease." He offered a tight smile.

"Daniel, this is Molly Brinks. Molly, this is Daniel Cardiff, the mayor's chief of staff."

Everything seemed to move in slow motion as Daniel turned to me, his smile becoming borderline salacious. I wanted to smack it off his face. "Molly. Nice to see you again."

Noah straightened his spine, shifting his gaze between us. "You two know each other?"

I blinked, wishing I could find a hole to bury myself in. I worried this day would eventually come. That I'd run into someone I used to have an arrangement with. I had shrugged those fears away. Most of the men I'd slept with in the past ran around in different circles. Now I was faced with a ghost of my past, and not even a good one. The idea of Noah learning about all my former indiscretions made me sick.

"Oh, yes," Daniel responded, still the slimeball I remembered him to be when he'd been my muse for a book about an up-and-coming young senator who fell for the daughter of his opponent. Things took a turn toward the end, making me attempt to write my next book without a muse to avoid going through the same drama with yet another guy.

"I know Molly quite well," he continued. The

smugness in his gray eyes made my skin crawl.

"Yes," I said quickly. "It's been a few years. How's your *wife*?" I tried to hide the irritation in my voice. "Is she here tonight?"

While my approach to dating could have been described as unconventional, at best, I refused to get involved with a married or otherwise attached man. Daniel lied to me, insisting he didn't have time for a commitment or any other serious distractions. I took him at his word. He didn't wear a band, and there was no tan line where one should be. I'd never felt as humiliated and guilty as I did when I saw him one day, a wife and two kids in tow.

"Unfortunately, she couldn't make it," he responded, oozing all the professionalism he could muster. This man was the reason I hated politicians.

"Please give her and the kids my best. The Museum of Science just opened a butterfly garden exhibit. You should take them."

His lips formed a straight line, his irritation with my comments loud and clear. "I'll be sure to do that." Adjusting his belt, he looked from me to Noah, offering him a curt nod. "I hope you both enjoy your evening."

"You, too," he responded, smiling as Daniel walked away. Once he was out of earshot, Noah turned to me. "What was that about?"

"Nothing," I insisted. "The butterfly exhibit is really cool. I figured his kids would enjoy it. Alyssa and Charlotte did."

He studied me. "Are you sure?"

My response to seeing Daniel was probably not the best. Still, I didn't know how to tell Noah all the shit I'd done in my past, all the men I'd slept with. Men could hook up with a different girl every night of the week and be lauded a stud. If a woman slept with the same guy for a long period of time but refused to have a committed relationship, as I had done for years, she'd be labeled a slut. I couldn't bear the thought of Noah thinking of me that way.

"Of course."

"You'd tell me if there were?" The compassion in his eyes made me want to tear up. Nevertheless, I lied.

"You know I would." Wanting to move on and forget about seeing Daniel, I stood on my toes, nibbling on his earlobe. "Tell me," I said in a throaty voice, "how are my panties? You seem to be keeping your hand in your pocket an awful lot this evening."

"Do you blame me?" His voice turned light. "I'm not going to lie, Molly. I really want to haul you upstairs."

"I won't protest. Just a quickie, then we can come back down and you can do all your doctor schmoozing."

"There's no such thing as a quickie with you. I told you before that you're a gift. You deserve to be pampered, to have all of your desires and fantasies catered to. I need all night to do that."

"All night?" I lifted a brow.

"That's right." He kissed me softly, sweetly, freely, with no reservations about who was watching. "All. Night."

"I do hope Sir Braveheart is nice and rested."

He threw his head back and laughed. "Come on. They're getting ready to serve dinner. Eat up. You'll need the energy." He placed his warm hand on my lower back and steered me toward a table.

~~~~~~~~~~

AS THE EVENING WORE on, I'd been able to relax and forget about the fact that a vestige of my past sat at the table directly behind me. Noah was right. His friends and colleagues had been impressed to hear I was a writer. Several of the females at the table had heard of me and read my column regularly.

Glancing at Noah to see the pride in his eyes as I discussed my writing, I felt empowered, emboldened. So much so that I even mentioned my alter ego, Vivienne Foxx. Much to my surprise, quite a few people, both men and women, were familiar with my books. Once word got out, the conversation at our dinner table turned down a path I hadn't been expecting. While most other tables probably discussed advances in Alzheimer's research, the purpose of the evening, our conversation had been a bit on the naughtier side. Before Noah entered my world, I never considered what I did to be a real profession. He changed all that. I began to realize that Noah had changed everything.

"I'll be right back," I said to him as we mingled by the bar with a few of his associates after finishing our decadent dinner of roasted lamb. If I didn't think I'd look uncivilized, I would have licked that plate clean.

"Are you okay?" Noah asked. I loved how concerned with my well-being he had been throughout the evening, even going so far as to keep clear of Daniel.

"I'm great, but nature calls."

"You're not going to come back and hand me a bra, are you?" He raised his eyebrows.

"No." I leaned toward him. "The only thing left is the dress," I murmured. "And the shoes and jewelry, of course, but what's the fun in that?"

"Try to keep the dress on." He winked.

"I can't make any promises."

Groaning, he stepped back. "On that note, I'll let you do what you need to do."

I kissed his cheek, then headed toward the restrooms. After I went about my business, I checked myself in the mirror, reapplying more gloss to bring my lips back to life. Once satisfied with my appearance, I headed back to the ballroom. As much as I wanted to finally have some alone time with Noah, I loved how he showed me off, how he looked at me with such pride and adoration, how his hand always seemed to find mine.

A lightness in my heart, I scanned the area for him, finding him standing by the bar. About to make another attempt to lure him upstairs, I strode toward him, my head held high, when Daniel's nasally voice made its way to my ears. I stopped in my tracks, my chest tightening as I watched him approach Noah.

"So, you and Molly?" Daniel remarked over the sound of a jazz quintet playing standards. "That's a thing?"

"Yes, it is," Noah responded.

Daniel whistled. "Careful with that one."

"What do you mean?" he asked curtly.

"I know Molly." There was a sort of innuendo in his tone.

"Aren't you married?" Noah shot back, picking up on what he inferred.

"My wife and I have an understanding. Sometimes you have to go elsewhere to satisfy your cravings, particularly when your wife is pretty vanilla in the bedroom. And Molly was certainly good for expanding my palate, but not for much else. That's just the type of girl she is."

When he put up his hands defensively, I could only

assume Noah shot daggers at him. At least I'd hoped he had. In truth, I would have much preferred Noah knee him in the balls, but he wasn't the type to get into a fight surrounded by colleagues.

"Listen, man. I don't mean anything by it. I'm just looking out for you. I've known you a few years and have seen the women you date. Molly's not it. I hope you don't expect more than just a fun time in the sack. She's not into relationships."

"Not that it's any of your business, but things are different with us."

An ache building in my chest, I stepped closer, their voices becoming louder.

"You can tell yourself that all you want. A whore can put on a nice dress and expensive jewelry, but at the end of the night, she'll still fuck you for money. Like I've always said, some women you date, other women you fuck. I'll let you decide which category the woman you *think* is your girlfriend falls into."

Unable to listen to any more, I spun on my heels, slipping out of the ballroom as inconspicuously as possible. I couldn't help but think there was some truth to Daniel's words. Maybe I was fooling myself to believe I could have a normal, healthy relationship with someone like Noah. Maybe I *wasn't* the type of girl he should date.

Stepping out of the lobby, I drew in a breath of the city air. It was a Saturday evening in late July and the downtown area swarmed with people in search of a good meal, a stiff drink, or something in the middle. I was in search of something, too. I just didn't know what. Clarity? Answers? Reassurance?

My brain playing Daniel's words on repeat, I was lost in my mind as my legs carried me across the street and toward the Common. It was as if they were on autopilot, taking me exactly where I needed to be at that precise time. Just as they had done back in April when I ran into Noah in this very park. I came to a stop beneath the same exact tree and lowered myself onto a nearby bench.

A sudden movement out of the corner of my eye caught my attention and, just like that day all those weeks ago, I was treated to the sight of Noah running toward me. This time, he appeared frantic, agitated, worried.

"Noah." I shot up, pulling my bottom lip between my teeth. I hadn't expected him to find me out here. I had every intention of going back to the gala. I just needed a minute to figure out how to make him see me as the woman he'd gotten to know the past few months, not the woman Daniel described to him. "How did you know where I was?"

"I saw you leave the banquet room and tried to catch up to you. One of the women you met earlier, Karen, was out front having a cigarette and noticed you cross the street." He shrugged. "Once I heard that, I had a feeling you'd be here."

"I guess this place kind of helps me think."

"About what?" He stepped toward me, worry etched on the lines of his face.

"Us," I answered honestly, then paused, avoiding his eyes. "I heard what Daniel said to you." I peered at him, bracing myself for him to end all this.

His expression softened. "He was just running his mouth, like a typical politician."

"Still defending my honor, are we, Dr. McAllister?" I asked in a small voice.

"Always, Molly." He took my hand in his and placed

a soft kiss on my knuckles. "Always."

I met his benevolent gaze, losing myself in the sincerity within. Then I pulled away, lowering myself back to the bench, staring at what I'd been calling "our tree".

"There was some truth to what he said," I admitted. Noah sat beside me, studying me. "Before you, I didn't date. I guess I never saw the purpose in it. I had no desire to go through the hassle of getting to know someone when it would never work out. So I'd just have casual flings."

"Who hasn't done that?" he argued. "Most adults I know go through that stage. It's part of figuring out who you are as a person."

I cocked a brow. "Noah McAllister, I didn't peg you for a player."

He shook his head, a blush building on his cheeks. "I wouldn't call myself a player, but med school can be somewhat grueling. It was impossible to have a real relationship with someone, but I still needed to blow off some steam. A lot of my fellow med students did the same thing."

My tone turned serious once more. "I wasn't in school, but I still had these arrangements."

"And Daniel was one of your arrangements?"

"I had no idea he was married. I met him in a bar by City Hall," I explained, leaving out the fact that I used him as a muse. "I thought he was handsome, mature." I shook my head. "I couldn't have been more wrong about him. One day, when I was at the Museum of Science with Drew and the girls, I saw him there with a woman and two little kids. Then I noticed a ring on his finger, which he never wore when he was around me. The next time we planned to get together, I confronted him and ended it. Apparently, no one's ever told him no before." I rolled my eyes. "Let's just say he had some choice words for me. You got a little glimpse at what those were earlier." I gestured across the street toward the hotel.

"So that's why you came out here?"

"I guess I'm worried you'll look at me differently now that you know the truth about my past. The Molly he knew is not the same Molly you know."

"I already know that."

"You do?"

"Of course." He wrapped his arms around me, pulling me into his chest and planting a soft kiss on the top of my head. "Do you think I'd toss away what we have just because some pompous asshole started throwing around accusations about the girl you used to be? I'm not that shallow. I get you have a past. So do I. I don't care about any of that. Hell, one of your columns is titled 'Confessions of a Serial Dater'. I knew what I was getting into when I started dating you, Molly."

I looked at him, cringing slightly. "See, that's the thing. I didn't really date these guys. We only got together to, ya know…"

"That doesn't matter," he assured me. "Everything you've done in your life, including the guys you had these so-called arrangements with, led you to this very spot on that Saturday back in April. Miraculously, my past led me to this same exact spot. Anything that happened before that moment is inconsequential. The only thing that matters is the now. Nothing else. And right now, I just want you."

Clutching his cheeks in my hands, I brushed my lips with his, my body relaxing at the contact. "Even if you found out something horrible about me?"

"Like what?"

"I don't know." I pinched my lips. "Like maybe I had a strange fascination with clowns and had an entire room in my apartment devoted to the creepy fuckers."

"Then I'd get you a pair of clown shoes to add to your collection."

"What if I'm secretly one of those people on *Hoarders* and have an attic filled with animal carcasses?"

"Then I'd hire a dump truck to clean all that stuff out so you can have a fresh start."

"But what if I had horrible taste in music and made you listen to '80s power ballads around the clock?"

"Molly, I already heard the story about you dancing around to Air Supply in your younger days, yet I'm still here."

I gave him an indignant look. "You can't sit there and tell me you don't enjoy the sultry tones of Russell and Graham."

He cringed. "I'm a bit scared you know their names."

I smiled, deciding now was the perfect moment to serenade Noah with a few bars from "All Out of Love".

"No! Stop!" He covered his ears, his face contorted in pain. It did nothing to dissuade me. I sang louder and with more conviction. Passersby stared, but I didn't care. Noah tackled me so my back lay flat against the bench, but I still sang. "I can't take it anymore!" he bellowed.

Laughing uncontrollably, I finally stopped singing when I couldn't recall any more of the lyrics. Noah loomed over me, his fingers brushing my forehead. His smile faded, a warmhearted expression covering his face as he seemed to study every inch of me.

"Hey," I breathed, the atmosphere between us

turning charged.

"Hey," he responded.

"I'm not wearing any underwear," I reminded him.

He groaned, burying his head in my neck. "Don't you think I know that? That's all I've been able to think about since you put them in my hand."

"Maybe it's time you stopped *thinking* about it and actually *did* something about it."

His teeth skimmed my flesh, fire burning in its wake. "You know what, Miss Brinks?" He leaned back. "I do believe you're right."

Chapter Twenty-Seven

EVERY INCH OF MY body was on high alert as Noah led me down the hallway on the top floor of the hotel, coming to a stop in front of the very last door on the right. Withdrawing a keycard from his wallet, he inserted it into the door. When it buzzed, he opened it, revealing a large living area, the lighting dimmed.

Allowing me to enter in front of him, I walked past a lush sofa and reading chair, heading toward the windows. I took in the view of the Boston skyline. The lights of the city were magnificent from this high.

Noah came up behind me, his breath hot on my skin. "Beautiful," he murmured, snaking his arm around my waist and pulling me against him. I could feel his erection on my back.

"It is, isn't it?" I responded, leaning my head on his chest. I closed my eyes, lost in the feeling of his fingers delicately tracing over the silky material of my dress.

"I was talking about you, Molly." He swept my blonde curls away from my neck, exposing the sensitized flesh on my nape, my little hairs standing on end. A shiver ran through me, the tension that had been building all night making me feel as if I were ready to fall apart from even the most virtuous of Noah's touches. "You're beautiful."

He spun me around and, before I could respond, captured my mouth with a kiss. His tongue swept against mine, his motions measured, deliberate, resolved. He breathed into me, making me feel alive. I ran my hands through his dark, silky hair, playing with the little curls at the ends.

His lips traveled from my mouth down my jawline, nibbling slightly. I craned my neck, giving him better access. He took my lobe between his teeth, his tongue tracing circles on the flesh behind my ear. My core lit on fire from the contact.

"That's the spot, isn't it?" he murmured, his voice husky.

"Yes." I raked my fingers up and down his back. My mind was a blank slate…other than thinking we both wore too much clothing. "Let's go to the bedroom," I begged.

"Not yet." He placed his hand on my back and pressed me against him. "You promised me a dance."

"But there's no music."

"There's always music when you're around."

I sighed, melting into his embrace. How could I deny him whatever he wanted when he said such endearing things? I'd never met a man who could be so romantic one minute, then tell me all the salacious and wanton things he wanted to do to me the next. And I loved every heartfelt and erotic word that fell from that suggestive tongue of his.

He swayed his hips, and I followed his lead. This felt so natural, so right. Our two bodies moved together in perfect harmony, almost as if I knew what song was in his head…and heart.

He began to hum, bringing a smile to my face. It was guttural, masculine, deep. When he finally put words to the music, I rested my head against his chest, lost in the drumming of his heart. Listening to him, enclosed in his embrace, made my soul happy.

"'Bewitched, Bothered, and Bewildered'?" I raised a brow. "Any reason for this choice in song?"

"It seemed fitting for how I feel about you…" He leaned closer. "Completely and unmistakably bewitched."

I met his eyes, swallowing hard. "Do you remember the first time we danced together?"

His movements grew bigger and more assured as he spun and swayed with me through the suite. I marveled at how well he danced, then I remembered he had four sisters. I was certain he'd been forced to dance with them more than he'd like to admit.

"How can I forget?" He licked his lips. "You wore a stunning red dress. Your perfume smelled of lilacs and baby powder. All I could think was how much I wanted to kiss you and how unfair life was that this beautiful, remarkable woman I could never have would cross paths with me. I went to sleep that night dreaming about what your lips would taste like, thinking I'd never have the chance to taste them myself." His words took the breath from me. "I never could have imagined they'd taste as sweet and perfect as they do."

Our lips locked as he expertly led me into the bedroom, one hand placed on my lower back and the other tangled in my hair, supporting my head. It was such an insignificant little detail, but it showed how much he truly did treasure me. With all the other men, there was no passion, no hunger, no romance. I never wanted it. But with Noah, I had all that and more; however, it still wasn't enough to satisfy my cravings.

"Your lips are so soft," he hummed, tracing a thumb against my mouth. "I can't get enough of them. So sweet. So intoxicating. So mesmerizing."

"Holy shit." I quivered, arching my body into his. "I think I just came from your words alone."

"I'm glad to know I can turn you on," he said coyly.

"You do more than turn me on, Noah. You make me feel like I've been stranded in the desert for days without a drink. Now that the mirage of a fountain is so close, I'm desperate for it." I raised myself onto my toes. "I'm desperate for you." I ran my tongue across his neck, inhaling his heady aroma.

"You'll have me. Seduction is an art, a science. One that should not be rushed." His lips hovered over mine, the light tingle of his breath on my skin sending tremors through me. I'd never felt so ready to fall over the edge in my life.

He spun me around, gingerly lowering the zipper of my dress. He peppered kisses across my shoulder blades. "Michelangelo took his time painting his masterpiece on the ceiling of the Sistine Chapel, just like I'm taking my time with you." He skillfully tugged the straps of my dress down my arms. The heat of his fingers on my skin sent a current through me. "When I'm through with you, I want to be the only thing you think about for weeks." My dress fell from my hips, pooling at my feet. "When you shower, I want you wishing I were there with you." His hands roamed my body as I stood naked...except for my jewelry and shoes. "When you fall asleep, I want you to imagine me beside you."

I leaned my head back against his chest, lost in the sensation of his hands and erotic tongue. My heart rate increased as his fingers skirted my stomach, slowly and leisurely making their way farther south. I tried to squirm away but he pulled me against him, keeping me blissfully locked in place. The instant he touched me between my legs, I feared I would shatter into tiny pieces.

His breath danced on my neck, making my core ache. His hand continued roaming past my waist. My chest heaved, the heat of his skin so close unraveling me. He pressed his mouth against the crook of my neck. "When you touch yourself, I want you to be thinking about all the things I did to you tonight."

Before I could react, his fingers found my center. Every nerve ending in my body fired at the same time. I thrust against his hand, a slave to my pleasure.

"God, I've wanted to do this all night." His voice turned harsh, brutal, his motions becoming more unyielding. My lips parted and I released a noiseless gasp. "All evening, all I could think about was how easy it would be to slip my hand under the table and make you come."

"Why didn't you?" I shifted my legs farther apart, chasing the orgasm I saw in my sights.

"Because no one gets to see how fucking beautiful you look when you come except me, Molly. I want every single one of your orgasms, including this one."

He slipped a finger inside and I clenched around him, my cries of relief echoing in the luxurious bedroom. His carnal words and tone turned me on in a way I hadn't expected. Noah was right. Seduction was an art, and he was a fucking master.

I spun around and crushed my mouth against his. I feverishly lowered his tuxedo jacket down his arms, then struggled with the buttons of his dress shirt. He grabbed my wrists, preventing me from ripping his clothes from his body.

"Patience," he crooned in a sly voice. He raised my arms over my head, locking his lips with mine. He pushed me toward the bed. When my knees hit the mattress, he released his hold on my wrists, supporting my back as he lowered me to it. Kicking my heels off, I scooted up toward the headboard, keeping my eyes glued to Noah's.

He licked his lips and loosened his bowtie, then unbuttoned his shirt at a laborious pace. He knew I was on edge, desperate to feel him, yet his motions remained unhurried. Finally, after what felt like an eternity, he shrugged out of his shirt and I was treated to the sight of Noah's defined chest. I couldn't believe this exquisite man was all mine. Noah was the complete package. Not only was he quite nice to look at, he had a beautiful heart.

He climbed onto the mattress, slinking up the length of my body. To my surprise, he pulled that blue necktie out of his pocket, a flirty expression on his face.

"Told you we'd be putting this to use." He winked, then lowered his head, kissing me. Confirming my suspicions he'd done this type of thing before, he effortlessly secured my wrists together with the tie and hoisted them over my head. He opened the nightstand drawer and removed an eye mask. "I'm glad I planned ahead," he murmured as he slipped the mask over my head, shrouding my world in darkness.

They say when one of your senses is impaired, it heightens the rest. That was certainly true. My sense of hearing and touch were amplified a hundredfold as the sound of our breathing grew more pronounced, the feel of his fingers delicately tracing down my body making me jump and writhe. I was exposed, vulnerable, completely at Noah's mercy…and it was the best feeling in the world.

Not being able to see made my skin come alive with

awareness. I could feel the heat of Noah's breath against my flesh as he seemed to travel around my body, a whisper from me. The anticipation made me want to combust.

His lips hovered over mine, tickling my mouth. "I'll be right back."

"Back?" I said in surprise. "Where are you going?"

He kissed me softly. "To get something I think you're really going to enjoy."

"Your cock is something I'd really enjoy. I don't need anything else," I panted with desperation.

"You're my masterpiece, Molly. I need to take the time to savor your perfection."

"Fuck," I breathed, squirming into the mattress. "I'm pretty sure I just came again."

He chuckled. "My plan is to make you come over and over again all night long." He placed a quick kiss on my lips, then I felt the mattress shift. His footsteps grew quiet, followed by the sound of our suite opening and closing. I had no idea how he could remain so composed when I was ready to fall apart. I squeezed my legs together, shifting and twisting to find some sort of relief from the dull throbbing. It didn't work. I doubted anything would put out the fire Noah had kindled with his words, his body, his seduction.

Finally, I heard the door open and close again, footsteps getting closer. Almost instantly, a familiar mouth was back on mine, his tongue invading me. "You look amazing like this," Noah whispered. "I can't believe you're all mine." He placed something heavy on the bedside table. I heard the sound of clothes rustling, then he climbed on top of me again. The feel of his flesh on mine sent me into overdrive.

"Say you're mine," he said, his voice husky.

"I'm yours," I murmured.

"God, I love hearing you say that." He kissed me again, the passion in that one gesture stealing all my oxygen. Too soon, he pulled away, the sound of rattling ice making its way to my ears. Then I felt the heat of his breath on my chest. He dragged his tongue across my skin, pulling a nipple between his teeth.

"Do you trust me?" he asked in a quiet voice, tugging and sucking on my breast.

"Yes," I answered. I would have confessed to taking the Lindberg baby just to feel that man.

"Good." I could hear the smile in his voice. Instantly, he pressed a cold object against my other nipple, his tongue still working on the one he had in his mouth. I moaned, arching my back off the mattress. I had no idea what to make of everything. There was something about the coldness of the ice on one nipple and the heat of Noah's mouth on the other that made every inch of my body tighten with anticipation.

Noah was an angel and the devil. He was fire and ice. He was my beginning and my ending.

He ran the ice down my body, his talented tongue following in its wake, warming the frigid chill. My mind was a blank as I succumbed to the pure bliss rolling through my body.

"Noah, please," I begged. "I need to feel you."

"You do feel me." He traced his tongue around my belly button.

"No. Inside me. I can't take it anymore." Every second that passed without him giving me what I needed was pure torture. An ache I didn't think could ever be satisfied consumed me.

He shifted his weight and I heard the glorious sound of a packet ripping open. Finally, I felt him settle between my legs, pressing his erection against my aroused flesh. I braced myself. His mouth found mine, then he eased inside me. I swore I heard angels singing. Or perhaps I was moaning.

His motions were gentle as he pushed into me, then withdrew. I would have given anything to reach out and touch him, to rake my fingers down his back, to feel his muscles as they rippled under my hands.

"You're incredible, Molly." He buried his head in my neck, his teeth scraping my skin. "God, you have no idea how difficult this past month has been."

"I think I do," I panted, wrapping my legs around his waist. "We could have done this weeks ago," I reminded him.

"No, we couldn't." He pulled back, continuing his tender motion. His fingers traced my face. When he removed the eye mask, I was treated to the sight of Noah hovering over me, a look of adoration in his gaze. "It wouldn't have been like this, and this is fucking amazing."

His mouth captured mine as he reached up, loosening the tie around my wrists. I ran my fingers down his back, digging my nails in as I deepened the kiss, meeting his motions. Tightening my legs around his waist, I forced him onto his back, his eyes momentarily becoming wide with surprise, then turning hooded as I increased the rhythm.

I leaned back, lost in the sensation of him filling me to the brim, a current running through me. My eyes rolled into the back of my head, and I was close to the edge of falling over.

"Keep your eyes on me, Molly," he murmured, his tone provocative.

I returned my gaze to his. He reached up, brushing

his hand against my cheek. I melted into him, marveling at how different he was from any other man I'd ever been with. He was selfless in the bedroom, making sure I felt just as much pleasure as he did. He knew precisely what to do to make me crumble into pieces, just as I was about to do at that moment.

My breath hitched as I fought my impending orgasm. Noah sensed it and gripped my hips, driving into me with more intensity. He pressed his thumb against me. The feel of him rubbing me and moving inside me was my undoing. I moaned out his name just as he found his own release.

I fell on top of him, both our bodies slick with sweat, my legs sore. My breathing still heavy, I raked my fingers through his hair, peppering kisses across his jawline.

"Damn, Molly," he crooned finally. Our chests heaved, the only sound in the room that of our labored breathing and the whirring of the air conditioner. I hoisted myself off him and lay on the bed beside him. He pulled me against his chest and I played with the little tufts of hair. "I hope it's not rude of me to say, but I really like fucking you. You have no idea how hard it was for me not to come the second I was inside you."

Meeting his gaze, I smiled, giddy, lightheaded, sated. "I take that as a compliment."

Chapter Twenty-Eight

THE SMELL OF BACON and freshly brewed coffee invaded my senses and I fluttered my eyes open. A subtle glow filled the modern bedroom with simple furnishings. My clothes lay crumpled in a ball on the floor, memories of the previous night flashing through my mind. I didn't think I'd ever tire of falling asleep beside Noah...and all the benefits that went along with it.

My stomach growled, the aroma of fried pig making me salivate. As much as I didn't want to leave the bed, I was famished. Stepping onto the hardwood floor, I found Noah's button-down shirt and put it on. I swam in it, but as I'd learned over the past few months, he loved when I wore his clothes. I loved wearing them, too, basking in his scent that was like an aphrodisiac to me.

I padded out of his bedroom and down a set of stairs in the stunning colonial he owned in the Boston suburb of Melrose. It was September, and we had become nearly inseparable. We stayed at my apartment some nights, but I preferred Noah's house. As did Pee Wee, judging by the way my slobbery hound currently followed Noah around the kitchen, begging for table scraps.

"Pee Wee, you're underfoot," he admonished. My dog simply lifted a paw, giving Noah that pathetic look no one with a soul could deny. Shaking his head, Noah grabbed one of the pieces of bacon and tossed it to him. I didn't even think the dog chewed it before swallowing.

I leaned against the doorway, just watching this beautiful man maneuver around the kitchen. He was truly a sight to behold. There was nothing sexier than a man holding a spatula, wearing only a pair of boxer briefs.

Before Noah entered my life, I would have turned my nose up at couples doing stupid couple things — having breakfast together, holding hands in public, feeding the ducks in the park, pretending they were tourists in the city they called home, and planning weekends away at a bed and breakfast. This was no longer the case. We'd become that cheesy couple I used to feel sorry for. I'd been convinced they were missing out on so much fun and excitement by committing themselves to each other. I'd shunned the idea of being in a serious relationship because I thought the adventure would end. I was so wrong. I'd never felt as fulfilled as I had these past few months.

Noah was my perfect match in every sense of the word. He never turned his nose up when I suggested we do something crazy, like attend random open houses where we would use terms we'd learned from my complete obsession with home improvement television to comment on each house.

"It's a beautiful entrance, isn't it, muffin?" he would say to me.

"It certainly does make a statement, but I had hoped for something a bit grander, like at our summer home in the Hamptons."

"How many bedrooms does it have?" he would ask the realtor. *"Because my wife has quite the appetite, if you know*

what I mean."

For the first time in my life, I was with someone who understood all my quirks and idiosyncrasies. We weren't one of those boring couples I saw sitting across from each other at restaurants, discussing last night's episode of *Wheel of Fortune*, not realizing they had absolutely nothing in common. Noah and I had fun and genuinely enjoyed each other's presence. We didn't have to sit at a stuffy restaurant and make small talk to learn about each other. There were no stilted conversations about our high school crush or our most embarrassing moment. None of that mattered. All I cared about was living in the now, not about what awaited me in the next hour, week, or year.

Noah turned back toward the stove, and I took the opportunity to silently pad into his kitchen. Sneaking up behind him, I stood on my toes and wrapped my arms around his bare torso, planting kisses on his broad shoulder blades. I could feel him smile by the way his body relaxed into mine. Being in a relationship was a funny thing. I'd spent so much time with Noah, I could tell what expression he wore without even looking at him. And I knew, at this moment, he had a look of absolute peace and contentment on his face.

"Morning," he murmured, then slowly turned around.

"Morning."

"I hope I didn't wake you. I just figured you might be hungry after last night's activities." He winked.

"You figured right." I feathered my lips against his. "Although I would have rather had another taste of you first."

He moaned, deepening the kiss. "How about after?"

"I can deal with that."

"Good. Now, go sit. Food's almost ready." His hand roamed down my side, then landed on my ass, giving it an unexpected squeeze. I squealed, then headed to a little breakfast nook just past his large eat-in kitchen. I lowered myself into one of the chairs at the bistro table, smiling to see he'd already prepared my coffee the way I liked it...just a hint of cream and no sweetener.

Noah approached, carrying two plates of food. He placed one down in front of me, then sat opposite me.

"Thanks for cooking."

"I love making you breakfast. Hope the eggs are to your liking."

I grabbed my fork and sliced into the egg, the yoke spreading all over my plate. "Extra runny, just how I like them."

We barely spoke as we ate our breakfast of eggs, bacon, and potatoes. Once we'd finished, Noah placed his napkin on his plate and met my eyes. He reached across the table, grabbing my hand. There was something new in his gaze. A ball of unease formed in my stomach.

Over the past several months, we'd kept everything light and fun. There were no serious conversations about where our relationship was going. Now, as I saw the sincerity in his expression, felt the delicate way his thumb caressed my knuckles, I feared our relationship was about to turn down a road I wasn't prepared for.

"Molly," he began, a look of peace on his face, at odds with the horror that filled me. "There's something I've been wanting to tell you for a while now, but I—"

"Look at the time." I jumped up from the table, tearing my hand from his. "Don't you need to get to work soon? You cooked. I'll clean up." I hastily cleared the plates, feeling the heat of Noah's gaze studying me as I rushed into the kitchen.

I turned on the faucet, hoping the sound of the rushing water would drown out whatever he wanted to tell me. I knew what it was. Over the past several weeks, I'd used every trick in my book to evade this precise conversation. I saw it in his eyes. I felt it in the way he held me. I heard it in his voice. I just didn't think I could bear to listen to those words fall too freely from his lips. It would change everything. Those three words had a tendency to destroy people.

When I started seeing him, I knew this was a probability. I simply hoped it wouldn't happen for a long time. Wasn't there some sort of time requirement before being allowed to say those words? A few months wasn't long enough. How could someone develop such strong feelings in such a short period of time?

After rinsing the plates and putting them in the dishwasher, I went about wiping down the counters. But I could still feel Noah's eyes watching my every move. I looked up to see him leaning against the island, his brow furrowed.

"Molly," he repeated, his voice soft.

I bit my lip, desperate for a way out of this conversation yet again. In my experience, there was one thing that always worked.

A sly smile crawling across my lips, I threw the dishtowel on the counter, then sauntered toward him, heat in my gaze. Raising myself onto my toes, I brushed my lips against his. He groaned, sneaking his hand beneath the shirt I wore, pressing me against him. He ran his hand up and down my side with light fingers. My flesh prickled with goosebumps.

"I need to shower," I murmured. "Care to join me?" I raised a brow, then retreated from him, swaying my hips as I walked out of the kitchen and up the stairs. When I disappeared into the master bathroom, I breathed a sigh of relief, thankful to have successfully skirted the conversation I didn't think I'd ever be ready to have.

Shrugging out of Noah's shirt, I stepped toward the glass shower, which could easily fit at least six people, and turned on the water. I knew I couldn't avoid this discussion for much longer. I just needed time to wrap my head around what this would mean.

Lost in my thoughts, I didn't even hear Noah approach as I stood with my eyes closed, my entire body taut. His hand brushed my hip, then he spun me around, his expression still too tender for my liking.

"Molly, I—"

Before he could say anything else, I forced my mouth against his. He stiffened momentarily before melting into the kiss. He pulled me toward him, our naked bodies flush with each other as steam filled the bathroom.

With careful steps, he backed me into the shower. Our mouths never broke contact. The sensation of Noah's lips on mine and the cascading water surrounding us made me crave him even more. I deepened the kiss, my nails digging into his back.

He tore away from me, his chest heaving. When he stepped toward me, a carnal and fiery expression on his face, my heart raced. With each step he took, I retreated until my back hit the tile wall. The coolness momentarily soothed the heat burning inside me.

With hooded eyes, he gripped my hips, then hoisted me up, forcing my legs around his waist. "Is this what you want?"

I nodded, words escaping me.

"You're insatiable," he murmured, his lips meeting mine once more as he slid into me.

I closed my eyes, savoring the sensation of fullness as he moved inside me. It didn't matter how many times we'd done this, every time was new, unmatched, more pleasurable than the last. Being with Noah was an experience. One minute, he'd be the caring, compassionate man he was when I first met him as my father's doctor. The next, he'd be ravenous, greedy, voracious, his carnal tone and rough, calloused hands bringing me higher than I thought possible. His appetite was just as ravenous as mine, and he always seemed to know exactly what I needed. Noah was a drug, and I an addict who would beg, steal, or maim someone just to get it.

I used to have a plan, a schedule, a routine. I'd get up, wake Drew, have coffee, then write until it was time to visit my father. In the evening, if I felt like it, I'd see whomever my unknowing muse was at the time. Since Noah, that had all changed. There was no morning wakeup call for Drew. There was no coffee by myself. I rarely stepped foot in the café lately. I'd even convinced myself it wasn't the end of the world if a day or two went by that I didn't go visit my father.

I'd become everything I swore I never would...a woman who made all her decisions based on someone else. I'd always been fiercely independent, but over the past several months, I'd become dependent on Noah for my happiness.

"Look at me, Molly," Noah said, breaking me out of my thoughts. His voice was soft, yet demanding.

I met his gaze. His movements were gentle and well-choreographed, the emotion and depth in his eyes too much for me to handle. I forced his lips back to mine as

I thrust against him, trying to pick up the pace. My body and motions pleaded with him to give me something else, something less meaningful, something less frightening.

"Slow down," he soothed. "I want you to feel me, Molly."

"I do, Noah." I ran my hands through his wet hair, tugging at it, unable to make sense of all the sensations and thoughts running through me at that precise moment. "God, I feel you. I feel so much."

"I feel so much, too." He smiled, then licked his lips before kissing me. The way his tongue caressed mine was tender, restrained, benevolent.

I opened my mouth, a tiny exhale of air escaping my lungs. I never understood what would cause someone to be so overcome with emotion during sex that they would tear up. In that moment, I did. It wasn't that my heart was so full it was going to burst. I just felt so much that the only way to soothe the fire in my veins, the ache in my core, the tingle on my flesh was with tears.

"Oh, Molly," Noah moaned, kissing my face, my neck, my chest.

My breathing increased, everything about this moment so much more than I ever thought intimacy could be. I was wound tight, my body perched perilously on the peak, waiting for that final push to make me crumble before Noah's talented body.

Clutching my face in his hands, he held my head in place, not permitting me to hide from him. The simple act of our eyes glued to each other was more penetrating, more sensual, more erotic than him moving inside me. He dug his hands into my cheeks with more vigor, his gaze fiery.

"God, I love you, Molly," he cried out, shuddering

inside me. He crushed his lips against mine, his declaration and the sudden invasion of his tongue in my mouth my undoing. I let go, my brain a slave to the rest of my body.

In the aftermath, as I slowly returned to earth, I didn't know what to think. I remained motionless, my eyes glued to the opposite wall of the shower, wishing with everything I'd simply imagined those words flowing too casually from his mouth...but I knew I hadn't.

A loud ringing echoed in the bathroom. "Shit," Noah groaned. Letting out an aggravated breath, he reluctantly helped me find my footing. "I have to get that."

Avoiding his eyes, I nodded, thanking the gods for intervening. "Sure. Sure." I turned from him, grabbing the loofah.

"Molly?" His voice was full of concern. "Is something wrong?"

"No. No," I answered in a clipped tone. "I'm fine."

I sensed his eyes on my back for what was probably only a second, but felt like hours. Finally, the door to the shower closed and he left me to answer his phone.

I released the breath I'd been holding, looking down at my trembling hands. Most women would be over the moon if the man they'd been dating for the past few months finally said that four-letter word. Not me. It didn't matter that I knew the real story behind the motto I'd placed an unhealthy dependence on throughout my life. A big part of me still believed love wasn't real, that it destroyed everything. Why had so many of my friends left their marriages? Why had some of their husbands cheated on them? Why had they been abandoned to take care of their kids? Why did my brother have to sacrifice everything he'd ever dreamed of because the woman who promised to be at his side in sickness and health had no intention of holding up her end of the bargain? I didn't care that my father and brother chose to look past all of that, still holding onto the hope of finding love again. I didn't want that to be me. I didn't want love to destroy me, too.

The door to the shower swung wide and I spun around to see Noah fully dressed, a frantic air about him.

"Is everything okay?" I asked.

He opened his mouth, then closed it, turmoil in his steel blue eyes.

"Noah?"

"I just love seeing you naked," he said finally, a smile forming on his lips. "I have to go into work. You can stay as long as you'd like. I'll call you later. I love you, Molly." He kissed my cheek, pausing for a response. When I remained silent, he blew out a breath, then left.

I remained still, listening for the faint sound of the front door closing. Once enough time had passed and I knew I was alone, I sank to the floor, allowing the water to run over me, despite the fact my skin had begun to prune.

Pulling my legs into my body, I did something I hadn't in years. I cried. And not just a few tears. I cried big, fat, ugly tears, gasping to breathe through my sobs.

I'd always thought I was a normal twenty-nine-plus-one-year-old independent woman who shunned traditional relationships so I could experience everything young adulthood had to offer. Now the realization I was anything but normal washed over me.

I never shed a single tear when my brother was injured, when family members passed on, even when my father got his diagnosis and I had to watch the deterioration of his brain over the past few years. None of that broke me. The one thing that finally ended up being my undoing was a man I cared about more than I should telling me he loved me.

Chapter Twenty-Nine

I FRANTICALLY RAN UP the steps to my apartment. All I wanted was to surround myself with some sort of normalcy to help sort through the chaotic thoughts circling my head. The ache in my heart had only grown stronger as Noah's voice repeated those three little words over and over in my mind. Was I so traumatized by my mother leaving that I broke down at the idea of someone loving me? I had no problem telling Drew, Brooklyn, my dad, and family I loved them. They said the same to me daily. It never made me have a complete meltdown. Why couldn't I let someone who wasn't family love me, too?

Opening my apartment door, I let Pee Wee in, then flopped onto the couch with him. This was exactly what I needed right now...the unconditional devotion of my furry friend. Dogs were the perfect companion. They would never promise to always be there for you, then just decide you weren't enough and head in search of greener pastures. They would always greet you with a smile and more excitement than you probably deserved. They'd never get bored with you. Men would do all that and more. I wasn't afraid of being alone. I'd been alone my entire life. I just didn't want to go through the same heartache my dad and Drew did.

My phone buzzed and I fumbled through my bag, searching for it. My pulse quickened when I saw it was the nursing home. I let it go to voicemail. I couldn't talk to Noah right now. His declaration had shifted the course of our relationship. Everything had been perfect. We had fun. We joked around. We didn't take ourselves or each other too seriously. At least I didn't. That was all gone now.

I curled into a ball on the couch. Able to sense my distress, Pee Wee licked my face, giving me the comfort he knew I needed. There was only one more thing that would make my moment of wallowing in a pit of despair even more pathetic and cliché…chocolate.

I reached for the canister of M&Ms. As I was about to open it, my phone rang again. I shot it an angry sneer. My expression changed when I saw it wasn't Noah, but my editor. I'd all but forgotten she had scheduled a call with me this morning to discuss the final manuscript I'd sent her the previous week after securing a few more extensions.

"Hi, this is Molly," I answered, trying to sound as professional as possible, not as if I were in the middle of a nervous breakdown.

"Molly, it's Tara." She coughed, making me pull the phone away from my ear as she expunged all the shit from her lungs. "Listen, I read what you sent over. In fact, I read it all in one sitting. I couldn't put it down."

I stood up, my pulse quickening. I'd worked with Tara on over a dozen books at this point. She'd never so much as complimented anything I'd sent her before. She was brutally honest to a fault. Her first words to me were usually along the lines of, *"It's got good bones, but needs a lot of help. And do you realize to accomplish some of the bedroom scenes, your hero would need to grow an extra appendage or two?"*

"Thanks, Tara," I responded.

"Don't thank me," she barked back. "I forwarded it to the head of the editorial team and she's in agreement with my assessment. It's a damn good story." She paused as I braced myself for the punchline I knew was coming. "But, like I told you months ago, it's just not what we publish here. We've already granted you quite a few extensions so we'll need to work nearly 'round the clock to turn this story around. You'll see my ideas in the manuscript when I send it back this morning."

Her words knocked the breath out of me, although I knew this was a strong probability. I'd been saddled with nearly complete rewrites before and it never fazed me. I saw it as a challenge. But I didn't want to rewrite this one. I could agree to some minor tweaks to make the story more compelling, more emotional, more gripping. This one was personal for me, a story I felt very strongly about.

"It's still a romance, Tara," I pleaded. "I think there's still some really good bedroom scenes."

Tara sighed. "That's certainly true, but we simply don't do this kind of story at this particular imprint. Our goal here is to deliver something that's sinful, sexy, and sensual."

"So just sex then?" I replied, feeling indignant.

"No. You can do sinful, sexy, and sensual without even getting into the bedroom. A little angst is okay, but there's too much heartache here. And where's the happily ever after? I have no closure."

"I'm not sure how the story ends yet. This is just the first part."

"The *first* part?" she shot back.

"Yes."

"It's over 90,000 words, which is about 10,000 more than we'd like, and you're telling me there's more?"

"Yes. I'm thinking it'll be more of a duet or a trilogy."

Tara sighed again, louder this time, exhibiting her obvious irritation with this news. "Listen, Molly. This is a good story, or I guess the beginning of a good story. But we can't go forward with it like it's written. We don't do heavy drama. We don't do heartbreak. And we certainly don't do series. You can keep the characters and the original premise, but everything else needs to go. I'm sure there will be enough left over to piece this story back together once we get rid of most of the drama."

I pulled my lip between my teeth. "What if I don't want to make the changes you're suggesting?"

"Then we won't be publishing this book. You'll forfeit whatever advance you've received, and it will nullify the remainder of the books we've contracted with you."

I considered what she said. This was my third contract with this publisher. This particular manuscript was the first book in a five-book deal. I'd be losing practically everything. Having to pay back the hefty advance would pretty much deplete my savings.

"I know it's a lot to take in," Tara said, breaking the silence. "I'll send the manuscript back with my suggestions so you can see what I'm talking about. Review it over the weekend. I'll call you Monday to discuss this further."

The line went dead and I sank back into the couch. Noah's stupid declaration of love was now the furthest thing from my mind. Could I throw away all my hard work over the past several months just to put out yet another book with the same regurgitated story and repetitive sex scenes? Or should I stand by my work, publishing contract be damned?

I searched through the contacts on my phone for my agent, then paused. I knew what she'd tell me to do. She'd recommend I give my publisher exactly what I'd promised them so I didn't destroy the relationship she'd helped cultivate over the past several years. Not to mention she stood to profit a considerable amount from this deal with her cut of the royalties she was guaranteed. I knew I had breaks in my publishing schedule that would allow me to release a book independently without violating any non-compete clauses in my contract. I could rewrite the book with different characters and release it then. I hated that idea, too.

I shot off the couch, grabbed my purse, and dashed down the steps. I needed Drew's advice. He'd always been the practical one, and I needed him to tell me what to do. My head told me to do what my editor wanted. My heart told me to stand my ground and back out of the contract. My head usually won, but this time, my heart was much louder.

I burst through the glass doors of the café and made a beeline for the counter.

"Molly," Aunt Gigi said. Her brow furrowed at the frantic expression on my face. "Is everything okay?"

"Where's Drew?"

She tore her eyes from me, scanning the display cases to see if anything needed to be restocked. "He's not here."

"I see that. Where is he?"

"Out," she answered evasively.

"Out where?"

"Why don't you call him and ask? I'm not his secretary."

"That's true, but you know everyone's business. Just tell me where he is."

She let out a sigh and placed a dishrag on the counter, wiping it down. "He's been trying to talk to you about this for a while now, but you've been a bit...preoccupied."

I shrank down, a pang of guilt making its way to my chest. This was yet another reminder of how much I'd changed since I began dating Noah. I'd neglected everyone I once held dear. All for some guy. Drew had reached out to me several times over the past few weeks, wanting to get together for a drink, but something always came up...like Noah's erection.

"Talk to me about what?"

"He bought a house in Needham. He closes on it today."

My eyes widened. "What's wrong with the apartment?"

"Molly, you and I both know that place is too cramped for those two girls. They need somewhere to run around and play outside."

"There are neighborhood parks all over the place!"

The idea of Drew leaving Boston made me panic. We had the perfect arrangement. Now it seemed like everything was ending.

"And why would he commute so far when he could just walk right downstairs to the café?"

Aunt Gigi studied me again, pausing, her lips pinched. "He hasn't really been working here the past month."

"What?" My mind raced. "What are you talking about?"

"Your brother wanted to be the one to tell you, but it appears that ship has sailed." She drew in a long breath, blowing it out as she spoke. "He finally took the coaching job he was offered at Boston College."

"What about the girls?" I argued. This change was too much for me. I'd grown accustomed to having Drew and the girls next door. For the past several years, he'd been one of the few constants in my life. The thought that I'd no longer be able to walk down the stairs from my apartment and into the café to see him was more than I could handle.

"He found a nanny who will be with them when he can't. He'll get most of the summers off, apart from some recruiting trips. When he's out of town, they'll stay with Leo and me. Or you, if you're around."

I shook my head, trying to process everything.

"Molly…" Gigi placed her hand on my arm, giving me a compassionate look. "You couldn't expect Drew to stay here forever. It was a great arrangement while he got back on his feet after Carla, but those girls need better than a city apartment that's only 1,000 square feet. He stayed these past few years because of you."

"Me?" I blinked repeatedly.

She nodded. "He didn't know how you'd react to him leaving, so he stayed. Did you really think he needed to live in such a tiny apartment when he could certainly afford something much larger with the substantial hockey salary he'd collected for years?" She shrugged. "Now that it appears you've found someone, he doesn't feel the pressure to stay anymore."

"What if this thing with Noah doesn't work out? What happens then?"

"You'll be fine." She gazed upon me fondly. "But I don't think you have to worry about that, my dear. I've seen how that man looks at you. He's got it bad."

I gaped at her, immediately reminded of the four-letter word Noah had said to me earlier today. This morning now seemed like an eternity ago. So much had happened in such a small amount of time. It wasn't even noon yet, and not only was I dealing with the notion that Noah loved me, but now my brother had taken a new job and was moving. I still had no idea what to do about my book, either.

It was days like today that reminded me why I hated being an adult.

"I have to go." I abruptly spun around and darted out of the café, ignoring Aunt Gigi's assurances that everything would be okay. I didn't see how.

The sun warmed my skin as I stomped down the sidewalk, unsure of where to go. I glanced around the streets of the North End, a decadent aroma unique to this close-knit neighborhood filtering out of the restaurants lining the street. How could Drew leave all this? This wasn't just a place to live. The North End was home.

I pulled out my cell and dialed Drew's number, listening to it ring repeatedly, only to be greeted by his voicemail. I was aware this wasn't as big a deal as I made it out to be. I'd still see him. I had the most flexible job in the world. I could easily make the twenty- or thirty-minute drive to Needham and work there, the girls running amuck in the background. Hell, I could probably convince Drew to make sure there was a guest room for me.

It wasn't the idea that he was moving on that made me unsettled. It was the realization that I refused to do the same. I'd become so set in my ways, I didn't want to change for anyone or anything. Change scared me. It always had. I wondered whether Aung Gigi was correct in thinking I'd gotten over my fear of abandonment because here I was, wandering the streets of Boston, nearly having a panic attack at the idea of losing Drew and the girls.

My phone buzzed, snapping me out of my anxious thoughts. Hoping it was Drew, I snatched it out of my bag, almost dropping it on the sidewalk. A scowl crossed my face when I saw it was the nursing home once more. I could only deal with one problem at a time. Right now, my most pressing issue wasn't my writing career or the idea that the man I'd been casually dating loved me. It was losing Drew.

I turned into Columbus Park and plopped down on a vacant bench, finally letting out a breath. I closed my eyes, using the time to think. When my phone buzzed again, I glanced at the screen. Relief washed over me when I saw Drew's photo pop up.

"Drew," I answered. "What—"

"Molly," he interrupted, a quiver in his tone.

"Drew?" I repeated, dread forming in the pit of my stomach. "What is it?"

"It's Dad."

Chapter Thirty

BARELY ABLE TO BREATHE through the lump in my throat, I rushed into the nursing home, ignoring Reggie at the desk, and ran frantically through the maze of hallways. I'd walked this same path countless times before. It never seemed to take as long as it did this afternoon. Hesitating briefly when I finally reached my father's room, I pressed my hand against the closed door, unsure of what to expect once I crossed the threshold.

With shaky hands, I pushed the door open and stepped into the living area. It appeared precisely as it had the last time I saw my father. A copy of *The Great Gatsby* sat on the side table, a shoestring marking where we had stopped about two-thirds of the way through.

I continued past the sitting area and approached the bedroom. When I saw my father's palliative care team surrounding his bed, my heart caught in my throat. I raked my gaze over my father's body as he lay there, his skin a blueish tint, his breathing shallow. I shook my head, wiping at my nose. Nothing made sense.

Five days ago, the executive director, Dr. Connors, had alerted us that my father had come down with the flu. I was concerned, particularly because of his fragile state, but they assured me it was mild and he'd been responding well to antibiotics. Unfortunately, due to his increased vulnerability to catching another infection or illness, he hadn't been permitted any visitors while it ran its course. Yesterday, Dr. Connors had called Drew with an update and indicated my father was feeling better, that it should only be a few more days before he could have visitors again. How could he have gone from improving to barely alive in the span of less than twenty-four hours?

I released a small cry. Drew's head shot up immediately from where he sat in a chair, holding my father's hand.

"Molly."

"What happened?" I squeaked out, meeting Drew's bloodshot eyes.

He wiped his cheeks, then cleared his throat. "It's his time, Molly."

Color drained from my face. I heard what Drew said. I just couldn't register what his words meant. He could have been speaking Chinese. I looked around the room, wanting someone to explain to me how a man who seemed healthy and normal a week ago could now be struggling to breathe.

"Ms. Brinks." Dr. Connors, an older man with graying hair, stepped toward me, sympathy etched on the lines around his eyes. I didn't buy it for a second. He didn't care. This was just another day at the office for him. He'd go home tonight, probably pour a glass of wine, watch whatever TV shows he liked, and forget a family had been torn apart just hours ago.

"He was showing signs of improvement yesterday. An orderly tried to wake him for breakfast this morning, but was unable to. He noticed he was having difficulty breathing. It's our belief he came down with pneumonia. He's been in acute respiratory failure all morning." He shook his head. "Because his body had been fighting the flu for the past week, he had nothing left when the pneumonia hit. His immune system was too weak."

"Then give him something! More antibiotics! Something!" I shrieked.

"More antibiotics won't help at this point," Dr. Connors stated very matter-of-factly. "We tried providing oxygen without the use of extraordinary measures, but it's not enough. The oxygen level in his blood is too low. As you know, your father has a DNR, or AND, in accordance with his advanced directive, so we can't intubate. All we can do is make him as comfortable as possible."

I shook my head, fighting back the tears that wanted to break free. I felt dizzy. Every time I tried to capture a breath, my lungs constricted, not allowing me enough oxygen. I couldn't imagine what my father was enduring.

"I'm sure you two would like to say your goodbyes." He nodded to the care team and they filed out of the room, leaving me alone with Drew and our father.

I wanted to pinch myself so I would wake up from this nightmare I found myself in. This wasn't supposed to happen. I knew Alzheimer's was a terminal disease, but there was a small part of me that thought by giving him the best care possible, it wouldn't be for him. He was my daddy. He was invincible. He was supposed to live forever.

Drew got up and led me to a chair, helping me sit down.

"What about Aunt Gigi?" I looked at him. I'd been so distraught after his phone call I didn't even think to stop by the café to tell her.

"I called her after I got in touch with you. She

337

knows."

"Is she coming?"

He shook his head. "She's already made her peace with it. She said she'd rather remember Dad as he was the last time she visited and brought him some of her Braciole." A small smile appeared on his face. My father loved Gigi's Braciole.

Returning my eyes to my dad, I tried to stop my chin from quivering. I'd read his healthcare directive over and over again. He wanted to die with dignity, not be kept alive for days or weeks because of a machine helping his lungs breathe or his heart beat. When he was diagnosed, he knew the risks associated with this disease. This was what he wanted. It didn't make it any easier.

I knew it was selfish, but I didn't care if my father didn't want to be hooked up to machines. If they could keep him alive, I didn't give a damn how long those machines breathed for him. Maybe all he needed was a little bit longer until he could breathe on his own. I knew I was grasping at straws, but I just couldn't come to terms with the idea of saying goodbye to him. What was I supposed to do without him?

I hooked my fingers through his cold, frail hand, holding out hope for some sign of sustainable life. "Wake up, Daddy," I begged quietly, wiping my tears. Leaning down, I placed a kiss on his pale cheek. "We still haven't finished reading *The Great Gatsby*."

I wrapped my arms around his still body. Regret filled me. I would have given anything to go back in time and hug him a little tighter, tell him I loved him a few more times, spend a little more time with him instead of rushing off on whatever date I had planned that night.

"Don't go," I whispered.

A movement out of the corner of my eye caught my attention. I shot my head up to see Noah rushing into the room, his gaze frantic. "I came as soon as I could," he said, out of breath.

I stood up and he pulled me into his arms. I buried my face in his chest. Despite my confusion regarding my feelings toward him, this was what I needed. Only his arms could give me the reassurance I needed that I was strong enough to make it through what was arguably the worst day in my life. Everything seemed to be falling apart.

Dr. Connors barreled into the room. "Dr. McAllister, I don't think—"

"I'm not here in an official capacity," Noah interrupted, his face flush. "I signed in as a visitor."

Dr. Connors formed his lips into a tight line.

"He can stay," Drew insisted. "My father granted me power of attorney. I'm allowed to make any healthcare decisions on his behalf that aren't covered in the DNR or advanced directive. This man is part of our family."

"This facility dictates our visitor policy, not any power of attorney you may have."

"Are you really going to argue about this when our father is about to take his last breath?" Drew's temper flared.

Dr. Connors glared at him, then blew out a frustrated sigh, his irritation with the situation clear. "Fine." Instead of retreating, he stayed, probably worried about Noah being present. Within moments, a few members of the palliative care team returned, an eerie silence falling over the room.

"Will it hurt?" My voice ripped through the stillness. I looked up at Noah. He opened his mouth to respond, but Dr. Connors cut him off.

"No, Ms. Brinks."

I turned my attention to him. "How do you know?"

"He's been given a sedative to make him comfortable."

"So that's it? You give him drugs to make him comfortable, but do nothing to fight the infection or help him breathe?"

"Ms. Brinks," he began, "we've been over this. We've given him all the antibiotics we can. Your father has specific instructions regarding what lifesaving measures he wants. Our hands are tied." He shook his head. "We can't go against his wishes."

A shaky breath echoed in the room and all eyes turned to my father. I pushed out of Noah's embrace and rushed to the chair beside the bed, taking my dad's hand in mine. He wheezed, the staff looking on as if this were normal.

"Will someone do something!" I bellowed, looking up through my tear-filled eyes. "He's dying." I shot my gaze to Noah. "Please," I begged in a small voice. "Don't let him go."

He pinched his lips together, the lines around his eyes creasing with worry. He slowly shook his head, then opened his mouth. He spoke, but I couldn't make out the words. All I knew was he refused to intervene. In that moment, I despised him.

Relentless tears streaming down my cheeks, I rested my head on my dad's hand, clutching it tightly as Drew rubbed my back. I didn't care that a room of mostly strangers witnessed my meltdown. I couldn't hold it in any longer.

I didn't know how long I sat there, trying to comfort my father as his breathing became more and more shallow. A movie of all the fun times we shared played in my mind — the trips to the beach, sledding down the steep hills at the park, swimming in the town pool during the summer, reading. Who was I going to read with now?

A hand shook my shoulder. I sat up and looked into Drew's eyes as he stood over me, tears staining his cheeks. Noah stood just beyond him, unease on his face. I blinked repeatedly, realizing the room had grown silent. Too silent.

"He's gone, Molly," Drew choked out.

A chill trickled down my spine at those words. I turned my eyes back to my father, no longer able to make out his chest rising and falling through my blurred vision.

Dr. Connors approached and pressed his stethoscope against my father's chest, listening for way too many anxious seconds. Straightening, he checked his watch, then looked at one of the nurses, who was holding a clipboard.

"Time of death: 12:39, September six."

In a daze, I stared straight ahead, barely processing what just happened.

"Take your time," Dr. Connors said with sincerity. "When you're ready, someone will be waiting to discuss the next steps." He nodded at the care team and they filed out of the room.

I looked at Drew, terrified at the notion he was all I had left. He touched my elbow and helped me from the chair. "I may as well get this over with and talk to someone about what we have to do now." He ran his hand over his weary face. "Will you be okay for a minute?"

Still in a daze, I simply nodded.

He placed a soft kiss on my forehead. "I'll be right back." He retreated from the room, his shoulders slightly slumped.

Once Drew left, Noah stepped forward. "Molly, I'm so—" He tried to hug me, but I slinked away.

"I don't want your apologies."

Betrayal flowed through my bloodstream as all the pieces clicked into place. The phone call Noah received this morning. The hesitation in his eyes. The sympathy etched on his face. I couldn't help but think this was why he left so abruptly. He knew my father was on death's door when he kissed me and swore he loved me, yet had said nothing.

Spinning on my heels, I rushed out of the room, down the maze of corridors, and out of the building. The sadness that had consumed me as I watched the man who gave me life draw his last few breaths had been replaced with unparalleled anger, obscuring my vision. My suspicion that Noah was most likely aware of my father's condition this morning made the ache in my heart even more pronounced.

"Molly! Wait!" a voice called out as I barreled through the parking lot and toward my car.

I paused just outside my car door, fire in my gaze. "What do you want, Noah?" I wished a tornado would come and whisk me away to Oz or somewhere. I had enough drama in the past few hours to last a lifetime. I kept running through all the stupid jokes my father used to tell that made me laugh until I cried. Now they only made me more upset. I could still hear his warm voice in my head telling joke after joke, regardless that I'd already heard them a thousand times.

Why didn't the melons get married? Because they cantaloupe.

Did you hear about the guy who broke both his left arm and left leg? He's all right now.

People wonder why I call my toilet The Jim instead of The John. It's so I can say I go to The Jim first thing every morning.

Fighting back my tears, I took a long breath, my eyes becoming narrow slits. "I can't even stand to look at you, Noah," I choked out. "You just watched me say goodbye to my father and you did *nothing*!"

"Molly…" He reached out for me, but I avoided his touch.

"I begged you, Noah! You saw how upset I was, yet you let him die."

"Do you think I wanted to be in that position? I wasn't here today as a doctor. I came to offer you support," he explained, his shoulders falling. "Even if I *were* here as a doctor, I still couldn't go against your father's wishes just because you wanted me to."

"I get it. Your job responsibilities come first. Now I know why you didn't say anything when you got that phone call this morning. You knew my dad was dying and said *nothing*." I spun around, opening the door to my SUV. I knew I sounded completely irrational, but I was upset, angry, at a loss. I needed to take it out on someone.

"You know damn well that's not true, Molly!" His voice was strong, almost violent. He clutched my arm and forced me to face him. "I had absolutely no knowledge of your father's condition until Drew called me!" He loosened his hold, lowering his voice. "I was called to the hospital on an emergency case…a young woman who'd been having unexplained seizures. When Drew called to tell me what was going on, I rushed right over."

"Yeah. Sure," I scoffed.

"Goddammit! It's the truth!" He gripped my biceps

once more, fire and pain in his eyes.

"Molly?" a voice called out. "Is everything okay?"

Releasing his hold on me, Noah jumped back as we both snapped our heads to see Drew heading toward us, his eyes wide with concern. I took the opportunity to make my escape. I jumped into my car, slammed the door, and peeled out of the parking lot. Glancing in the rearview mirror, I could see the surprise and confusion plastered on both their faces.

Chapter Thirty-One

"MOLLY," DREW WHISPERED, NUDGING me as I sat in an uncomfortable chair, staring at a giant photo of my father that had been placed on an easel. His dark eyes had so much life. His smile was contagious. Anyone could see how much charisma he had. He looked nothing like the man he'd become in his later days.

A blank expression on my face, I turned to Drew.

"We need to start. We can't wait any longer."

"Five more minutes?" I begged.

"We've already waited five more minutes...several times."

Biting my lip, I closed my eyes.

"If you don't feel comfortable speaking, I can do it for you," Brooklyn interjected, clutching my hand.

I faced her, giving her a small smile. I didn't think I would have been able to get through the past few days without Drew and Brooklyn. She'd pretty much been living at my apartment while I went through the motions of getting ready to say goodbye to my father. She'd even taken it upon herself to turn Noah away each and every time he came to see me. She never pushed me when I refused to talk to him, although I knew she didn't exactly agree with how I was treating him. She was a good friend...better than I'd ever been to her.

"I can do it," I assured her, then returned my eyes to

Drew. "We can start." I glanced past him to a chair with a reserved sign on it. I didn't know why I'd hoped my mother would be here. She'd never shown up to anything else in our lives. Why start now? I supposed I had some misguided hope that she still cared about my father. I guess I was wrong.

Drew offered me a tight smile, then nodded at the priest. Father Russo had been hesitant to agree to lead the memorial service since it was being held at the local Sons of Italy, not a church, and my father had been cremated, but Aunt Gigi worked her magic, as she always did, and the Father had come around.

When Father Russo approached the podium and started the service, I zoned out, as I'd often done over the past several days. I'd lost count of the number of times Brooklyn caught me standing in the hallway of my apartment, staring into space. I would have given anything to have just a few more days with my father. To have spent more time with him when I was growing up. To talk to him more, instead of locking myself away in my room.

After listening to several people say a few words, I felt a squeeze on my arm. I shot my eyes to Drew. "It's time, Molly," he said.

"Oh." I looked at the small stage, Father Russo's eyes encouraging me. I gingerly raised myself onto my unsteady legs and made my way up to the podium. I scanned the large number of people who had come to pay their final respects. Judging by the sheer size of the crowd, it was more than apparent Vincenzo Brinks...or Enzo, as most people called him...was well-liked in our tight-knit community.

"When I was eight, my father bought me my first journal," I began in a small voice. "I needed a way to let out my feelings, and being an eight-year-old girl without a mother limited my options. So I began to journal. And I still journal to this very day." I clutched the podium, briefly looking down before returning my eyes to my father's friends and family.

"Four days ago, after I watched Dad draw his very last breath, I went back to my apartment, feeling lost. I'd never known a world without my dad in it." I struggled to fight back my tears. "Needing the comfort of an old friend, I took out my journal and started to write. But I could only think of four words… *My father is gone.* I wrote those words over and over." Biting my quivering lip, I shook my head. "Even after seeing pages and pages of that one line, the truth of it didn't sink in. Standing up here, I can admit it still hasn't. I don't know if it ever will. Every time I've gone down into our café, I feel him there. I can hear him singing as he wipes down the counters. I can see him interacting with the customers, telling those stupid jokes over and over again. And I can feel the love he had for life.

"My father didn't have it easy. I couldn't imagine having to raise two kids on my own." I looked to Drew, Alyssa and Charlotte beside him. "But everything happens for a reason. My Aunt Gigi always says that God doesn't give us anything we can't handle. And my dad handled raising us with more enthusiasm than I think we deserved…at least *I* deserved. All little girls look up to their fathers. He's our point of comparison for all men we meet in our lives. Although I didn't realize it at the time, my father set the bar very high. I wish I had told him that."

I looked around the crowd, seeing tears trickling down so many people's faces. I couldn't help but think my father would have hated this. He didn't want people to mourn his passing. He would have wanted them to celebrate his life.

"If you've ever been to the café, you know my father loved his jokes. Whenever someone came in and looked like they were having a rough day, he'd work his magic." I smiled warmly at my memories of sitting behind the counter with him, watching him interact seamlessly with everyone. "I certainly have some of my favorites. I'm sure you all do, too. Who wants to share one?" I asked, completely going off my prepared speech.

An older man toward the back raised his hand, then stood up. "What's the difference between roast beef and pea soup?" He paused. "Anyone can roast beef, but nobody can pea soup."

A small chuckle rippled through the audience. It warmed my heart. As the laughter died down, someone else stood up. Then another. And another…until nearly everyone had shared a joke, including Alyssa and Charlotte.

"Why don't teddy bears ever order dessert? Because they're always stuffed."

"Why did the scarecrow keep getting promoted? Because he was outstanding in his field."

"If money doesn't grow on trees, why does every bank have so many branches?"

"Two men broke into a drugstore and stole all the Viagra. The police better be on the lookout for two hardened criminals."

With each joke, the laughter became louder and louder.

Aunt Gigi stood up, the tears that had been flowing freely replaced by a bright smile. "What car does Jesus drive? A Chrysler."

Drew raised himself from his chair. He always hated my father's jokes. Now I think he realized the importance of them. "It's game seven of the Stanley Cup. A man makes his way to his seat on center ice. He sits down and notices the seat next to him is empty. He leans over and asks the person on the other side of the empty seat if someone's sitting there. The man tells him no, the seat is empty. 'That's amazing,' the man says. 'Who would have a seat like this for the Stanley Cup and not use it?' The other man responds, 'The seat belongs to me. My wife was supposed to be here with me, but she passed away.' 'I'm so sorry to hear that,' the man offers. 'Couldn't you find someone else to take the seat? A relative or friend, perhaps?' The neighbor shakes his head. 'No. They're all at the funeral.'"

The audience roared with laughter. Once it all died down, I approached the podium again. "When I was younger, I remember asking Dad why old people had so many wrinkles. He told me it was a way to show they lived a good life. Each wrinkle was a memory they wanted to keep close for when they had trouble remembering. My dad had a lot of wrinkles." I swallowed past the lump in my throat. "Because of that, I know he had a good life. Thank you for being a part of it."

I offered the crowd a small smile, then returned to my chair. Drew draped his arm over my shoulder, planting a soft kiss on my head. "I'm proud of you, Molly Mae. Dad would have been proud of you, too."

I looked into his eyes, struggling to keep myself together. "Thanks, Drew."

"You bet, kid."

I snuggled into his chest and clutched Brooklyn's hand, reveling in their warmth, kindness, and support.

It was more than I deserved, but I was grateful for it.

After the service ended, I played the dutiful daughter, mingling and sharing stories with the rest of my father's friends. A few of the staff from the nursing home even made an appearance. I'd been concerned Noah would show up. I didn't know if I could stomach seeing him. Not today. I didn't think I ever could after everything.

As I listened to one of my father's childhood friends regale the crowd with a humorous story of my father stealing bras off of the neighborhood clotheslines and hoisting them on the flagpole at the high school they attended, a movement in the doorway of the function hall caught my attention. I shot my head toward the entrance, my back stiffening. The air rushed out of my lungs when I saw Noah standing there in a dark suit and that damn blue tie.

Blinking repeatedly, I turned back to the small group. "Will you please excuse me?"

My father's friend nodded, then continued with his story, tears of laughter dotting everybody's eyes.

I scurried away, slipping into the women's restroom. I knew it was childish of me, but I had no desire to speak with Noah. I still couldn't forget his look of hesitation when I begged and pleaded with him to do something to keep my father alive. I couldn't help but think if he had put my needs first, my dad might still be here.

As I was about to lock the door, it burst open. Noah came barreling inside, startling me.

"Noah, what are you—"

"I need to talk to you, Molly, and it appears this is the only way that's going to happen." He widened his stance and crossed his arms, blocking the exit.

My eyes narrowed. "Now is *not* the time. This is my father's memorial," I hissed.

"Then, by all means, please tell me when the right time will be! I waited until the service was over to come here. I've tried seeing you countless times over the past few days! I've barely been able to eat! I can't sleep! I've been so worried about you, but you just keep shutting me out." He approached me, placing his hand on my bicep. "Please, talk to me," he begged, his voice soft. "I'm falling apart without you."

Closing my eyes, I shook my head, struggling to fight my body's impetuous reaction to his skin on mine.

"I love you, Molly."

I flung my eyes open. The same unsettled feeling that formed in the pit of my stomach the first time he'd said those words returned. "No, you don't," I shot back, freeing myself from his touch. "What you feel for me… It's not love. Real love isn't real life. If you really loved me, you would have done something to keep my father alive, but you didn't."

His jaw tightened as he ran his hands through his hair in obvious frustration. "You know damn well I couldn't intervene. You're just trying to find any reason to push me away. You're hurting and you're scared, but you can't stand there and say what I feel for you isn't real." His eyes narrowed. "I've never felt something so real in all my life, Molly."

"Is that true?" I peered at him through curious eyes and took a measured step toward him. A serene look passed over his face, our chests almost touching.

"I wouldn't say it if it weren't." He lowered his head toward me, licking his lips. "I know you feel the same way about me. That's why you've been taking your grief and anger out on me. Because you love me, too."

"Noah," I exhaled, then closed my eyes. His lips nearly brushed with mine before my expression

351

hardened. "You couldn't be more wrong," I hissed, pushing against his chest. "You think this is real?"

Every voice in my head yelled at me to stop what I was about to do, but I was still hurting. And I wanted Noah to feel the same pain that was ripping me open.

"Of course it is."

"Nothing about us is real. The feelings you think you have for me are based on a lie," I confessed, an ache in my throat.

"What are you talking about?"

"I *used* you," I sneered, my lips forming a tight line. I tried to fight back the tears rolling down my cheeks. It pained me to do this, but I couldn't stop the words that fell from my mouth. "The book I've been working on is a forbidden romance. I had writer's block. Nothing helped. I tried everything that had worked in the past, but I was still completely uninspired...until I began spending time with you."

His eyes widened, his jaw dropping as he absorbed what I was telling him.

"*That's* why I spent time with you. Because I was able to write again. *That's* why I kissed you. *That's* why I fucked you. And now that my book is done, I don't need you anymore," I choked out through my tears, barely able to say the words.

"You... It's not true. You're just saying that because you're upset."

I shook my head. "It's all true. Every last word." I avoided his gaze, not wanting him to see through my lies, to see that I *had* developed feelings for him...feelings stronger than I ever thought possible.

"You can think that all you want, but your eyes don't lie, Molly. I see the love in them. I see the desire. I see the passion, the yearning, the hunger. You can't fake that."

"All the guys I slept with before you, even your buddy, Daniel... I used them, too. I've been doing this for years. You don't know how good I've gotten at making people believe I have feelings for them. And that's all I did with you." I swallowed hard, my chin quivering at the notion. "It's not my fault you're too blind to see what's been right in front of you all along."

"I'm not blind at all, Molly. I see you. I see you so fucking clearly. I see a woman so scared of being in love, she's lying to herself about her feelings. Even if what you say is true, I don't give a damn you got close to me because of a book. If that's the reason, I'm grateful. As much as you want me to believe otherwise, at some point, this stopped being about your book and became something bigger."

I shook my head, vehemently denying his accusation.

"You know damn well you care about me, that you love me."

I began to shake my head again, caught by complete surprise when Noah cradled it between his hands. He crushed his lips against mine, trapping my body against his. I tried to fight him, banging my fists against his chest, but I was no match for his strength.

He pulled out of the passionate exchange that left me breathless and lightheaded. "Tell me you feel nothing!" he bellowed. My knees almost buckled at the hunger in his eyes. People could probably hear us, but neither one of us made an attempt to reel in our overwrought emotions. "Tell me you don't feel even so much as a tingle or spark every time our skin meets."

I simply stared at him, unable to form any words. This time, my brain refused to let me admit something that wasn't true.

"Tell me each time our lips touch, it doesn't make you crave more." He brushed his lips against mine softly. A current ran through my veins, my body betraying me. "Tell me that I never gave you an orgasm so intense, you fucking cried."

Memories of the last time we were together flooded back. The passion. The emotion. The power. The tenderness. Noah was right. I *was* scared. Fear always made people do things they'd regret. Just like fear made me push Noah away when I should have been running toward him.

"Tell me you don't care about me and I'll go," Noah's husky voice whispered. "Tell me you'd rather throw it all away."

Biting my lower lip, I took a deep breath, pushing out of his embrace. "There's nothing to throw away." I met his eyes, struggling to get the words out. "Because I feel *nothing*." I spun on my heels and scurried out of the bathroom.

As I darted through the function hall, Drew and Brooklyn attempted to stop me, but I didn't listen. I couldn't be there anymore. I just wanted to curl into a ball and have my daddy assure me everything would be okay. But that was no longer possible.

Tears streaming down my cheeks, I stormed out of the building.

"You know what, Molly?" Noah's voice called out as I hurried down the busy sidewalk. It was a perfect September day. The sun was shining and there was a crispness in the air. It was the type of day my dad always loved.

I stopped and faced him, remaining silent. He stepped toward me, and I straightened my spine, doing everything I could to rebuild the wall he had disassembled, brick by brick, over the past several months.

"I thought you were this beautiful woman with an even more beautiful soul. So many of my patients are abandoned in nursing homes, their family forgetting about them. Here was this young, vibrant woman who made sure to take the time to visit her father every single day. Where's *that* woman? Because that's the Molly I've been dating these past several months, not the Molly I see today. The one who's just trying to make other people hurt like she does."

"That woman was a lie, Noah." I turned around, feeling like someone had just ripped my heart out as I looked on with morbid curiosity.

"I don't believe you."

With a deep breath, I glanced at him over my shoulder. "So it goes."

He shook his head, his Adam's apple bobbing in his throat. "You don't…"

Observing the disheartened look on his face, I knew he remembered our conversation that very first night together, the meaning those three words carried.

"So. It. Goes," I repeated, more firmly this time. Then I continued down the sidewalk toward my apartment. I expected him to run after me.

He never did.

Chapter Thirty-Two

I SIPPED MY COFFEE as I stared at Brooklyn sitting in the reading chair in my living room, her eyes scanning the final page of my manuscript. Three weeks had passed since I'd last seen Noah. I tried not to think of him too much. Instead, I'd hidden myself away in my apartment and completely rewrote Avery and Jackson's story into what my publisher wanted…sexy, sinful, sensual, with no love. It was now a story of Avery's sexual awakening instead of an emotional one.

Sighing, Brooklyn placed the last sheet of paper on top of the pile that had accumulated throughout the morning as she read the final three chapters of the book I'd finished in the middle of the night.

"And?" I raised my eyebrows, anxious for her opinion.

"It's good, Molly."

"But?" I could sense there was more.

She scowled. "But it's not nearly as good as the original story. There's no connection here. It was pretty much just a lot of really kinky sex. I don't think I'll ever look at a stapler the same way again. Still, it's nothing special. The original was full of so much love and passion, it jumped off the pages and held me hostage. I felt like I was part of their story. I went to bed dreaming about them. I didn't here." She met my eyes, a guarded look on her face. "I want to feel their love again."

"Their love was a farce," I argued, unsure of whether I was talking about myself or the characters I'd made up.

"You can't honestly believe that."

"Why does everyone say that?" I shot back, jumping off the couch. I paced in front of her. "There was nothing real about Avery and Jackson's feelings for each other. Avery simply felt bad for him because of his mother's mental state. Jackson used that to get in her pants."

"But somewhere along the way, he fell for her. It was a *real* connection that I know both characters felt, regardless of what they tried to convince themselves and everyone around them. You...I mean, Jackson and Avery love each other. And I'm not just talking about a high school fling kind of love. I'm talking about big, fulfilling, soulful love. A love to put all other loves to shame. A love unmatched even by Elizabeth Bennet and Mr. Darcy." She narrowed her gaze at me, then softened her voice. "You're just too proud to admit it."

"If he really loved me, how could he just let my father die?"

Brooklyn jumped off the couch. "He had no choice! He's bound by the ethics of his profession, Molly! You're just using this as an excuse to push Noah away. You're scared, I get that, but don't throw away something many of us would do anything to have." She lowered her eyes. "Including me."

I glowered at her, my jaw clenching. I seemed to be having this same conversation with everyone lately...Drew, Aunt Gigi, Brooklyn. These were people who were supposed to support me no matter what. All they had been doing was trying to convince me I was wrong. I wanted to surround myself with people who would encourage me, not tell me I was just one big fuckup. I wanted people to agree with me that maybe, just maybe, my mother had been right all along. That she may have been onto something when she insisted that real love wasn't real life.

Tired of feeling like an intruder in my own life, I grabbed my purse and headed toward the door.

"Where are you going?" Brooklyn called out.

"To see someone who's not going to berate me for being me," I answered, my face flushed with anger. "I'm going to see my mom."

I slammed the door to my apartment and darted down the stairs before she could talk some sense into me. I swallowed hard when I nearly ran into a moving truck parked in the street. I continued past it, doing my best to ignore it. I couldn't stomach another reminder that everyone had abandoned me.

Hopping into my car, I cranked the engine, plugged the last address I had for my mother into the GPS, then pulled into traffic. It was somewhere in western Massachusetts, about ninety minutes away. I just hoped she hadn't moved since my birthday in February.

I didn't know what possessed me to think this was a smart idea. I had little to no communication with this woman since she left us all those years ago. What made me think she'd want to see me now? What made me think I *needed* her now, especially when my actual family had been nothing but supportive throughout the years?

I almost came to my senses a few times during the drive, particularly after I made the mistake of reading a few of Drew's texts when I stopped to get gas. He urged me that dropping in on our lovely mother was the last thing I needed to do. My pride and stubbornness prevented me from listening to him. I needed some sort of reassurance that I hadn't allowed my fear to ruin what was one of the best things to ever happen to me, that the love Noah swore he had for me wasn't real.

Pulling my car off the Mass Pike, I followed the GPS through what appeared to be a pleasant middle-class community. Perhaps my mother wasn't this horrible woman the rest of the family made her out to be. The stories they continued to tell about what she was currently doing with her life painted an appalling picture, but there was nothing offensive about this charming suburb.

I drove past a medium-sized college campus, then through a historic downtown area that was typical of so many small New England towns. As I followed the GPS, the suburban landscape gave way to a more rundown section. I passed what was probably a factory at some point, but had long since been abandoned, front doors hanging on by rusty nails. Dilapidated cars covered in grime were parked in driveways. I tried not to be too judgmental. Perhaps this neighborhood had been plagued by the housing and mortgage crisis all those years ago.

When my GPS indicated I'd reached my destination, I slowed to a stop, apprehensive. I put my Audi in park outside a one-level white house with vinyl siding that probably hadn't been power washed in over a decade, the roof in serious need of repair. A voice inside me shouted to go back home, but I couldn't ignore my own curiosity. I hadn't seen this woman since I was a little girl. I wondered whether she was anything like the image in my head.

Stepping out of my car, a smell that reminded me of an old scrap metal yard hit me hard. I made sure to lock the car, then walked up the gravel drive toward the front door. It was just past one on a Thursday afternoon, a time of day most people would be at work. I considered the likelihood that my mom wouldn't even be here. Perhaps it was a blessing in disguise I hadn't really thought this through. The last thing I probably needed was to see this woman, a woman who didn't want me all those years ago. Why would she want me now?

As I was about to ring the bell, the screen door, which contained no screen, swung open. I was surprised it didn't fall off its hinges.

"Well, fuck me living," a woman with curly blonde hair and bright blue eyes muttered.

She came out of the darkened house and onto the stoop. Her orange and leather-like skin made it obvious she had spent far too much time in the sun or in tanning beds over her lifetime. She was slender, although no amount of good genes could help when gravity took over. She wore a tight black tank top and a pair of cut-off denim shorts. Everything about her appearance and clothing choices made me suspicious she was desperately trying to pretend she was in her twenties, not her fifties.

"I can't believe you're here!"

Much to my surprise, she pulled me into her arms. I weakly returned her hug, unsure of what was happening. The faint scent of alcohol made its way to my senses. Coupled with her slurred speech, I had a feeling she'd already been hitting the bottle today. That probably accounted for the warm welcome.

"Gosh, Molly." She stepped back, holding me at arm's length.

My stomach rolled at the idea I could be looking into my future. We were the same height, had the same color and style hair, the same blue eyes. Growing up, I'd always felt as if I didn't belong, the rest of my family dark-haired with olive-toned skin. Not me. I'd always been told I took after my mother. Now I saw it. We were twins, separated by several decades.

"How long has it been?"

"Twenty-six years," I mumbled.

She furrowed her brow, then quickly recovered. "Well, we'd better make up for lost time." She grabbed my hand and pulled me into her small house. A cloud of smoke seemed to hang in the air, ashtrays filled with old cigarettes on every usable surface. It smelled like a hole-in-the-wall bar in a state where you could still smoke inside. I'd probably get lung cancer if I spent too much time in this house.

She sat down on a torn brown sofa and patted the cushion next to her. I pulled my lip between my teeth, feeling as if the walls were closing in on me. I considered leaving and forgetting I'd ever come here, but an outside force pushed me forward.

I gingerly lowered myself onto the edge of the sofa, avoiding what looked like a questionable stain on the cushion. Despite her less-than-optimal surroundings and objectionable cigarette addiction, this woman was still my mother. I felt the need to give her a chance to redeem herself, although the only interest she'd ever shown in me was keeping my feet warm with a crappy pair of slippers every year.

"So what brings you here, Molly Mae?"

My heart warmed at her use of my name in a singsong voice. It rolled off her tongue with such ease, as if no time had passed since she held me in her arms and sang me to sleep at night.

"I just needed to get away," I confessed, fidgeting

with my hands in my lap. "No one back home seems to support me."

"I'm sure that's not true," she insisted. "What about Drew? He's always been incredibly supportive of you, hasn't he? At least that's what your father always told me."

"Not this time." I rolled my eyes. I struggled to hide my disgust when I noticed a torn condom wrapper underneath the coffee table, a crusty used rubber poking out beneath it. No child should be faced with the idea of their mother having sex. For all I knew, I was the result of an immaculate conception. But it didn't feel like this woman was my mother. I felt no connection to her.

"Tell me what's really going on."

I took a breath, then launched into everything. I brought her up to speed on my writing and how I refused to get too attached to any man, simply using them as a muse. Then I told her all about Noah. How he was dad's doctor and I began spending time with him because I was working on a forbidden romance, but that things changed between us.

"No one will listen to me when I say I never loved him," I said, finishing my story. "I guess I just wanted to talk to someone who will believe me when I say none of it was real."

"So let me see if I have this straight." My mom cocked her head. "You write really sexy romances and have dated guys for the sole purpose of using them as inspiration for your writing, but this last guy seems to have fallen in love with you."

I nodded. "Until I told him it wasn't real."

She studied me, a serious expression on her face. For a minute, I expected her to side with Drew and

Brooklyn. Then she laughed, a wide smile growing on her face. Pulling me against her, I inhaled the combination of vanilla body wash, cigarettes, and hairspray.

"The apple certainly doesn't fall too far from the tree, does it?" She got up and headed into the kitchen that probably hadn't been updated since the 1970s. "It doesn't matter I wasn't around to raise you. You figured it out all on your own." She returned with two shot glasses containing some dark liquid, handing one to me.

"Figured what out?" I'd come here to get some advice, not get drunk.

"You're right. This man couldn't possibly love you."

"Why?" I asked, my heart sinking in my chest, much to my surprise. The idea of Noah *not* loving me hurt more than I thought it would.

"What people think of as love isn't real. It's a temporary feeling caused by hormones and nothing else. Like I've always said..." She held her shot glass up and I hesitantly followed suit. "Real love isn't real life." She threw back the glass. I simply watched her, my stomach churning.

When she saw I hadn't drank my shot, she grabbed it out of my hand and threw that one back, as well. Her face turned up in a grimace before she recovered.

"Come on." She jumped off the couch, tugging me up.

"Where are we going?"

"We're going to make up for lost time. It's not every day your estranged daughter appears on your doorstep and you learn she's exactly like you." She draped her arm over my shoulder. "That's a damn good reason to celebrate. The world needs more smart people like us, ones who see all this bullshit for what it truly is. Could you imagine waking up next to the same person for the rest of your life?" She made a fake gagging sound as a look of absolute disgust crossed her face.

All I could think was it wouldn't be so bad to wake up next to Noah the rest of my life, considering he had proven to be a big fan of morning sex. Come to think of it, waking up in Noah's arms had been one of the things I'd missed most these past few weeks.

"No," my mom continued. "We're the smart ones, Molly. Variety is the spice of life, after all." She dragged me out of the house.

I had no idea what was going on, but I somehow ended up behind the wheel of my car, driving back toward town.

"Take a left up here," she ordered when I reached a stop sign at the end of her street.

"Where are we going?" I asked, putting my indicator on.

"To one of my favorite spots." She winked. "There's a benefit to living in a college town."

My brain shouted at me to turn around and drop her back at her house, then return to Boston, but my intrigue kept me going. I followed her directions and, within ten minutes, pulled up in front of a bar in the downtown area. It seemed odd to be going to a bar in the afternoon on a Thursday, but as we entered, the place filled with college students watching the Sox game, it appeared we were late to the party.

A collective shout of "Josie" echoed as we stepped inside. I should have left then, but I didn't. It was like watching an out of control car careening toward a crowd. As much as you knew you should do something to stop it, you were rooted to the spot, watching.

I heard a crunch beneath my feet and looked down,

noticing the dark linoleum floor was covered with peanut shells. I refused to go to places like this when I was *in* college. What would possess me to want to be here now?

"Don't call me mom or any of that shit," she whispered into my ear as I attempted to come to grips with the fact that the woman who gave birth to me was a regular at a college bar. "Just call me Josie. Nothing else. Got it?"

I turned to her, my jaw slack, but before I could respond, a guy who didn't look like he was old enough to drink approached, slinking his arm over her shoulder.

"Who's your friend, Josie?"

"This is an old acquaintance from when I used to live in Boston," she answered, gripping my arm hard, her nails digging into my skin. "Molly."

Mr. Barely Legal grinned at me. "Nice to meet you, Molly." He took my hand, licking his lips as he eyed me up and down. I couldn't help but feel incredibly creeped out. "Any friend of Josie's is certainly a friend of mine. You two look like you could be sisters."

I pulled my hand away, my skin crawling. "Thanks." I turned to my mom, only to realize she'd already abandoned me.

"If you're worried about talking to me because of Josie, don't be." He slid his finger down the back of my sundress. "We just hook up once in a while. She likes to hit-and-run."

I faced him, my eyes wide. Nausea settled in my stomach. "How old are you?" I asked in disbelief. This all felt like a bad dream.

"Twenty-two." He beamed, as if proud to have managed to stay alive that long. "What can I say? I've got a thing for MILFs. Well, I guess it's cougars in Josie's case since she doesn't have any kids."

"What?" My voice rose, heat crashing over my body. I didn't know why I was so hurt when I found out my mother had been telling people she didn't have kids. She had abandoned us years ago. Still, part of me wanted to think there was some redeeming quality about her.

"Don't worry. I like women my age, too."

I shook my head, swallowing hard. I scanned the bar, seeing my mom across the room, laughing and smiling with another group of barely legal college students. Fire in my gaze, I stormed toward her.

"You tell people you don't have kids?" I demanded, seething.

Irritation covered her face. She grabbed my arm and pulled me to an empty corner, obviously not wanting anyone to overhear our conversation. "What does it matter?" she hissed.

"It matters to me! How could you just leave us so easily?"

"Because that was a time in my life I'd rather forget," she shot back, her tone harsh. "I didn't want any reminder of it. Unfortunately, I'd given birth to two such reminders. So yes, I left, and I didn't look back."

"Is that why you didn't go to Dad's memorial service? I waited for you. I thought maybe you'd care enough to make an appearance!"

With a smug look, she crossed her arms over her chest. "Your father was dead to me the second I drove away from that crappy little house. Like I said, I cut all ties to that time in my life."

I opened my mouth, heat washing over my body. "But you send me slippers! Why would you do that if you didn't care?"

She furrowed her brow. "Slippers? What the fuck are you talking about?"

"Every year on my birthday, you send me a pair of slippers. I still have them all!"

She shook her head. "That wasn't me, Molly. If memory serves, Drew was the one who always got you slippers for your birthday." She threw back a small glass containing an amber liquor. "I never sent you anything," she scoffed, then pushed past me, rejoining her so-called friends.

A knot formed in my throat as I stared at this woman who carried me in her belly for nine months. She was convinced I'd turned out exactly like her. Seeing what my future held if I continued on the same path was the slap in the face I needed. I refused to believe this was what I'd become.

Chapter Thirty-Three

THE SOUND OF THIN blades cutting through ice met my ears the second I stepped into the rink. I hadn't been around the ice since my brother was injured. It felt oddly comforting to be back here.

I headed past the stands, a few students watching the team practice. I had a feeling they just wanted to catch a glimpse of Drew. I often forgot he was still a bit of a celebrity. He'd always just been my brother…the same person who put bubble gum in my hair, who ran over my Barbies with his Hot Wheels, who put worms down my shirt.

My eyes fell on the ice, a slow smile building on my lips. The fact he was covered in padding and a helmet didn't matter. I could spot Drew by the way he skated across the ice so flawlessly. This was where he belonged, not hanging out in some café and bar, wishing things were still the way they used to be.

I climbed up the aisle in the center of the rink. A whistle blew, stopping the players. Drew summoned them toward him. I probably should have waited until practice was over, but I didn't know how long that would be. Standing on a row of bleachers so he'd see me, I shouted, *"Drew!"* My voice echoed against the rafters.

Drew shot his eyes up, scanning the rink. When he noticed me, his shoulders relaxed. "Okay, everyone.

Take five. We're going to do this again, so whatever you need to do to pull your heads out of your asses in the next few minutes, do it."

Removing his helmet, he skated toward the edge of the rink, opening a small door and stepping off the ice. I hurried toward him. Out of the corner of my eye, I noticed a few of the players looking me over. Drew must have noticed, too.

He faced them. "This is my sister, assholes. If any one of you so much as looks at her in a way I don't like, you'll need a permanent ice pack on your nuts."

"Drew," I hissed, jabbing him. "You're the coach. Are you allowed to say shit like that?"

He smirked. "My coaches said a lot worse."

I shook my head. "Men are Neanderthals."

"But you can't live without us."

"Ain't that the truth," I remarked, hugging my body to try and warm myself. A sundress wasn't exactly the proper attire for an ice rink.

"Good to see you, Mols," he said, studying me. "You look...better."

"I just got back from seeing Mom," I blurted out.

He briefly closed his eyes. "So you went through with it."

"I don't know what I was thinking. The second I got in my car, I knew it was a stupid idea, but some sort of morbid curiosity kept me going." I looked down, biting my lower lip. "I should have turned around."

Drew pulled me against his padded chest, kissing the top of my head. I allowed the warmth of my brother's arms to comfort me, just as they had throughout my life.

"I understand more than I think you realize, Mols." I felt his chest rise and fall. "I've been there, too."

369

I craned my head, meeting his dark eyes. He raised his brows, as if trying to tell me something. "You…"

"When Dad got his diagnosis." He looked away, his voice softening. "I figured she'd want to know. Since she gave birth to his children, I thought she at least deserved to hear about it in person and not over the phone." He returned his gaze to me. "Boy, was I wrong."

I stepped away from him, unsure how to feel about this new information. Why didn't he tell me? Why didn't he take me with him?

"What did she say?"

"You can probably guess." He shook his head. "She pretty much said it was none of her concern. She just wanted to forget about that part of her life and everything it entailed…" He trailed off. "Including us. That's why I didn't want you to go there, Molly. I didn't want you to have to experience that woman's cold heart firsthand."

"How could she have so much disdain?"

Drew hesitated, then turned from me. "Scully!" he shouted. One of the guys skating on the ice looked in his direction. He appeared older, so I assumed he was also on the coaching staff. "Run practice for a few minutes, will ya?"

"You got it, Coach."

Drew grabbed my hand and led me into the stands. I had no idea how he walked with skates on, but it didn't even faze him. Once we were settled, he glanced at me. "Did anyone ever tell you about Mom's family?"

I pinched my lips together. "Not really. Just that they were pretty religious, which was why Dad married her when she got pregnant."

"That's certainly true, but it's only part of the story."

He paused, staring into the distance, then turned back to me. "Her father was an officer in the Marines. Served in Vietnam. He ran his family the way he ran his unit...with order, discipline, and from what I've been able to find out, sometimes an iron fist. The things he'd witnessed in Vietnam changed him. When he came home, he wasn't the same man he was when he left. He was beaten down. And he ended up beating his family down, too." He gave me a telling look.

My eyes widened at the hidden inference.

"His wife, who was once full of life and love, became a woman too scared to open her mouth."

"How did you find this out?"

"On a whim, I Googled her one day. I found some old articles from around the time I was born. There was a big story here in Boston...a woman shot and killed her husband, a Vietnam vet. Her name was Molly Micelli."

I stared blankly ahead. "She named me after her mother."

"According to various reports, after she shot him, she called 911 to report it, then went about cleaning the house."

I wrinkled my forehead, not understanding.

"The officers reported that when they asked why, she responded she knew company was coming and her husband would be upset with her if anyone saw the house in the supposed disastrous state it was in. It didn't matter that her husband was lying in a pool of blood in the bathtub. The police reported the house was almost immaculate, museum-like, but she didn't see it that way.

"After investigating further, they found so much evidence of psychological abuse, she was never charged with his murder. No jury would have convicted her based on everything she and her kids had endured. Imagine how you'd feel if you grew up in a house where it was more important your bed was made each morning to a precise standard than it was that you get into a good college. This family lived this way for years. No wonder mom never really cared about any of us. She'd never known how it felt to be loved."

I shook my head in disbelief. "Why didn't you tell me any of this before?"

"I guess I wanted to protect you from finding out the truth."

"Like with the slippers?" I shot him a sideways glance.

"You figured it out?"

I nodded slowly. "When I asked Mom why she wasn't at Dad's funeral, she gave me the same speech she apparently gave you. That she'd rather forget about that chapter of her life. So I asked why she'd send me slippers every year when all she wanted to do was forget about Dad, you…" I swallowed hard, "and me." I met Drew's eyes. "That's when she told me she didn't send the slippers and it was probably you."

"It was both me and Dad. Apparently, when you were a baby, your feet were always cold," he reminisced, a twinkle in his eye. "But you hated socks. According to the story Dad told me, when your first birthday rolled around, he asked what I wanted to give you, so I said a pair of slippers. As the years went on, you thought they were from Mom for some reason. When Dad and I saw how happy you were at the thought that Mom still cared about you, we didn't have it in our hearts to tell you otherwise. We thought we'd be able to stop as you got older. When you turned sixteen, Dad *did* stop." He paused, shaking his head. "That night, I heard you crying in your room. The next day, I went out, got a pair of slippers, and sent them to our house, making it appear like Mom sent them. I've been doing it ever since."

I wiped away the tear falling down my cheek. "I don't deserve a brother like you, Drew."

"Yes, you do." He draped his arm over my shoulders, and I rested my head against his chest.

"No, I don't. I'm a horrible person. Mom said I turned out just like she did. I can't help but think there's some truth to that. I walked away from what was probably the best thing to ever happen to me. And why?" I shook my head, unable to recall how everything in my life had come unglued so quickly.

"We all do things we're not proud of when we're upset, when we're grieving. Believe me, you are *nothing* like that woman who gave birth to us. You're kind. You're caring. I see how you are with Alyssa and Charlotte. You're beautiful on the inside and out. Don't let anything Mom may have said to you make you think otherwise. She doesn't know you, not like I do...like Noah does."

Pulling away from his chest, I stared at the ice, releasing a heavy sigh. Being here with Drew brought back so many memories from our childhood when I would spend hours at the rink during his practice, reading book after book. Afterwards, Dad would take us to a neighborhood diner where we ordered the biggest plate of cheese fries they had. I wished I had appreciated those moments more.

"So what are you going to do?" he asked, breaking the silence.

I shrugged. "Beg for forgiveness?"

"Sounds like a good plan." He offered me a small smile, then stood up. He held his hand toward me and I grabbed it, allowing him to help me to my feet. As we approached the ice, he placed a soft kiss on my forehead, then put his helmet back on. "Just promise me one thing."

"What's that?"

"Be honest. No more games. No more lies."

"I can do that."

"Good. I'll be around later if you need to talk. The girls want to show you their new bedrooms one of these days, too."

"Sounds good, Drew. Thank you."

"Anytime, Molly Mae." He began to skate away.

"Hey, Drew!" I called out. He stopped, glancing back at me. "This suits you. You belong on the ice."

He grinned. "Thanks, Mols."

Chapter Thirty-Four

I FIDGETED WITH THE skirt of my dress as I walked up the paved path and under the archway of Forest Hills Cemetery. The early autumn sun had almost disappeared beyond the horizon, but still cast a beautiful glow over the landscape. As I crested the hill, I almost laughed when I saw the movie they were showing tonight...*The Apartment.* It was a story about a man forced by the upper executives at his office to allow them to use his apartment so they could go on with their illicit affairs. It took forbidden romance to a completely different level.

After I left Drew, I knew exactly what I needed to do. I needed to finally talk to Noah. It was Thursday night, so I had a feeling he'd be in the exact same place he was every Thursday night.

Approaching the roped off area where everyone had set up their blankets, I scanned the crowd. Noah must have sensed my presence. Just like that first night all those months ago, his eyes shot straight to me, making my breath hitch. I considered the possibility he'd ignore me, but he wasn't the type to run when things got tough. He faced his problems head-on, something I vowed to start doing.

His expression not giving anything away, he raised himself to his feet and slowly made his way toward me. "Molly," he said in an even tone. "What are you doing here?" He glanced back to his blanket on the grass.

"I..." I stared at his windswept dark hair, the intensity in his eyes, the fullness of his lips. He looked so good. So handsome. So beautiful. So perfect. Why did I ever allow myself to run from him?

"You?" He lifted a brow, crossing his arms over his chest.

Looking down, I shuffled my feet, chewing on the inside of my cheek. I returned my eyes to his, everything I planned to say flying out the proverbial window. Instead, I did something I'd rarely done, if ever. I spoke from my heart.

"I saw my future today," I admitted in a soft voice. "And it had leather skin from too much sun, smoked way too many cigarettes, and wore vastly age-inappropriate clothes."

Noah wrinkled his brow. His expression was a mixture of amusement and confusion. "I'm not sure I follow."

"I'm not sure I do, either." I laughed nervously. My thoughts a scrambled mess, I paced the grass, clenching and unclenching my fists. "My mother's almost sixty, but still acts like she's twenty."

"You went to see your mother?" His eyes widened in surprise and a touch of concern.

"I was so tired of thinking no one supported me. In retrospect, it was probably one of the worst decisions of my life. This is a woman who lives less than two hours away, yet never made the effort to try and be part of my life." I stopped pacing, then stepped toward Noah. "I don't know what I expected. I guess I hoped to see that she had a good life, that her decision to leave my father and her family was the right one for her." I shook my head, looking away.

"And was it?"

"She'll never admit it, but she's so lonely, she'll throw herself at any guy who will look at her. She's a complete joke. I don't want to turn into her." I peered at him through apologetic eyes. "I don't want to run away from love anymore."

"But I thought love didn't exist." The pain I'd caused was still visible on every inch of him. "Do you still believe that?"

I inhaled a long breath, deciding to answer honestly for once. "All my life, I'd held onto that belief very firmly, that there was no such thing as true love, that what everyone else considered to be love was nothing more than an illusion, the result of hormones. For me, real love wasn't real life."

Noah's shoulders fell.

I reached out and brushed my hand against his arm. He met my eyes, a glimmer of hope in his gaze. "But I think it *can* be, if you'll just give me another chance."

He stared at me for several excruciatingly drawn-out moments as my heart remained completely exposed and laid bare for him to destroy or repair. He held all the power.

"Molly," he finally said with a sigh, stepping back. "I want to believe you, but how can I? When I look at you, I don't see a woman in love. I see a girl so scared of being alone, she's willing to do anything to make sure she's not." He shook his head. "I'm not interested in being with someone just for convenience, just because they saw what their future held and didn't like it. I want to be with someone who wants to be with me, who won't run when things get tough, who has no problem telling me she loves me."

I opened my mouth, searching for the words I

needed. I'd made a living off of always knowing what to say and when to say it, but when it came to my own life, I had permanent writer's block. Noah always had a way of making me completely speechless, but I knew this was my one and only chance to convince him I was no longer that girl who pushed him away to protect her heart.

"I took a fall and found out I could bleed," I confessed. "I should have told you how I felt when you said you loved me, but I didn't. You're right. I was terrified. My mother walked out on my father when I was four. Drew's ex walked out on him when Alyssa was two. They say things happen in threes. I was so worried it would happen to me, I did everything I could to make sure I'd never be in that position." I inched toward him, desperate to feel the heat of his body, to inhale his musky scent, to be in his universe.

"For the past few weeks, every time I've closed my eyes, I see yours staring back at me. I've missed everything about you...from the way you hold me when I go to sleep, to the way you kiss my head first thing in the morning. I miss the way you always held my hand in public, the way you brushed my hair out of my face so you could see into my eyes, the way you would kiss me in the middle of a crowded elevator for no reason at all." A lone tear trickled down my cheek as all the wonderful memories I'd shared with Noah rushed forward. "The way you made me feel more cherished and valued than I probably deserved. The way we danced when the only music was in our hearts." I swallowed through the lump in my throat. "I refused to admit it to myself because I was so fucking scared, but the truth is that I am completely and utterly in lo−"

"Noah?" A tall blonde wearing a flowing white top

and dark jeans approached, placing her hand on his shoulder.

My jaw dropped, my eyes blinking repeatedly. Struggling to recover, I plastered a fake smile on my face, my heart breaking into tiny little pieces as I realized he'd already moved on, that everything I'd just confessed had been for nothing.

I spun on my heels, my face burning with embarrassment as I ran down the walkway toward the parking lot. I reached into my purse, fumbling for my keys. My eyes welled up with tears and I swallowed through the throbbing in my chest. I wanted to scream and cry at the notion that this was too little, too late. Regret filled my heart, making it ache. I should have told Noah how I felt weeks ago. The minute he said he loved me, I should have returned the sentiment with enthusiasm. Instead, I shrank away and allowed my own fears to consume me.

Fear cost me the one man I knew I could spend the rest of my life with.

"Molly," Noah called out as I continued searching for my keys.

"What?" I whirled around, frustrated that my escape had been foiled by my bottomless pit of a purse.

Before I could react, his lips were on mine, taking the breath from me. I stiffened, confused, aroused, and a hundred different other emotions my brain couldn't adequately describe at the moment. His fingers tangled in my hair, his grip tight, like he never wanted to let me go. I had no idea what was happening, why he was kissing me just a few feet away from another woman, but at that moment, that didn't matter. If this was the last time I'd ever kiss Noah, I wanted to remember every sweep of his tongue, every brush of his hand, every beat of his heart against mine.

With incredible ease, he slowly pulled his mouth away, licking his lips. I stared at him, bewildered.

"Wha—"

"Tell me," he said, his chest heaving.

"Tell you what?" I asked.

He swallowed hard, his gaze fierce. "Tell me what you were about to say."

I tensed, pulling my lower lip between my teeth. This was one of the hardest things I'd ever had to do. Most people I knew gave their love freely with no reservations. Not me. I kept my heart guarded, always on the lookout for someone who would use my love against me.

"Please." He brushed his lips against mine again before meeting my gaze. "Please, Molly. Say it."

"I love you," I whimpered in a small voice.

Relief washed over his face and he brought me back into his arms, covering my mouth with his. His kiss was soft, reverent...loving.

"That wasn't so hard, was it?"

"It was easier than I thought it would be," I admitted, then tilted my head up. "Everything's easier with you."

He leaned toward me. "And everything's easier with you, Molly Mae." He cupped my cheeks, locking me in place. I wouldn't run even if I could. I was exactly where I wanted to be. "You may have used me as inspiration for your book..."

I swallowed hard as he ran his thumb across my lips.

"But you inspire me." His mouth found mine again and I lost myself in him, not caring that we were making out in a cemetery where hundreds of people could see us. Not caring that the blonde bimbo he'd probably been sleeping with watched us. Not caring about anything but the love I had for this man.

"What the hell is going on here?" a female voice hissed. We both jumped away from each other, whirling around.

"Morgan...," Noah began. He looked like a deer caught in the headlights. "This is Molly."

She placed her hands on her hips, eyeing me up and down.

"Molly?" She approached me. Before I knew what was happening, she wrapped her arms around me, hugging me tight. "Noah has told me so much about you!"

My eyes widened, confused. She stepped back, keeping her hands on my shoulders. "Are you joining us for the movie? Noah didn't mention it, but he's been a bit...distracted lately. We brought dinner with us. We've got enough for you, too, if you'd like."

I looked from her to Noah, wanting one of them to explain what was going on.

"Morgan is my sister." He smirked. "She and her husband just relocated here from New York."

"Noah's been telling me about cemetery movie night for years now. I had to see what it was for myself. I have to say, I'm hooked." She winked, then paused, eyeing both of us. "I'll give you two love birds a few minutes." She spun around and dashed back up the pathway toward the large projection screen. "But John said to hurry up or he's going to eat all the food!" she called out before disappearing back into the crowd.

"So..." I began as I turned to Noah. "She's not your girlfriend."

Grinning, he shook his head. "Definitely not. But I'm a little scared you seem to always assume I'm dating my sisters."

I laughed. "You're not seeing anyone?"

His grin grew bigger as he shook his head again. "How could I possibly date someone when I'm in love with another woman?"

"Even after everything I said to you?"

He wrapped his arms around me, nodding. "That's what real love is. It's knowing the other person is completely full of shit, but letting them figure it out on their own." He winked. "That's why I let you have your space these past few weeks. It was the hardest thing for me to do, but I knew if I had any shot with you, you needed to have this time to yourself."

"So all that stuff you said before about not knowing whether you could ever believe me?" I tilted my head, my eyes locked with his.

He shrugged, a twinkle in his gaze. "I just wanted to finally hear that four-letter word come out of your mouth." He let out a satisfied breath. "And it was more beautiful than I could have imagined."

The sincerity of his voice turned my legs into jelly. I didn't think people swooned in real life. I was so wrong because this man just made me swoon…and I swooned so damn hard.

He placed a softy kiss on my lips, then grabbed my hand, leading me back up the path. "Since we're overcoming our fears…" He looked at me, a mischievous smile on his face. "How about you say that other word, too?"

I scrunched my nose momentarily, then realized which word he referred to. I vehemently shook my head. "No. I will never!"

He stopped in his tracks, pulling me against him. He buried his head in my neck, nibbling on my earlobe. "Please, Molly," he whispered, his tone seductive.

All he had to do was press his body against mine, murmur in his sensual voice, use his tongue on my skin, and I was putty in his hands. His large, rough, talented hands.

"I'm thirty," I declared with a quiver.

A low rumble escaped his throat, the sound of his laughter bringing a smile to my face. He draped his arm across my shoulders and we continued back toward his blanket.

"That wasn't so hard, was it?"

"That one definitely hurt a little bit."

He faced me, holding my hands in his. "I love you, Molly Brinks, crazy tendencies and all."

"And I love you, Noah McAllister, even though you're complete rubbish in bed."

He cocked his head, giving me a coy look. "Is that so?"

"Oh yes. I've had to fake every orgasm with you." I avoided his eyes.

"Well, I guess I'll just have to keep practicing with you. Is that something you'd be interested in?" Snaking his arm around my waist, he lowered his mouth to mine. He nibbled on my bottom lip, the gesture causing a spark of electricity to run through my body.

"God, yes," I breathed. I had no idea how this man knew exactly how to make me want him even more, but he did.

"Good. Because I *really* like practicing with you." He abruptly pulled away. "To be continued." He winked, tugging me back toward the crowd.

I scowled playfully. "You're such a clamjammer." It had been so long since I'd been with Noah. I would have given anything to feel him again.

"Clamjammer?" He lifted a brow.

"It's the female equivalent to a cockblocker. You, Noah McAllister, are clamjamming me right now."

"Maybe," he murmured, his breath hot on my neck. "But just think how amazing that first orgasm, which you claim you fake, will feel after hours of pent-up sexual frustration. All evening long, with each brush of my fingers on your leg, each squeeze of my hand on your hip, each nip of my teeth on your skin, you'll be thinking of what's in store for you later."

"God, I've missed you," I panted, his erotic words giving me a high no drug could replicate.

He grinned. "Me, too." He wrapped me in his embrace, leaving a soft kiss on my nose. "I love you, Molly."

"And I love you."

"It's about time you finally came to your senses."

Epilogue

Nine Months Later

"KNOCK, KNOCK!" NOAH'S VOICE called out from the hallway before opening the door to my office.

My eyes burned from being glued to my laptop for the past however many hours, but my latest book was nearly finished. Welcoming the distraction, I looked up from my laptop to see Noah carrying two large boxes.

"Does it look like I need any more boxes in here?" I gestured around the room.

Boxes were piled high in nearly every corner of my new office in Noah's house. He'd been pestering me about whether I was ever going to get around to unpacking. I simply responded that I'd unpack as the need arose.

Deciding to leave my apartment in Boston and move in with Noah wasn't as big of an adjustment as I thought it would have been. I'd been practically living at his place anyway. This made it official. I couldn't have been happier to spend lazy Sundays on the couch with Noah, to welcome him home from a hard day at work with a home-cooked meal, clothing optional.

"No, but I think you'll want these." He winked and my eyes widened.

I jumped out of my chair, rushing toward him as he set the boxes on the floor. Grabbing a razor blade off my desk, I made quick work of the tape sealing one of the boxes closed, throwing all the packing materials everywhere.

A smile of satisfaction and accomplishment tugged at my lips as I held my book in my hands. I'd been writing and publishing for over five years. I'd never forget how I felt when I held my very first book. I'd been so proud of finally having a book with my name on it, or my pen name anyway, that I didn't reflect on everything. Instead of writing what was in my heart, I followed the herd and wrote what was popular, what was trendy. There was no substance to it. But the book I held in my hands now was different. This was all me, a story I wanted to tell.

I'd written my love story.

After considerable thought and support from Drew and Noah, I'd decided to forfeit my contract with my publisher. I didn't want to write what someone else told me to. I wanted to write what was in my heart. As much as I wanted to publish the first version of Avery and Jackson's story on my own, after speaking with my agent and having a lawyer review my contract with my publisher, I felt it best to table the book for now so as not to run into any legal problems down the road.

At first, I was upset at the thought of no one ever reading their story because of how personal it was to me. Then Noah had said something that gave me hope.

"*They can hold Avery and Jackson hostage, but they'll never be able to take our love away from each other. That's the most important thing.*"

That was when I knew how to fix this. I didn't need Avery and Jackson, not when my own love story was even better.

I nestled into the crook of Noah's arm as we gazed at

the cover of my book, my real name on it in big, bold letters. Able to sense what I was thinking, he whispered, "He would have been proud of you."

"I know," I responded through the lump in my throat.

If he knew about my alter ego, I'd often wondered if my father would have bragged about me the way he did Drew…if he would have remembered who I was even during those later weeks.

"When did you change the title?" Noah asked, picking up one of the paperbacks in the box. "I thought you were going to call it *Confessions of a Reformed Serial Dater.*"

"I was," I admitted. "But I think the new one's a lot more fitting." I shrugged, looking at the script of the new title, *Writing Mr. Right.*

"I agree." He nuzzled his nose into my hair, inhaling my scent. We'd been living together for nearly three months now, but he still knew how to make me grow weak in the knees to the point of hauling him into the bedroom for another round of "research".

"Read to me," he murmured, resting his hands on my hips as we swayed to the sound of nothing and everything all at once.

I closed my eyes, lost in the feel of his warm body against mine. He peppered kisses down my neck and across my nape as I began to recite from memory the first few lines of my book.

"No," he murmured. "I know how it begins. I want to know how it ends."

"'*It's about time you finally came to your senses,*'" I said, recalling the last line in the book.

Noah shook his head. "That's not what I'm talking about, Molly," he replied, his tone sensual as he

387

continued rocking his body against me. When I suddenly no longer felt his arms around me, a void washed over me.

I flung my eyes open. All the oxygen left my lungs and my heart sank into the pit of my stomach when I saw him on one knee in front of me. He reached into his pocket and withdrew a black velvet box. Flipping it open, he revealed a stunning round cut diamond.

My hands trembling, I shook my head. "Noah, please…" I grabbed his elbow and yanked him back up, imploring him with my expression.

"Molly, I thought…" Confusion covered every inch of his body, his mouth agape, his eyes wide with concern, the lines on his face furrowed.

"Noah," I sighed, then my lips turned up into a brilliant smile. "I don't want you to look up to me, and I never want to look down on you. For the rest of my life, I want to look beside me and see you there." I held my left hand toward him. A tear escaped, my heart nearly bursting with love at the thought of waking up every day with this beautiful, caring, passionate man at my side, supporting me, nurturing me, loving me…duck attacks and all.

Relief washed over him, his shoulders relaxing. "I had a whole speech planned, and this is kind of throwing it for a loop."

"I've learned one very important thing this past year," I began as he held the ring up to my finger. He lowered his lips to mine and slid it into place. Most women would probably be upset they didn't get some big elaborate speech with a declaration of undying and never-ending love from a man on one knee in front of them. Not me. This moment was exactly as I dreamt it would be.

"And what's that?"

Grabbing his cheeks in my hands, the sparkle of the diamond catching my eyes, I murmured, "Plans are made to be broken."

The End

If you're wondering about Drew and Brooklyn's story, be sure to check out The Redemption Series. Now complete and available.

She's my sister's best friend.
She thinks I've never noticed her.
She couldn't be more wrong.
Now I just need to prove it to her...before she says "I do."

Brooklyn Tanner and Andrew Brinks have a long history...one she wants nothing more than to forget. Considering he's her best friend's brother and single father to two amazing girls who mean the world to her, it's almost impossible.

When the man she's been dating proposes, she thinks it's exactly what she needs to finally close this chapter of her life. After all, over sixteen years have passed since she gave Andrew Brinks her heart, only for him to destroy it. Why should that matter now?

But it matters to Drew.

When he learns of her engagement, he realizes he has a decision to make. Does he finally tell Brooklyn the truth of what happened all those years ago? Or does he watch her marry another man to protect her from enduring any more pain?

Playlist

No Time For Lonely - LOLO
Days Like This - Kim Taylor
Paper Hearts - Silver Trees, feat. Bailey Jehl
Fallin' For You - Colbie Caillat
Where I Belong - Bobby Bazini
Sparks - Coldplay
Dance With Me - Griffin House
I Put a Spell on You - Nina Simone
Never Got Away - Colbie Caillat
Farewell - Rosie Thomas
Trouble - Coldplay
Desire - Meg Myers
Lifted Away - Joseph
I Like The Way This is Going - Eels
Tourist - Yuna
Miracles - Matt White
Bewitched, Bothered, And Bewildered - Ella Fitzgerald
Masterpiece - Josh Kelley
Addicted To Love - Florence + The Machine
Give Me Something - Emeli Sandé
Changes - Jack Savoretti
Fearless - Colbie Caillat
Without You - for KING & COUNTRY
Till I Fall Asleep - Jayme Dee
And So It Goes - Sara Gazarek
It Must Have Been Love - Kari Kimmel
Hit and Run - LOLO
I Never Told You - Colbie Caillat
Beautiful Lies - Jon McLaughlin

Acknowledgments

I wasn't supposed to write this book for at least five or six more years, but here I am, publishing book number ten, which ended up being *Writing Mr. Right*. The original title was *Blocked*. I had a rough premise in my notes, but this book became something else entirely. The inspiration came to me one day when I was going through responses to questions I tend to pose on my Facebook page. I had asked "What's your biggest fear?"

The responses were across the board — death, cancer, losing my family. There was one response that stuck with me — love. And Molly Brinks was born. What better way to write about a woman who has the same fears so many others do than to make her a romance author?

I had fully intended on working on a different book first, a more emotional contemporary romance featuring one of the characters readers first met in *Heart of Marley*. When I decided to change gears, I was already working on a very heavy, emotional book — *Vanished*. I needed a break from the heartache, and Molly's voice was shouting in my head, so I made the decision to work on a romantic comedy.

I think it's fitting I can celebrate my tenth release with this particular story — the tale of a romance author who believes real love isn't real life but then finds love where she wasn't expecting it. I've taken some liberties with a few things in the book but the fears

Molly has, personally and professionally, are real things I think many of us authors experience. The doubt. The drama. The loneliness. Bearing our hearts and souls for readers to rip to shreds. It's not easy, but I couldn't imagine doing anything else.

It's still a bit surreal to think this is my tenth book. It's been an amazing journey and I couldn't have done it without the love and support of my husband, Stan. He's been my biggest cheerleader since day one and he still is. On the same note, I need to send a HUGE thank you to my two wonderful nannies, Sharon and Julia. I'd be elbow deep in shit (no pun intended) if I didn't have these two women helping me with little Miss Harper Leigh. They love my little girl as they would their own and I'm truly blessed to have found them.

Writing a book is not an easy task and there are so many people involved. There's one small group of women I trust with my baby when it's just random babbling and they help mold it into the story it becomes in the final product. First, a big thank you to my beta readers… Joelle, Karen, Lin, Melissa, Stacy, Sylvia, Victoria - thank you ladies for taking the time and effort in reading this and giving me your valuable feedback.

I also need to thank the only woman I'd ever let touch my babies, Kim Young. She's edited every single one of my books and I couldn't imagine trying to do this without her brain and expertise. It's rare to find someone who cares about my book as much as I do, and Kim certainly does.

None of this would be possible without my wonderful team of admins who help keep my social media presence going when I lock myself away to write — Melissa, Victoria, Lea, Joelle, you girls are my rockstars. And a special shout out to my Burnham Bitches, who do more for me and ask nothing in return than any sane human should. #BurnhamBitches4Life. Another huge thank you to my Street Team, my Angels. It still amazes me how many people devote their time to promoting me and my books. Simply saying thank you seems so inadequate for all you do for me, but thank you!

None of this would be possible without all you amazing bloggers who volunteer your time to read, review, and promote all of us. You're the reason so many of us authors are able to stay independently published, so thank you!

Last but not least, thank you to you, my wonderful readers. Whether this is your first book of mine or your tenth, I am humbled by your support. I hope you'll stick with me for the next ten books, too!

Love and peace,

~T.K.

Books By T.K. Leigh

ROMANTIC SUSPENSE
The Beautiful Mess Series
A Beautiful Mess
A Tragic Wreck
Gorgeous Chaos
Chasing the Dragon (Deception Duet #1)
Slaying the Dragon (Deception Duet #2)
Vanished: A Beautiful Mess Series Novel

The Vault
Inferno

Heart of Light

CONTEMPORARY ROMANCE
The Redemption Series
Promise: A Redemption Series Prologue
Commitment
Redemption

The Dating Games Series
Dating Games
Wicked Games
Dangerous Games
Royal Games

ROMANTIC COMEDY
The Other Side of Someday
Writing Mr. Right

MATURE YOUNG ADULT
Heart of Marley

For more information on any of these titles and upcoming releases, please visit T.K.'s website:
www.tkleighauthor.com

About The Author

T.K. Leigh, otherwise known as Tracy Leigh Kellam, is the USA Today Bestselling author of the Beautiful Mess series, in addition to several other works. Originally from New England, she now resides in sunny Southern California with her husband, beautiful daughter, and three cats. When she's not planted in front of her computer, writing away, she can be found training for her next marathon (of which she has run over twenty fulls and far too many halfs to recall) or chasing her daughter around the house.

T.K. Leigh is represented by Jane Dystel of Dystel, Goderich & Bourret Literary Management. All publishing inquiries, including audio, foreign, and film rights, should be directed to her.